BEYOND THE VEIL

Mirabelle Maslin

ATHENA PRESS
LONDON

BEYOND THE VEIL
Copyright © Mirabelle Maslin 2004
The moral right of the author has been asserted

ISBN 1 84401 229 8

First Published 2004 by
ATHENA PRESS
Queen's House, 2 Holly Road
Twickenham TW1 4EG
United Kingdom

Printed for Athena Press

BEYOND THE VEIL

To Vanessa and Norman

Chapter One

They had met by a curious stroke of fate. Both were on a train journey to York. Both to attend meetings. They had been allotted seats that were adjacent. She was sitting in her seat by the window and hardly bothered to turn to see who had arrived to sit beside her. She had seen the reservation ticket said 'York' as hers did, but did not really give it a second thought.

She had her newspaper and was absorbed in reading an article on breastfeeding. She was relieved to see that it was well-written and included reference to a broad range of important aspects of the subject. She became aware of the person next to her making a throat-clearing sound, and vaguely realised that it must be a male person.

She sensed the rustle as he reached his newspaper out of his briefcase, and she saw him spread it out on the table beside hers before she once more became deeply engrossed in her reading.

After about ten minutes, he went off in the direction of the refreshment carriage. She glanced across at the paper which he had left open on the table, and noticed that it was exactly the same one as hers, and that he had it open at the article on breastfeeding. After some time he returned with two bottles of mineral water. He offered one to her and, surprised, she accepted, thanking him for realising that she must be thirsty. She had noticed that his voice sounded quite pleasant with no particular accent.

By this time she was engrossed in the obituaries. She was fascinated by these people whom others wrote about. It was at times quite difficult to fathom why anyone should want to write in such detail about people no one had ever heard of. Secretly she planned to write her own obituary and lodge it with her solicitor, who would have it published at the appropriate time.

It was a whole hour before she spoke again, and then it was to ask to get past him into the corridor. He noticed that she was of medium height and that her hair was brown, held in a loose plait down her back. She wore flat shoes with plain trousers. Her jumper was quite striking, as it was made from several shades of gold and yellow which in places were woven into pictures, but he could not quite make out exactly what they depicted.

She returned to her seat and continued her study. However, she had now turned to her conference papers. He tried to make some sense of what she was seeing out of the corner of his eye, but the subject was not one which he recognised at all. He gave up trying to guess and turned to his own briefcase. He pulled out a document headed 'Updates in the study of Mycotic Abortion in Dairy Cattle'. Later that day he would be giving his own paper on *Aspergillus fumigatus*. He had himself previously identified a new strain.

The train rushed on. His pen dropped to the floor, and in his struggle to reach it he brushed past her leg. That pen was so important to him. It had been a present from his wife, who had died some years ago. It was a good pen, and had many associations – all of them positive. He was hardly aware of her leg in his search for the pen. Noticing his struggles, she offered to retrieve the pen herself, for which he was grateful. To her surprise, it was exactly the same sort of pen that she herself had been given some years ago by an old college friend. As it was an unusual design, it led to conversation between them.

Having exhausted the subject of pens, they then explained to each other that each was attending a meeting in York. Soon they lapsed into a silence which continued until they bade each other goodbye at York station.

Much later that day, she was at the small hotel where she had booked a room. She was quietly relaxing in the corner of a snug sitting area, profoundly grateful that there was no musak assailing her sensitive ears. She was studying a small book very intently, and had not noticed that someone else had entered until he spoke. She half recognised his voice, but could not place it. She lifted her head reluctantly from her study, and saw that it was the man she had encountered on the train. As he stood there, she was more aware of his appearance than she had been on the train. He was of medium build, possibly six feet tall, with hair that had receded a little but was largely brown.

She was unwilling for her studies to be disrupted, but did not wish to appear unfriendly. She pondered for a moment, and then decided to speak honestly to him. She said that it was interesting that they had encountered each other again, but explained that it was necessary that she continued her studies, and was therefore unable to spend any time in conversation. He looked mildly surprised, nodded, sat down a few seats away and began to sketch designs in a pad he produced from his briefcase. From time to time he observed her concentration on her task, and then returned to his own.

At 10.30 she rose from her seat, nodded to him, and retired to her room. A few minutes later he went to his own room, having first ascertained her room number by asking at the desk, quoting the name he had memorised from some of her documents. Room 3; his was room 15, on the floor above and at the opposite end of the building.

He became filled with a sense of purpose. He was there only for this one night. He did not know how long she was staying, and in any case that was not relevant. In the morning he would be gone. He wrote to her, beginning with his name and address:

Dear Occupant of Room 3,

I would like to give you my name and address, so that if we are to meet again it would not be by chance.

Some weeks later he received a letter through the post, which bore handwriting he did not recognise. Puzzled, he opened it and read the contents:

Dear Sir,

Thank you for the note you addressed to Room 3...

Now, he had a name *and* an address. He felt unusually alert as he read what was on that sheet of paper – address at the top, signature at the bottom. The content of the letter was certainly brief. It thanked him for his note and for the sentiment attached to it. It commented upon the obvious, that their addresses were far apart. She did however add that it was possible that she would be staying with friends about fifty miles away from his address, at some time over the summer months.

He sat and mused. It was now early June. Most of his July and August was to be spent with his old friend in a country district outside St Petersburg. This had become his habit since his wife died. The last stages of her illness had spanned many weeks through the spring and into the summer, and he preferred to be out of the country each year over the anniversary of her death. Being in a different country, a different culture, helped him to endure that time. He let his mind drift back into the weeks preceding her death. She had suffered long bouts of pain. He had taken unpaid leave to nurse her. Before he had known how ill she was, he had been impatient. He had never stopped regretting that. All this had taken place nearly seven years ago. And now here he sat, feeling faintly disturbed. Over those seven years he had hardly noticed that there were two genders in the human race. If he had, it was a mechanical observation. Then this woman on the train – why had he noticed that it was a woman and not merely a person? Why was it that he had felt drawn to her in some indefinable way? He stood up and paced through the living room to the kitchen and back again. He had repeated this exercise many times before he realised what he was doing.

A fragment of memory of the ultimate closeness between himself and his wife slipped through his mind and was gone. He stood, puzzled, wondering what had just happened.

He picked up the letter from the woman on the train, and read it again. He knew very well what it said, but he had to read it again; he had to absorb the handwriting. He stared at it, and realised that he was studying it minutely for any small clue that would tell him more about the person who wrote it. He failed to find anything.

He was in a quandary. She had not specified any dates when she might be with her friends. There was no doubt in his mind that he wanted to see her. He picked up the special pen and wrote to her:

I have your letter. I would very much like to have the opportunity of seeing you. Please could you give me some idea of the date you might travel?

He put the note in an envelope, glancing at his watch. It was nearly

5 o'clock. If he hurried, he would just catch the last collection. He penned the address, grabbed a stamp from the few he kept under the clock, and jogged down the road just in time to see the post being collected from the 'VR' box which was set into the wall.

That evening he could settle to nothing. That night he lay wakeful. He tried listening to the radio, but he found he could not concentrate on anything. He tried reading, but the words blurred in front of his eyes. All the time he seemed to hear the sound of the train they had shared. All he could see was the article on breastfeeding. Why had he not saved that article? But why should he have? If he had the article here, his current state would be no easier. He realised that he was clutching at irrelevances.

Several days later she returned home from her study weekend. It had been fascinating. She had always wanted to expand her knowledge of lichens, and this had been her chance. Her mind was filled with new names – *Lecanora atra*, *Ochrolechia parella*, and many others – and with the images she had seen under the microscope. She made herself some soup, which she enjoyed as she opened the letters which were waiting for her.

She read his letter and felt slightly annoyed. She had not yet confirmed, or indeed decided, her dates. Surely this must have been apparent from her note to him? But she thought again, and realised that this was not necessarily so. Briefly she wondered why he had written to her so quickly. Then she unpacked and went to bed. She had to make an early start in the morning.

The days passed. Each night he tossed and turned, aware that he was in a state that was unfamiliar to him. The days were filled with work necessities. In the evenings he worked on repairs to his house. Some of the guttering needed replacing. This he did mechanically.

After five days, he e-mailed his Russian friend:

<Something unexpected has turned up. My dates of travel are not the usual ones. I will be in touch as soon as I know more.>

He knew his friend would understand. He would be a little surprised, but he would not mind. He went back to the guttering, and that night he was not so restless.

Five more days passed. He almost snatched the pile of mail from the hand of the friendly postman when he saw the now-familiar writing. He passed the time of day, disappeared into the house, and quickly used the letter-opener. The letter was very brief:

In haste. I hope to travel on July 14th. I have meetings to attend, but if you are at home yourself, then maybe you would be free to come across to join us on Saturday 21st. We have a small gathering of old college friends that afternoon, and you would be welcome.

The letter then gave the address where this would take place. Yes, it was about fifty miles from his home, by a fairly straightforward route. He e-mailed his friend in Russia:

<Will be with you by July 28th.>

This would be a full two weeks later than usual.

He carefully chose a card from a collection he had made from photographs of flowers. The one he chose was of red poppies. Inside he thanked her for her suggestion of July 21st, and added that he was looking forward to seeing her and her friends then. He noticed that now that date was fixed, he was able to concentrate his mind upon a number of matters that he had had to lay aside. There had been quite a number of days of rain. The garden needed much attention. The sunsets at this time of year were late – and were spectacular at times. He took some photographs. Since his retirement from full-time work as an agricultural consultant, he had continued to take on particular projects from his former employers. The most recent assignment became pressing, and he attended to it gladly. It absorbed his attention for more than a week. And all the while at the back of his mind there was the constant sound of the train journey – and the interweaving rhythms of the movement of carriages along rails.

Chapter Two

As the days grew closer to the 21st he checked his road atlas. Yes, the route was very straightforward. He had not visited that village before, but he would find it easily. He wondered what to wear... an afternoon gathering would surely not be formal. He chose unremarkable clothes – white shirt, dark brown sweater, dark grey trousers and a lightweight beige jacket – and put them ready, wanting to feel that he would not seem out of place.

The morning of the 21st was very wet. He dressed slowly and thoughtfully. He did not want to do anything other than contemplate the afternoon ahead. He checked the weather forecast on the Internet, and it was not encouraging. He had an early lunch and set off at 1.30. The drive was enjoyable, and he savoured thoughts of the moment when he would see her again. It pleased him that although he was driving along main roads the route seemed quite quiet, and he had the opportunity to notice some rather fine hedges which had been properly shaped to encourage bird populations to flourish. The continuing heavy rain did not affect his relaxed mood. He reached the tiny village, and asked a man under a large umbrella at a bus stop for directions. The house was easily found – only three down from the bus stop.

He parked his Peugeot 205 outside the house. It was the left-hand house of a semi-detached pair. He liked its appearance, and in particular he liked the climbing roses which had been trained up a trellis to the left of the front door. There was a slatted wooden fence along the front of the garden, and a golden privet hedge behind that. The wooden gate was hanging slightly askew, but it looked as if it would still swing on its hinges. The front garden had a small lawn surrounded by borders of plants which were very familiar to him.

He opened the gate and walked up the path to the front door. On any other occasion he would have spent a few minutes running his gaze around the familiar plants; but now he seemed to have no further interest in the garden, and he rang the bell. The door was opened by a man whom he guessed was about the same age as himself. He gave his name and was welcomed into the house. He was shown into the sitting room, and was offered a drink of fruit juice, which he was glad to accept. The man who had let him in encouraged everyone in the sitting room to introduce themselves. No sign yet of the woman on the train. Everyone was very relaxed, and made efforts to include him in their conversation. It was obvious to him that they all knew one another very well. Evidently they had all kept in touch since their college days. They spoke of their work, their interests, their children, their homes and their holidays. Still no sign of the woman on the train.

A telephone rang. He could hear half of a conversation. The man who had let him in came into the room and relayed the message that she was not able to join them. Her car had broken down; she had stayed overnight in a hotel, the car repair had been promised for lunchtime; but there was a delay. She would therefore miss the gathering and have to go tomorrow straight to her meeting. He heard sympathetic sounds from the others. He himself was struggling with feelings he could not name. After a few minutes he managed to ask his host if he knew the name of the hotel where she was. 'I'm afraid not,' was the reply. To his embarrassment he felt weak, and he had to sit down. He asked to use the bathroom, and as he went through the hall he saw the telephone. He noted that everyone else was safely in the sitting room. Quickly he lifted the receiver, keyed 1471, and scribbled down the number he heard on a till slip he found in his pocket. On his return from the bathroom, he made his excuses.

'I feel a bit unwell. Must go now. Thank you for your hospitality,' he explained, and left.

Back in the car he took his mobile phone out of his pocket, and phoned the number he had written down. He asked the receptionist for the name of the hotel, and for precise directions. It was some distance away, he realised, as he studied his road atlas. However, if he drove without a significant break, he should get there in a couple of hours. That would mean his arriving at about 8 p.m. He hoped that she would be eating there, and that he would catch her before her evening meal.

He drove very determinedly. He realised that he had not asked if there was any accommodation available at the hotel tonight. It did not really matter. The main thing was to find her, to see her, and spend the evening with her.

She was disappointed to have missed the reunion. However, this feeling of disappointment took up little of her thoughts. It was important that she spent time on further preparation for the study meeting the next day. Her car was now repaired, so the journey tomorrow would not be a problem. She had been feeling tired; uncertainty about car repairs always left her feeling drained. She had known what was wrong with her car, but it had needed a mechanic to repair it.

She decided to stay in her room. Although there was a comfortable chair, she preferred to lie on the bed. She had her briefcase close beside the bed, and she leaned over and reached inside it. She was reluctant to take out her papers, and instead took a small book from the back pocket of the briefcase. It was the same book that she had been studying at the hotel in York. It had a hard back of a deep red colour and there was an intricate pattern embossed on it. The edges of the pages looked slightly blackened – a feature one would not have expected. She opened the book near the beginning and instantly became absorbed in what she saw. She was unaware of the passage of time.

Eventually he arrived at the hotel at ten past eight. His journey had been reasonably uneventful. There had been a tolerable delay on a small country lane when he had had to wait for a flock of sheep being moved to another field. He had watched with interest how well the collie dog kept them moving in the right direction without alarming them.

He found the place. It was a small hotel, bearing the name the Traveller's Arms. Not uncommon, he thought to himself as he parked his car in the forecourt, but it was written in a rather unusual style of lettering, one which he did not remember ever having seen before.

He entered, ordered a drink of lemonade, and went to sit near an open fire. Although it was midsummer, the evening had a chill to it and he was glad of some heat. Having relaxed a little, he looked around him. There were no people in the room. The walls were lined with bookshelves, and there was a piano at one end. He was surprised to discover that it was a Blüthner boudoir grand. Running his gaze round the bookshelves, he noticed quite an extensive collection of music, and he began to look through it all. He was further surprised in that the music was not the usual mixture of popular songs that one might encounter in such circumstances. He found works by Bach, Hummel, Chopin, Debussy and many more. On an impulse he picked out a book of Chopin Nocturnes and sat down to play. The years melted away, back to the last time he had played these – during the months of his wife's final illness.

He was so engrossed in his playing and his memories that he did not notice a member of the hotel staff until he was standing right beside him. He jumped and stopped playing.

'Will you be dining here tonight, sir?'

A simple question, but one which left him in some confusion. He felt exposed and caught out. At first he could not think what to say, and then he muttered, 'Yes, thank you… yes, I will.'

He was handed a menu from a table at the side of the room, and he chose mechanically. Home-made soup followed by chicken and green vegetables. Not long afterwards he was called to a small table in the dining room.

He had hoped to see her somewhere, but as there was no sign of her he decided to ask:

'I was intending to meet a friend here this evening, her name is Ellen Ridgeway.'

'Oh yes, sir,' came the reply, 'she booked in earlier today.'

In her room upstairs, Ellen gradually became aware that she was feeling hungry. She was mildly irritated by this, feeling it as an intrusion. She looked at her watch and started. Hours had passed since she lay down. It was now nine o'clock. She had better go downstairs and order something to eat. It did not need to be much. She sat up, slipped on her sandals, and put her book into the serviceable handbag that she used for essentials. She enjoyed running her hand down the solid mahogany banister rail on her way. For a moment she wished she could slide down; as a child she had loved to do that at home.

As she entered the dining room she saw him at once, sitting at the small table near the window. She felt a mixture of emotions – surprise, puzzlement and something that verged on anger and frustration. She had counted on having this evening to herself. To be honest, she had been slightly relieved when she found she could not attend the reunion that afternoon. She would have been happy to see her friends, but was not particularly looking forward to seeing the man from the train again. She had been glad that he would have been well received by her friends, and she felt that was sufficient under the circumstances.

She saw him look up from his soup, and she watched the pleasure on his face as he saw her. She made herself walk across to speak to him.

'Mr Thomas…' She held out her hand in a formal way.

'Miss Ridgeway… Ellen… It's good to see you again. Please call me Adam,' he replied as he took her hand. He noticed immediately that the hand invited no prolonged contact, so he made no attempt to make this anything other than a formality.

'I had so looked forward to seeing you again that I felt I wanted to drive over here.'

He made no attempt to explain to her how he had identified where she was staying. He hoped that she would assume that her friend had told him.

'Would you like to join me?'

She hesitated visibly, and he gave her time to assemble her thoughts. He could see that she was undecided. She told him how tired she was, that she had come down for something light to eat, and that she would need to sleep soon as she was to leave early in the morning. In the end she agreed to share his table while she too had a bowl of soup.

'I'm sorry to have missed the reunion,' she said. 'I had a nasty moment when I realised there was a problem with my steering this morning. However, it's all fixed now.'

'I was disappointed when I heard you couldn't make it,' he said. 'I'll soon be leaving to be abroad for a number of weeks.'

He noticed that she seemed reassured by this latter piece of information, and he continued. 'Yes, I'm visiting an old friend near St Petersburg, and I hope to be there for about eight weeks.'

He noticed that she was beginning to look more relaxed now.

Her soup arrived. It was a mixed vegetable soup. She realised that she was quite thirsty, and that soup had been a good choice. Her mind fixed upon the little book she had in her bag, and he noticed from her face that her thoughts were turned quite inward. He did not disturb her, and concentrated on his soup which was now quite cold. It was sufficient to share time with her; he did not feel they particularly needed to converse. He did not wish to intrude upon whatever was preoccupying her.

She slowly finished her soup, and he suggested that she stayed and had some chicken.

'No... no thank you... not now.'

He tried again. 'Some green vegetables?' She wavered, and then showed some interest.

The waiter came, and Adam ordered extra vegetables. They sat on in a silence that felt a little less lacking in connection, although he noticed that she was still very preoccupied. Still it felt as if her presence alone was sufficient, and he was content. Sensing this, she was not on edge, and thought her own thoughts. The waiter brought his chicken, her empty plate, and a dish full of green vegetables decorated with strands of fried seaweeds.

They ate slowly, in silence. He sensed that she would be uncomfortable if he said he would stay the night at the hotel, so he soon mentioned that he was intending to drive home, leaving in about an hour. She expressed the hope that he did not find night driving stressful. He shrugged. It was not an issue for him.

He puzzled as to why he felt so at ease with himself and with the situation. If anyone had asked him earlier to describe how he thought he would feel in such circumstances, relaxed is not a word which would have occurred to him. Here he was, once more sitting with the woman from the train, almost next to her. Here he was, eating with her. He was going to leave in a very short time, and then he was going to Russia. Why did he feel so calm and confident? It did not make sense. However, he wasted no further thought pondering the question. She seemed quite relaxed and composed as she ate her vegetables.

They finished. She had declined coffee. He must leave; she must go upstairs. The handshake lingered fractionally. She thanked him for making the effort to drive to see her. He thought quickly. Should he suggest some possible meeting on his return from Russia? He sensed it was best to say nothing, and they left the dining room; he to his car, and she to her bedroom.

She needed to spend more time with her book, and with her papers for tomorrow, but now there was none. It was important that she slept. She set her clock for 6.30 a.m. That would mean that she would not be rushed in the morning. It was a travelling clock, the case of which was white plastic. It had been her trusty companion on many of her journeys, and she found it comforting.

Adam drove home, quite slowly, savouring the memory of the feeling of calm he had experienced sitting and sharing the time with her.

Chapter Three

Ellen woke to the jarring sound of her alarm, and was soon turning on the shower. She liked those where the height of the shower head was adjustable. They were more commonplace nowadays, she had noticed. To her relief this one was exactly to her liking, and she had to resist the temptation to put off the time when she reached for the towel.

Breakfast was something that did not interest her. She would eat some fruit in the car later as she drove to her meeting. She settled her bill, and carried her possessions to the car. She had an overnight bag, her briefcase and the handbag she had carried the evening before. Anxiously she checked her handbag and briefcase until she found her book. Having found it in her handbag, she carefully transferred it to the zipped pocket of her briefcase, where she felt it would be safer.

The first part of her journey led her to a small market town, which she skirted round, and then drove southwards for about a further five miles. Locating a familiar cul-de-sac, she drove to the end of it and parked her car. She walked up the path to the door of the house at the right-hand end of the row of terraced cottages, and knocked.

'Nearly ready,' she heard a voice shout, although it was somewhat muffled.

Some minutes later a youngish woman of about her own age emerged carrying a stick and a large shoulder bag, both of which she put down on the doorstep to enable her to reach out affectionately to her friend. The two women embraced each other in a way that had grown through years of contact.

'So this is the stick,' said Ellen, picking it up to examine it in detail. The younger woman nodded.

'I had tried to visualise the carving on it from your description,' said Ellen. 'I see you described it very accurately.'

She noted that the carving was just below the middle of the

stick, and seemed to depict two simple figures seated facing each other. Although faceless, the two figures gave the impression of being in close communication. Ellen could not quite grasp what produced this effect. She thought the stick was made of ash, and she liked the relatively light colour of it.

'Tell me again exactly how you came by it,' she suggested.

'I was on holiday in Scotland last September,' her friend explained, 'and at the end of the fortnight I was driving through East Lothian to follow the A1 to the North of England to stay with my aunt on my way home. I began to feel very sleepy, and knew that I must stop for a while. A walk would revive me, so I turned off down a narrow side road and parked at a wide gateway. I walked about a mile along the road, and was just about to turn back to the car when I noticed that the hedge was full of blackberries – or brambles, as the local people call them. Fortunately I had a small polythene bag in my pocket, and I started to gather some of the berries. I was so engrossed that I was startled when I heard somebody greeting me. I looked up and saw an old man with an old woman whom I guessed was his wife. They were approving of my task, and they suggested that I might be thirsty, and invited me to their home, which was a little farther along the road. I was indeed thirsty, and since my small bag was nearly full, I accepted their offer.

'We walked together to where they lived, which was a small section of some old farm buildings near an implement shed which housed a number of rather dilapidated bits of machinery, which I couldn't recognise at a glance. They invited me to sit on a wooden bench at the front of their house, and the old woman brought a mug which was made out of rough pottery. She encouraged me to sip its contents, and as I did, my mind filled with sensations that seemed new to me. The sensations were something that I experienced in the same way as I experience beautiful colours, but of course I knew that I was seeing nothing other than the fields and trees outside their home. The cool liquid had a fresh taste which I can only describe as being full of vibrance, but was something I did not recognise at all. I wanted to say something, but I could not think of any words.

'The man sat on an upturned log quite near the bench I was

sitting on, and the woman sat next to me. Each of them now held a roughly-made mug, and we sipped in companionable silence. I really had no idea how much time passed, and I did not have any thought of my watch. All I know is that after some time the old man stood up and said, "I have something for you." He disappeared inside his home, and returned a few minutes later with a long wooden box. He put it on the ground in front of me, and I saw to my surprise that it contained a number of walking sticks. Each of them was of a simple style. The type of wood was different for each stick. He pointed them out – "Cherry, hawthorn, ash…" I was immediately drawn to the ash stick. I had no interest at all in the others. When I look back, I'm surprised at this; the person that I am would have normally examined each stick in detail, but the only one which had any meaning at all to me was the ash stick. The old woman was looking at her husband, nodding to him.

'"It's yours," he said, and he picked it up and handed it to me. I felt no protest in me, and I offered none. I ran my finger along the length of the stick, and it was then that I became aware of the carving on it. I studied it closely, and the couple smiled to each other and then to me in an approving way.

'"It was right that you came," they said, and they gathered up the mugs and started to move towards the door of their house. I set off back to my car, and it was only when I saw it that I thought to look at my watch. Exactly three hours had passed since I had left it.

'And so since then I have kept that stick here. I usually keep it beside the fireplace, but I do occasionally take it out with me when I'm walking. I seem to sense when I should do that. There seems to be no pattern to the occasions when I find myself using it. I remember when I got to my aunt's house in Alnwick I had no desire at all to say anything about the stick. I left it in the boot of my car, carefully wrapped up in a blanket I keep there for emergencies.'

'Thank you for telling me about it again,' said Ellen. 'You included a little more than before, I think. I do feel a bit envious of your experience, but I'm really glad that it happened.'

'I'm sure that it has a particular meaning for me,' added her companion. 'Yet I notice that I feel no sense of urgency about discovering what that is. No urgency at all.'

Together they walked down the path to Ellen's car. 'Would you mind sharing the driving?' asked Ellen. 'I'd really appreciate a break from it. Oh, by the way, I've had a problem with the steering, and had to find a garage that would take it on at short notice. Fortunately I did, and it's fine now, but I missed that reunion I was intending to go to.'

'That's a real shame! I know you were looking forward to catching up on all the news with your old friends.'

'Thanks,' said Ellen. 'Actually, I'd like to talk to you about someone else I was supposed to meet there – a man I met on a train. It's a slightly strange story, but I certainly wouldn't put it in the same category as the story of how you came by your stick! I feel a bit uncomfortable about the situation with this man, though, and I'd really welcome the chance just to turn it over in my mind by explaining it all to you. I don't suppose I'll end up being any clearer, but it's important to me that someone else knows; and I can't think of anyone better than you!'

The two women noticed very little of the scenery over the next twenty miles as Ellen told her story. Together they puzzled about the possible meaning of it.

Having exhausted the subject of Adam, the man on the train, they fell silent for some time. The silence was broken by Ellen's friend, Eva. She mentioned that she was feeling hungry, and knew that not far ahead was a car park with a footpath leading from it to a viewing point. She suggested that they could eat their fruit there. The day was now quite warm, and Ellen readily agreed. She parked the car in the shade of an oak tree by the side of the car park. Ellen expressed concern about leaving anything of value in the car. She transferred her book from her briefcase to her bag, and then felt she could leave the rest of her possessions, apart from the fruit which she carried in a separate bag. At first Eva thought that leaving her stick in the car would not worry her, but as Ellen locked the car, she changed her mind, and took it out of the blanket to keep with her.

It was now eleven o'clock. There were no other people about. The footpath had fields on either side. On the right the crop was clearly barley, on the left there was a field of hemp. Ellen was glad to see the return of this crop. This particular variety was not one which could be used for anything other that the production of fibre. She hoped that clothing made from hemp would become more readily available, and she commented on this to Eva.

After about a mile, the path rose steeply up a rocky place. The climb was only about seventy metres, but at the top there was a clear view in all directions but one. There was a viewfinder to help identify various features, but both Ellen and Eva preferred to sit on one of the three benches and enjoy the view, unfettered by the need to name any particular landforms.

They shared a banana, an apple, a pear and some seedless grapes. Eva had brought a flask of rose-hip tea. This was a very welcome addition, as by now they were both thirsty.

'What a pity we can't stay here all day,' sighed Eva. 'I'm not particularly looking forward to the meeting. My main reason for coming was so that we could have more time together. I haven't seen you for ages! It must be about three months since you last came to stay.'

'I know what you mean, Eva, this place feels perfect at the moment. However, I probably didn't remember to tell you that I'd promised to give a short presentation at the meeting, and I really can't back out. Apart from that, Jane will be there. Do you remember my speaking about her? She's the friend who, when I saw her at the last meeting, confided that she had recently had an experience of automatic writing.'

'No,' replied Eva. 'You didn't mention that before. Did she tell you what the writing said, or the circumstances she was in at the time?'

'I think we should make our way back to the car,' replied Ellen. 'I can tell you more while we drive the last leg of our journey. If I started now we'd be rushing, and I don't want that.'

Eva found that her stick was quite useful on the steep path down. She was worried about slipping and falling. She had once had quite an awkward fall which had damaged her back, and it had taken a long time to heal. The stick ensured that she would not fall this time.

They hurried along the path between the fields, reached the car, and loaded in their possessions. Eva adjusted the driving seat and the mirrors. Although she was of a similar height to Ellen, she preferred to be closer to the steering wheel. They calculated that they had just sufficient time to reach the village of Bishop Thorsford to meet the others without needing to hurry. As they rejoined the road, Ellen began to recount all that she knew about Jane's experience of automatic writing.

'When I last saw Jane it was at the last study meeting on agricultural land use. The usual group of us had gathered at Peggy's home. It was at lunchtime, when we were discussing the poor food-conversion ratios that milk production from cattle has in current farming practices, that I noticed that Jane was doodling on her A4 pad. At first I felt irritated by this. It felt like an unwanted intrusion into our discussion. I tried to contain my irritation by asking her about it, and was surprised to find that she was pathetically grateful that I had asked. She told me that there was something on her mind that she would like to talk to me about, that it was nothing to do with the subject of our meeting, and that she was hesitant about confiding it as she was worried about my reaction. I reassured her that I'd be interested to hear anything she wanted to tell me, and I settled myself and opened my mind to whatever she had to say.

'I remember it all quite vividly, so I can tell you almost verbatim what she said. She said: "It was about three weeks ago. I'd been feeling exceptionally tired for no apparent reason. I'd been reading a book that a friend of mine had given me for my birthday last year. The book was written by a woman who had a son who had never been able to speak properly. He made sounds that no one could understand, and as an adolescent he had become almost violent in his frustration about not being able to make people respond to him in the same kind of sounds. His hearing had been tested regularly throughout his childhood, and as far as the tests showed, he certainly heard sounds of a range of pitch. He would tap his right hand each time he heard a sound through the testing headphones, and he would raise or lower his left hand to give a rough indication of the pitch. I rarely read a book at all, and when I do, I read in a way that others would think to be very slow. The book was describing the mother's struggle to keep in some kind of meaningful contact with her son. I won't describe the details of this

– suffice it to say that I became aware that my tiredness had started not long after I read the first few pages of the book. One evening, when I had just finished chapter three, I felt thirsty and sipped a glass of water. I next decided to write up the events of the last couple of days in my diary; and in order to do that, I went to bed and propped myself up on pillows. It was not long before I was comfortably installed with the bedside light as my only source of illumination. I began to write, recalling what I had accomplished, and the feelings I had had about it. I'd had no contact with people apart from exchanging short greetings as I went for a longish walk the day before. My eyes soon felt very heavy, but I was still able to continue writing, or so it seemed to me. In fact, writing in this position seemed to be remarkably easy… I woke several hours later, wondering why the light was on. It didn't take me long to realise that I must have fallen asleep while writing my diary. It was more or less in the same position as before I fell asleep. I was just in the process of closing it to put it on one side prior to switching out the light, when I noticed something odd. I looked at the page I'd been writing on, and I saw that although it certainly started with some description of the day before, it continued in something that looked as if it was *meant* to be writing; but the marks the pen had made were not anything that made sense to me at all! The marks did not follow the lines of the page but appeared in spiral arrangements, each spiral being about three inches in diameter. I turned over the pages and found more spirals. I counted them and found that there were nine in total. When I examined these more closely, it seemed to me that some of them had been formed from the centre of the spiral working outwards, and others had been worked inwards from the outer edge. On further inspection I noticed that some had been worked anticlockwise and others clockwise. There was a further form, a double spiral. This then meant that there were five kinds of spiral. I then studied the marks which made up each spiral. Although fascinated, I soon felt defeated, and fell asleep. I could study them with a fresh eye the next morning."

'Until now, I had been sitting listening, making no comment. However, at this point I asked, "Do you have that diary with you?"

'She said, "No, I never take it out of the house."

'Then we were interrupted by our hostess saying that as lunch was over we should continue with the other item listed for discussion. She introduced the next speaker, Mark, who led a stimulating discussion on developments in berry harvesting in Finland. This ran well over the time allotted, and there was no further time for private conversation before the meeting broke up and we all left. So that's as much as I know,' Ellen concluded.

'Did you not contact Jane afterwards?' asked Eva.

'I tried to,' replied Ellen, 'but she didn't answer the phone; and I later heard from a mutual friend that she had gone to stay with her sister for several months to help with the new baby. She could still travel to work from there, so it wasn't a problem for her to stay for as long as her sister needed. Her sister's husband was working abroad unexpectedly and unavoidably.'

'So,' said Eva slowly, 'this is the first time you'll have spoken to her since that day…'

'Yes, that's right,' replied Ellen.

Chapter Four

Adam had arrived in St Petersburg on July 30th. His friend Boris had been curious about the change in the usual date for his arrival, but he had not pressed Adam for any explanation. He was eager to show Adam the mass of tapes that he had been able to assemble so far. The previous summer they had spent time discussing a project which was now well into its first phase. They first conceived this project as they sat sharing memories of their student days spent in London together. Adam had been remembering how they had for some time made a private study of Romanian folk songs together. Adam and Boris had admired Bartok's collection of Romanian music, and had been determined to add their own efforts to his. Adam's great-grandmother had been Romanian, and he had always had contacts with cousins who lived there. He had written to three of his best-known cousins with a request that they asked all the older people they knew to record on tape any songs they could remember from their youth.

This proved to be a rich source of music, much of which had not to their knowledge been written down previously. Adam and Boris worked together to document this music. Sadly, they had never reached the stage of preparing it for publication. They had had no more time, and they also felt that there would be no market for such a volume. On that evening last summer, Boris had leaped to his feet, and rushed out of the room. He returned a little later with a flat parcel covered in faded brown paper and tied up with dirty ribbon.

'I had completely forgotten about it,' he said, 'but I have had it safely packed in an old chest in which I keep the few rare manuscripts I have collected over my life.'

He untied the ribbon, opened the paper, and there they could see once again the results of their labours of those bygone years.

'Things have changed quite a lot since then,' Adam reflected. 'People in the UK are showing increasing interest in this kind of thing. Let's look through it all again.'

They spent the evening playing through a number of the songs. They took it in turns to improvise an accompaniment on Boris' piano, while they both sang enthusiastically.

At about 1.30 in the morning they both collapsed into bed, exhausted but content.

The next day plans started to form. With the time they now had available, why not prepare these songs for publication? Why not start to collect songs from other sources?

They made lists of people to contact. They decided to start with the contacts Boris had amongst teachers of music, inviting contributions from all over Russia. They drafted letters to let them know that they were hoping that any interested students would gather songs from local people by recording on tape.

Since those first letters had been sent last summer, Boris soon found that many enthusiastic students had contacted friends about the project, and tapes had been arriving from locations more widespread than Adam and Boris could ever have hoped for. Although Adam knew of this, he was astonished when he saw all the tapes heaped in a large cardboard box beside Boris' desk.

'Well,' he said, 'let's get to work as soon as we can. I'm here for eight weeks, and we can put all of our time together into this.'

'I agree,' replied Boris. 'I wanted to wait until you arrived to see how you felt, and I am relieved that you are as keen as I am to get started straight away.'

Every day, the two men would work through the morning, eat lunch, walk together for a couple of hours discussing something of what each had discovered that morning, have a snack, work on until about 8 p.m. and then finish for the day. The rest of the evening was spent preparing and eating a meal together.

The days passed in the low-built house well outside the suburbs of St Petersburg. The routine was the same each day, but the music was richly varied. Fascinating though it was, Adam became aware of a nagging feeling at the back of his mind that he could not quite grasp. At first the feeling was not at all intrusive, just a vague awareness that he was thinking of something in addition to the music. Then the feeling became clearer. After this it became very insistent, and he laid down his pen – *the* pen – the one his wife had given him all those years ago. And now he remembered Ellen, the woman on the train. He began to hear the sound of the train again, and it tried to weave itself, unsuccessfully, into the music. After struggling for half and hour or more, he broke the pattern of their timetable and spoke to his friend.

'Boris, would you mind if we took a break? I've something that I'd like to turn over with you.'

Boris looked up, surprised. 'Of course; let us take a longer walk today.'

They walked along, at ease with each other, although Adam was feeling uneasy within himself. What would his friend think of him when he told the story of his contact with Ellen? There was really very little to tell, and he feared that Boris would think he was unbalanced in some way, after admitting to being so drawn to someone who was barely an acquaintance.

Boris prompted him by asking, 'Has this something to do with the reason why your visit was later this year?'

Adam jumped as if he had been 'found out'. He had a strange sense of feeling exposed, although it was quite a natural question for his friend to ask. Indeed, it would not have been surprising if Boris had asked some time ago what had been the reason for his delay. He decided that he would just go ahead and describe to Boris the meeting on the train, the encounter in the hotel, the letters, the reunion gathering and his time with Ellen at the Traveller's Arms.

Boris listened without interrupting. When Adam had finished he said, 'I am glad you told me, and I look forward to anything else you want to tell me about this when you have returned home. One thing is obvious to me, you will certainly be seeing her again, and that time is not very far away.'

Adam felt calmed by this conversation, and had no further difficulty in concentrating on the transcription of the Russian songs. They had already been developing a good cataloguing system, and they both hoped that by the time Adam left they would have processed about thirty of the fifty tapes they had already received. A few more had arrived during the course of Adam's stay. They were pleased about this, and they both started to discuss plans that Adam should return in the spring of the following year so that they could keep the work going. In the interim, Boris would continue to contact students who might gather songs in the form of recordings, and Adam would research the possibility of publishing their old collection of Romanian songs in the UK.

Chapter Five

Ellen and Eva were nearing Bishop Thorsford by noon. They had been sitting in silence over the last few miles.

'Apart from wanting to learn more about Jane's spirals, I'm glad we're coming after all,' said Eva. 'A meeting of this kind, where the background and training of each of the people are so different, but the subject matter is of common interest, is potentially so much more stimulating than the meetings and conferences I usually go to. Now, please can you remind me of the directions to Peggy's house?'

'It's the second turning on the left,' answered Ellen. 'Then drive down to the end of that road. Peggy's house is down a track which leads from there. If I remember correctly, we'll be able to park at the front of her house.'

It took only a few more minutes to reach the beginning of the driveway to Peggy's home. Once they were on the driveway, the house was clearly visible through the avenue of lime trees. She had lived there since she was a child. She was an only child, and her parents had been killed in a road accident just as she had planned to leave home. She had never married, and had filled her life studying environmental issues and supporting organisations and groups who tried to initiate changes in existing systems of land use in order to preserve or restore the balance of nature. She had continued to maintain the large walled garden at the rear of the house in much the same way as it had been managed for generations. This included the use of companion plants for pest control. About ten years previously she had started to take an interest in biodynamic methods, some aspects of which she had incorporated into the annual cycle of management of her garden.

Eva parked the car next to a vehicle which was completely unfamiliar to her. On closer inspection she and Ellen came to the conclusion that it was the prototype of something new. Although the front door of the house stood open, Ellen rang the bell, and she and Eva waited until Peggy appeared and welcomed them in.

'It's good to see you both,' she said as she took them into the room they always used for meetings.

It was a large room to the right of the front door. It had a bay window which looked out past the nearest lime tree and across fields. 'I'm afraid some of the others couldn't come after all,' she continued. 'Jane phoned to say that she had tripped on an uneven pavement, and she's damaged her ankle. It happened yesterday; she had to go to hospital. She had a three-hour wait in casualty before being X-rayed. They bandaged it, and she's resting at home. She has friends who come in to help, so she's managing okay.'

'I'm very sorry to hear about that,' said Ellen. She turned to Eva. 'Perhaps we could visit her on our way back? It would be a bit of a detour to get there, and it rather depends on whether you can spare the extra time. I could certainly manage it myself. What do you think?'

Eva pondered for a while. 'It'll be difficult for me to rearrange things to free up the time we'd need, but I think I want to try. Will you leave it with me and I'll let you know later? I'll have to work out what to do. After what you told me about Jane's experience with the spiral writing, I'm keen to see her, particularly since she's at home and will have her diary with her there.'

Peggy did not hear this part of the conversation. She had moved across to welcome another member of their group who had just arrived.

Out of the twelve members of the group, only five had been able to come. This was an unusually small number. Several people had had to cancel at short notice, either through illness or some other misfortune. Apart from Ellen and Eva, there was Peggy herself, Mark, and Barry, who was the owner of the curious vehicle.

The five decided that even their minimal formalities were inappropriate on this occasion. Peggy had prepared some cold food for lunch. This consisted of large bowls of mixed salads with special dressings made to recipes devised by Peggy herself. She had experimented over the years with the ingredients, most of which she grew in the walled garden. People who had been lucky enough to taste them found it hard to describe the beneficial effect which these combinations had upon them. A certain vibrance seemed to

31

flow from the food. The effect seemed to come from both the way it was grown, and the way the foods were combined in each dish.

After lunch it was decided to use the material collected by Ellen for her short presentation as a focus for deeper discussion. They hoped that openings for further investigation would arise from this. Ellen told them of the contacts she had made with schools where a successful kitchen garden had been created. She had visited a primary school where children tended the garden lovingly, under the supervision of a school auxiliary. She had brought photographs of the children harvesting the produce and taking it to the cooks who, with further help from the children, incorporated it into the school lunches. Apart from discussion about the most successful foods produced in these gardens, the main interest of the group of five was on the development of a system whereby more schools could be encouraged to enter similar schemes, and be supported in the early stages of development.

At six o'clock, Peggy reluctantly drew the time to the attention of the others, and they realised that they would have to draw the discussion to a close and leave.

'What's your decision about detouring via Jane's house?' Ellen asked Eva.

'While you were eating lunch I made a phone call, and I've reorganised things so that I can,' answered Eva. 'The other thing I wanted to mention is that as far as I'm concerned, you're welcome to stay the night with me, then you won't have to drive through the night to get home.'

'That's good of you,' Ellen replied.

'Not really,' smiled Eva. 'I'd like to have you, and if our plans go well, we'll have spoken to Jane and seen her diary, and I'm sure that you and I will have plenty to talk about after that.'

'I think the best thing is if we phone Jane now,' suggested Ellen. She asked Peggy if she might use her phone, consulted a list of numbers on a card in her purse, and rang Jane's number. An unfamiliar voice answered. For a moment Ellen felt non-plussed, then she asked to speak to Jane.

'Yes, of course, I'll hand you over,' said the voice. 'Is that everything you need then, Jane? – Okay... bye.'

Ellen then heard Jane's familiar tones saying, 'Who's that?... Oh, Ellen! It's really good to hear you... you want to come and see me?... Great, are you sure?... That would be nice... You have Eva with you?... That's right, we've not met, but do bring her. I'm rather immobile at the moment... Peggy told you? Right then, I'll see you both in about an hour. The key will be in the usual place under that broken plant pot. Do you remember? Yes. All right then.'

Ellen and Eva thanked Peggy for her hospitality, and prepared to drive off. They sat and watched in both amazement and amusement while Barry lifted up the top of his strange vehicle, climbed in, and slid off almost noiselessly down the road.

'He must be battery-powered,' remarked Ellen.

Eva smiled. 'Yes, I'd heard that he'd been experimenting with a one-person, lightweight vehicle of this type. I wish that we'd had a chance to ask him about it. I know that he has a wind generator on his land, so I expect he charges up batteries overnight.'

The evening was warm and the air was clear and pleasant. They drove with the windows open to enjoy the effect, and chatted in an anticipatory way as they looked forward to the possibility of seeing the spiral writings in Jane's diary.

Jane lived on the outskirts of the small town of Castle Brimswich. Her bungalow was of a style that suggested that it was built about thirty years ago. Ellen remembered the way to it without any difficulty. She drew her car up in front of Jane's garage. The scent of lavender was quite obvious as they got out of the car and their legs brushed past the low bushes along the path up to the side gate. Ellen led the way round to the back, found the broken plant pot with the key underneath, and unlocked the back door.

'Jane, we're here!' she called as she made her way through the kitchen into the hall, Eva following close behind.

'Lock the back door behind you, please,' returned Jane, 'and then come into the sitting room on the left. There have been some burglaries locally in the last few months, and I don't want to take any risks.'

Ellen locked the door. She and Eva found Jane sitting with her right leg raised on a stool with a pillow on top.

'I was told that it was best to keep it up,' she explained ruefully. 'I really do feel a fool. Fortunately the X-ray showed I had not broken anything, but the ligaments are badly torn, and here I am laid up like this. I feel it was all my own fault for not picking my feet up when I walk.'

'Don't blame yourself like that,' said Ellen, 'it doesn't help; and anyway there are places in pavements where the paving stones are very uneven. I'm sorry that this has happened to you. You must be feeling quite shocked.'

'Well, now you mention it, I have to say that I feel I just can't get warm.'

'Have you got a hot-water bottle anywhere?' Eva asked, concerned.

'There's one in the bedroom, just on the floor inside the door. Yes, I'd be very grateful if you'd fill it for me. But I should at least say hello, and that it's nice to meet you, before you start rushing around on my behalf!'

Eva grinned, and went off to put the kettle on for the bottle. She rummaged around in her bag and produced a small bottle of white tablets. A few minutes later she returned to the sitting room, put the hot-water bottle behind Jane's back, and sat down on the sofa next to Ellen.

'Jane,' she began, 'have you ever taken homeopathic medicines?'

'Not personally, but I know a few people who use them.'

'Well,' Eva continued, 'would you be willing to give one a try right now? It might help.'

Jane thought for a moment or two. 'Tell me exactly what you have in mind first, and then I'll decide.'

Eva explained. 'I happen to have with me some tablets of a homeopathically prepared medicine called Traumeel S. You may have heard of homeopathic Arnica being used in cases of shock and bruising.'

'Well, as a matter of fact that does sound familiar,' said Jane, 'and I do remember my mother saying that Arnica was used for sprains in the gym when she was at school.'

'Oh good,' Eva continued. 'Well, Traumeel S has Arnica in it, but it has a number of other constituents too. I first heard of it from a masseuse from Spain. She gave it a glowing reference, and I've found it to be excellent. I'd say that it's more effective than Arnica alone.'

Jane decided to give it a try.

'When did you last have anything to eat or drink?' asked Eva.

'About half an hour ago.'

'Well, that's fine, you can take some straight away.'

'What do you mean?'

'It's important when one takes a homeopathic remedy that there's no food or drink in the person's mouth. Half an hour is a good space of time to ensure that the mouth is clean. It's also important to have nothing after taking the remedy, preferably for a further half-hour.'

'Okay then,' said Jane. 'Here we go.'

Eva tore a clean piece of white paper out of a writing pad she saw on the low table and folded it. She gently tapped the bottle of tablets as she tipped it towards the white paper until two tablets landed in the fold. 'It's better not to touch them,' she said. 'I'm going to drop them from the paper into your mouth. Let them dissolve slowly under your tongue.' She leaned over and dropped them into Jane's mouth. Jane obediently moved them under her tongue, and held them there as they dissolved. This did not restrict further conversation, and they moved to other subjects.

'I'm really pleased to see you both.' Jane's enthusiasm was obvious. 'I can manage, but it feels a lot better to have people coming in. I got such a shock when I fell, and you might think it silly, but I'm afraid of falling again, even though I've plenty of furniture to hold on to.'

Ellen's voice was warm and concerned. 'It's perfectly understandable that you would feel like that. Try not to worry. Perhaps we should start off by discussing how long we might stay. For myself, I can certainly stay until about 10.30 this evening. If we leave then, Eva and I would arrive at her house at midnight. Is that okay for you, Eva?'

'Yes, that would be fine. I don't have an early start in the morning.'

Jane looked pleased. 'I'd be grateful for that. I could get into bed just before you leave. Now do tell me how the study day went; I was so disappointed to miss it.'

Ellen and Eva gave Jane a description of the day. Jane asked so many pertinent questions that they all expressed further regret that she had not been there. Such questions would have been an important stimulus to the group discussion.

Time slipped by quickly. Eva glanced at her watch, and was astonished to see that it was already after ten o'clock.

'Oh no!' she exclaimed.

'What's the matter?' asked Jane.

'The automatic writing!' Eva felt a little embarrassed at having blurted this out, and she coloured.

'Oh, has Ellen been telling you about it?' asked Jane.

'Yes indeed, and to be truthful I'm eager to hear more about it,' admitted Eva.

Ellen smiled. 'Actually I think this time I might not have gone to the study group if it had not been for the automatic writing. I haven't had a chance to tell you yet, but I tried phoning you after you'd told me about it at the last meeting.'

'Oh… and of course I was at my sister's for a long time after that,' said Jane.

'The study group proved to be well worth attending, and I'm very glad I went,' Ellen continued, 'but I really want to talk about the writing again. However, you must be exhausted, and we must go.'

Jane pondered. 'Look,' she said, 'I've a proposition to make to you both. Tomorrow is Sunday. I assume that neither of you is working. Do you have any other commitments?'

Ellen and Eva looked at each other and shook their heads.

'I've a spare room with a double bed in it. I'd be very happy for you to stay the night if you don't mind sharing the bed. This would of course mean that I'm not alone – which I'd appreciate, as I do feel rather wobbly. In the morning we could have some time talking about the writing, and I can tell you where to find the diary that I was using at the time. What do you think?'

Ellen turned to Eva. 'If we leave here at about lunchtime, we could get back to your house by about 3 p.m. If I could have a break there for an hour, I can drive on home, and get there for about 6 p.m., which would suit me very well. Is that all right for you?'

'I think that would work out very well,' returned Eva. 'Now that's settled, let's put Jane to bed.'

'There are spare nightclothes in the cupboard in that room,' Jane offered. 'I'm happy for you to use them. I always keep something for unexpected overnight stays, together with spare toothbrushes!'

'You *are* well organised,' chorused Ellen and Eva. 'Now, let's get you tucked in.'

The next morning Ellen woke first. She slipped out of bed quietly in order to avoid disturbing Eva, who looked so peaceful and relaxed that she was determined not to wake her. She took her clothes into the bathroom, showered and dressed there, and then proceeded to the kitchen where she made a start by boiling the kettle. Looking for something to drink, she came across a selection of herb tea sachets, but in the end opted to have a mug of hot water. She made her way down the hall to Jane's bedroom. It was half past eight, not too early to put her head round the door to see if she was awake. She tapped lightly on the door, and Jane's voice answered in tones which clearly showed she was pleased that someone was up. Ellen went into the room.

'Hello,' she said. 'How did you sleep last night?'

'Surprisingly well,' came the reply. 'I think I'll get up now. I've been awake here for about half an hour, thinking about that spiral writing. The more I thought about it, the more I found I was looking forward to discussing it with you both. I haven't mentioned it to anyone else since I told you about it; my mind has been taken up with so many other things. I haven't even finished reading the book which I still believe was a factor in the appearance of the spiral writing. I'll tell you where to look for that book and the diary. I'd appreciate it if you'd get them while I wash and dress.'

'That's fine by me,' Ellen replied. 'But what about something to eat and drink? And we should think about waking Eva.'

'My ankle doesn't feel too bad this morning,' Jane remarked. 'I'd expected it to be more painful than this. Perhaps those tablets Eva gave me last night have had some effect… I must ask her more about them. I'll be careful, though. I'll take my time getting dressed. Would muesli be all right for your breakfast? I mix it up myself.

There's a large jar of it in the pantry. Can you wake Eva on your way to the kitchen? The book and the diary are towards the left of the top shelf of the bookcase in the room where you slept. The diary has "Diary" written on the spine and the book is called *Communications* by Frances Ianson.'

By about nine o'clock, they were all sitting eating muesli. Eva had insisted that Jane should keep her ankle up, so the stool and pillow arrangement had been reassembled.

'How is it that you are so knowledgeable about these things?' asked Jane.

Eva laughed. 'It is my work,' she said. 'I trained as a doctor, and then took a course in homeopathy.'

'I'd like to hear more about that,' Jane rejoined eagerly.

Ellen smiled. 'Oh dear,' she said. 'Amongst friends there is never enough time to talk about all the things one wants to. I think we'd better stick to our original plan, and then move on to other things if there's any time left. I have the book and the diary here, I found them just where Jane had told me to look. Now we've finished breakfast, let's take the bowls to the kitchen, and make a start.'

Ellen took the bowls, and when she returned she opened the diary.

Chapter Six

Ellen stared at the spiral shapes. Although Jane had described them to her, the impact of seeing them herself was quite different. There were indeed nine individual spiral forms. Eight of these were simple spiral shapes, but the ninth was a double spiral; and where the two spirals almost met, the line of each spiral was straight instead of curved. Although there was only enough room on each page for two spirals, there was a small diagram which seemed to indicate how they should be arranged. The double spiral was the central form; the other eight spirals were arranged round it. There was an inner arrangement of four and an outer arrangement of four, each of which was opposite a gap between two of the inner spirals. Each of the two sets of four spirals contained one of each of the four types: one formed anticlockwise from the middle outwards, one anticlockwise from the outside to the middle, one clockwise from the middle outwards and one clockwise from the outside to the middle.

Having studied the spirals this much, she handed the diary to Eva, who herself stared silently at the shapes for some time.

It was Jane who broke the silence.

'Not only is there the puzzle of the spiral shapes themselves, but also there is the way the lines of the spirals are formed. I really am astonished at how precise and intricate these workings are. I had my usual ball-point pen, which produces quite a fine line, but I find it amazing that I apparently produced these intricacies while half lying down, and using a fairly ordinary pen.'

Eva started to describe a section of the first spiral that appeared after the handwritten description of Jane's day had petered out. The line was sometimes a series of tiny dots or small dashes; sometimes it was a continuous line with tiny regular markings off either one side or the other, and sometimes both. She followed the line a little farther, and found that in places there were even some minute sub-spirals. The farther she followed the line, the more kinds of marking she noted.

'I think I should let you have a closer look at this now, Ellen,' she said.

The next hour was spent in silence. The diary was passed between them at intervals, so that each could have a chance to make further study of the construction of the spirals.

'Apart from being fascinated by the pattern,' said Ellen, 'I feel that looking at the spirals is affecting me in some way.'

'Do you know,' said Eva, 'I was just about to say exactly the same thing. I was sitting here trying to work out how I'm being affected, but I just can't put words round it.'

'Of course,' said Jane, 'I've seen them before; but I haven't looked at them recently. Because I have seen them before, I'm really in a different position from both of you. Yet despite having seen them before, the fine structure of the spirals is still a surprise to me – but maybe this will be less so than for you. However, I feel affected too in a way I don't seem to be able to pin down.'

'Ellen!' said Eva suddenly. 'You remember the stick?'

'Yes,' replied Ellen. 'Why?'

'Do you remember when I was telling you the story of how I came by it, I described how the old woman had brought me a drink?'

'Yes, of course.'

'Well, I have a sense that the effect that looking at the spirals is having on me is a bit like the way I was affected by the drink the old woman gave me.'

Jane interrupted: 'Please will you explain what you are both talking about?'

'Oh, I'm really sorry,' replied Eva and Ellen almost in unison.

Ellen continued, 'I'll stay quiet while you tell your story to Jane. Better still, perhaps I could go and get the stick out of the car.'

'I didn't leave it in the car!' laughed Eva. 'Remember how I take very good care of it? I brought it into the house! I'm surprised you didn't notice. It's behind the door of the room where we slept.'

Ellen fetched the stick, and handed it to Jane to look at, while Eva started to tell its history.

When the story was finished, Jane was eager to ask more about the drink. 'Did you see the old woman prepare it?' she asked.

'No,' replied Eva, 'she made it inside and brought it out to me.

Although it was still warm, it seemed to have a cool flavour. Its taste was different from anything I've drunk before or since. There was a definite and particular energy, or vibrance, associated with it. I couldn't tell the colour because of the dark earthenware mug it was in. When I was drinking it, and for a while afterwards, although I knew that everything was the same, my perception changed, so that my experience of everything felt much more profound. For example, as I said to Ellen, I was aware of perceiving beautiful colours, although I still saw the leaves and fields in their usual shades of autumn. When I look at the spirals I see them as they are. I can describe their structure to you and you would agree with me; but there's something else happening too. I'm not seeing beautiful colours on this occasion, but I do have a feeling of a deeper sense of perception without having any way of describing it further.'

Jane was listening intently to everything Eva said. She thought for a few minutes. 'I do think my own experience is like that too. I wish I could say something more, but there seem to be no words.'

Ellen was sitting very still and looking slightly detached but relaxed. Jane spoke to her, but she did not seem to hear. Jane and Eva looked at each other mutely, wondering what to do. Eva put her finger to her lips, and Jane nodded slightly. They both looked at Ellen once more. By this time her eyelids had begun to droop. After a while, her lips started to move, almost imperceptibly. Jane and Eva stared at her. The movement of Ellen's lips became progressively more pronounced, until it seemed she was mouthing something. The movements of her mouth did not seem to relate to any words, and she made no sounds.

Jane and Eva glanced at each other, nodded, and then continued watching Ellen. Ellen began to make some slight sounds. Eva and Jane leaned forward, listening intently, and then looked at each other once more. They shook their heads; neither could make out what the sounds were. Gradually the sounds faded; gradually the movements of Ellen's mouth ceased. She sat completely still with her eyelids half shut for several minutes.

She then started to rub her eyes. 'Oh, I feel a bit odd,' she said. 'What time is it?'

Jane looked at her watch. 'It's nearly half past twelve.'

'Just about lunchtime then,' said Ellen.

Jane and Eva stared at her.

'What's the matter with you two? Why are you looking at me like that?' Ellen burst out.

Jane and Eva patiently explained to her exactly what they had seen happening to her. Ellen gaped, first in disbelief, and then with dawning acceptance of what had been described to her.

'I'm feeling quite chilled,' she said. 'I'll just go and get an extra jumper and a mug of hot water.' She soon returned, looking rather pale.

'I still feel a bit odd. I wonder why I went into that peculiar state you described. All I remember is that I was studying the minute pen strokes that make up the double spiral shape, then the next thing was finding you two staring at me. You've explained how I was behaving, but I have no memory of it myself at all.'

The three were rather shaken by this turn of events. Together they decided that since time was pressing, Eva would make them all something to eat, and that when they had eaten, she would drive Ellen's car for at least the first half-hour. They all agreed that it was better for Ellen not to drive until she had recovered a little more. They wished they had more time to discuss the configuration of the spirals, their reaction to them, and in particular what had happened to Ellen. It was difficult to guess when they would all be able to meet again, but they agreed to keep in touch. Ellen and Eva made sure that Jane had everything she needed to hand. She assured them that another friend would be calling in the mid-afternoon. After that, they said goodbye.

In the end, Eva drove Ellen's car all the way to her house. They had intended to share the driving, but Ellen still felt a little odd, so Eva continued. Ellen spent an hour relaxing in Eva's house before driving home. She phoned Eva when she got in to let her know that she had arrived safely. Eva had asked her to do this because she was concerned. She had tried to persuade Ellen to stay the night, but Ellen had been adamant that she was feeling fine by then, and anyway she had to start work again the next day. Although she had an independent income from her late father's estate, she now had considerable responsibility in the running of a charity which supported homeless people, and those who found it difficult to make the transition between places in long-stay hospitals and community living. She knew that she would not be able to take any more time away from her work for some weeks. She spent the evening unpacking and organising things in such a way as to keep housework to a minimum, as she knew she had a heavy schedule facing her.

Chapter Seven

'The first day of September,' mused Adam. 'I find it hard to believe I've been here for more than four weeks already. I'm glad I have nearly four more weeks left. Quite a number of new tapes have been arriving, and we now have sixty-five in total. It has been good to find that students have been so enthusiastic about gathering these songs, and that the people who sing them have not been too reluctant to be recorded.'

'It is so good to have you here,' said Boris. 'I am glad we have more time, and that I will not have to wait until next summer before you return. Our idea of your returning next spring is ideal for me and for our project. How long do you think you will be able to stay then?'

'I'll have to look into it in more detail once I'm back home, but I hope that I'll be able to be here for about five weeks.'

Boris relaxed. 'That's excellent!' he said.

The days continued to pass in the pattern that the two had laid out for themselves. They studied side by side; they walked together every day discussing new material they found on the tapes, and they cooked and ate in the late evenings. The rhythm of their lives carried a feeling of timelessness, but nevertheless Adam was vaguely aware that the days he had left to work here were becoming fewer. He consulted the calendar – September 21st – only seven days left, and then he must board his plane to return home.

He turned to Boris. 'Old friend,' he said, 'I'll miss you and our work here together a lot. I feel that this time we've had has brought us closer together than ever before.'

'I agree,' said Boris. 'Although I know that you are going to try to find a publisher for our earlier work, and that has to do with our shared life, it is not the same as working together here. While you are away I would prefer not to work on any of the tapes. Do you mind? I will collect up any new ones that come in, and store them carefully, together with those we have which we have not yet processed. We have done well. We have already finished thirty-eight tapes, which is more than the thirty we thought we would cover. I hope we shall do another two each by the end of this last week.'

'I'm glad you won't be working on them while I am away,' said Adam. 'I realise I would prefer it that way too.'

In the afternoon of the next day, just after their daily walk and snack, Adam picked up his next tape. He loaded it into the tape deck, put his headphones on, and switched it on. At first there was a solo voice, a rich tenor, which was soon joined by what was obviously a large gathering of people. He was aware from the beginning that this was a different type of music altogether from any that the other tapes had revealed. While they worked, Adam and Boris rarely spoke to each other, but on this occasion Adam stopped the tape and touched Boris' arm urgently. His friend realised that there was something important happening, and immediately switched off the tape he had been working on and turned to Adam.

'What is it?' he asked.

'I want you to listen to this,' said Adam. He started to play the tape through the speakers.

'The origins of this music are clearly quite different from any of the rest I have been working on,' said Boris.

'That's exactly my experience,' said Adam, 'so I wanted you to hear it straight away. Shall I play some more of it?'

Adam ran the tape back to the beginning, switched it on, and then played it for about ten minutes. After this, they sat in silence for a while, staring at each other.

'I don't really know what to say,' said Adam, 'but I think I'd like to hear it again.'

Boris was keen to hear it again too, and suggested that this time Adam did not stop the tape.

The two men sat almost motionless as they shared the experience. The only movement was when they reached out to each other to join hands. Boris ran the tape back to the beginning.

Without referring to Adam, he started it once more. Again they sat almost motionless, holding hands. About halfway through, Boris noticed that Adam's hand seemed colder than before. He turned to look at his friend, and was surprised to see that his eyelids were drooping. He felt a little concerned, but said nothing. A few minutes later, he noticed that Adam's lips seemed to be moving very slightly. His hand was still cold. Boris let the tape keep playing, and he sat and observed his friend. By now Adam's mouth was moving quite obviously, and his throat too was moving, as if he were singing, but there was no sound.

The tape finished. Boris continued to hold Adam's hand, reluctant to break that contact while he was in this state. His mouth was no longer moving, but his hand remained cold and his eyelids drooping. Boris sat and watched him carefully. He appeared motionless except for his breathing, which was very slow and measured. Boris decided that the best thing was to sit and wait. Although he did not understand what was happening, he did not feel there was any reason to worry about Adam's health. Instinctively he sensed that it was important not to interfere in any way with what he was experiencing.

From time to time he looked at his watch. Ten minutes had passed since the tape ended, then twenty, then thirty. Then Boris became aware that Adam's hand was slightly warmer. He waited another ten minutes, during which Adam's eyes opened fully, and his hand and his breathing became normal for someone who was fully conscious.

Adam turned to Boris. 'Now that we've had a chance to absorb the music on that tape, tell me what you think of it.'

'I have something else I have to talk to you about first,' answered Boris.

'What do you mean?'

'Well,' said Boris carefully, 'first I want to talk to you about what I saw happening to you.'

'What are you talking about?'

Adam was clearly puzzled, and Boris was then sure that he had no awareness of the change that he had undergone. He suggested that they made a drink for themselves, and went to sit on the bench outside to talk about what had happened.

Sitting side by side in the late afternoon sun, the two men relaxed as they gazed across the fields to the ancient birch woods beyond.

'Now tell me,' said Adam.

Boris described everything from when he had noticed how Adam's hand had become colder. Adam listened without interrupting. He trusted his friend completely, so that although he felt incredulous, he also knew he was hearing the truth.

'You say that you first noticed my hand was colder about halfway through the tape?' asked Adam.

'Yes, I did,' confirmed Boris.

'I do remember that after the first time we listened to the whole side of that tape I had a feeling of wanting to talk to you about something; but I so much wanted to hear it right through, I decided to wait. I can't remember what I would have said to you, but I do remember the feeling. Perhaps we should listen to the tape again.'

'I think we should,' said Boris, 'but not now. I think it would be wise to leave it until at least tomorrow.'

'I think I agree,' replied Adam. 'Perhaps we should leave the tapes for today. Shall we cook early and then spend the evening playing chess?'

'But first shall we make some more of that vegetable stew we enjoyed so much last week? I have just remembered I froze some fresh young nettles in the spring this year; we could add these,' said Boris.

'Excellent!' replied Adam enthusiastically.

Later in the evening the two men were sitting and setting out the chess pieces. 'I've always admired this set,' said Adam, 'where did it come from?'

'Have I never told you before? My grandfather carved these pieces himself. He died before I was born so I never saw him do it. My grandmother told me that it was one of his hobbies after he became too old to do heavy work. He used to sit on the bench outside in the afternoons and work on these pieces. Time did not matter at all to him, and he did it solely for his own enjoyment. Fortunately his eyesight remained very good; and this, along with his carving skills, meant that he was able to produce these beautiful and intricate designs.'

They played the game slowly, with much discussion between moves. The game was not central to their conversation, it was a pleasant addition. They reminisced about their student days, laughing out loud at some of the events they each recalled. They drew up a list of possible leads for Adam to follow when trying to get a publisher for their early collection of songs. After finally completing the game of chess, they played duets on Boris' piano, delighting in having the freedom to stop and repeat passages that they particularly enjoyed. They finished with Schubert's 'Fantasie', and then leaped up and hugged each other.

It was late. Tomorrow they would listen to that tape again.

Although Adam was tired, he could not settle. He tried reading a gardening magazine from the collection that Boris had thoughtfully left on a small table beside his bed. Blueberry bushes floated around in front of his eyes as he tried to doze. Eventually he fell asleep, but he kept waking, aware that he had been hearing once more the sounds of that train… the train where he had first met Ellen.

When morning came he was glad to get up. There was no sign of Boris yet, so he walked in the garden and watched a bird having a dust-bath in a particularly dry patch that had yielded a crop of potatoes earlier that summer. He was reluctant to eat breakfast until his friend joined him, so he eventually sat on the bench and sipped a glass of water. His mind went back to what Boris had told him of the state he had entered when they listened to that tape yesterday. As he reflected on it, he began to doubt whether it would be the right thing to listen to it again today. They had only a few days left now before he had to leave, and it was important that they continued to process the remaining tapes. Perhaps they should lay that one aside for now, and work on the others. He did want to know more about what had happened to him and why. He wanted to remember what he had been going to say to Boris after they first listened to the whole side of the tape. But he had a feeling that if they started to concentrate on that, it might well take up most of the time they had left. Being completely honest with himself, he also felt reluctant to investigate this further at a time when he would soon be parted from his friend.

When Boris appeared his face showed concern. 'Adam, you look really tired this morning,' he said, as they went indoors.

Adam explained about his disturbed night, and then went on to share his thoughts of this morning about the tape. 'You may be right,' said Boris. 'Although I am keen to learn more about what happened to you, let us just leave it for now, work on two of the remaining tapes, and I will put yesterday's tape in this cupboard.' He opened a long narrow glass-fronted cupboard which was near the fireplace. It had five shelves in it. He put the tape on the top shelf, along with some delicate glassware.

They began work once more. Adam found that he could not focus on the task as he had been able to do before. He kept finding himself staring out of the window. He could hear the music on the tape he was supposed to be studying, but it seemed to be much in the background. Again he could hear the sounds of the train. Again he heard some passages he remembered from that tape of yesterday. His thoughts ran past the chess set of last night which was carved in that strange and unusually intricate way. Even the delicate glassware he had glimpsed in the cupboard this morning was having a greater impact than the sound of the music he was supposed to be studying.

At length he turned to his friend and said, 'I think I need to go outside this morning. I don't feel I can do any more work at the moment.'

'Shall I come too?' asked Boris, concerned; his friend looked so tired, and almost unwell.

'I think I need to be on my own for a while this morning,' said Adam. 'There are so many things on my mind. I think I need to walk about slowly for a while. Actually, I feel in a state of shock, but I don't really know why. Your telling me what happened to me when we listened to yesterday's tape has affected me a lot; but that's not all.'

He stood up slowly and heavily. Although the air was quite warm, he put on a coat, and walked out into the garden. Boris watched him go. He understood that Adam needed to be alone for a while, but he made a mental note of the time, and decided that if Adam had not returned in about an hour and a half, he would go out and look to see where he was. He assumed that he would take one of the usual routes they followed on the walks they had shared each day. Boris noted the direction Adam took, and then resumed his work. He was becoming more and more aware of just how much he would miss Adam when he returned to the UK at the end of the week.

Adam took the route that led him towards the ancient birch woods. It did not seem to be a conscious decision, his feet merely seemed to take him there. As he proceeded down the path between the fields, all the different parts of the jumble of thoughts in his mind continued to appear and disappear, unchanged. He felt very tired and dispirited. He was barely aware of the vegetation along the sides of the path. This was unusual; his eyes were normally alert to the array of grasses, wild flowers and even certain of the mosses. He felt so weary. No, it was beyond that; he felt at the end of his energies. Despite this, he continued to make his way very slowly towards the edge of the woods. Gradually the slow rhythm of his walking movements began to still the jumble of thoughts in his mind. He was able to think about each thing separately, and to ponder on the meaning of each without feeling he had to come to any conclusion. He reached the birch trees and was enveloped in their cool shade. The shapes of the branches calmed him, the gentle movements of the leaves made precisely the sound he needed. Without having to think about which direction to take, he followed one of the paths that was so familiar from his shared walks with Boris.

As time passed, he began to feel that not only was it all right to have these things to think about, but also he was feeling a sense of fascination about them instead of being totally overwhelmed. He began to look forward to a long process of savouring their existence in his life. He felt he could pull them out and think about them again whenever he wanted to.

He noticed that his pace had quickened a little, and he began to think of Boris and the rest of the tapes. Perhaps he would be able to complete one more before he had to leave. He walked briskly back to the house. Boris looked up and smiled in welcome; he was pleased and relieved to see some colour in his friend's cheeks. Adam sat down in a businesslike fashion, and the two worked on until lunchtime.

The end of the week came. Boris drove Adam to the airport and waited with him as long as he could; a long hug, and then they parted.

Adam's flight home was uneventful. Next week he hoped to be making a number of phone calls which would start off the process of finding a way to get that early collection of songs published.

Chapter Eight

It was October. Jane's ankle felt fine, so much so that she rarely thought of the day when she had tripped and fallen so awkwardly that she had thought it was broken. After Ellen and Eva had left, her friends had provided enough help, and she had been very glad of their support. She made her way around her home very gingerly at first. Fortunately her work as a secretary for a firm on a local industrial estate was a job where she could sit down most of the time. A friend from work had offered her transport, and consequently she had needed to take only two days off.

Although thoughts of her ankle had more or less faded, memories of that Sunday morning she had spent with Ellen and Eva looking at the spirals in her diary had not. She looked forward to being able to arrange a time when the three of them could be together again. Telephone conversations about such matters would be possible, but unsatisfying.

Last week they had been in touch with each other, and had realised that it would probably be the first weekend in November before Ellen and Eva could come to Jane's house again. It was important to them to wait until they all had a whole weekend free. Ellen and Eva planned to arrive sometime on the Friday evening, and hoped to stay until mid-afternoon on Sunday.

Feeling slightly frustrated by the long wait, Jane wondered what she could do. Then it occurred to her that she had never finished that book she had been reading at the time the spiral writing appeared in her diary. Why had she not thought of that before? She went to the bookshelf to look for the title: *Communications*.

'Ah, here it is!' she muttered to herself, remembering the author's name, Frances Ianson.

She quickly became absorbed in the book again. Why had she not thought of finishing it before? She had been so affected by Ellen's reaction to studying the spirals, and indeed her own reaction to them, that she had not thought again about the book until now.

She started to read it from the beginning again to refresh her memory. This time it seemed to her that the son was very intelligent, and was very upset that no one could understand what he was saying. Jane felt frustration. His mother was obviously a caring, concerned woman who loved her son; but she had been affected by the attitude of the education authority, who had assessed him as having below normal intelligence. It seemed to Jane that everyone was missing the point. They were all trying to make the boy speak as they did, when the real task was for them to study *his* language, because it was through the understanding of this that they might learn much that was of great value. His behaviour, deemed to be 'difficult', was straightforward frustration and distress. Jane found herself speaking out these words, as she felt strongly about his situation.

She now wanted to know more about the sounds that the boy was making. Would these sounds be described in more detail later on in the book? She was tempted to skip through the chapters to see, but thought better of it, and continued reading through the book.

'There's no rush,' she told herself. 'What I should really do is to read just a few pages each night. After all, look what happened to me before, after reading only a few pages! There's more to this than meets the eye. This is no ordinary book, and I must allow time for my reaction to it to emerge.'

Ellen's life was very busy as she had predicted. She had to be careful not to drive herself to do more than she could truly manage. There was always more work than she could cover, and never enough hours in the day to get through it. She always made sure that there was some time at the end of each day when she could sit and reflect.

She had always been of an independent nature. She was an only child. Her mother had died when she was only four years old. Although the house they lived in was not specially large, it did have one particularly large room to the rear. It had been used as a music room when her mother was alive. She remembered little of this, but had vague images of her father and mother playing duets on the piano. She also remembered how friends had been invited round to play quartets and quintets. She was never excluded from these evenings. She remembered the warm atmosphere, and how everyone always wanted her to stay and be a part of it. They would show her their instruments, and helped her to play simple tunes. She would eventually fall asleep in her small rocking-chair listening to them play, and her father would later carry her up to bed. Ellen had had a close relationship with both her parents when she was small. After her mother's death, she and her father were together in their great grief.

After her mother's death, her father had not been able to play music any more. After Ellen started school, he eventually converted the music room into a room which was both a library and a study. He was a lecturer in certain Middle Eastern languages at his university. His own father had lived in Arabia for about five years when he was a young man. He too had had a gift for the languages of the Middle East. He had collected a number of books on his travels. Many of these books had previously been stored in the loft, and Ellen's father gradually brought them down into the library and unpacked them.

He spent much time in this room. The door was never closed, and Ellen always knew that she could join him whenever she wanted. They had many shared interests, and as Ellen grew up they would sit up late, deep in discussion.

He had died very suddenly, just after Ellen's twenty-seventh birthday. On his way back from the post office, he had been knocked down by a lorry which had swerved to avoid a young child dashing into the road after a pet dog. The child and the dog were safe, but Ellen's father was seriously injured. He was rushed to hospital, but died within a few hours. Ellen was heartbroken. He had been her father and her best friend. She was so distraught that she was unable to continue with her work as a teacher of biology at the local secondary school. The education authority had held her position open for as long as they could. She had been a very skilled member of staff, and they did not want to lose her. However, she simply could not focus on her subject any more, and much to everyone's sadness, left her job.

It was very fortunate that her father's assets were such that when reinvested they produced sufficient income for Ellen to live comfortably. She was not an extravagant person, and found that she had enough for her needs with something to spare. She was very grateful indeed for this. Although her friends kept in regular contact with her, at first she spent much time alone. She would sit in the library, sometimes crying, sometimes staring at the photographs of her father and mother that she had put on her father's desk, and sometimes staring at all the books.

At first her friends would bring food round for her to try to tempt her to eat. After some weeks she started going to the local shop to buy essential stores, but still she spent most of her time indoors in the library. The first significant change came when she found herself looking through the catalogue of the books her father had prepared. Although it was well advanced, he had not completed it. She gradually began to familiarise herself with it, little by little, day by day. The work he had done was very methodical, and Ellen found it easy to track down any books that interested her from the reference numbers. She had of course already used some volumes from the library, but it had always been her father who had suggested those which might interest her, and she had never needed to explore the library herself.

She became deeply engrossed in familiarising herself with his whole collection. She was unaware of its monetary value; to her each book was a gem.

One evening she decided to light a fire in the library to keep her company. This was the first time she had thought of this. In her early memories she had a vague sense that when her mother was still alive and the room was full of friends and music, a fire had been lit on the colder evenings. Today, she had prepared the grate before darkness fell. It was evening. She took a match, and lit the twists of newspaper upon which she had built kindling wood with some coal on top. Flames leaped up and the wood started to crackle. She noticed immediately that she felt less alone.

She decided that she would devote that evening to examining some of the books which her father had not catalogued. There were some shelves in the corner at the left of the window where the books appeared as if they had not been arranged in any particular order, and indeed she had not seen any that were numbered in her father's familiar system. The top shelf seemed to carry works which had been brought back from her paternal grandfather's travels. She could not read any of them as they were written in script that meant nothing to her. The next shelf bore books of a similar kind. She worked her way downwards, and as she became level with the window sill, her hand fell on a book that looked markedly different. It had hard backing of a deep red colour, embossed with an intricate pattern, and the edges of the pages were slightly blackened. There was no wording on the spine. The flyleaf merely bore a signature she did not recognise. The handwriting was such that it certainly did not approximate to anything that looked familiar. She turned the pages, and was surprised to see that many of them, in fact most of them, appeared to be blank.

She came upon individual pages from time to time which carried very fine engravings of patterns which seemed to her to be the network of veins found in a leaf.

'Yes,' she said to herself, 'this page carries one which definitely looks like the veins of a leaf from a beech tree.'

She was fascinated by this book. She could not understand why the patterned pages appeared so infrequently. Presently it came into her mind to check the number of blank pages between each patterned page. The first pattern appeared on the eighth page, the first seven pages appearing blank. The second pattern appeared on the tenth page after the first pattern, so that meant that there were nine blank pages in between the first and second patterned pages. The pages themselves were quite fragile to the touch, and reminded her of pages of the Bible that had belonged to her mother. She continued to examine the book, counting the number of pages between the patterned ones. To her surprise, having gone from seven to nine they then went to seven and then to nine again, and continued in that way. Each engraving seemed to be different, but each of them appeared to represent the pattern of veins of a single leaf. Having felt sure that she recognised that of a beech leaf, she thought she could also identify an oak leaf. She was not sure of the others.

The fire died down, but she did not notice as she was so absorbed in the book. She kept turning the pages and studying the engravings, but more and more she seemed to study the pages that appeared blank. At first she did not question this, but as she became more drawn to these pages, it occurred to her to wonder why. She noticed that although the blank pages all appeared to be the same, she felt in herself quite different when she looked at certain of these pages.

She began to feel very tired, and glanced at her watch. It certainly was late, and she decided to go to bed, taking the book with her.

From that time onwards she always kept the book beside her, and she liked to have quiet time during which she could study it undisturbed. Adam's unexpected appearance at the hotel in York, and his later appearance at the Traveller's Arms, had disrupted her precious time with the book.

She mused upon the fact that she was now aware of a number of mysteries close to her at the moment. Apart from her red book, there was Eva's stick and there was Jane's spiral writing. Another thing that puzzled her was the chance meeting with that man Adam on the train to York, and his slightly irritating but apparently harmless interest in her. She had been very relieved when at the Traveller's Arms he had told her that he was soon leaving for a destination in Russia, and would be away for some time.

Chapter Nine

Adam's journey back home to Britain had been uneventful. Although he missed his friend Boris, he soon settled back into his own home, full of plans of how to interest publishers in the collection of Romanian songs. He sent e-mail messages to Boris every few days to keep him abreast of his ideas, and to keep up the feeling of sharing their lives, albeit from a distance. Of course he was making plans for his return in the spring, and he had realised that if he found a publisher for the Romanian songs, such a contact would perhaps be interested in the large collection of Russian songs which they were still gathering and documenting. He wrote to a number of publishers, and to a number of friends whom he felt might advise him.

While awaiting replies, he was able to think about certain aspects of his time with Boris. There was that amazingly beautiful chess set which had been carved by Boris' grandfather. He wished now that he had taken some photographs of the pieces. He had never seen chess men like that before. Then there was the delicate glassware, and that special tape. Although he knew that it had been a wise decision to leave further examination and discussion of the tape and its effects for the spring visit, in some ways he was impatient to learn more about what it all meant. He reminded himself that just because he was in Britain it did not mean that the experience with the tape had gone away. He had had a reaction. Boris had described some of it to him, and the rest he remembered. There was plenty to think about in all of that. An attempt to rush into a premature understanding would not necessarily bring any enlightenment. Having thus reassured himself, he felt he was able to return to his programme of small home repairs that had been shelved when he went off to see Boris.

He had been back home for about three weeks. The nights were drawing in, and he found he needed more heat in the evenings. He saw in the newspaper that cheap rail tickets were available on the East Coast line from Edinburgh. York... York, how could he have forgotten? Ellen Ridgeway... the woman on the train. He could see now how preoccupied he had been thinking about his experiences while with Boris, and in particular that experience with the tape. It had put all thoughts of Ellen out of his mind.

He sat and remembered the fragments of contact he had had with her. He went through his memory of that short time they had spent together on the train. What was it about her that had drawn his attention? In the years since his wife's death he had not led an isolated life, and he enjoyed contact with people in many situations. Yet Ellen was someone whom he had noticed in a way that was difficult to define. Her general appearance was not remarkable; but there was something about her which led him to notice her through the invisible veil he had put round himself. What was it? He searched his mind but could find nothing.

He moved to remembering how they had met in that hotel in York, entirely unexpectedly. She had been so engrossed in her book. After that encounter, although he did not feel that he knew her any better as a result, he was certain that he did not want to lose touch with her. Why was that? He did not know her. There must be something unusual that he had noticed which was drawing him, but what was it? He had taken a step that was quite out of character when he had put that note under her door.

He remembered how he had been on edge until he knew that he would be seeing her again and had some idea of when that would be. He remembered the feeling of anticipation when the day of the reunion with her college friends was near. He remembered how shocked he was when he learned that she would not be coming after all. He remembered how, resourcefully, he had obtained the number of the hotel from which she had phoned, and how he had travelled there unheralded to see her. He remembered how she had given no sign of being pleased to see him, and he felt she had only managed to tolerate his presence once she knew that it was very temporary. She had never appeared openly unfriendly. She was polite. There was a gentle warmth about her, although it was not directed towards him at all. He had a sense that she was in some way detached from her surroundings, and from him. Present,

59

but detached; a curious mixture, and one which left him with a subtle feeling of uncertainty, and a slight unease.

Since his return home he had heard nothing further from her, and he began to think that if contact were to be made it would have to be he who initiated it. He was glad that he had spoken to Boris about the situation. It was good to have a friend he could rely on to discuss his thoughts and feelings. Boris had seemed sure that he would see Ellen again, but he had not said anything about how he thought this might happen. Since the effect of that tape, the special tape, had overwhelmed him, that experience had predominated in his mind, and he and Boris had not spoken again about Ellen.

It was getting late. He should go to bed now because he had to be up early in the morning to let workmen into the back garden. He had planned for some time to have a small conservatory built at the back of his house, and tomorrow was the day when the foundations were to be laid.

Before he went to bed, he decided to send an e-mail to Boris to get his advice about whether or not to write to Ellen, and if so, what he might say.

The ring of his alarm clock woke Adam from sleep. He felt rather odd, and soon realised that he had woken from a dream. He switched on the bedside light, picked up the pencil and pad which he kept handy, and began to write.

I feel very strange. I have just dreamed about Ellen. She was reading her red book. She was sitting on a low chair at one end of a long room, and seemed unaware of me. I started to walk towards her quite slowly and softly, so as not to disturb her. I seemed to be walking a very long way without getting any nearer to her. I became aware that she was surrounded by bright light, the source of which I could not see. I walked and walked but got no closer. Eventually I called her name. She jumped and looked up as if frightened. She seemed to see me, stood up, and disappeared through the wall directly behind her chair. After this I found that my walking resulted in my reaching her chair. I could see no sign of a door in the wall. I picked up her book from the floor where it had fallen when she stood up. I looked inside and saw only blank pages. Then I started to feel faint… and the next thing I was aware of was the ringing of my alarm clock.

Adam felt very disorientated. He made himself get up and get dressed. It was Saturday morning. Time was short before the arrival of the workmen. He was quite glad when they arrived, at exactly 8 a.m., to start work. The small firm that was doing the work was able to employ men who were available at weekends. This suited Adam well. He showed them everything they needed, and then wandered rather aimlessly around his house. He found the sounds of the workmen reassuring, and was very grateful for their presence. His dream was still with him, and he felt as if he were in two parallel lives with no apparent link except for Ellen, who was someone whom he had really seen; she was not just a dream figure.

He wandered from room to room until he realised that he felt quite cold. He then made a hot drink and sat with it in his study. Sipping the hot liquid helped him to feel he had more substance, and he began to think that it might help him further if he sent another e-mail to Boris telling him of the dream. Although it was still very vivid and present to him, he went back to his bedroom to get the notes he had written about it before he sat down at his computer.

He started to type a message to Boris. Despite the hot drink he was feeling chilled, and went to get a thick fleecy jacket from the hall. He typed the message quite slowly, carefully trying to record exact details of the dream. He was trying to recall more about the appearance of the room where Ellen was sitting, and the chair on which she sat. He tried to describe precisely how he had felt in the dream, and how he was feeling now. He experienced some relief as he became absorbed in the writing. He realised that it had been a good thing to tell his friend; and also the writing of this message meant he had a more accurate record of the dream and its immediate effects than he would have had from the notes alone.

The room in the dream had very little furniture in it he remembered. He had a vague sense that there were a few chairs, but he could not remember them clearly at all. They did not seem to be significant. The room was certainly very long, like a gallery in a large mansion or stately home. He felt that there had been windows all down the wall to his right which would have made the room very light by day. He was sure that in the dream the general lighting had been quite dim, and it had felt as if it were late evening.

There had been no other people there in the room. Ellen's chair had been positioned near the far left-hand corner. He did not have any idea about the source of the bright light which surrounded her. He was very aware of how bright it had been, and how it had meant that from quite a distance he could see that it was that red book she was reading. He remembered the strange sensation of walking and walking towards her but getting no closer, and that he could only reach her chair after she had disappeared. The feeling he had while trying to reach her was a mixture of anticipation and anxiety. When she disappeared he felt numb until he picked up the book. At that point he had felt a rush of warmth in his body, followed by the feeling of faintness as he discovered that the pages of the book appeared to be blank.

He reflected on that faint feeling. Why should he have felt like that when he looked at the pages of the book? Blank pages would not normally have that effect. Then there was the anomaly that Ellen had been studying that book very intently, and was studying blank pages. Why? He realised that now he was feeling quite muddled. Was he remembering the hotel in York, or the room in the dream?

He finished the message to Boris and sent it off. He was glad to see one from Boris appearing in the in-box. He hoped it would be a reply to his message of last night. Perhaps his friend had written some helpful advice about whether or not to try to contact Ellen. Boris had written:

<Thank you for your message. I will think about what you wrote, and hope to reply soon. At the moment my mind is full of a dream that I woke from last night, and I am eager to let you know about it. This is what I remember:

I had woken very suddenly, feeling hot and disturbed. The image that was in my mind was the shelf where my special glassware is kept. Very intense white light seemed to emanate from the shelf and the glassware. Everything else in the room was dark, and the only thing I was aware of was that shelf. I felt so agitated that I got out of bed, went to the bathroom to splash cold water on my face, and went to look at the shelf. Of course the whole room was dark. I switched on the light, and it was at that point I remembered that this shelf is where I put that special tape for safe keeping. I thought that it was important to write to you about this, since the tape is something that matters a lot to us, and we still do not know the meaning of it.

Let me know what you think.

Boris>

Adam got up from his chair and paced round the small study. Then he went through to the hall and to the back of the house where the men were hard at work. The ordinariness of their noises was very welcome.

So, he and Boris had each had a dream that night, dreams that seemed very significant. The dreams had been on the same night, a few hours apart. Both dreams had involved seeing unexplained white light. It was clear that both he and Boris had been deeply affected by something.

Adam felt that he needed to go out. He would walk down to the local shop and buy an extra newspaper. The shop was about a mile away, and the walk would give him time to think about the dreams; and he hoped that he would encounter some of his neighbours and pass the time of day. He felt the need for such contact. As he turned down the road there was a shout from behind him. He looked back and was glad to see the familiar face of Matthew, a friendly neighbour. They walked down the road together, Adam talking about his decision to have a conservatory added to his house and how glad he was to see it beginning. Matthew was very interested. He had been thinking about adding something similar to his own home.

'Why not come round and have a look at the plans?' suggested Adam.

'Thanks, that would be really good.'

'How about coming now, then. Or would you rather leave it to the evening?'

Matthew pondered. 'I think that this evening would be best for me. I've a number of things to see to today, and I'd like to get these done first.'

Before the two men parted they had arranged that Matthew would come round any time after 8 p.m., and would stay on for the evening. They could discuss conservatories, and then go on to other things.

Adam had been very glad of this contact. He looked forward to a companionable evening with Matthew. Now he would go to the library. Although it was Saturday, it was open until 1 p.m. He wanted to change his books and to pick up information about evening classes. Although autumn was advancing, and courses would have started weeks ago, he felt sure that he could find a suitable class to join even at this late stage. Afterwards he could pick up a newspaper which he could read in the evening, while he was waiting for Matthew to arrive. He also hoped that during the course of the day he might receive another e-mail from Boris.

Chapter Ten

Ellen looked at her diary. Yes, she had remembered correctly: it was only ten days now before she and Eva would return to Jane's bungalow in Castle Brimswich. She must remember to phone both Eva and Jane this evening to confirm the arrangements. She left herself a note on the kitchen table, and rushed out of the house to drive to a meeting about a new shelter for homeless people in Sheffield.

She arrived back quite late in the evening to find that there was a message on the call-minder from Eva.

'Hi Ellen! I'm just phoning to confirm arrangements for the weekend after next. I've been in touch with Jane, and she's looking forward to seeing us. Give me a ring when you get this message. Bye.'

Ellen was glad to hear her friend's voice, and decided to phone back straight away before she made something to eat.

'Hello, Jane, thanks for the message. I'm just in… Yes, quite a long day. I'm hoping to arrange my diary so that I can come to your house at around 6 p.m. … Oh, thanks; it would be really helpful if you could have some food ready that we could eat on the way to Jane's. I know that she likes to eat early, and there's no way that we can get to her in time to join in with her meal.'

'That's fine,' said Eva. 'I'm glad to have everything arranged. By the way, Jane tells me that she has been reading more of the book by Frances Ianson. She'd like to discuss it with us sometime over that weekend.'

'It does seem likely that her absorption in that book had something to do with how she unconsciously wrote the spirals into her diary,' said Ellen. 'But there's no way of telling just how much can be attributed to that, and how much to other factors.

'Thinking about it just now, there's the effect of being absorbed in a book, and there's the effect of the material in which one is absorbed.'

She hesitated, wondering whether to say anything to Eva about the red book, her precious red book…

'Is there something on your mind?' asked Eva, who had sensed that the silence was not just a casual break in the conversation.

'Oh... yes... there is,' replied Ellen, 'and I'd like to talk to you about it, but not in a phone call.'

'Of course, I'll make a note in my diary that you've something to tell me.'

'Do you remember that walk we had on the way to the meeting at Peggy's?'

'Yes, I do.'

'Do you remember how before we set off I transferred a book into the bag I was taking with me?'

'No, not really. My mind was taken up with wondering about whether or not it was safe to leave my stick in the car.'

'Well, the book that I was transferring is the thing I want to tell you about.'

'Okay, I'll make a note of that too,' answered Eva cheerfully.

After Ellen had put the phone down, she felt uncertain about what she had done. In a way she wished she had not said anything to Eva about the importance of her book. It was so very personal, so very, very personal. Eva knew everything about the circumstances of her father's death, and the withdrawn state that she had endured after that; but Ellen had never told anyone yet about the importance of the red book. She did not particularly hide the book from people, but she had never indicated that it was something that was unique in her life, and that it was very precious to her because of how she had found it.

If she changed her mind about confiding in Eva about it she was sure that Eva would respect her decision, and would not press her for an explanation; but now that she had mentioned it she knew that she would feel a tension inside herself around Eva if she decided not to tell her about it after all. It was difficult. On the one hand, it would be an important step to tell someone whom she trusted about something that was so important to her; but she did worry about how she would feel having kept this to herself for so long. There was no way of predicting the outcome. She knew that Eva would be interested and sympathetic. Of that she could be sure; but beyond that there was no way of telling.

At that point she made a firm decision that she would not go back on her agreement with Eva. She was suddenly quite clear that now was the time to share what little she knew about the book, and see what came of it. Having made this decision, she could then see that there was something in her that had been using her absorption in this book as a way of avoiding facing feelings about her father's death, now more than seven years ago. When she talked to Eva about the book, she knew she would have to face even more deeply the grief of her loss.

She had a light meal, listened to some music, and went to bed. She had an early start in the morning, since she had to travel to a meeting two hours' drive away to arrive by 9 a.m.

The time passed quickly, and the day of her journey to Eva's soon came. She found she was almost impatient with the morning's work, longing for the late afternoon to come so that she could load her weekend bag into the car, and drive to Eva's house.

At last it was four o'clock. She had felt somewhat guilty about her relative lack of concentration on the day's work. She normally gave all her attention to the task in hand, particularly when it involved making decisions about the well-being of the disadvantaged people in the various communities in which she worked.

She put her files into the section of her weekend bag which she reserved for such items, put on her coat, and went to the car park to collect her car. She found it quite quickly, but to her dismay saw that someone had positioned their car carelessly when parking, and she could see no way out unless this, or one of the other cars next to hers, was moved. She felt frustrated, and began to feel angry until she told herself to bear in mind that this might be some kind of emergency. The car was a silver-coloured VW Golf Estate. She made a note of its registration number, and was walking back to the office block, when it occurred to her to return to the VW to see if there was anything in it that might identify the owner.

Just then she saw a man coming across the car park pushing a child in a wheelchair. He appeared to hurry when he caught sight of her. As he came closer she could see he was in his late thirties or early forties, and was wearing a thick navy jumper and worn jeans. The child in the wheelchair was a girl. It was hard to guess her age as she looked pale, thin, and as if her growth process had been disrupted.

The man called out to her. 'Terribly sorry! Have I boxed you in? I was just collecting my daughter, and there was nowhere to park.'

She could see that he was flustered and embarrassed, and she did her best to reassure him.

'That's okay,' she said. 'I'm on my way to see friends for the weekend, I've hardly been delayed at all.'

She watched as he very gently lifted his daughter into the back of his car into a booster seat, and put the safety belt round her. She wondered about offering to help with the wheelchair, but decided against it, since she felt that he must be adept at handling it himself, and she did not wish to appear to be rushing him. The man kissed his daughter's cheek, shut the door, folded up the wheelchair, and put it into the back of the car. She wanted to ask him about his daughter, but did not wish to appear intrusive. Instead, as he opened the door to get into the driving seat she said, 'Safe journey!'

'Thanks,' he replied. 'I appreciate that. We're just setting off to see someone who may be able to help with my daughter's condition. Safe journey to you too.'

Then he drove off.

Ellen slowly got into her car. The image of the girl's thin pale face had impressed itself on her mind, and she kept thinking about her as she drove to Eva's cottage. It was soon dusk, and then quickly dark. The day had been overcast, and there was no sunset.

As she neared Eva's cottage she began to feel very weary. She made a mental note to ask Eva to share the driving on the way to Jane's. She saw a lay-by and drew into it, thinking that she would sit for a few minutes before the last ten minutes of the journey. She realised that she had been looking forward so much to this weekend, to being with Eva and Jane again, that she had not taken time from her busy schedule to reflect on what the weekend might signify to her. It certainly was not merely a weekend away with friends. On the drive here so far, her mind had been full of the thin girl in the wheelchair, not about the weekend. She sat and tried to clear her thoughts. Then she remembered how she had spoken to Eva about her red book, and how she had resolved to go ahead with talking to her friend about it, telling her all she knew. In her weary state, this seemed very daunting; and she began to wonder if she could do it, in addition to concentrating on whatever the weekend revealed about the spirals and Jane's researches on Frances Ianson's book. Her head began to nod forward, and she realised that she had been very wise to stop the car for a while, even though she was going to arrive at Eva's later than she had planned.

When she looked at her watch she realised that she must have dozed off. About twenty minutes had passed since she stopped the car. She did not feel so tired now, but she felt muzzy. She decided to walk round the car a few times to try to clear her head. The air was cool, almost crisp, and she found that she benefited greatly from pacing about for a few minutes. Now she felt fully competent to drive on.

She arrived at Eva's about an hour later than she had planned. Eva had not been worried. She knew that Ellen could have been held up for a variety of reasons, and she had been sitting ready with the things she needed, listening to the radio.

'Sorry I'm a bit late,' said Ellen as she hugged Eva.

'That's no problem at all,' replied Eva. 'I'll phone Jane to say we are on our way. Would you like me to drive for a while?'

'I'd really appreciate that. I was going ask you if you'd mind.'

Eva phoned Jane, loaded her things into Ellen's car, and adjusted the seat. 'Before we set off, can I just show you that our food is in this basket?'

Eva drove most of the way to Jane's house, stopping with Ellen only long enough to eat her share of the food she had brought. Jane was very pleased to see them both and welcomed them in. They were all tired, and after sitting drinking herb tea while catching up on some of their news, they went early to bed.

Chapter Eleven

Adam's trip to the library had been fruitful. He had found a number of leaflets about evening classes which looked promising. One in particular attracted him. It advertised a series of talks by a retired historian, Professor Barnes, whose specialty had been in studying ancient artefacts held in British collections. From the description, it looked as if he had very broad interests. Now it was the second weekend in November, and Adam had obviously missed a number of the talks. He counted them; he had missed five, but there were still five to go, and the first of these was to be on Monday evening. The venue appeared to be a private address. Perhaps this was the professor's own home. He noticed a footnote on the leaflet which said 'numbers limited'. He felt a stab of disappointment. He guessed that all the places would be taken. He searched the leaflet for a phone number and found only an e-mail address.

Trying to be positive, he decided to search the non-fiction section of the library for a book about general archaeology. Having consulted the computerised catalogue, he discovered that the book held in the adult section was already out on loan, but that there was a book in the junior section. On a whim he decided to find it; and having given it a cursory glance, he borrowed it, and walked home at a brisk pace, as he was by now feeling hungry.

On his return, he was impressed to see that the workmen had already done a lot of the basic preparation for the foundations of his conservatory. The foreman explained that since the days were so short at this time of year, they had agreed to take only short breaks, so that they could work on until about 3.30 in the afternoon, when they would finish for the day. He said that they hoped to return at eight the following morning, as there was much they could do before the rest of the materials were delivered on Monday morning.

Adam made himself a simple meal of beans on toast, and sat

down meaning to look at the paper as he ate. Instead, he found himself inspecting the book he had brought from the library. It was then he noticed that it had actually been written by Professor Barnes, the man he hoped to hear speaking on Monday evening. The preface explained that he liked to write for young people, since he himself had become interested in ancient artefacts in his early adolescence, and had found it difficult to find any literature to inform him and stimulate his interest. As Adam turned the pages, he realised that the book was written in a way that showed the obvious enthusiasm of the writer, who had not oversimplified the material in any way. He felt considerable respect for the professor, and hoped even more that there would be a place available on Monday evening. Having finished his lunch, he went into his study to e-mail the address on the leaflet. He had been so absorbed in the thought of the series of talks that he had not been thinking about his dream of the night before, and the messages that he and Boris had exchanged.

He realised he had left the leaflet on the table in the other room, and remembering Boris, he decided first to see if there were any more messages from him. Yes, indeed, there was one.

<Hello Adam,

I have just returned from a long walk. I felt I needed to go out to think about the dream I had last night, and the one that you described in your message to me. It does feel to me as if there is some connection between these, but what it is I do not know. On a purely practical front, we had our dreams within only a few hours of each other. The other feature is that we both experienced a sense of very intense bright light. The special tape – when we listened to it together and you went into that strange state – I do not think I told you all of what I noticed about you. Remember how at first we had planned to listen to it again and discuss it some more, but thought better of it, and postponed it until next spring? You will recall that I explained to you that for a while your mouth and throat were moving as if you were singing. Well, I made a note of some of the words that your mouth seemed to show. After I had been thinking about your dream I went and found that list of words. I wanted to be sure that I was remembering correctly. Please take into account that I had jotted things down that you seemed to mouth, and I cannot be certain that I had got the words right. The list included the name 'Ellen'. I knew when I wrote it that that was the name of the woman you had spoken to me about.>

Adam studied the message with intense interest. So, it had seemed to Boris that he had spoken or sung Ellen's name while he was in that strange state! He wondered what the other words were that Boris had written down.

At that point he remembered that he should e-mail the address on the leaflet, and he went to get it from the other room. He wrote a message saying how much he would like to be able to attend the talk on Monday evening, and asked if there would be a place for him. He thought he might write a message to Boris too, but decided to leave it until later. Instead, he would review the progress he had made so far about making links with publishers about their collection of Romanian songs.

Time passed very quickly. The workmen had left several hours ago. Adam glanced at his watch, and realised that Matthew would be arriving soon. He put his work on one side. He ate some soup followed by fish with steamed vegetables, and then sat down to read his newspaper while he waited for the doorbell to ring. Matthew arrived a little later, carrying a small packet, which proved to be a bag of nuts for them to share while they talked.

Chapter Twelve

Ellen had a disturbed night. She seemed to wake every hour. Something was affecting her, but she could not be sure what it was. She did not feel she could wake Eva, who again was sharing Jane's spare bed with her, and she had tried not to move about much in case she woke her. At last morning came, and she could hear Jane moving about, so she got up to join her.

'Did your ankle recover fully?' she asked.

'Yes, thank goodness, and I've had no further trouble with it at all.'

'Another thing I wanted to ask about was your sister's baby. I think you told me it was a girl. How old is she now?'

'She must be about a year old. Let me see… she was born on November 21st, so she'll have her first birthday quite soon.'

'How is she?'

'I'm glad you asked me,' answered Jane. 'My sister phoned me last week, and we had a long conversation about her.'

By this time Eva had joined them, and was immediately interested. 'What was your sister saying?' she asked.

'It may sound strange, but she's worried about the fact that Emily – that's what she decided to call her daughter – is a very quiet child. She is content to sit and watch what's going on around her, or to play quietly with her toys. The thing she likes best of all is an abacus that my sister bought for her. They were in a toy shop one day last month, and Emily became very excited. This was so unusual, and my sister Clare picked Emily out of her buggy, and lifted her over towards a number of toys on a stand. It became very clear that the only toy that Emily was drawn to was an abacus. Clare assumed it was the colour of the beads that had excited Emily, as they were very bright. She was happy to buy it for Emily, and Emily clutched it to her all the way home. Since that day, Emily likes to have her abacus with her wherever she is, and she spends much time quietly moving the beads backwards and forwards.'

73

'I can't say anything that would explain what she's doing, but I wouldn't worry about it,' said Eva. 'If Emily appears to be calm and relaxed, I think there's no cause for concern. The fact that she's watching what's going on around her is a very good sign.'

'Why do you say that?' asked Jane.

'If she's watching in a non-anxious way, then there's a good chance that she's absorbing what she sees as part of her developing understanding of life. Does Clare have plenty of friends?'

'Yes,' replied Jane. 'She's a friendly and sociable kind of person. She decided to be a full-time mother for as long as she could, and she's involved with a community project in addition to having a varied social life.'

'Who looks after Emily when Clare is tied up with these things?'

Jane laughed. 'Clare has taken Emily with her everywhere as much as possible, she loves her so much. She has always made sure that Emily sees other children, including some of her own age.'

'Do you have a photograph of Emily and Clare that we could see?' asked Ellen.

'Yes, I have one that she sent last week. I'd been wanting one for a while, and Clare was finishing up a film before she could send me this print.'

Ellen and Eva looked at the photograph of Emily in Clare's arms. Her face seemed to have a calm radiance about it, together with sense of wisdom beyond her age. Ellen commented on this, and Eva agreed. Ellen turned to Jane.

'When did you last see them?' she asked.

'Oh, about a month ago.'

'Would you agree with what Eva and I are saying about Emily in the photograph?'

'Well, yes, I would. Yes, I think you're right.'

'Jane,' asked Eva, 'will you tell Clare that I think her daughter is a lovely child, and that I'd really like to hear more about her as she develops?'

'Me too,' added Ellen.

Jane looked pleased. 'I'm sure that she'll feel supported by that. I've known other people who feel their child seems different from others of the same age, and it can produce quite a bit of concern at times.'

74

Eva looked at Jane and said very firmly, 'Such differences can be very important, and often crucial. I'm glad that we'll have the opportunity to encourage and reassure Clare.'

'Do you have a small frame for this photograph?' asked Ellen. 'It would be nice to have it on your mantelshelf.'

'Unfortunately not,' replied Jane. 'The frame I have is really too big. I could use it for now, but it doesn't look quite right.'

'I'll have a look around for a suitable one when I'm out and about, and send it to you when I find one. Would that be okay?' suggested Ellen.

'Thanks, I'd like that very much.'

Having eaten a late breakfast and tidied the kitchen, the three women went to sit in the front room of Jane's bungalow, the room where they had studied the spirals months ago. Jane had her diary and the book by Frances Ianson on a low table by her chair. Ellen had brought a different book into the room with her. She looked slightly agitated.

'Ellen, are you feeling worried after what happened last time?' asked Jane.

'I might be,' answered Ellen. 'But the thing I'm aware of is something else. I have a book here which is very special to me, more special than I can explain to you. When I was speaking to Jane on the phone some time ago, I referred to this book, but she hadn't particularly remembered my having it. I decided then I'd say that I wanted to talk to her about it when I met her this weekend. I felt anxious and agitated afterwards, for reasons which I'll explain to you both; but I did decide that I'd go ahead and talk to her when I saw her. However, I was held up and arrived late. As a result I was rather tired at Eva's, and I knew that it was not a good time to try to talk.

'I didn't sleep very well last night, and one of the things that was going on in my mind was how to talk about this book, and what it means to me. In the night I decided to speak to you both this morning, asking if you would mind if I spoke about it some time this weekend. I want you to think about it carefully, because I don't want it to get in the way of our agreement to study the spirals and their effect on us – and to find out from you, Jane, more about the book by Frances Ianson. I always take this book of mine with me in my bag wherever I go, and I look at it regularly, but I have never ever spoken to anyone about it before, and it's a big step for me to take.'

Eva and Jane stared at Ellen. It was Jane who spoke first.

'Look, Ellen,' she said, 'if you'd like some time on your own with Eva this weekend to talk about your book as you had planned, I'm more than willing to arrange that. There are things I can do in the loft here, or I could go out and you can have my home to yourselves. It's obviously really important to you. If we run out of time when we're talking about the spirals, we can always arrange another weekend, there's no rush. I sense that you need to make a connection about your book before you can concentrate on the spirals, and I don't want to get in the way of that.'

Jane stopped speaking for a moment and laughed gently. 'Did you hear what I said?' she asked. 'I heard myself talking about your making a connection about your book. I think that this is something I'm more sensitive to now that I've read most of that book by Frances Ianson. Remember, it's called *Communications*; and that it's about the connection between a mother and her son.'

Ellen looked relieved. 'Thank you for being so understanding. To be honest, what I'd really prefer is that I talk to you *both* about it. The more I thought about it last night, the more I realised that not only would it be better for me to speak to you both, but also it would be wrong not to include you, Jane. The reason why I'd thought only of telling Eva is because she already knows a lot about my personal past, and it's that background I need to share with you first before I talk about the book. Can I ask you both if it would be okay for me to take some time right now to talk about this book before we consider the spirals?'

There was no hesitation from either Jane or Eva in their agreement to this, and Ellen began to talk, rather slowly and hesitatingly at first, about her life before her mother's death. When she had finished speaking, Jane asked if she minded being asked some questions. Ellen was open to this, and found she was encouraged by Jane's interest. She continued her story, moving on to the change of the music room into a library, her father's slow cataloguing of the books, and then to his sudden death.

'I'd known that your father died as a result of an accident,' said

Jane, 'but I hadn't known before exactly what had happened. How on earth did you manage after that?'

'I didn't manage well at all,' answered Ellen; and she went on to describe how she had not been able to work, nor been able to see people for quite a while.

'I can see that there's quite a bit more to tell,' Jane interrupted gently. Then she asked, 'Would you like a break now, and I can make some hot drinks for us; or would you like to carry on?'

'If it's all right for you both, I'd prefer to carry on a bit more now.'

Then Ellen described how she had gradually turned to her father's task of cataloguing the books in the library, and how she had found this book, the book with a dark red hard cover with fine engraving embossed into it, and the unusual feature of the blackened edges of the pages.

Jane and Eva had been asking quite a number of questions during the latter part of Ellen's story. Although Eva had known the circumstances of the death of Ellen's father, and had been one of the people who had supported her in the first stages of her isolation in unbearable grief, she had not known anything at all about the collection of books from the Middle East, and Ellen's having found this book in that section of the library.

Ellen's agitation had gradually dissolved, and she was now feeling quite relaxed. She was ready to suggest that Eva and Jane might like to examine her book themselves.

She handed the book to Eva, who opened it and slowly turned the pages. At first she looked very puzzled, as she saw nothing at all on them. Then she came to a page bearing a leaf-vein pattern and gasped. 'It's beautiful!' she exclaimed. 'Look, Jane!'

She passed the book across so that Jane could see. Jane stared at it and then passed it back. Eva continued to turn the pages, feeling puzzled once more, until she found another of the leaf-vein patterns. Again, she handed it across to Jane so that she could see. By this time she was becoming accustomed to the fact that many of the pages appeared blank. She carefully turned them until she came to each of the patterns. After studying them, she passed the book to Jane.

Having looked through the book in this way, Eva handed it back to Ellen.

'I'd like a little time to think about what I've seen in this book,' she said.

'Me too,' added Jane.

'Then I've a suggestion to make,' offered Ellen. 'I see it's already lunchtime. After eating something, I'd like to go out for a walk. It'll get dark early, but the sky's clear at the moment, and I'd like to see some of the general area where you live, Jane. There are a couple more things I'd like you to know about my book, and I could tell you about them as we walk.'

Jane and Eva were happy to fall in with this, and soon they were walking towards the small reservoir which lay about a mile from Castle Brimswich. Jane had suggested that they walk in that direction as there was a track that was good underfoot, and was wide enough for them to walk abreast of each other.

'What were those other things that you were going to tell us about your book?' asked Eva eagerly.

Ellen explained. 'The first thing I want to say is that I've found there's something significant about those blank pages. I saw you looking puzzled when you first saw them. I was puzzled too, and I still am; but one thing I began to notice was that there are a set number of blank pages between the leaf-vein patterns. At the beginning of the book there are seven blank pages before the page with the first pattern; after that there are nine blank pages followed by a further pattern, then seven blank pages. The number of blank pages alternates between seven and nine throughout the book. Of course I've no idea why that is.

'The second thing is far less tangible. After I'd been examining the book for a while, I decided to concentrate on some of the blank pages. I was already absorbed in the book, and it didn't feel strange to be examining blank pages; but I began to realise that I felt different in some way when I was looking at certain pages in particular. After this, I found I wanted to carry the book in my bag wherever I went, and wanted to have some quiet time with it each evening. When you told me about how you want to keep your stick safe, Eva, and how you often like to take it with you even when there's no apparent use for it, I began to wonder if your feeling about your stick was similar to the feeling I have about my book.'

'This is fascinating!' Eva exclaimed. 'I really hadn't taken in anything about your book when you were telling me the story of Adam, the man on the train, and how you saw him subsequently. Did you tell me that you were looking at your book on both occasions when he appeared in the hotels you were staying in?'

'Yes,' said Ellen. 'I did find it hard to be distracted from my book, but I think I handled the situations reasonably well. I gave him a little of my time, but didn't let his presence intrude too much. I think that the time he came to find me at the Traveller's Arms he noticed that I was uncomfortable, and made sure that he didn't press me for prolonged, or further, contact.'

'Could we fill Jane in about Adam?' asked Eva.

'Oh yes, of course.'

Ellen was a little embarrassed that so far she had not remembered to tell Jane anything about the man on the train. She hurried to tell her all that she had told Eva on their journey to Peggy's house. She added that she had heard nothing further from him.

'Would you like to see him again?' asked Jane.

'I don't know,' mused Ellen, half to herself. 'I have his address, but I've no desire at all to contact him.'

Adam and Matthew were sitting in the dining room with the plans for the conservatory spread out on the table.

'When did you make the decision to build this?' asked Matthew.

'Oh, I've been thinking about it on and off for quite some time. As you know, my garden is quite long, and an extension won't leave me feeling cramped for enough garden space. In fact, I'm quite glad to swap part of the lawn for more floor space. The vegetable patch at the far end of the garden is unaffected. In recent years I've seen a few different types of conservatory, and I began to wonder about having one myself. I've put quite a lot of thought into it. I researched a number of "ready-made" versions. The price of these was quite attractive; but the designs were not really what I wanted.

'Finally I approached an old school friend who's now qualified as an architect. After inheriting money from a distant relative about ten years ago, he gave up his job as a bus driver, and began to study to be an architect. To be honest, I wondered if he'd stick it out, as it takes many years to become fully qualified. He's self-employed, running a small business doing certain specialist jobs. I really admire what he's achieved. He was happy to design a conservatory for me. I gave him a few pointers about the kind of thing I wanted, and I'm more than satisfied with what he's drawn up. He's developed good links with local builders, which is another plus for me. The whole thing will cost me about twenty-five per cent more than a ready-made package; but it's well worth it for the individual design, and the exact size I was wanting. I have a security light on the back here so we could go out and have a look. The builder is only working on the foundations at the moment, so there's not much to see, but you'll get some idea of the size.'

The two men went outside.

Matthew was impressed. 'I must admit I feel quite envious,' he said. 'I can't afford anything like this myself at the moment. Also there's a chance that my work may be relocated. I'll just have to dream about how nice it would be to have a conservatory, and there it will have to end.'

'I hope your job is secure,' said Adam earnestly. 'That's the most important thing.'

'There's no sign of redundancies in the offing, but I feel that if it's suggested that I'm relocated, I've just got to go with that. I think I have to appear keen and enthusiastic about any changes.'

'Tell you what,' said Adam, 'I'll give you the name and address of my friend, and if you ever need any alterations or additions to your home in the future, you could contact him. His fees are very reasonable, and he does have some creative solutions to problems people have with buildings. I've seen a few of the things he's been involved in.'

'Thanks very much, that's really helpful.'

Adam and Matthew made their way into the sitting room where Adam had laid a fire.

'I don't normally light a fire when I'm on my own, but I thought we could enjoy one together this evening. It won't take long to get going.'

Adam struck a match, and lit the coils of newspaper which lay beneath the criss-crossed kindling sticks.

'There's something else I wanted to show you,' he said. 'I picked up a leaflet in the library after I left you this morning. I'll just go and get it.'

He soon returned with the leaflet in his hand.

'Ah, Professor Barnes,' said Matthew.

'You know him?'

'Not personally, but I've been to a talk that he gave. It must have been about three years ago. It was unusual in that it was held at his house. The gathering was limited to twenty people. I see this leaflet says that the numbers are limited. It doesn't give a postal address, only an e-mail address. I wouldn't be surprised if it's at his house. Do go if you can; he's such an interesting person. Of course, he has a large collection of artefacts in his house. The time I saw him speak he got quite carried away, and he brought out all kinds of fascinating things from his collection for us to see.'

Adam explained that he had already sent an e-mail in the hope that he would be offered a place; and the conversation turned to other subjects as the evening progressed.

The fire burned quite brightly, providing a deep, relaxing warmth.

Ellen, Eva and Jane had returned to Jane's bungalow after dark. Their walk had taken them further than Jane had intended. They had circled the reservoir as planned, but Ellen and Eva had then expressed an interest in seeing a standing stone in a field about three quarters of a mile off the track. They had noticed the signpost to it on their way to the reservoir and had remarked on it at that stage, but had elected to circle the reservoir first, and see what time they had left after that. When they reached the signpost it was nearly dusk; but there was still enough light to see the way to the stone. Having made that detour, by the time they reached the bungalow it was late in the afternoon.

They removed the mud from their shoes, and sat down to discuss how to proceed.

'The first thing I want to say,' said Jane, 'is that I'm really glad that you told us about that red book and showed it to us, and that we have spent time talking about it. I know it has delayed our getting back to the subject of the spirals, but I'm convinced that your red book is equally important. I'm glad too that you've told me about that man.'

'I agree,' added Eva. 'And although I already knew about Adam from what you'd said before, I found it helpful to hear you going over the details again. In fact, I think there were one or two things you said this time which seemed new to me.'

Ellen asked Eva what she meant.

'When you told me about Adam as we travelled to Peggy's that day, you didn't say anything about being relieved that your car had developed that steering fault, and you hadn't been able to get to the reunion. The other thing I noticed this time is that when you spoke about the Traveller's Arms, you referred to the lettering on the sign being of a very unusual style.'

'Thanks for pointing that out,' said Ellen. 'I'd been looking forward to seeing my friends at the reunion, but as the time came nearer I'd begun to regret having written to Adam saying that he was welcome to join us. I had a strong feeling that I didn't want to see him, and the steering fault provided the ideal solution to my dilemma. Imagine my shock when I saw him in the dining room of the Traveller's Arms! On the subject of the lettering, I haven't got anything else to add. Thanks for reassuring me about all that I've told you. It means a lot to me. I'm eager now to hear from you, Jane. I want to know what you have to say about Frances Ianson's book, now that you've had time to study it further.'

'Let's go into the sitting room, and make ourselves comfortable,' suggested Jane. 'The central heating came on while we were out, so it should be warmed up by now.'

The three settled themselves in the firm but comfortable chairs which made up most of the furniture in the room.

Ellen remarked on the design of the upholstery. 'It looks like tapestry,' she said.

Jane explained that it was actually a copy of a design from a seventeenth-century tapestry. 'I was so pleased to find it,' she said. 'I have the details written down somewhere, and I can look for them later if you want. It meant that the chairs cost more than I'd planned, but I didn't mind at all because I ended up with something that really appealed to me, rather than something that was merely acceptable. Any evening when I'm sitting on my own, I can find myself mentally tracing the intricacies of the pattern, and I count the number of different shades of green and brown which appear. I like the repeating pattern of the small hunting party in the glade, and how the glade appears as an insert in the yawning mouth of a lion. As you can see, the colours are predominantly greens, browns, rusty yellows and some red. I find that combination very pleasing. I expect you'll have also noticed that the pattern repeats down the back of each chair, and across the seat from the back to the front. The rest of the design on the chairs is dense forest that's full of mythical creatures.'

Jane picked up *Communications* from the low table. 'I've read right through the book since I last saw you both, and I made some notes as I went along. I thought it would be helpful.'

'Good,' replied Ellen. 'I told Eva about the mother trying her hardest to maintain some meaningful contact with her son.'

Jane went on: 'Most of the rest of the book was a detailed account of how the mother, convinced that in order to help her son she must learn the meaning of the sounds he made, devoted much of her time to that end. All her previous attempts at helping him to communicate had been to try to get him to make the sounds from which normal speech is built. In her new approach, she first tried her best to imitate some of his sounds, "speaking" them back to him. She soon discovered that this led to a rapid escalation in his agitation. She then made a short tape-recording of some of his "speech". When she played it back, he became very angry, snatched the tape and destroyed it. She realised that he had experienced this in the same way as when she had tried to imitate his sounds. She felt upset about this, wishing that she had been more aware of the possible effects of her actions.

'Having thought further, she tried to coax him to record some of his sounds himself. She did this by letting him see her recording her own voice and playing back the sounds. He watched quietly while she repeated this, then he reached out for the equipment. Very slowly and deliberately he made a series of sounds on the tape, repeated them, and then handed the equipment back to his mother. After that, he stood up and went quietly to his room.

'Every night when she was in bed, about to go to sleep, Frances would put on her headphones and listen to the sounds her son had recorded for her. To begin with she'd listened through the speakers of the sound system, but she felt much more affected by listening through the headphones. From the beginning she had decided to listen to these taped sounds with an open mind. Somehow she sensed that in order to help her understanding she needed to let go of any conventional explanations which came into her mind.

'As the days went by, she noticed that there was a marked difference in her son. He appeared calmer than she had ever known him to be. This gave her encouragement. She was no nearer to understanding his sounds, but since the need to understand them appeared to have reduced, she felt less driven by her desire to do so. She began to guess that it must be that her son now knew that she was joining him in his sounds, and that it was this that had calmed him. She began to consider how she could open her mind further when she was listening to the sounds on the tape, and she began to take time to relax before she went to bed. She would walk slowly down the hallway, trying to make her footsteps glide along as smoothly as possible. When she got to the end of the hallway she did not turn, but reversed her gliding footsteps until she returned to the spot where she had begun. She would repeat this exercise at least twenty-one times before going upstairs. She found that by this means, she was increasingly more relaxed each time she went to bed to listen to the tape.

'One Monday evening, after about a month of trying this exercise, she noticed that as she listened to the sounds her son had taped for her, she could hear something else, something faint and distant, but unmistakable. She removed the headphones and noticed that the sound continued. There was no break in it at all. She put the headphones on and off again. The sound was definitely there, whether or not she was listening to the tape. She got out of bed and went across the landing to the bathroom. The sound was still there. She returned to her bedroom, and at that moment she realised that her experience of the sound was as if it were *inside* her head. She sat down on the edge of her bed. The nearest description she could apply to the quality of the sound was that it was a humming. But it wasn't a hum. She tried to think what the source of the sound might be, but she could not come up with anything.

She tried to imagine constructing an instrument which would make a sound like that, but her mind produced nothing. Her head was full of the sound. She was clear that it was exquisitely beautiful, but could think of no further words to describe it. She lay in bed, full of the beautiful sound. As the hours passed, the sound was increasingly present to her, and she knew that there was a swelling ocean of sound gently surging and intermingling with that central "hum". There were no instruments that she knew of that could produce this.

'At some time in the middle of the night, she heard her son walk along the landing. Her bedroom door opened, and she could see the shape of his body moving towards her bed. His normal habit was to spend the nights sitting staring out of his bedroom window; and she had long since given up any attempt to encourage him to lie down to rest. Now he came straight to her bed, lay down beside her, and seemed to fall asleep almost instantly. His gentle breathing reassured her as it mingled with the beautiful sound in her head.

'When daylight came, he woke and smiled at her, a smile that was the embodiment of peace. His face seemed to glow with a gentle radiance. He stood up, kissed her cheek, and went back down the landing to his room, where she could hear him making almost inaudible sighing sounds, very like the sound of a low wind passing through the branches of the oak tree outside in their garden. From that time on, her son slept beside her every night in a state of calm, his face emitting the gentle radiance. In the daytime he began to work in their large garden which had, over the years of turmoil, become completely overgrown.

'I was a bit disappointed,' said Jane. 'I'd hoped that the book would record something of what the son was doing in the garden, but it only gave a very short description. It did say he'd gradually transformed the garden, and that in his spare time he devised strange structures out of wood and rushes that looked like small instruments of some kind which he hung in the trees. I do wish that she'd described these in more detail. One thing I was extremely interested to discover was that as he cleared the garden, and started to plant some herbs and vegetables, instead of planting in rows, he planted, believe it or not, in spiral patterns!'

'*Spiral patterns!*' exclaimed Ellen and Eva together. 'Surely this must have some connection with the spirals in your diary.'

Ellen and Eva looked at each other and laughed at the way they had said exactly the same thing in the same way at the same time.

'I came to that conclusion too,' said Jane. 'But again, there's no detail of the spiral patterns he used. I do find it frustrating.'

'When was the book published?' asked Ellen.

'About five years ago. I'll just check.' Jane turned to the front of the book to see the date. 'Yes, five years ago.'

'Where did you get the book from?' asked Eva.

'Well,' answered Jane, 'that's a bit of a story in itself. A friend of mine had picked it up in a second-hand bookshop. She was looking for something to read while on holiday. She got a bargain – a handful of paperback books, for only £3. However, on examining them at home, she had no interest at all in this one. It was just by chance she mentioned it to me, and I immediately felt that I wanted to read it. She made me a present of it. She said that I could have it for my birthday!'

Jane glanced at the clock. 'Goodness,' she said, 'look at the time, I thought I was beginning to feel hungry.'

It was eight o'clock. So immersed had they been in their conversation that they had lost all track of time. After further deliberation, it was agreed that they would prepare something simple to eat, and then turn to the matter of the spirals in Jane's diary. They decided not to worry about how late they sat up. Ellen and Eva would be leaving in the middle of the afternoon next day, so leaving the spirals until the next morning did not seem a good idea. It was definitely best to look at them tonight, staying up as late as they needed to, feeling free to sleep on longer in the morning and get up late.

The fire was burning low. 'Do you play chess?' asked Adam, as he got up to add a few well-chosen pieces of coal.

'Hardly,' replied Matthew. 'When I was a boy a cousin of my father's taught me the basics, but it's a game that I've not pursued. In some ways I regret it.'

'I have a set here,' said Adam. 'Shall I get it out and we could have a game?'

'Okay – if you promise to remember that I'm a novice!' laughed Matthew. 'When I say that I hardly know the basic moves, I'm being completely honest.'

Adam stood up and walked over to a low cupboard to the right of the fireplace. He bent down, opened the wooden doors, and lifted out a smallish wooden box, together with a flat rectangular board that turned out to be a folded chess board.

'As you can see, there's nothing fancy about my set,' he said, as he laid the board on the coffee table and took the sliding lid off the box.

Together they arranged the pieces on the board.

'By the way, earlier this year I saw a most amazing chess set.'

'Where was that?' asked Matthew.

'As usual, I was spending most of the summer with my friend Boris outside St Petersburg.'

'Mm… you've spoken to me about Boris before. Weren't you students together?'

'Yes, that's right. I've stayed with him every summer since Maria died.'

'I'm sorry to sound crass, but was Maria your wife?'

'Don't apologise. I'm not surprised that I haven't used her name before. After she died I found I couldn't even mention her name. Boris has been very good to me. He suggested that for the first anniversary of her death I should go out to visit him. I went, and I stayed for two months. I've done that every year since then.'

'I'd like to ask you more about what happened, but perhaps you don't want to talk about it any more.'

'Actually, I'd really like to talk to you about it. Would you mind? I don't want to burden you.'

'Fire away,' said Matthew. 'Just tell me as much or as little as you want. I've got the impression that you moved to this house not very long after her death. If I remember rightly, that was about five years ago.'

'Yes and no; she died just over seven years ago, and I moved into this house five years ago.' Adam leaned back in his chair. 'Can I start by telling you about her illness, and see how far I get?'

'Of course.'

'The last Christmas of Maria's life was a very difficult one. I'd always looked forward to Christmas. I sang in a choir, and played in a small amateur orchestra. You can imagine that there was always plenty on in the weeks before Christmas. Although she didn't play an instrument, Maria was very musical indeed. Her appreciation of music was profound. The way she spoke always demonstrated to me that she was able to sense and understand sound in a way that was far beyond my own capacities. When I look back, I realise that I had become too reliant on her support and encouragement. I wish I'd known this when she started to show the first signs of something being wrong. She didn't come to the performances before and during that Christmas period. All she would say was that she felt tired. I couldn't get anything out of her at all. I can see that even the way I'm telling you about this now sounds irritable, and I feel ashamed. I can feel the old upset coming up in me that she didn't seem interested any more. I have to say that I feel so embarrassed and ashamed that I'm wondering about leaving it at that. Perhaps we should just get on with our chess.'

'Look, mate,' Matthew broke in, 'it's fine by me. I'm not Mr Perfect either. I've had my limitations, and I still have plenty. Just spit it out, and you might find it helps.'

Matthew's very direct interjection reassured Adam, and he continued.

'I used to snap at her. I used to say she didn't care about me or about music. She would sit and say almost nothing while I berated her. Her face was pale, but had a yellowish tinge. I wish that I had taken more notice of that sooner. Maybe things would have been different now if I had. I used to slam out of the house, and when I returned she would be upstairs asleep. Mercifully, I never went so far as to wake her up, but I certainly felt like doing it. The more I speak about this just now, the more I can see how I was so very dependent on her perceptions and feedback about my musical involvements. Without it I felt like a husk, but I tried to hide that from myself by trying to force her to respond. She simply wasn't able to; she was ill, and I was ignoring that fact.

'The previous summer she had had a very bad dose of flu. Do you remember that year? Many people were hospitalised in that outbreak. Fortunately I never caught it myself. It took her weeks to recover from it to the point of being able to return to her work as a tax inspector. I had helped her while she was ill. In the evenings I used to sit by her bed and we would listen to music, exchanging a few thoughts and ideas. We were very close then. Why then was I so unkind to her at Christmas? I think the main thing was that she rarely spoke, and there was something about that that inflamed me. I didn't take in that there was something wrong, and that she needed help. I just assumed that she was trying to upset me and deprive me.

'The Christmas break was over, and January came. Maria looked at me straight in the eye and said, "Adam, I know that I can't go back to work, and I have a strong premonition that I will die very soon. I'm sorry that I've not been able to say anything to you, and I can see that has been upsetting for you. The tiredness I feel is beyond any other tiredness I have ever felt, and it robs me of speech. It took me all my energy and concentration to keep going in to work, and by the time I got home I was virtually mute. I thought it would pass. I thought it was just a further effect of the flu you helped me with in the summer; but the break from work over Christmas did not help me at all. In fact, as time goes on I feel worse." And she collapsed back in her chair from the huge effort she had made to say all this to me.

'I was stunned, completely stunned. When I recovered a little, I went straight to the phone to make an appointment with our GP, and then to phone another old friend whose brother was a doctor. I know I should have sat beside Maria to talk to her and make these decisions together, but I needed help myself, and selfishly, but maybe also wisely, organised that first.

'It gradually emerged that Maria had developed a form of liver dysfunction which was very difficult to diagnose. It took many hospital visits and tests to identify, after which we were told there was nothing that could be done. With the agreement of my then employer, Jack, I reduced my working hours to half-time so I could be with Maria. But I needed time at work in order to be able to keep going. Friends clubbed together to organise a rota so that Maria nearly always had someone in the house with her, or at least only a phone call away. She died in the July, and ever since then I've stayed with Boris each summer.'

Matthew quickly understood that the rather abrupt and

truncated end to the account meant that Adam had reached the limit of what he could cope with saying.

'Thanks for telling me,' he said. 'Did you take early retirement from your job when you moved here?'

'Yes, after Maria died, I went back to work full-time, and continued until I moved to this house.'

Matthew would have liked to ask more about Adam's work; but again he sensed that this was not the time.

'You mentioned a chess set belonging to your friend Boris,' he said. 'Tell me about it, I'm intrigued.'

Adam, who had become quite visibly tense, relaxed a little as he recalled the intricately carved pieces, and recounted what Boris had told him of how his grandfather had come to carve them.

When he had finished, Matthew said, 'Well, I'm quite willing to make a fool of myself, let's have a game, and then I should be going.'

The clock on the mantelshelf showed that it was half past eleven, but neither Matthew nor Adam was concerned. There was no need for either of them to end the evening.

Refreshed by their simple meal, Jane, Ellen and Eva returned to the sitting room where the diary was waiting on the low table – the diary which contained the spirals. Jane lifted a large brown envelope down from a shelf behind her chair. From it she produced a number of sheets which she handed to Ellen and Eva.

'I thought it would be useful if I made some copies of the pages in my diary where the spirals appear, so that you can each have your own. As you'll see, I've also enlarged the small diagram which appears to indicate how the spirals should be arranged.'

'Right,' said Ellen. 'Here I have four pages each showing two spirals, and these are enlarged copies of the pages in your diary. Then there's another page with the double spiral. The fifth page I have here is the enlarged version of what we're referring to as the layout diagram. Can you remind me? I think it appeared in the bottom right-hand corner of the page bearing the double spiral. Am I right?'

'Yes,' replied Jane. 'When I copied the double spiral, I put a piece of paper over the diagram so that it doesn't show on the copied sheet. Maybe I shouldn't have done that, although it seemed a good idea at the time.'

'I'll just make a note about that,' Eva commented, 'then I'll remember. It was a very good idea of yours to make these copies. Thanks very much.'

'I've just thought of something else,' Jane added. 'I wish now that I'd copied each spiral separately so that we could make a layout of spirals as indicated in the diagram.'

She paused for a moment; then continued. 'I know what I can do. I've made three copies of the pages. I can cut the individual spirals out of the spare copies. I've a white dust sheet I can spread on the floor, and we can arrange the spirals on it once I've cut them out. I'll be back in a minute.'

Jane returned carrying the dust sheet under one arm, and a pair of scissors in her hand.

'I know that this is rather makeshift, but it should give us a better idea of the effect,' she said.

She cut out the spirals, leaving as large a margin as possible around each of them, while Ellen spread the dust sheet on the carpet.

'Do you think we should take the diagram to be just a rough guide, or to be something that's accurate?' asked Ellen. 'If the latter, then one of us should work out the scale of the diagram, and be ready to measure the distances between the spirals as we place them on the sheet.'

'Good idea,' said Jane. 'I think that it's best to assume that's the case. Eva, would you mind doing that? I suspect that this is more your area of expertise than ours. Certainly my mathematical skills are a little rusty!'

'Of course,' replied Eva. She reached for her handbag, and from it she produced a tin containing a number of articles including a compass and a ruler, and some well-sharpened pencils. She quietly got to work, using both the original diagram in Jane's diary, and the enlarged version. As a result of her labours, she was soon deftly placing the spirals on the dust sheet.

Ellen had been watching all of this with deep concentration. 'Jane,' she said, 'I think that your idea of the white dust sheet was very good. It covers an area far larger than we need to arrange the spirals themselves, but I'm sure there's enormous value in having nothing immediately around the spirals to distract the eye.'

Eva put her things away in order to join Ellen in her examination of the completed layout. Jane knelt down on the floor to be closer to it.

Eva glanced at Ellen sharply, then touched Jane's hand and whispered, 'Ellen is starting to go into a different state again – like she did the last time we were here. Do you think that we should try to stop it?'

'I don't know,' replied Jane in a low voice. 'My worry is that we don't know how far into the state she's already gone. We can't really tell from just her appearance. If she's well into it, it may be a big shock to her if we try to bring her out of it.'

'I think that you're probably right. Maybe the best thing we can do is to make sure that neither of us looks at the layout meantime. We can watch Ellen closely. I think I'll shut the door properly so that the room is warmer. Remember how Ellen was quite cold when she came to last time.'

They watched as Ellen's eyelids drooped, and, as before, her lips started to move. At first the movements were tiny, and there was no sound. This again was something that Jane and Eva had seen before. Then Ellen began to make some sounds. Her lips moved quite slowly and deliberately. Jane and Eva strained forward in an attempt to make some sense of what they saw and heard. Jane noticed that Eva was making a few notes. She herself could not glean anything from the movements of Ellen's lips and the sounds she was making, and she turned her attention to Ellen's hands, which seemed to be shaking... no, not shaking, vibrating. She made a note of this, and continued to watch. She glanced across to Eva again, who was concentrating on Ellen's mouth, and listening to the sounds. Jane was reassured that her own observation of Ellen's hands was useful. She noted that their vibration gradually diminished at the same time as the sounds she was making faded away.

'I think she'll be coming out of it soon,' Eva whispered to Jane. 'I'll go and get a blanket to wrap round her as soon as she can see us again.'

She slipped out of the room, and was soon back carrying a

cellular blanket from the cupboard in Jane's spare room. Soon after this, Ellen opened her eyes and commented about how cold it was in the room.

'Why are you both looking at me like that?' she burst out. 'Oh no!' she said, as the likely explanation dawned upon her. 'Have I been in that state again? Why on earth does it happen, and why does it happen to me? Last time we looked at the spirals you both were affected, but not to the same extent as I was. Why didn't you stop me?'

Jane explained how quickly it had taken over, and why they had decided not to intervene. She added that they had not studied the spirals themselves while she was affected.

'Oh, I didn't mean to sound critical. Thanks for doing your best. It was very thoughtful of you to avoid looking at the spirals while I was in that state. Who knows, if you hadn't done that, with this being the first time we were looking at the full layout, we might *all* have been affected, and there would have been no one left to see what had happened!'

'Jane and I made a few notes,' said Eva. 'We can go through them with you once we've got you warmed up.'

By this time Ellen was shivering, and Eva wrapped the blanket round her while Jane went off to make her a hot drink.

'Just sip it slowly,' she said as she came back. 'The important thing is to really take our time with this.'

Jane collected up the spirals from the floor and folded up the dust sheet, while Eva put her set of copied sheets back into the envelope along with Ellen's. They all agreed that it was best to put them out of sight for a while, certainly during the time they discussed what had happened to Ellen.

The fire had reduced slowly to a few glowing embers as Adam and Matthew played their game of chess. There were times when Matthew sensed that Adam was choosing moves that prolonged the game, but he did not question this. The atmosphere between the two men was very relaxed, and that was sufficient. The game of chess was comparatively incidental.

Concentrating for a while on the positions of the pieces, neither of them had spoken for a good twenty minutes. Then

Matthew suddenly remembered that he had wanted to ask about Adam's previous work, but had not wanted to interrupt him at the time. He looked at Adam.

'I meant to ask earlier,' he said, 'but it slipped my mind. What was your work before you moved here?'

Adam leaned back in his chair. 'I've had a rather chequered career,' he said. 'Before I retired and moved here, I worked as a consultant in a firm which had been very successful in supporting farming communities. Government-funded advisors are one thing; but the highly motivated multi-disciplinary team that we had developed over the years provided better advice from an integrated perspective, and farmers usually found our services cost-effective.'

'That's very interesting,' Matthew replied. 'How did you end up in that kind of work?'

'I came from a farming family, although my main interest at school was music. My parents were highly critical of this, as they needed my help on the farm, and they regarded musicians as people who never had 'proper jobs'. Before I left school I'd got a place at music college, but my father wouldn't let me go. Instead I studied farm management at the local agricultural college. I must say that I found it very interesting. I learned a lot that I couldn't have learned just by working at home. However, I felt very unhappy that I had no time to develop my music. I started to have rows with my father, and eventually got my parents to agree that if I did well in my course, they would let me do a further course, this time at music college. That's where I met Boris.

'Violin and piano are the instruments I played. Although I did well, my performance skills were not up to a professional standard, and in the end I went back home to help my father. About five years later I met Maria, and we soon planned to live together. We wanted to have our own home. By this time, my younger brother had become very active and enthusiastic with plans for developing the farm. He and father got on very well together. Then I found the job I told you about, and Maria and I got married and moved into our own home. I was glad to be away from the farm. My work was interesting, and I had time to play music with our friends. Maria was always very involved in all of this, and we had a good life together.'

'Thanks for filling me in, Adam.'

'That's okay. You work in IT don't you? Has that always been your patch?'

'Yes. It suits me very well except for the uncertainty. In all the jobs I've had, there's always been some chance of being relocated. Have you been working at all since you retired?'

'As a matter of fact I have. The firm I worked for contact me from time to time for specific jobs. I don't have to take them on, but generally I do if I'm not going abroad. There are also times when I'm invited to give talks and lectures here and there.'

Adam paused as he thought of the train to York, Ellen, and their subsequent meetings. Matthew noticed that he appeared distracted, and looked down at the chess board to give his friend time.

Adam continued. 'I don't think I mentioned it to you earlier, I'm also currently involved in a project with Boris.'

'What's that?' asked Matthew with interest.

'I'm not sure if it'll go anywhere, so I'd be glad if you don't mention it to anyone at the moment. Inspired by the composer Bartok, Boris and I collected quite a number of Romanian songs in our student days. My great-grandmother was Romanian, you might be surprised to hear. When I was visiting in the summer of last year, Boris unearthed the manuscripts from the bottom of a chest. We began to think about getting these published; and we've started on another larger project, which involves collecting Russian songs.'

'Have you got a publisher interested yet?' asked Matthew.

'I've written to a number of them, but I haven't heard anything back so far.'

'Well, let me know how you get on with it. It's a rather specialist area, and one in which I have no contacts, but of course I'll keep my ear to the ground now that I know you're looking. Perhaps we'd better polish off our friendly game of chess now, as I should be going.'

He grinned across at Adam and winked.

Adam laughed. 'Ah, you've noticed my ploy of trying to keep the game going,' he said. 'We could put it away now, if that's all right by you. I've rather lost the thread anyway.'

Matthew helped to pack the pieces back into the box, and collected his coat from the hall.

'I hope that you get your place at Professor Barnes' talk on Monday. Thanks for the evening. Bye now.'

Adam let him out. He closed the door and walked slowly down the hall. It had been a good evening – a very good evening, he felt. He remembered talking to Matthew about Maria. How could it be that he had broken his long silence? How could it be that it had seemed quite easy? If this afternoon he had sat and tried to plan to speak to Matthew about Maria, he would surely have failed to come up with anything, would have felt defeated long before Matthew arrived, and would certainly have said nothing at all about the subject.

He had some vague realisation that having spoken even the little he had shared, he felt a bit better; certainly not worse. He had always imagined that speaking about her would inevitably make him less able to cope with having lost her. This evening he had discovered that this was not true. He looked back and remembered how his pain had been so great he had told himself that he could never ever speak about her again, and that that was the only way to cope. He had believed that talking about her would only make the pain more intense.

Unwilling to go to bed straight away, he turned into his study.

'I'll just check my e-mails,' he said to himself in a low voice.

A few minutes later he saw that there was a reply from the address on the leaflet about the talk on Monday, and a new message from Boris. First he opened the one about the talk. It read:

> <We have a spare place. One of our number has had to drop out for the rest of the term.
>
> Hope to see you on Monday. Please confirm.
>
> Edmund Barnes>

This was followed by an address. Adam picked up his street map, and found that he would be able to walk there in about fifteen minutes. He felt pleased and encouraged, and sent a quick message to confirm that he would be there.

Next, the message from Boris:

<Dear Friend,

Am not yet in bed – up very late – wanted to send you a quick message – nothing special to say, except I would really like a game of chess! B>

Adam was startled, then laughed, and sent a quick reply:

<Have just finished a game with a neighbour who was round for the evening!

Will be in touch. A>

Not long after that he was in bed and switching off the light. He had set his alarm clock for 7.30 a.m. as the workmen would arrive at eight.

'Tell me everything you noticed,' said Ellen insistently.

'Are you sure you're ready?' asked Eva. 'I think that we should wait until you're properly warmed up again.'

'I am,' said Ellen. 'And I'm keen to get on with this now. Tell me what happened.'

'Well,' said Jane slowly, 'the first problem is that neither Eva nor I know exactly when you started going into that state.'

'Yes,' said Eva, 'all my concentration was on making sure that I was placing the spirals on the sheet in the way indicated on the diagram. I was making precise measurements, and at the same time I was trying to see exactly which spiral to place in each position.'

'And all my attention was on the emerging pattern,' added Jane. 'When Eva pointed out what had happened to you, we decided the best thing was to keep you warm, and wait. It was very similar to last time, as far as I could tell. Eva was watching your face very intently, so I concentrated on the rest of your body. As before, you were pale; but this time I noticed that your hands were vibrating.'

'Vibrating!' exclaimed Ellen.

'Yes, that's the word that best describes it,' confirmed Jane. 'The palms of your hands were about six inches apart, facing each other; your fingers were curved inwards, and the tips of them were about two inches apart. What did you notice, Eva?'

'When I saw Ellen's lips moving and some sound coming from them, I concentrated solely on that. I used to make a hobby of lip-reading and have developed a moderate skill. It's surprising how useful it can be! I can't claim to have a full grasp of what Ellen was trying to say, but by connecting the lip movements with the small sounds, I did note a few words that I felt fairly sure about.'

'What were they?' asked Ellen, eagerly.

Eva looked uncertain. 'I don't want you to think that I'm sure I've got this right. It suddenly feels like quite a big responsibility.'

Ellen thought for a moment. 'Yes,' she said. 'If you tell us what you think I was saying, it could affect us all quite a lot. And if you've got it wrong, then it could be affecting us all in a wrong direction.'

'Perhaps I could tell you first what the subject seemed to be,' suggested Eva. 'Then you'll have a better idea of my dilemma.'

Ellen and Jane looked puzzled, hesitated, and then agreed.

'You seemed to be saying the name *Adam*, several times,' said Eva bluntly.

Ellen stared at Eva. She was at a loss as to what to say.

It was Jane who broke the silence. 'Perhaps I'd better add here that the name of the young man in Frances Ianson's book was Adam.'

Ellen looked instantly relieved. She did not want think of the man on the train. She did not want to be thinking about him at all. She wanted to make some sense of the spirals. She wanted to learn more about the meaning of the special pages in her red book, and she wanted to understand the significance of Eva's stick; but she did not want to think about the man on the train.

'What else was I saying?' she asked.

'The other words were less distinct. I'm fairly sure that one of them was "light". I thought you said "sound of light", but that doesn't seem to make sense.'

'Can we think a bit more about what happened last time?' asked Ellen. 'I remember that you said you felt a bit strange, Jane. It seemed that you were the least affected of us, and we thought that this was because you'd seen the spirals before. But that might not have been the reason after all, because this is the second time I've seen the spirals, and you both say I had a reaction similar to last time. In fact, what you describe suggests that in some ways my reaction was more intense.'

'Yes, that's right,' said Jane. 'Last time your lips were moving, but without sound. This time you made faint sounds. Last time I don't remember seeing your hands vibrating, but this time I did. Can you say something about *your* experience last time, Eva?'

'Yes, of course. You may remember how I thought there was some connection between the way I felt when I looked at the spirals, and how I'd felt when I was with the old couple who gave me the stick? The feeling then had come on after I'd finished the drink the woman gave me. Since the last time we looked at the spirals, I've often thought about this. If I'm correct, we could assume that there's a connection between the spirals and the drink, but I can't think of one.'

'Ye...s,' said Ellen slowly. 'But not being able to think of a connection doesn't mean there isn't one. It could mean there's one we aren't aware of yet.'

'There's a lot about all of this that we don't know or understand,' said Jane. 'Look at how the spirals appeared in the first place. Remember, I'd hardly started reading that book before the spirals appeared in my diary, and I still don't know how they got there. I think we've all assumed that I drew them while I was asleep, but we can't be sure. I'd only read three chapters of the book, and not all on that night. And there was that strange unaccountable tiredness I'd been suffering that I realised started soon after I began to read the book.'

'How long had you had the book?' asked Ellen.

'As you know, I was given it for my birthday. After that it lay on my bedside table for about a week, then I read the introduction. It was after that I found I was feeling tired all the time. I thought I might have some viral infection, and maybe I did; but no symptoms were apparent apart from the strange tiredness. About a week later I read the first two chapters, and a few days after that, on the night of the spiral writing, I'd read chapter three. When I look back, I'd say that the strange tired feeling wasn't there any more after the spirals appeared in my diary.'

'Can you tell us exactly what's written in Chapter Three?' asked Ellen.

Jane picked up the book and explained how Chapter One was the account of the son's behaviour – behaviour which people were finding difficult. She said how it went on to describe how the mother did her best to deal with the situation. Jane described how in Chapter Two the son's hearing was tested. Ellen and Jane listened quietly to all of this, and then waited while Jane prepared to read Chapter Three out to them.

This chapter was a very moving account of how the mother searched her soul for any way in which she might be to blame for her son's condition. It described how she alone believed that his behaviour was due to distress, and not because of any intention to frighten or harm people. She could not understand what was happening; but she knew he needed help, and she was determined that she would find a way to communicate with him.

When Jane had finished reading she put the book down, and the others noticed that she had tears in her eyes.

'Today when I read this,' she said, 'I know what affects me most. It's the mother's determination to make a meaningful connection with her son, however impossible that might seem to be.'

'Do you think that was what led to the appearance of the spirals in your diary?' asked Ellen. 'We know that when the mother had connected with her son, he began to work in the garden; and he planted herbs and vegetables in those spiral layouts. It's a pity the book doesn't give us details of those, but maybe it isn't necessary. Maybe the spirals that appeared in your diary are in a different form – something more to do with you. That would make sense. The spirals he laid out had arisen from the link between him and his mother. The spirals which we believe you drew while you were asleep could be your response to reading about the mother's ultimate commitment to something that seemed impossible.

'If all that is true, then the next thing to think about is why I've been so deeply affected by the spirals. What was it that I was trying to communicate? … "Adam", "sound of light" and the vibration in my hands are the only clues so far. We know that the name of the son in the book is Adam, but as you know the man I met on the train was called Adam too. Which of these two people I was referring to I don't know. It could be either or it could be both. Eva, when you said I'd been saying that name, I wanted to discount the possibility that I was referring to that man, but I have to admit that I think he's significant here. Don't ask me why… I just have that feeling. Have you got any more thoughts on why the spirals affected you in the same way as that drink the old woman gave you, Eva?'

'No, not really; but as I said that, something came into my mind. I suddenly seemed to know that my mind had been opened in some way by that drink, in the way necessary for me to be able to choose the right stick. Do you remember how I told you that I had no doubt about which stick to take? All the sticks were well made, but the only one that had any real attraction for me was the ash one with the small carving on it. If looking at your spirals, Jane, opens my mind in the same way, I wonder what that means? Is it to aid me in making some other choice? I just don't know.'

It was not much later that the three women agreed that they were unlikely to get any further with the many remaining questions that night, and they bade each other goodnight.

Adam, very relaxed from his evening with Matthew, had expected to fall asleep quickly once he was in bed. He was surprised to find that this was far from the case. His mind started to fill with images of Ellen – Ellen Ridgeway, the woman he had met on the train. She had mostly been out of his thoughts since he had exchanged e-mails with Boris regarding the dream about her. He had been preoccupied with other things. But now his mind was flooded with thoughts and questions. He remembered her politeness and her warmth of tone, but also the sense of her detachment, and her underlying unwillingness to engage with him in anything other than formal conversation. He remembered how, when he saw her at the Traveller's Arms, she had seemed almost panicked by his presence, until she knew that he would soon be leaving. He remembered watching her concentration as she studied her book at the hotel in York. There was something odd about that book, he remembered. From what he could see, there was little or nothing on many of the pages. Perhaps the print was very faint, so that he had not been able to see it from a distance. Yes, that would explain it. But then he thought about how the book she had been reading in the dream had blank pages. And what about the train…? Why had he been so drawn to her almost immediately?

There was no apparent reason for this. He searched his mind again and could find nothing. Yet not only had he noticed that it was a woman sitting next to him, but also he had been affected by her presence. Nothing like that had happened to him since Maria's death. And the way he had been affected by her presence was not something he could put his finger on. If someone asked him to describe precisely what it was, he would not be able to say. There had, of course, been the coincidence about the pens; but he only learned of that later in the journey. He had definitely felt affected by her presence before he knew about the pens. He had tried his best to explain it all to Boris in the summer. It was in no way similar to the attraction he had felt when he first met his wife, Maria. He remembered that very clearly, and his sense of sitting next to Ellen on the train was not in the least like that. Yet sitting next to Ellen, he had had a flash of memory of his long and happy intimacy with Maria. So why was that?

He wished he could switch off these thoughts and go to sleep. He needed to be up for the workmen in the morning; but sleep was impossible. The thoughts and questions continued unabated. Next, it was back to that dream. Fragments of it mixed themselves up with memories of the two hotels where he had seen Ellen. The long gallery-type of room in the dream became mixed up with the room at the Traveller's Arms where he had been surprised to come across the piano. The book that Ellen was reading in the dream seemed to be the book she was reading at the hotel in York; but now, when he thought about the dream he was sure he could, after all, see something on the pages: shapes. Shapes of what?

He got out of bed, went to the bathroom, and paced around for a while. His bedside light provided little comfort as he got back into bed, but he left it on. He remembered with a wry smile that on the few occasions he had been ill as a young boy, a bedside light had been brought into his sparsely furnished bedroom, and had been left on all night in case he needed to get up.

'I'm not ill,' he muttered to himself, 'but I'll just have the light on anyway.'

He stared at a picture that he had hung on the wall opposite his bed. It was the one thing he had painted at school. The class had been told to copy a print of a painting by Sisley. What was his first name? It began with an 'A'. Ah, Alfred... Adam mused to himself as he thought about the picture. He smiled as he remembered how the teacher had congratulated him on his efforts, before pointing out that he had failed to include the figure of a woman that appeared in the centre of the woodland scene. He had never felt the need to add that figure; but he had kept his picture. When he had come to this house five years ago, he had found it sandwiched between some sheets of music. He had felt keen to have it framed, and, facing his embarrassment, he took it to an art shop, and chose a good frame for it. He had found the result quite satisfying.

Staring at the picture seemed to calm him he realised with surprise; and after a while he was able to switch off the light, turn on his side, and fall asleep.

He woke briefly in the night, sweating. He knew he had been dreaming. He was sure he could hear the sound of a train, in fact he was sure that he was on a train. But he was not. He was in bed. Exhausted, he slept again until his clock woke him in time to get up for the workmen.

As he shaved, he heard a thought in his head almost as strongly as if it had been spoken. *Shall I get in touch with Ellen again now?* He answered himself firmly: Look, the best thing to do is to get ready for the workmen, let them round the side of the house, eat your breakfast, and then e-mail Boris. You need to think sensibly about this.

Later, eating breakfast to the sound of men's voices accompanied by digging and clanking, he felt more able to think clearly. He jotted down a few notes. The first thing was to get this conservatory finished. The builder had promised that everything would be in place well before Christmas.

Let's assume that I must be around until the end of the year, Adam continued to himself. This would take account of any unforeseen delays. The next thing I must decide is when I'm going out to spend time with Boris again. We'd agreed it would be in the spring, but exactly when we'd not said.

He got out his diary for the next year, and looked through the commitments he had made. There was a work project which would take up most of February at a guess. There was a lecture he had agreed to give on January 21st. As things stood, after February

103

he was free. He would send an e-mail to Boris suggesting that he travel there sometime after the middle of March, and stay for at least five weeks. He pencilled this into his diary and carried it through to the study, where he wrote suggested dates into an e-mail and sent it off. When he heard back from Boris, he would know whether or not to contact work to say that he would not be available over that period.

'Over the next few weeks, I must follow up some of the people I contacted about publishing our Romanian collection,' he said out loud. 'I've put out a lot of feelers, but have heard nothing back so far. If the dates I've suggested to Boris are okay, I'll ask him what he thinks about a plan that's coming into my mind about writing to Ellen Ridgeway soon, to ask if there would be any possibility of meeting her some time in January.'

Having made these decisions, Adam was able to concentrate on preparing more letters to send to publishers. Time passed quite quickly. By the end of the morning he had a reply from Boris suggesting that he came out some time in the third week of March, adding that he could stay as long as he wanted.

Pleased to get this news, Adam wrote straight away to his former employers to let them know he would be unavailable for about three months after completing February's project. Then he concentrated on a further e-mail to Boris, to decide more precisely how he might approach Ellen, if indeed Boris did not advise against it.

Now, I have that lecture to give on the 21st, so I shouldn't suggest anything that week. A thought struck him. Where is it I have to go this time?

He got out the road atlas and the lecture invitation, and stopped.

'Why am I so dense at times!' he exclaimed, glad that the workmen could not hear him from outside the house. 'That lecture is only about forty-five minutes' drive from the village where Ellen lives. I'd planned to go by train, but I could drive instead. Why don't I write to her saying that I'll be in the area, and ask if it would be possible to meet up?'

Adam wrote on the computer the kind of letter he thought he might send, and then sent it across to Boris, attached to an e-mail that said:

< Have blocked out two months in my diary from the third week in March. Will book travel arrangements nearer the time. Please tell me exactly what you think of my sending the attached letter to Ellen. I have only just realised that the lecture I'm giving in January will be quite near where she lives. It does seem like a good opportunity for getting in touch with her. >

He sent it off and then went to the kitchen, having called out to the workmen that he was putting the kettle on, and would brew them some tea. And there was that talk by Professor Barnes tomorrow evening to look forward to.

The work outside continued to progress well. The men left at dusk, and Adam went for a walk to stretch his legs. He took the route which followed a fairly steep rise for about half a mile. He liked to feel he was stressing his breathing for a while. There was still enough light for him to see the track. He knew it well, and did not need to fear losing his way. He walked briskly. Things seemed to be falling into place, and he felt almost an eager anticipation about what might lie ahead.

When he got back to the house, he hurried to the computer, eager to see if there was a response yet from Boris about his plan to contact Ellen. Yes, there it was!

< Dear Friend,

I am already looking forward now to seeing you in March.

Regarding your letter to Ellen, just send it and see what it brings.

B >

Chapter Thirteen

It was Jane who woke first the next morning. As there was no sound from the others, she decided to get up and go out for a while. Her head was aching a little, and she thought that a brief stroll would clear it. It was raining, but it was quite mild for the time of year. Unwilling to wear her waterproofs for a short outing, she used the large umbrella that she kept handy at the back door. It had been left behind by a golfing friend who, having noticed its absence on her return home, had phoned and cheerfully informed Jane that she was welcome to keep it, as she had several others she had collected over the years. Jane chose a route that would take her about half an hour. That should be long enough, she thought.

As she walked, her mind went over all that had happened since Ellen and Eva had arrived on Friday evening. There was a lot to think about. One thing was very clear to her, there was far more to be understood about the spirals and the effect they had had on each of them, although she had no idea of how that would come about. She realised how glad she was to have Ellen and Eva as friends, and that they had taken such an interest in her spirals. She had looked forward to this meeting ever since they last met, but now she also felt a little concerned. The spirals were having a very obvious effect upon Ellen. Although Eva appeared less affected, there was no way of knowing if that effect was really of a similar intensity. She became aware of a nagging doubt in her mind.

It was through me that those spirals came into being. It was because of me that Ellen and Eva have seen them. What if all this results in Ellen or Eva being harmed in some way? she said to herself.

At this, her head cleared. This worry must have been what was affecting her when she woke up this morning, but she had not been able to see what it was until now. She immediately made up her mind to speak to her friends as soon as possible, and she walked briskly back to the house.

She entered by the back door to find Ellen and Eva sitting in the kitchen with hot drinks, deep in conversation.

'Oh good, you're up! I've got something I must say to you both,' she said.

Ellen and Eva smiled. 'Snap.'

'Let's toss a coin to see who goes first, then,' suggested Jane. 'But I want you to know that what I have to say is quite a serious matter.'

Ellen took the lead. 'No need for coins,' she said. 'What we want is to ask when you'll be free to meet again. We're in agreement that our discussions are very important to us, and that we want to pursue them and continue to examine your spirals.'

Jane relaxed. 'I want to as well, very much, but I do have a worry. I realise that where the spirals are concerned, I feel responsible for any adverse effects that they might have on either of you.'

Ellen and Eva stared at Jane, and then looked at each other.

'For my part,' said Eva, 'that had never entered my head. What about you, Ellen?'

Ellen shook her head. 'I suppose I can see how you might think that; but you have to remember that you didn't force either myself or Eva to be involved. We were both interested and asked to see the spirals. In addition, you know that we fixed this trip specifically to study them and their effects. It's my view that we have equal responsibility.'

'I'm entirely in agreement with that, Ellen,' Eva added emphatically.

Feeling reassured, Jane took a mug, filled it, and sat down.

'Jane,' asked Eva, 'I've been wondering if you'd be willing to lend me your copy of Frances Ianson's book. I'd like to read it myself before we meet again. Your description of the contents came over very well, but I'd like to read the whole book.'

'Of course, I'll just go and get it.'

Jane returned a few minutes later with the book in one hand, and a polythene bag in the other.

'No, wait a minute,' said Eva. 'I've a better idea. I'll take down the precise details, and try to get a copy for myself. I've found a number of good sources of books on the Internet.'

She took out a pencil and a small notebook from her bag, and carefully copied the details into it.

'You're very welcome to use this copy,' said Jane encouragingly.

Eva shook her head. 'No, I'd definitely like to get one of my own. Perhaps I can borrow yours later if I draw a blank.'

'Would you like to borrow this copy then, Ellen?' asked Jane.

'It's good of you to offer, but I think I'll wait and see what Eva comes up with. We'll always have access to your copy here, Jane; and I hope that we'll eventually end up with one each. The more I think about it, it does seem obvious that we should have a copy each.'

'Okay,' agreed Jane; and she returned the book to the sitting room where her diary and the photocopies of the spirals still lay.

'I've got an idea,' said Eva thoughtfully. 'How about meeting at my house next time? I haven't got a spare bedroom, but I do have a sofa bed in the living room. You'd both be welcome to use my bed in the attic, and I could sleep downstairs.'

Jane looked surprised. 'I'd assumed that if you wanted to meet again it would be here, but I'd like to see where you live, Eva. As you know I don't drive, so I'll have to work out how to travel across. It shouldn't be too difficult. I can get a bus to the train at this end. I can always use a taxi at your end if I need to. If I come to you, it'll mean that Ellen has only one journey instead of two. Let's have a look at our diaries and see what we can arrange.'

'I know it would be wise to have a reasonable gap between our meetings,' Ellen mused. 'But to be truthful, I'm eager to meet again quite soon if we can arrange it. What do you two think?'

'I agree,' replied Eva, as she slowly turned over the pages of her diary.

'I certainly would like that,' said Jane, 'and although like you I'm eager to meet again soon, I think we should be careful not to hurry things. A lot has happened in each of the two visits that you've made here, and I think we all need time to mull it over in the context of our ordinary lives, however eager we might be to rush ahead with it all. I know I need some more time to think through my feeling of being responsible. You have both been very reassuring, and I accept everything you've said; but I do need time.'

'What have you got in mind?' asked Eva.

'Fortunately, the Christmas period is usually a quiet time for me, and this year is no exception. I won't feel under any pressure, and I'll have time to think through all that has happened. The only thing I'm definitely committed to is my usual visit to see my sister, Clare – you know, Emily's mother. I'm looking forward to seeing them both. It'll be just the three of us, because unfortunately this year her husband will be away again. His work takes him all over the world.'

'Eva, I'm beginning to see your suggestion of meeting at your house next time is a good one. Not only will Ellen not have to travel so far, but also it will reduce my remaining sense of responsibility.'

'How about towards the end of January?' asked Ellen. 'Personally I don't think that would be rushing things. What do you both think? The last weekend would be the best for me.'

Eva and Jane consulted their diaries. 'That would be fine for me,' Eva said slowly, pencilling in the dates. 'I feel comfortable about the gap of over two months. It feels right for me. How about you, Jane?'

'Yes, fine for me.'

'Now that's all sorted out, would you mind if we have an early lunch?' asked Ellen. 'It would be best for me if I could drop Eva off by mid-afternoon, and then I'm not too late getting back home myself.'

Chapter Fourteen

It was Monday. Adam had leapt out of bed eagerly at the ring of his alarm clock. The workmen had arrived punctually as before, and were hard at work. There were two reasons why Adam was feeling particularly good today. The first was that he was looking forward to the talk this evening, and the second was that he was going to write a handwritten version of the letter he had planned to send to Ellen, which Boris had approved. He was very grateful for the input of his friend. Without that he knew that he would have been likely to waver for days about whether or not to contact her, and then still not make a decision.

After breakfast he took out his writing pad and began:

Dear Ellen,

I hope this letter finds you well. I have been invited to give a lecture in Alnwick in the afternoon of January 21st. I shall be staying overnight in the locality before returning home. I shall travel by road.

I note that you live less than an hour's drive away. It would be a simple matter for me to detour if you happen to be free for us to meet for a couple of hours. Do let me know. I can fit in with anything you might suggest for after 7 p.m.

Yours sincerely,

Adam Thomas

He addressed the envelope, put the letter inside, sealed it and found a stamp. A few minutes later he was walking briskly down the road to the post box. He felt brighter now. Although he had been well occupied since he last saw Ellen, and she had not been consciously in his mind very often, the continuing effect of her upon him was nevertheless significant. Taking some positive action about seeing her again seemed to have cleared his mind in a way, akin to the effect of having told Matthew about Maria.

Back at the house he saw the post had been delivered in his absence. Amongst the bills and circulars he saw an envelope the contents of which he could not guess. He opened it to find a letter from Carillon Music, suggesting a meeting on January 10th to discuss their possible involvement in the publication of the Romanian songs.

Oh good, breathed Adam to himself, they are a very small concern, but that won't matter. In fact, I think I prefer something like that; there's a likelihood that I can be more directly involved, and that would be more interesting.

He sent an e-mail to Boris to let him know.

The whole day passed in a very pleasant way, and soon it was time for him to set off for the talk. Not wanting to risk being late he had given himself plenty of time, and in the event arrived earlier than he felt was polite. He walked up and down the street a few times, admiring the style of the large stone-built houses that stood on each side of it. It was difficult to see much of the finer detailing of the buildings, because although there were street lights, the houses stood back from the road, and the large gardens contained a selection of bushes and trees which obscured any hope of a clear view.

He checked the number on the wooden side gate which opened on a path leading to the front door. Number 9. He opened it, went through, and closed it behind him. There was no one else about. He made his way up the path, and found by the door a large iron handle which looked as if it were a bell pull. He tugged at it rather tentatively but heard no sound. He waited. After a minute or two he pulled it again, this time more determinedly. He heard the surprisingly deep tones of what must have been a large bell, and soon after that the door was opened by an old man dressed in brown trousers and a Harris tweed jacket, which bore large leather patches on the elbows. It was difficult to guess how old he was. His remaining hair was pure white, but he stood very straight, and had an air of well-being.

'I am Professor Barnes, Edmund Barnes,' he said. 'And you must be Adam Thomas. Do come in and meet the others.'

His voice was quiet and cultured, with an almost indiscernible accent. Adam was aware of standing in a large hallway with a log fire burning in a fireplace on one side of it.

'Take the door that's third on the left.'

Following the instruction, Adam was surprised to find himself in a large room with a vaulted ceiling, which gave a feeling of being in a small chapel. There were a number of people in the room seated on benches. It was heated by a large wood-burning stove situated on the wall at the back of the room, near where he had entered. He noticed to his surprise that all the other people in the room were men. At a glance he guessed that their ages ranged from about forty upwards to eighty, and possibly beyond.

Adam felt a little puzzled. He had arrived early, but it looked as if everyone else had arrived long before. He did not feel able to ask about this. One of the men motioned to him to take up a seat on the end of a half-empty bench. Edmund Barnes walked to the front of the room, and addressed the group.

'I'm glad you were all able to come again this evening. We have an addition to our gathering, Adam Thomas, who contacted me at the weekend, and has taken up the place that had become vacant for the rest of the term.'

His voice wavered a little as he said this, and Adam began to wonder if the reason for the absence of the missing person was something unpleasant.

'This evening,' he continued, 'I will be talking about ancient signs, and forms of writing such as hieroglyphs, runes and cup and ring marks.'

He turned to the makeshift blackboard that had been erected at the front of the room, and began to make a series of marks on it, most of which Adam did not recognise. But he soon became totally engrossed in what the professor was saying. He had brought a small notebook and a pencil, and he did his best to make sufficient notes to prompt his memory about things he intended to follow up once he had time.

'And now,' said the professor's voice eventually, 'much as I would like to continue, I must finish for this evening. You are all welcome to stay for a cup of tea and a biscuit if you wish. I must leave you in about half an hour.'

Adam realised that this was a polite way of indicating that they should all leave some time in the next twenty minutes. He turned to his neighbour.

'Have you attended all this term's talks so far?' he asked.

'Yes, I wouldn't miss them for anything. This chap is so experienced, it's like sitting with a talking encyclopaedia.'

'How many more talks are there in this series?'

'Just one. The professor has had to reduce the number this term.'

Adam felt a stab of disappointment; he felt hungry for more of what he had been learning. It was not just the content of the talk, it was the fascinating way in which the information was conveyed. At least there was one more Monday. Perhaps he could ask then for details of where Professor Barnes would be speaking next…

Lost in thought, he made his way slowly back home.

Chapter Fifteen

Ellen's Christmas was going to be very busy. She was always heavily involved in overseeing food and shelter projects for the homeless. It suited her very well. Although her involvement was genuine, she was also aware that the time this work occupied was a time she used to dread, as after her mother's death Christmas became a time when she and her father felt most isolated. People used to invite them round, but in general they could not face going. Her father was obviously uncomfortable in the presence of a husband and wife, and Ellen not only felt that discomfort with him, but also suffered much pain in watching children in warm contact with their mothers. Yes, these mothers were kind and sensitive towards her, but they were not *her* mother; they were the mothers of other children, and they would not be there at *her* bedtime.

It had been about two years after the death of her father that she was first asked to help with one of the voluntary projects. After that year she quickly became involved in the organisation of several others; and over the five years since then, workers and homeless alike looked forward to being alongside her in her tireless commitment to those less fortunate than herself.

There was much to prepare through December that absorbed most of her time and energy. At this time of year she often let her mail mount up for a few days, and then would allot an hour or so to sort through it. At the end of the first week in December she had quite a pile of letters and cards, and in the evening she sat down to look through them. Here was a card from Eva with a gold star on it on a deep blue background. It was quite striking. Inside there was a note:

> *I have traced two copies of Frances Ianson's book and have ordered them both. A copy should be sent direct to your address. This will be my Christmas gift to you. I hope it arrives soon. Please let me know when you get it. Love, Eva*

Ellen threw away a number of items that were obviously advertisements for things in which she had no interest. But what was this? A letter, the address on the front written in handwriting that was vaguely familiar, but which she could not place. She opened it and unfolded the page inside. She froze. It was from Adam, the man on the train. *Oh no!* She had nothing against him, but she also knew that she did not want to have to think about him. He was suggesting that they might meet. January 21st. She stuffed the letter in a rack where she put things about which she was undecided, and turned to the rest of the heap. She wrote a cheque for the man who had recently repaired her roof. She filed the itemised accounts for her phone. January 21st...? She picked up her diary. That was a weekday, not many days before the weekend when she would be seeing Jane and Eva again. She told herself not to think about it at the moment, and to concentrate on the rest of her task. She had promised herself that she would spend an hour with her red book before she went to bed tonight, and she did not want to give that up.

At ten o'clock she put away the remaining items in a drawer, and sat next to the radiator with her red book. The procedure each time she did this was almost exactly the same. First she would sit with her eyes closed for a few minutes, then she would open the book at the beginning and study the first leaf pattern. After this, she would slowly turn over the blank pages until she found the next leaf pattern, and so on. Having studied the first nine leaf patterns, she would then study the blank pages. She had learned over a long period of time that there was always one of the intervening pages that seemed to affect her differently from the others. The position of such pages in relation to those bearing the leaf patterns varied, but there was always one somewhere. Each of the blank pages that affected her seemed to have depth. Although each page was flat and blank, it was as if her eyes could see into the page. She marvelled at how each time this happened, it felt as if it had never happened before, although of course she knew it had.

This evening, for the first time, she realised that she had not studied the rest of the book in any detail. How strange; until now she had concentrated only upon the first nine leaf patterns and the intervening pages. On an impulse she turned the book over, and opened the back cover as if it were the front of the book. Instead of methodically searching for the leaf patterns to study first, she chose blank pages at random. She looked at a number of such pages with no apparent effect. Then something happened. The page she had been looking at had nothing on it at all, but when she looked away she was aware of a visual pattern in her mind, a very faint pattern made up of minute dots.

When she thought about it, the only association that she had was of some faint spore-prints left from mushrooms and toadstools she had tried to identify many years ago. What was this? The pinprick pattern faded in her mind. She looked again at the blank page, and then looked away once more. Once again, the faint pinprick pattern came. She suddenly felt very weary. It was no use puzzling about it just now. She had a heavy day ahead, and more beyond that. Best to put the book away in its place on the shelf to the left of the fireplace and go to bed.

As she undressed she was glad that she had told Eva and Jane all she knew about the red book. When she saw them again, she could tell them what had just happened. She wished that she hadn't got that letter from Adam. She felt in a quandary about what to do.

Tired as she was, she spent a restless night, waking several times to find the duvet on the floor beside the bed. She was aware of having dreamed, but could not remember anything about her dreams. She felt quite tearful, but was not sure why.

The next morning, driving to her first meeting of the day, she nearly went through some red lights, and that made her decide that she would phone Eva that evening to discuss what to do about Adam's letter.

Her decision helped her through the day, and back at home, having eaten, she keyed in Eva's number. She was disappointed to find that there was only a call-minder message. Having left a brief message to the effect that she hoped Eva would call as soon as she could, she settled down to work through more of her papers; but being very tired, she fell asleep across her desk.

The ring of the telephone penetrated her awareness, and she struggled to remember where she was and what time it was, as she lifted the receiver.

'Hello, it's Eva here.' The familiar sound of Eva's voice brought Ellen into full consciousness.

'Eva, it's good to hear you! I'd fallen asleep at my desk. I've got a couple of things I wanted to mention to you.'

'I'm glad you phoned and left a message. Funnily enough, I wanted to phone you myself this evening. Something rather unusual has cropped up, and I'd like to tell you about it.'

'Of course, tell me about it, and then I'll tell you what I was wanting to speak to you about.'

Eva explained that she had had a letter from a friend of hers, who was also a colleague. She was well known as having an unusual degree of intuition in sensing how best to help people whose sickness defied conventional medicine. Very recently she had been approached by a man who had heard of her, and had driven a very long way to see her. He came unheralded and had brought his daughter with him, begging that she would see them both. She was in the middle of a clinic, but instinctively she realised that she must see the girl. She asked the man to return that evening. She spent two hours with them, taking notes of the background. The girl was very thin, pale and weak. Although she was twelve years old, she looked more like a child of about eight. She spent some time trying to sense the energies around the girl, but was met with patterns she had never encountered before. She was therefore extremely reluctant to suggest any treatment for her at that time. The girl's father was at his wits' end, and begged her to do something. She explained to him that if she tried to treat the girl while not understanding the nature of her illness she might do harm, and she could not therefore contemplate intervening at this stage. She had written in the letter to me that as he pressed her more and more, she suddenly became aware that she should write to me, and ask if I would see them. There was no explanation in the letter as to why this was.

Eva continued. 'I wanted to tell you about this, Ellen, because somehow I know that if I talk about it to trusted people, then I'm more likely to be able to help the girl. I phoned my friend, and agreed to see her and her father. She phoned him with my number and address. She got his permission to send me a copy of the notes she'd made during the consultation. He rang me yesterday, and I'm seeing him with his daughter in two weeks' time. I asked him if I could discuss the case with colleagues of mine, and he gave me permission to talk to anyone I wanted. I know that two weeks might seem a long time for them to wait, but I also know I need time to prepare for this. I'm seeing them just before Christmas. I'm going to phone Jane in the next couple of days to tell her as well.'

'I was going to suggest that,' said Ellen. 'I'm very glad you're going to. Please let me know how it goes when you see them. It's okay to phone me any evening after about 9 o'clock.'

'Thanks. Now tell me what it was you wanted me to know.'

'I've had a letter from Adam,' Ellen burst out. 'He's suggesting that we meet. He's going to be in Alnwick on January 21st and wants us to meet in the evening. I don't know what to do.'

'How do you feel about it?'

'Muddled and agitated. I wish he hadn't written. I don't want anything to do with him.'

'That may be true,' said Eva, 'but he has made a big impression on you. He's been on your mind enough for you to want to talk to myself and Jane about him.'

'You're right I suppose. If he were of no consequence to me, I'd hardly have thought to mention him. I must try to work out why I feel so agitated. I think it was that third meeting that did it. The thought that he would drive all the way to the Traveller's Arms in the hope of seeing me, unnerved me. However, the time we spent together there was not unpleasant. He put no pressure on me at all.'

'I have an idea,' said Eva. 'How about writing to him to say you may be away from home at that time. After all, it's just days before you're coming down to stay with me for our next meeting with Jane. You could say that you'll get in touch once you're clearer about your existing plans. That would also be true. That way you'd have given him a fair response, and one which gives you more time to think things through.'

'That's a very good idea. I'll write something to him tomorrow and get it off.'

'What was the other thing you wanted to talk to me about?' asked Eva.

'Thanks for reminding me. You remember the red book?'

'Yes, of course.'

Ellen went on to explain to Eva about the night she had turned the book round, and tried to describe the impression of the pinprick pattern in her mind.

'I can hear what you're saying,' said Eva, 'but I can't really picture the pinprick pattern.'

'I'm not surprised,' said Ellen. 'It eludes *me*, and I was the one who sensed it. Don't worry about it though, it's good to have had the chance to let you know about it.'

'Well, do get in touch if anything else emerges.'

'Thanks. Well then, we may have more things to say to each other soon. Bye for now.'

Ellen put the phone down. She had been deeply affected by Eva's situation about the girl in the wheelchair. She hoped that Eva would be able to help that girl. She was glad of her support about the letter from Adam, and also about her recent experience with the red book. She decided not to delay replying to Adam. The post could be quite slow at this time of year. She picked up her pen and started to write on a sheet of her pre-addressed notepaper.

Dear Adam…

She put the pen down, feeling a little odd. She got up and walked round the room. She stared at the pen where she had laid it on the desk.

Come on now, you don't need to feel funny about the fact that you're using the pen like the one Adam dropped on the train. Just sit down and write the letter!

She sat down and started to write again.

Thank you for your letter…

She stopped, got up, and walked round the room again. There was something else bothering her. Suddenly she remembered the man in the car park – the man with the girl in the wheelchair, the man with the VW Golf Estate. And she remembered how he had told her he was going to see someone who may be able to help his daughter. Surely that could not be the man that was taking his daughter to see Eva? Surely not! But the description fitted so well. The timing was right, the man who was going to see Eva saw her colleague recently; the description of the girl seemed to fit – thin, pale and looking about eight years old. But surely not… it was too much of a coincidence. She put it out of her mind, and continued with her letter.

I have a prior engagement at the end of January, and am therefore not yet sure if I am available on the 21st. I will let you know.

Yours sincerely,

Ellen Ridgeway

She put it on the stand in the hall on her way upstairs to bed, so that she would see it in the morning and not forget to post it.

Chapter Sixteen

As the day drew near for Eva to see the man and his daughter, she noticed that she felt quite anxious. She had spoken to Jane about a week ago, and had been helped by her response. During that conversation Jane had confided that she felt that Eva's help when she had hurt her ankle had not just been the wise choice of Traumeel S, but had been something to do with Eva's whole attitude, and the kind of person she was. Although she appreciated that her ankle injury was minor compared with the plight of the girl, she had wanted to impress upon Eva that the quality of help she had received from her was something that she rarely encountered. Like Ellen, Jane had encouraged her to phone to talk things over whenever she wanted. She had even given her her sister Clare's phone number, saying that she would be there from Christmas Eve until just before New Year. She was not sure of the date of her return. She planned to wait until her brother-in-law was back home before returning to her bungalow in Castle Brimswich.

The case notes had arrived from her colleague just a few days ago, and Eva had studied them several times. Her friend had, as always, been very thorough. She had conducted a number of standard tests alongside her own particular observations. The father had taken with him a copy of his daughter's medical file. She had taken copies of this and had included a full copy together with her own notes in the packet she had posted to Eva. She noted that the girl, Hannah, had appeared healthy until she was seven years old. She had then become quiet and withdrawn, finding it increasingly difficult to eat, and needing to sleep for long hours each day. She had kept attending the local primary school for a few months, but became unable to do the work. She had not attended school since the end of the autumn term just after her eighth birthday. The only mention of her mother was a note saying that when she and her father had been asked about her, they had both stared blankly, and said nothing at all. A later enquiry about the mother had elicited exactly the same response. Eva's friend had thought that it was best not to press the matter at that stage, given that the girl's state seemed so precarious.

However, there was another piece of information that impressed itself upon Eva's mind, and this was a reference to the time when Hannah was born. Hannah had been one of twins. Eva made a note to ask Hannah's father more about this. Her instincts told her that this was a crucial clue to Hannah's current illness, but at this stage she could not guess why. She was a little puzzled as to why her colleague's notes contained no further information about the twin. It would have been usual for her precise and methodical friend to have asked questions about it, and to have documented the answers. As she puzzled, she realised that the reference to Hannah's being one of twins appeared in the notes soon after the information about their lack of response when asked about Hannah's mother. It was now obvious to Eva that the reaction of Hannah and her father to being asked about Hannah's mother was so extreme that her friend had thought it unwise to follow a line of questioning about the birth of Hannah and her sibling, as it would inevitably involve further reference to the mother.

Eva was now clearer why her colleague, who was more experienced than she in the field of general medicine and alternative approaches, had thought to suggest to the father that he brought his daughter to see her. An idea began to form in her mind about the kind of approach she might take. Of course, this would depend a lot on how things evolved at the appointment. The notes she had received documented a very thorough and broad examination. She would not need to repeat any of this. She knew she could rely on the skill of her colleague. She would devote the interview to trying to learn more about the mother and Hannah's twin. She knew that this final objective of gaining more information might not be achievable in only one meeting. However she also knew that a very careful, sensitive and gentle approach from her about the whole situation might well start a process which led to conversation about the mother and twin at a later meeting. The more she thought about it, the more she knew that one of the keys to any improvement in Hannah's condition lay in forming a link of basic trust with her.

The notes revealed that the father and daughter always appeared to have good communication. This could be the case; but Eva knew that when someone has been ill for a long time, it is possible to develop a very good level of communication between the carer and the sufferer *about the symptoms of the illness and how to cope with them*, when in fact there is much that is crucially important that is not being communicated at all. In this case, where the carer was the father and the sufferer his daughter, this was even more likely to be an issue.

Two days later, at 9.55 a.m. precisely, a VW Golf Estate drew up outside Eva's house. She had specifically decided to suggest they met at her home, as she had sensed from the outset that Hannah and her father had probably had too much of hospitals and offices.

She welcomed them in. Hannah's father carried her through the door, and settled her down on a small chair that Eva had thoughtfully placed in a prominent position.

'Mr Greaves,' she said, 'it's good to meet you.'

She took his hand for a moment.

'Hannah, I haven't spoken to you before, only to your father, on the phone, but I expect he's told you about me.'

Hannah stared at Eva with eyes that appeared hooded and slightly glazed, a condition that detracted from the unusual blue colour of her irises. She inclined her head slightly as if assenting, but said nothing.

'Would you both like a drink of something?'

'I'd appreciate a glass of water,' said the man. 'And I've brought Hannah's bottle with me.'

He produced a plastic bottle of the kind joggers frequently use, with a plastic nipple at the end.

Eva went into the kitchen, and came back with a glass of water which she handed to the man, while she placed a small table within reach of both her visitors.

'We agreed on the phone that I'd make two hours available for this meeting, but do tell me at any time if you feel we've done enough for one day.'

It may have been her imagination, but she thought she observed a tiny change in Hannah's rather rigid and frozen state.

She continued. 'As you know, I've received a copy of all the medical notes you made available, and I've also read through my colleague's notes. There are one or two things I'd like to ask you to expand on, but there's no rush.'

Here Eva noted that Hannah darted a quick glance towards her father before returning to her glazed state.

'With your agreement, I'd like to start by asking you both a bit about your daily life, and how you're managing things. I know it can be a bit complicated when one or more members of a household are less able to do things for themselves, particularly when it spans quite a long time. Can you tell me about your daily routine, Mr Greaves? And perhaps Hannah would like to add things along the way when she wants.'

Eva smiled at Hannah in a way that indicated she required no response to her suggestion.

'I'm not sure exactly what you want to know...' Mr Greaves began.

Eva looked at him calmly. 'I want to know exactly what you feel you want to tell me,' she said. 'That's the most important thing at the moment.'

He continued, rather mechanically at first; but appeared to relax a little as he described their daily routine. It emerged that he and Hannah lived on their own. After she became unable to go to school, he had left his job as a senior nurse, and had built up a business working from home. He researched and marketed aids for disabled people, from simple things like drinking mugs to the more complex, which included specially designed chairs and beds.

Hannah slept in the same room as her father. She had been in her own room from when she was five until she was seven, but after that she always slept in his room. She really could not bear him to be out of her sight; and it caused him terrible pain on the few occasions when he had to leave her in the care of a kind neighbour or friend. He said nothing about their life before Hannah was five, and Eva did not ask. She merely made a mental note of this, and made small sounds and gestures which encouraged him to continue.

He described how he would get them both up in the morning; and how, after breakfast, which for Hannah was a few sips of apple juice, she would sit quietly in the room and watch him while he worked. In the afternoons, he would take Hannah out for a walk in her wheelchair, and then would sit with her and try to do a little of the kind of schoolwork she could manage; but she quickly tired, and would shut her eyes to indicate when she had had enough. He also mentioned that he was grateful that his business had allowed a situation where he could take time to go with Hannah to her hospital appointments, and to any other possible source of help.

Eva noted that he said nothing more about what Hannah ate or drank. Again she made no comment, and asked no questions. He had made no mention of relatives, only of friends and neighbours. Hannah had said nothing at all while her father was speaking, and had sat with that same glazed expression.

Thus far, Eva had made no attempt to steer the conversation. Now she decided to intervene a little, and see what happened.

'Mr Greaves,' she said, 'how did you come to hear of my colleague, Mrs Braid?'

'It was through my nursing connections,' he replied. 'I've kept in touch with a number of people in my profession.'

'Ah yes, of course.' Eva paused. 'Of course, you probably don't know anything about how I know her.'

'No, she didn't say.'

Eva chuckled, and she noticed that Hannah and her father looked startled.

'I first knew Patricia when we were children. She lived next door to me for a few years when we were both at primary school. I lost touch with her after she moved away, but we met again about four years ago when we were both on an advanced course in homeopathy. I didn't recognise her, I'm embarrassed to say, but she recognised me.

'Perhaps this was partly because I've never married, and I have an unusual surname. We've kept in touch ever since, mostly as friends, but sometimes as colleagues.'

Hannah's father had appeared very interested in this information, and when Eva had finished, he added spontaneously, 'That was lucky for us!'

He looked at Hannah, who Eva felt glared at him with what little energy she had behind those hooded eyes. Eva noticed that

Hannah's thin body stiffened momentarily, and then began to tremble.

Making a swift decision, Eva turned to Mr Greaves.

'Do you mind if I leave you for a moment? I've something upstairs that you might like to see,' she said.

Without waiting for an answer, she swiftly went to the stairs and up to her bedroom, where she lingered for a little while. Then she reached for a photograph album on the shelves beside her bed, and returned, making her footsteps on the stairs sound louder than they normally would.

When she came into the room, Mr Greaves was holding Hannah's hand. Hannah jerked a little as she entered the room, and motioned for her father to pull his chair closer to her own.

Eva opened the album, and found what she was looking for. She turned it round and held it towards Hannah's white, closed face, pointing to a photograph of two girls aged about seven years.

'I thought you might like to see this, Hannah. It's a picture of Patricia and myself when we were both seven.'

Hannah stared and stared at the picture as if nothing else existed.

Eva took a chance and said, 'I missed Patricia terribly when she moved away soon after that picture was taken. We were both at an age when we would have needed help to keep in touch with each other. Somehow I couldn't tell anyone just how much I missed her; I think I didn't really know myself until much later. By that time, I had no contacts who knew where she was living.'

Hannah's eyes were opening wider and wider.

'Have – you – told – her – how – much – you – missed – her?' she said, slowly and deliberately, staring straight at Eva.

'No, not yet, but I do plan to,' Eva answered, slightly unnerved by the girl's very direct approach.

'You must – as soon as you can!' The girl was insistent.

Eva thought quickly, then she said, 'Thank you very much for helping me to see that. I really appreciate your advice. I'll be speaking to her tomorrow evening.'

'About me?' questioned Hannah.

'Yes. But I promise that the first thing I'll tell her is what you've helped me with. After that, she and I will talk about you, and try to think of ways we can help you to feel a bit better than you do at the moment.'

'Daddy,' Hannah asked, 'please can we tell this person about Dawn?'

Mr Greaves swayed in his seat. For a moment Eva thought he was going to faint. He gathered himself, and nodded his head slowly.

'Of course we can,' he said very slowly, as if speaking from the end of a long tunnel. 'Do you want me to tell her, or shall we tell her together?'

'I want you to tell her.'

Mr Greaves began; and Eva learned that when Hannah was conceived, her parents had been aid workers living abroad in a small village far from a town. The pregnancy had proceeded apparently quite normally, and since there were women of the village who were skilled midwives, the couple had no anxieties about the approaching confinement. However, about two hours after Hannah was born, her mother gave birth to another child, who was much smaller, and who lived only for eight months. This had been completely unexpected. They had called the child Dawn, as she was born just as the sun began to rise.

Hannah's father's face had softened as he remembered those short months of his other daughter's life. He described her as being tiny but perfect. She hardly ever cried, and would lie and gurgle happily. By contrast Hannah had been a restless baby, who was always eager to be carried about to see everything that was going on. As the months went by, they were worried because although Dawn appeared healthy and contented, she hardly grew at all. One morning, he woke very early. He had a feeling of unease, and got straight out of bed to look at his daughters who were sleeping in an alcove in the bedroom of the small building they all shared. Without thinking, he bent to pick Dawn up. He stayed stooped over her with a rapidly growing realisation that something was very wrong. She looked so peaceful and beautiful that at first he doubted his instincts. Surely she was only in a deeper sleep than usual? But no… There was no movement – no movement at all. Not even a whisper of a breath. She was dead.

He had picked her up, and gently cradled her in his arms.

Hannah, who was asleep in the same room, began to stir, and he wondered what he should do. Without pausing to question his impulse, he picked Hannah up too, and cradled her with her dead sister. It was obvious that Hannah knew her sister was dead. She lay quite quietly in her father's arms with Dawn, reaching across to the lifeless body, and patting it gently from time to time. By this time his wife was stirring, and she called across to him. He had had to tell her that Dawn was dead. She had stared at him; and then uttered a howl which seemed to go on forever, sounding like some unearthly creature. After that, she took Hannah from him, and seemed on the surface to be a perfect mother. Together they stayed close to Hannah, right through the small funeral service. They continued caring for Hannah, and with their work. She continued to behave like a perfect mother, and a perfect aid worker. But Mr Greaves knew that something was seriously wrong. He, who knew her so well, knew that she was playing a part; she was in reality detached from her life; but the only overt symptom of that was that she never, ever referred to Dawn again.

Mr Greaves had stopped speaking.

Eva asked, 'Where is Dawn?'

'There's a little grave just outside the village where we were living. She had lived and died there. It was her home.'

'I can't express just how glad I am that you both wanted me to know about her,' said Eva with tears in her eyes. It's very important to me that you trusted me with her life, something that's so private and special to you both.'

'You are safe,' said Hannah, simply.

Eva took a deep breath. 'Mr Greaves… Hannah…' she said, 'I'd like to suggest that we all meet again next month. I have a little more time just now, but I have a feeling that it would be best to leave further talking until next time. With your permission, I'll get my diary and we can arrange something. I know that you've quite a long journey to get here. Would you like to suggest a date, and I'll see if I can fit round that?'

Hannah and her father looked at each other and nodded.

'Please, do you have any apple juice?' asked Hannah.

'Of course.'

Eva went into the kitchen, and poured a small amount of apple juice into the bottom of an unusual crystal glass and returned with it. Hannah carefully took one small sip, and even more carefully put the glass on the table next to her.

Mr Greaves had taken his diary out of his pocket and was studying it.

'How are you fixed around the third week in January?' he asked.

'That's fine. That week is very flexible for me. I'm studying at home. Name the day and time.'

Having agreed a time, Mr Greaves gathered his daughter up in his arms, while Eva opened the door. She bade them goodbye, and then watched while he gently settled Hannah in her seat. They did not turn towards her as they drove off. Eva was glad of this.

It's important that any change is very slow, she said to herself.

Chapter Seventeen

Jane was looking forward to seeing her sister again. Although they spoke on the phone, sometimes at great length, spending time together was something she missed greatly. Clare was only eighteen months younger than Jane, and as children they had fought a lot. Things changed when they moved from the primary school they had both attended. They had had a choice between two secondary schools: Clare had chosen one, and Jane chose the other. It was from then that they began to develop a firm friendship with a very obvious affection for one another. They were of similar ability academically. Their shared interests included history and art, which they both enjoyed immensely. They were both interested in needlework, and had tried out various forms of embroidery, which had culminated in their creating a tablecloth with a feast of colour in floral designs. They had laughed when they finished it, deciding it was far too beautiful to use on a table! Everyone who saw it declared it to be a visual banquet.

Clare's husband, George, was an engineer who worked on oil rigs as a troubleshooter. He could be away for long periods of time with almost no notice. He was much sought after, as he was extremely adept at divining and remedying problems. Neither he nor Clare particularly liked the fact that he had to work away from home, but they had both agreed from the outset that there was no way round that at this stage in their lives. They kept in touch regularly by e-mail and fax.

This time, George had had a few weeks' warning of the next job; and because of this Jane and Clare had been able to plan their Christmas together well in advance. George was very happy to know that Jane would be with Clare and Emily. He and Jane had always got on well together. George was an only child, and he remembered when he was quite small how he envied other children who had brothers or sisters. As he grew older, he had longed to have a sister, and now he felt he had one in Jane.

Jane packed a few clothes. She would not need many, as she would have the use of Clare's washing machine; and if she needed anything else, there were always things of Clare's that she could borrow, since although in features and colouring Jane and Clare were quite different, in height and build they were remarkably similar. The only other things she had to remember to take were the presents she had bought for Clare and Emily. She had posted George's gift weeks ago, so that he had the option of taking it away with him. The journey to Clare's present home was quite an awkward one. She had moved when Emily was about six months old, and Jane's journey there involved a bus, a train, and then another bus. Travelling light was a considerable advantage.

It had been easy to choose gifts for Clare and for George. She had bought for Clare a book about famous tapestries in museums and stately homes in the UK. For George, after secretly consulting Clare, she had bought a copy of John Bunyan's *The Pilgrim's Progress*, in a small format. Clare had explained that he wanted such a copy to carry with him on his travels. A gift for Emily had required much more thought and deliberation. She had wanted to get something that was suitable for her age, but something that might help to further develop the kind of interest she was showing in the abacus Clare had told her about. Jane had racked her brains a lot before she had an idea. And she had to remember that the gift should be something that was safe for a child of only just over one year.

Some time ago Jane had attended an evening class in woodwork; and there she had met a man who made wooden toys as a hobby. She had been so impressed by the few toys he had brought to show some of the parents attending the class, that she had made a note of his address and phone number. Although Clare and George had no children then, she had known that they certainly wanted to become a family, so she had noted these details in her diary. Contacting him about her idea, she had asked him if he would be able to do something for her for Christmas, and indicated that what she had in mind was a selection of wooden blocks, some of which were less common shapes. He had said he would be able to do that. He had a lot of orders, but was now retired from his full-time employment, and loved to spend his days making toys.

Encouraged by this conversation, she wrote out a list of the ideas she was having. Her plan so far had been to ask him to make a collection of wooden shapes such as cubes, spheres, hemispheres, cylindrical blocks and triangular blocks. One more shape had come into her mind, a tetrahedron. She had then started to think of size. They must be too big to put in the mouth of a small child such as Emily, but not too large to grasp in a small hand. She had got out her ruler and pondered. Four centimetres seemed to be a realistic measurement to aim for. If each edge of the cubes, the diameter of the hemispheres, the height of the cylindrical blocks and the height of the triangular blocks were four centimetres, she could also ask for each edge of the tetrahedra to be the same. She had posted to him her list together with diagrams to be sure he could follow what she had written.

Two weeks later the toy maker had phoned, inviting her to come round to see what he had made. The result had been more than satisfactory. Not only had he been able to produce a selection of the shapes she had requested, but also he had thoughtfully taken the sharp edges off all the shapes, which was something that had not occurred to her to ask. He had told her how much he had enjoyed working on this project, and urged her to let him know how Emily reacted to the set, adding that he would be pleased to make more for her any time. Before Jane left he had told her with obvious enthusiasm that he would be willing to experiment with more complex shapes.

In the evening before she set off, Jane carefully wrapped the box up with the clothes she was taking with her, and packed them in her lightweight bag. The box and its contents certainly made up the bulk of the weight that she would be carrying.

The following morning, she was up early to catch the bus at the crossroads to travel to the station to catch the train. The journey proved to be a pleasant one. Most of the travellers she met were, like herself, on their way to spend Christmas with relatives; and there was an air of anticipation of happy times. The journey passed quickly, and by the middle of the afternoon she was ringing the bell of Clare's house, which stood at the end of a quiet cul-de-sac. Clare opened the door with Emily in her arms, and the sisters greeted each other happily, with Emily joining in by patting Jane's cheeks with a large smile on her face.

When Jane commented on how accepting Emily was of her although she had not seen her since Easter, Clare explained that she had been talking to Emily about her and showing her photographs of her, saying that she would be coming very soon.

'Come and sit down,' said Clare. 'I'll put the kettle on and we can catch up a bit. You may have seen through the window that I have a Christmas tree in the sitting room. Emily loves to watch the tree. I think the way the coloured lights reflect on the baubles fascinates her. I have most of her toys and books in there too. Here, you take her, and I'll be back in a minute or two.'

She passed Emily into Jane's arms, and went into the kitchen. Jane carried Emily into the sitting room, and Emily instantly pointed to the Christmas tree.

'Tee, tee,' she said excitedly, and struggled to get down out of Jane's arms.

She took one of Jane's hands and pulled her towards the tree.

'Tee, tee,' she said again, insistently.

When she and Jane were standing by the tree, she stood very still, gazing at it with a rapt expression. Although Emily's attention was focussed on the tree, Jane noticed that the abacus which Clare had told her about was carefully laid down on the floor not far away.

Clare reappeared carrying a tray of things to eat and drink.

'Here you are,' she said. 'I have some of your juice here Emily.'

Emily turned round, smiled, sat down on the floor next to her abacus, and returned her attention to the tree. Clare put her cup down on the floor beside her, together with a small dish of raisins.

'We could sit and chat for a few minutes, and then we could read some stories to Emily,' said Clare. 'She loves her books, and I'd like to see what you think of the ones she has. Of course, some of them are those we had as children, but there's a much wider selection now.'

The rest of the day passed very pleasantly with stories followed by supper and Emily's bath time – a time of great hilarity and much splashing. There was an e-mail from George saying that he hoped Jane had arrived safely, and telling them both to give Emily plenty of kisses from him. Emily was tucked up in her cot, with her beloved abacus tucked down the side of the mattress.

The sisters chatted their way through the rest of the evening, oblivious of the time, until Jane yawned and glanced at her watch.

'Goodness!' she exclaimed. 'It's after midnight. Merry Christmas, Clare!'

'Merry Christmas! But I think we should get to bed now. Emily sometimes wakes up quite early, and I forgot to tell you I've invited a neighbour for a Christmas meal, so I'm planning a bit more food preparation than I'd otherwise have done. I've been assuming that you'll help out.'

'Of course I'll be very glad to. Who's our guest?'

'Well actually it's two guests. A friend who lives just along the road has a son who's a little older than Emily, and her husband is on duty for Christmas and Boxing Day. He works in A and E at the local infirmary. She'll see almost nothing of him, and we thought it was a good idea if we all got together. What do you think?'

'That's an excellent idea. I'll look forward to seeing them. In the morning you can give me a list of the things you want me to make, and I'll get to work.'

'I asked her if she wanted to come round when David, her son, has had his midday rest, and spend the rest of the day with us.'

'Oh good. Then we'll have plenty of time together. It'll be nice for me to get to know at least one of your neighbours. When we're speaking on the phone that will be one person whom I'll be able to recognise from a name. By the way, I've brought a present for Emily which I might save until Boxing Day. She'll have enough excitement before then with the parcels you have for her, and having visitors and a special meal.'

'That's fine,' said Clare. 'Now let's get to bed.'

Christmas Day passed very pleasantly. Jane enjoyed doing the food preparation in the morning, while Emily opened some parcels at the kitchen table with Clare's help. In between parcels she had 'helped' by putting things in bowls and jars. In the afternoon, before dark, Jane, Clare, Emily and their two guests went to feed the ducks on the local pond. Their special meal was very successful, with Emily and David sitting side by side in high chairs, enjoying a wonderful game of handing small pieces of food to each other, in between tasting and eating some of it.

It was Boxing Day. Jane woke with a sense of anticipation, and she got up to join Emily and Clare at breakfast.

'I haven't told you before,' she said, 'but I got something made for Emily. It's a bit of an experiment actually. After you'd told me how much she loves her abacus, I'd begun to wonder if there was something I could get that was associated with that. I thought a lot about it, and in the end I had something specially made for her.'

Clare listened quietly with interest.

Jane continued. 'I'll just go and get it from my bag, and we could give it to Emily now.'

She went upstairs and returned with the box.

'Can I put it on the floor in the sitting room?' she asked.

'Yes, of course,' answered Clare.

She lifted Emily out of her high chair and put her on the floor, where she toddled after Jane.

'Here you are, Emily,' said Jane. 'I have a present for you.'

She put the box down on the floor not far from the tree, and sat down next to it. Emily sat down beside her and looked at her. Jane patted the box.

'This is for you; you can open it,' she said.

Emily patted the box and looked at Jane.

Jane opened the lid a little, and said, 'Look, the lid comes off.'

Emily leaned forward to help Jane to take the lid off. Putting the lid to one side revealed the selection of wooden shapes. Emily sat very still and stared at them for a long time. Then she reached forward very slowly and selected two hemispheres, held them together, and laughed. She put them carefully to one side and chose shape after shape, matching the faces of the shapes in various combinations. She was completely absorbed in what she was doing, and Jane and Clare sat quietly and watched her.

After some time, Clare turned to Jane saying, 'What a wonderful present. Thank you so much for thinking of it.'

At this, Emily put down the shapes she was holding, moved into a crouching position, and threw herself into Jane's arms. Jane hugged her tightly and gave her a kiss. Emily wriggled back onto the floor, and was once more deeply absorbed in her experimentation.

'The man who made these for Emily told me he was willing to

make more any time, and that he was also willing to try making more complex shapes.'

'That's wonderful!' replied Clare. 'I must tell George about the shapes, and how Emily is using them. I'm sure that he'll be keen to be involved in deciding about any additions to the set.'

It was no surprise to Clare when later that day she was taking Emily up for her bath, that she insisted the box of shapes had to come upstairs along with the abacus. In her cot, Emily was not satisfied until the open box had been placed on a chair beside her cot, so that she could see the shapes and reach out to them if she wanted. When Clare went upstairs later to check that she was asleep, she called Jane up to see what she found. Emily was fast asleep with a tetrahedron clutched in each little hand.

Chapter Eighteen

Ellen was sitting with her feet up on a stool in the library. Christmas Day had been the usual exhausting rush, which was what she preferred: the less time to think about the past the better. She always continued to make sure that she was overstretched over the festive season. She could bear to think about the Christmases of her childhood once January 6th was gone each year, but not before. The people she worked with over this time of year were impressed with her dedication to making midwinter a less gloomy prospect for deprived people. She was indeed dedicated to that end; but it had the dual purpose of meeting her sense of responsibility to society, and numbing the pain of the sudden loss of her father. Christmas with him had always been a time of gentle intimacy. That dark time of year had somehow comforted them both, and they had felt that her mother was never very far away at those times. But once her father was dead, Ellen lost the feeling of connection with both of her parents; and this was a cruel blow.

She looked over to the mantelshelf where stood a small picture frame containing no picture. She was very pleased with this frame. She had seen it in a shop quite by chance only a week ago; and she remembered her promise to Jane that she would look out for a frame that was suitable for the photograph of Emily. As soon as she had seen this frame, she knew straight away that it was just what she wanted. She had left it out on the mantelshelf so that she would not forget to take it with her when she went to Eva's house. It was quite a plain frame, but the narrow strips of wood of which it was made were of good quality, and had a faint gold line in the moulding.

She dozed for a while, but woke with a jerk. Something was bothering her – nagging at the back of her mind. She was looking forward to seeing Eva and Jane again. The weeks would pass quite quickly, and she did not feel impatient at all.

Then she remembered. The man on the train. Adam.

She tried to thrust all thought of him back out of her mind; but the more she tried, the more he seemed to be there.

'Can't you just go away for a while?' She spoke out loud.

Exhausted as she was, she got out of her chair and paced round the room. She knew she did not have to make a decision today about whether or not to meet him next month. There was no rush. But the need to decide seemed to hover over her like a heavy black cloud. She tried to do a deal with herself.

'I'll write to him on January 6th. By that time I'll have decided what to do.'

That sounded good at first; but she found it did not ease her state of mind. It was just a collection of words. In fact, it dissolved into a meaningless jumble in her head.

She tried again. 'I'll think about it for ten minutes each evening until I'm clear about what to do. Then I'll write to him.'

Again that sounded good... very good.

What a sensible approach, she thought.

Sensible it might have been; but it had offered her only five minutes of respite from the pressure that had been building up inside her head.

Eva! I'll phone Eva. No, I can't, she'll be busy; it's Christmas Day...

Ellen paced around the room several more times, looked at her watch, noticed the increasing pain in her head, and lifted the phone. She keyed in Eva's number.

'Hello.'

She heard Eva's voice, and felt a sense of immediate relief. She knew now what she had really needed. She needed to talk the whole thing over again, without pressure or worry about what to decide.

'Eva, I'm so glad you're still up. I know it's rather late, but this decision I have to make about whether or not I meet Adam next month is weighing heavily on my mind. In fact I've ended up feeling terribly tense, and I'd really appreciate a chance to go over it all with you again.'

'That's fine by me,' replied Eva. 'I wasn't going to go to bed yet. Do you want to talk now?'

'If you don't mind. But tell me first, how did your meeting with the girl in the wheelchair and her father go?'

'I've been meaning to phone you to tell you a bit about that. Mr Greaves and his daughter Hannah did come as arranged, and I'm beginning to see a possible route to pursue. They're coming back in January to talk again. I won't take up time with details just now. When you come here at the end of January I'll have seen them again, and will have a better idea of things. Perhaps you and Jane would let me have some time to talk it through when we're all together. I'd find that helpful I know. I've been thinking about them quite a lot. By the way, did I ever tell you the colleague who referred them to me was a childhood friend of mine?'

'No, you haven't mentioned that before.'

'Yes, I lost touch with her and met her many years later on a course we both attended.'

'That was a quite a coincidence,' said Ellen.

'Yes, life can contain many coincidences,' answered Eva. 'There are always unpredictable surprises in the offing!'

'Why did you say that – and in that way?' questioned Ellen.

'To be honest, I've a hunch that man you met on the train is bringing something into your life that's entirely unexpected, and could never have been predicted. Already there have been two coincidences: there was the fact that you met him on the train, both of you travelling to York, and also the fact that you both spent the night in the same hotel in York. You can see that he at least has certainly been affected by that. He's made attempts to keep in touch with you. Look how he drove all that way from your college reunion to see you at the Traveller's Arms. What do you really feel about him and the situation as it stands?'

'I feel edgy and uncomfortable.'

'It must be a bit more than that if you've got a headache thinking about it,' Eva reminded her as kindly as she could.

'I know, I know,' Ellen replied wearily. 'I can't say more than that. There doesn't seem to be anything more to say; but there is. I feel in such a muddle about it. I just wish he hadn't written. Before that, the discomfort I'd felt about him had been offset by the fact that he'd always behaved in a way that didn't alarm me. However, since receiving this letter I've felt alarmed.'

'You're getting a bit closer to what's bothering you now,' said Eva. 'Keep on talking. He wrote that letter to you recently, and now you feel alarmed. Why do you think that could be?'

Ellen groaned. 'I just don't want to have to cope with him!' she burst out.

Eva waited before she said anything else.

'No one is forcing you to meet him, you know,' she said calmly. 'You can just write back and say you aren't free. You could be more blunt if you wanted. You could say that you'd prefer he didn't contact you again.'

'It's all my fault that I'm in this situation.' Ellen's voice was almost a sob. 'I should never have replied to the note he put under the door of my hotel room!'

'One thing is clear to me,' Eva's voice was soothing, 'this man is not putting any pressure on you and never has. That's maybe why you felt you could reply to the first letter he sent. To be honest, I was quite surprised when you told me about that on the way to Peggy's. When you said you'd later received a letter from him, I'd expected you to say you hadn't replied.'

'Why was that?'

'Well,' Eva continued gently, 'since your father died, I've never known you to respond to any man in a way that invited dialogue of any kind. You've always been polite and courteous; but whatever you've done or said has, by implication, discouraged further conversation or contact. You've even been like that with male colleagues and friends whom you knew before your father's death; but those people have understood why you were distant, and didn't take it as a signal that they shouldn't keep in touch with you.'

'Why didn't you say all this before?' Ellen sounded flustered.

'There was no need,' answered Eva simply.

There was a long silence. Eva noticed that Ellen's breathing sounded upset, but made no comment.

'So you were surprised that I wrote back to him and invited him to come along to the reunion?'

'Yes.'

'And you were not surprised that I was sad to miss the reunion, but relieved that the problem my car developed meant I didn't have to see Adam?'

'Yes.'

'And what did you think when I told you about how he came to the Traveller's Arms?'

'As far as I was concerned I was glad to hear there was nothing in his behaviour that gave any cause for concern, taking into account how I knew how easily you could have been very upset by something like that.'

'Oh.'

Ellen fell silent again, but this time Eva did not detect any distress.

'Do you think it would be all right to agree to meet him then?' Ellen asked. The words sounded as if they were being squeezed out of her mouth.

'I'd have no worry about it on your behalf, if that's what you decide to do.'

Another pause; and then Eva continued. 'You know that I was talking about coincidences earlier on in this conversation?'

'Yes, of course.'

'Well, here's another one for you. When Mr Greaves was deciding when to bring Hannah to see me again, I asked him to give me an idea of when he'd be able to arrange to travel down. You see, he has to come quite a long way. The week he suggested was the one I'd already decided to take as a study week. This meant I was able to offer him any time during that week. Guess what day he chose?'

'I haven't a clue.' Ellen was puzzled. She had detected slight amusement in Eva's tone.

'I don't suppose it's January 21st?'

'Yes, you guessed first time,' Eva laughed.

'Something has just come into my mind to say, but I'm afraid to say it as I haven't thought it through,' said Ellen.

'What is it? You might as well tell me,' asked Eva.

'The problem of how you may be able to bring help into Hannah's life is very challenging. I can tell you're feeling less anxious about it at the moment; but with a case like that there are bound to be times when you'll be worried.'

'That's true,' Eva agreed.

'I'm finding the matter of Adam a very difficult challenge. Perhaps I should try to do something with that, instead of planning ways to run away from it.' Ellen paused. 'And there's something else I should tell you.'

'What's that?'

'I'm almost certain that your Mr Greaves and his daughter Hannah are the people whose car had blocked me in when I was trying to set off to pick you up the last time we went to Jane's. Does he drive a silver-coloured VW Golf Estate?'

'Yes,' replied Eva.

Ellen continued. 'After you'd spoken to me about your anxieties as to whether or not you would be able to help the girl who was being brought to see you, I began to remember the incident in the car park. The more I thought about it, the more it all fitted. The man was setting off to see someone about his daughter. This must have been when he was going to see your colleague. What you said to me about the girl's actual age and her arrested development seemed to fit exactly my memory of her appearance when I saw her.'

'What an amazing coincidence!' exclaimed Eva. 'But can we go back to the subject of Adam for a moment? Are you saying that you're going to try to follow that up, even though it's very difficult for you?'

'Well, yes, I think I am. What you've just told me about how I've been behaving since my father's death is news to me. I'd no idea. As your impression of the way Adam has behaved so far gives you no cause for concern, maybe I should just face my fears. If I feel the same in the morning as I do now, I'll write to him and suggest a meeting place for the evening of the 21st.'

'Remember there's no pressure from me,' Eva reminded her; 'and although I'd gained some confidence that I might be able to help Hannah and her father, I feel somehow comforted that it seems you've met them, albeit very briefly.'

'Good. And thanks for being there. It's been really good to talk to you tonight.' Ellen no longer sounded oppressed.

'I'm glad you phoned. It's been good to hear from you. Why not phone me again in the next few days to let me know what you finally decide?'

'I will,' said Ellen. 'Goodnight.'

Chapter Nineteen

Adam got out of bed briskly. He felt excited – very excited. Today was the day he was going to meet one of the directors of Carillon Music. The previous evening he had carefully packed some of the manuscripts he had brought back with him from his last visit to Boris. He had put them in a large file in a bag he had bought specially for the purpose. It was the kind of bag he had sometimes seen art students carrying, presumably to protect items they were producing for their portfolios.

He had also bought a new hard backed notebook in which he had listed all the main points he wanted to raise with the publisher, should the man he was seeing show the kind of interest that he was hoping for. He had been in frequent e-mail contact with Boris over the last few days – extending, refining and finalising the list.

He shaved, dressed and ate quite quickly, and then collected his road atlas and a street map which would help him to find the address of Carillon Music. He did not want to risk being late. The weather was mild for the time of year, and the forecast did not suggest any immediate change. He had calculated that the journey would take him about an hour and a half, but he had allowed two hours for possible wrong turnings and difficulties in parking. However, the journey was uneventful, and having reached the small town he stopped in a car park, from which he could see the office block where Carillon Music was located. He was too early to go in, so he sat and took a final look through the list in his notebook, before collecting the manuscripts in their bag from the back seat of the car, and walking over to the building. It was an unremarkable modern office block.

About fifteen minutes later, a secretary took him into a small bright office and introduced him to Gordon Quaver, who smiled, stood up, and stretched out his hand in a welcoming gesture.

'I'm afraid my partner has flu at the moment, so he can't see you. However, I have your file in front of me here, and have read the letter you wrote to us. By the way, my surname is not an affectation. It's my real name, my father's surname. He was a fishmonger. Do sit down and tell me more about your proposals. Before we start, perhaps you might like to know that over the last year we've begun to specialise in the publication of ethnic music. The market for such music is beginning to expand. There used to be only a very limited circulation, and that was confined almost entirely to recorded music. In recent times, there's been a growing demand for sheet music, and we've decided to take a bit of a risk and devote a relatively large percentage of our resources to this area.'

Adam began to relax a little. He had been so eager to come to this meeting that he had not noticed how tense he was. Already the situation was looking better than he could have hoped. In his best moments he had thought he would at least get some leads from this meeting, but now it was looking as if there was a chance that this firm themselves might be interested in the manuscripts.

'Perhaps the best thing would be if I go over what I've said in the letter I sent to you, enlarging on what I've written,' he said. 'Do stop me at any point where you want clarification.'

Adam explained how he and Boris as music students had been enthused by the work of Bartok, and had managed to make their own collection of Romanian songs that did not seem to have been documented previously. He recounted how their collection had lain at the bottom of Boris' chest until last summer, and how they had begun to think of seeing if it would be possible to get it published.

'But of course,' he went on, 'by far the greater and more exciting task is the one Boris and I are currently engaged in.'

'You don't mention that in your letter,' Gordon replied. 'What is it?'

'We've collected tapes of traditional songs being sung from all over Russia, and have been working on transcribing them.'

Gordon stared at Adam. 'How many tapes have you got so far?' he asked.

'When I travelled back home last autumn we had sixty-five. I keep in e-mail contact with Boris, and he tells me that more keep trickling in. We have at least another ten tapes.'

'How many of the tapes have been transcribed so far?'

'About thirty. We intend to start work again when I travel out at the end of March. I think I'll be able to spend about eight weeks with Boris then. We agreed that we only work on the transcriptions when I'm staying with him and we're working together.'

He went quiet for a moment, remembering the day he had come upon the tape that had affected him so much. He quickly decided that although he felt comfortable with Gordon, he would not mention anything about it.

He heard Gordon say, 'You intended to bring some transcribed samples of the Romanian songs with you.'

'Yes, indeed, I have them here,' replied Adam, as he unzipped the large flat bag.

'Would you mind if I look through them for a while and possibly photocopy one or two of them?' asked Gordon.

'I can certainly go away for half an hour, but I'm afraid I can't give you permission to copy any of them at this stage. I'd have to contact Boris about that.'

'Of course,' said Gordon. 'In my enthusiasm I'd not taken that into account. There's a café just round the corner. You should be able to get something to drink there. I don't recommend the coffee machine on the ground floor of this block if you value your health.'

'I'll do what you suggest, and see you in about half an hour,' smiled Adam as he passed some of the manuscript sheets across to Gordon, collected his things, and made for the door.

He returned to Gordon's office promptly, and Gordon greeted him warmly.

'I want to say straight away that personally I'm very interested in this project and in the one you're engaged on now. However, that's only a start. At this stage, all I can say is that I'll represent you and your work favourably to my partner once he's well again. I should let you know that there's an immediate problem with the manuscripts of the Romanian songs.'

At this point Adam cut in. 'I'm pretty sure I know what you're going to say. These transcriptions were written only for the personal use of myself and Boris. Consequently, they're too rough to give to a publisher in their present form.'

Gordon looked very relieved. 'That point had been worrying

me a lot,' he said, 'and not just because of problems in publishing the Romanian songs. Are your transcriptions of the Russian songs in a similarly rough form?'

'No, not at all,' Adam reassured him. 'Right from the outset Boris and I have been hoping that our efforts will eventually lead to publication, and our work is much more complete and precise. If your partner shows the same interest as you are showing, I'll work on a much more presentable version of some of the Romanian songs; and with Boris' permission, let you have a copy of them.'

'That's excellent. Leave it with me for now, and I'll get back to you once I've had a chance to speak to my partner. Here are the manuscripts I was looking at.'

He handed them carefully back to Adam across the desk.

Adam drove home slowly with a satisfied glow inside him. He looked forward to e-mailing Boris as soon as he got in. Why not sit down this evening and rewrite one of the Romanian songs into a finished form? he thought. Yes, I could do that, and then scan it into the computer, and e-mail it to Boris for his approval. The weather is mild, and I can put the heater on in the conservatory, and sit in there to do it. It's such a pleasant place to be.

Back home, Adam reflected once more upon how efficient the builder and his men had been. The conservatory had indeed been finished by Christmas, and he had bought some simple items to put in it. He might even phone Matthew to let him know the encouraging reception he had encountered at Carillon Music. Perhaps he could invite him round one evening to see the completed conservatory; and there was the subject of Professor Barnes to discuss further. He had only attended that one talk, but there was plenty to discuss. He had looked forward to the next one, but had received an e-mail from the professor to say that he had been called away urgently, and would not be back for some months. There had been no further explanation.

When he got in, he sent a long e-mail to Boris, and then phoned Matthew. There was no reply, so he left a message on the call-minder. He might be away at the moment, of course; he does have to go away quite often, Adam thought.

He put the heater on in the conservatory, and carried through a table and an upright chair. The desk light was the final item he needed; and after positioning that on the table, he went to the kitchen to make some food for himself, before starting work on the first manuscript.

Adam was very keen to complete the finished redraft of that manuscript, and sat up very late working on it. He was determined to reach the point where he could scan it and e-mail it to Boris. He did not mind how long it took him, and his concentration did not lapse. As he went to the kitchen for a glass of water, he promised himself that not only would he finish this one this evening, but also he would try to do two more tomorrow. This would mean that Boris would soon have three to look at and approve. Then all would be ready when Gordon Quaver contacted him again. He felt sure Boris would agree to Gordon having a copy of each of these three songs, but he could not be entirely sure that Boris would approve the versions he was writing out, without suggesting and discussing a number of amendments.

Adam had slept very soundly, so soundly that when he woke rather late, he wondered where he was. The familiar copy of the Sisley without the central figure steadied him as soon as he saw it. He glanced at his watch: 10.30. He remembered the events of yesterday and his plans for today. He rubbed his hands together briskly.

First, a walk, he thought. All that driving yesterday has left me in need of some exercise. I'll have a walk while it's daylight, and then return to the manuscripts.

He busied himself making up a sandwich to put in his pocket while he ate breakfast. He checked the computer, but there was no reply from Boris so far.

'I won't bother looking at the post until I come back,' he muttered to himself, as he left by the back door.

The weather had changed. The air was crisp and invigorating, and he soon got into his stride, heading for the riverside path leading to the low hills and woodland area which was his objective.

He returned to the house at about three o'clock, much refreshed. His boots were muddy, and he washed them before putting them on an old newspaper on the floor in the conservatory to dry. He hung up his coat, put on the kettle, and went to collect the post he expected to find lying inside the outer front door. There was a small packet, a number of items that looked like circulars, and there was a letter with a handwritten address. I wonder what this is? he mused.

He turned it over, but found no clue. He was just carrying it into his study to get the letter opener when he stopped with a sudden realisation. Of course he knew who this was from. His hands were trembling slightly as he carefully opened the envelope. He did not want to make the fatal mistake of cutting the letter in two by careless use of the paper knife. He had previously received Ellen's short reply to his letter, but it had told him nothing except that she did not yet know if she was free on the 21st. He had not been sure if that was a polite way of fobbing him off, or if it was genuine. It seemed now that it had been genuine, because here was a further letter from her. He read it eagerly.

Dear Adam,

Thank you for getting in touch and suggesting we meet.

I find I am able to meet you on the evening of the 21st. I enclose a leaflet about a quiet pub which serves light refreshments through the evening. If you look inside the leaflet you will find directions on how to get there. I can get there by about 8 p.m. There is no need to reply to this letter, unless it is to let me know that your arrangements have changed, or that you are not happy with my suggestion.

Yours sincerely,

Ellen

Adam sat down suddenly. He felt pleased, very pleased. After receiving the previous note he had felt fairly certain that he would *not* be seeing Ellen on the 21st, but now it seemed that he would. This letter even seemed warm when compared with the last one. He studied the leaflet, and made a mental note of the location of the pub. He should be able to find it relatively easily. He had not heard of it before, but he knew the locality slightly. He carefully put the letter and the leaflet in with the lecture notes he would be taking with him that day. He did not want to risk mislaying them, or leaving them behind. Satisfied, he turned his attention to the manuscripts again.

Late in the evening the phone rang. It was Matthew.

'Hello Adam.' His voice sounded crackly. 'I got your message when I phoned in to my call-minder.'

'Where are you?' asked Adam.

'Cornwall,' came the crackling answer. 'I'm here until nearly the end of the month. Can we fix a date when I get back?'

'That would be great,' Adam replied. 'Phone me again as soon as you get back.'

'Okay, bye.'

This break in his concentration allowed Adam to remember to check his e-mails. At last there were replies from Boris.

<Excellent news. Keep me informed.>

The second one contained a number of suggested amendments to the revised manuscript that Adam had sent. Adam smiled. He would look through these tomorrow. It was time to finish for the night.

Chapter Twenty

Eva was feeling good about her study week. The days she had had so far had proved to be invaluable. She had at last had time to concentrate on a number of books she had bought over a period of months, but had never had enough time to study to her satisfaction. She had bought them on the recommendation of colleagues who were practitioners of various forms of 'energy medicine'. The whole subject was fascinating, and very exciting. She was keen to develop her own views rather than merely following what she had read, or parroting what she had heard. She had sometimes suspected from her experience of researchers and practitioners that they could be conservative with the truth, if not actually dishonest. It was very important to her to build up her own sense and experience of the truth. The study of these particular books was the next step.

The last thing she read each evening was a section of the book by Frances Ianson that Jane had been reading before the spirals appeared in her diary. She planned to have finished it by the time Jane and Ellen arrived for their next weekend together, and to have reread some sections that she had found of particular interest. She was making a note of these as she worked through the book.

Ellen had let her know that she had indeed agreed to meet Adam. Consequently, yesterday evening she had phoned her to say she hoped it would go well. Ellen had sounded surprisingly calm and determined, which Eva felt was encouraging. She had asked Eva how she felt about the approaching visit from Mr Greaves and Hannah. Eva had confided that she was a little nervous, but had prepared herself as far as she could. She had been in touch with her colleague, who had been very interested and supportive of the direction she planned to take, and was keen to be kept in the picture. Eva had told Ellen that the more she had thought about her contact with Mr Greaves and his daughter, the more she was convinced that the very unusual configuration of energies her colleague had sensed around Hannah had something to do with the relationship between her and her father. Ellen had eagerly reminded Eva that the subject of Hannah and her father was one they had planned to discuss when they met. She too had been studying her copy of the book *Communications*. She had laughed when Eva had said how she was noting certain sections, because that was exactly what she herself was doing.

Ellen's last words had been, 'Not long to wait now! It won't be long before you and I and Jane are sitting in your living room. And we've quite a lot of ground to cover. So bye for now.'

All this had been passing through Eva's mind as she stood at the window waiting to see Mr Greaves' estate car arrive. She was glad that she had taken care to buy some fresh apple juice in case Hannah asked for some. In fact, she decided that once she had an idea of how things had been since she last saw them, she might let Hannah know that she had bought some for the occasion; but she knew it was a sensitive issue and would be cautious.

As before, the car appeared a few minutes early. Eva opened the door as it drew up, and waved to Hannah, who had turned round so she could see the house. Eva noticed that although she did not wave back, her hand had been raised slightly, just above the level of the bottom of the car window, before it dropped back, as if Hannah had had an impulse to wave that she just could not follow through.

'Hello, Mr Greaves, Hannah. Do come in.' Eva was smiling at them, a smile that was genuine.

All traces of the nervousness she had felt yesterday evening had gone. She realised then that the main cause of this had been worry about whether they would arrive safely for the appointment.

'We stayed last night at a Travelodge. There's one only forty minutes' drive from here,' said Mr Greaves. He looked fresh and relaxed. 'We found the staff very helpful, and we'll certainly use it next time we come to see you.'

Hannah's head moved as if in assent.

Eva was interested to note that they were already thinking in terms of keeping up their contact with her, and she felt glad about that. She herself might not be the person who could manage the treatment of everything Hannah was suffering from, but she had some confidence that her contact with the girl could support her in a way that might help a gradual process of improvement.

'How have you both been since we last met?' she asked.

'I had to take Hannah for a set of tests at the hospital two weeks ago. These are done every three months.' Mr Greaves looked at Hannah and stopped.

'When do you get the results of these?' asked Eva.

'I should have heard by now. Some take longer than others, and they wait until they all come in before writing to my GP. I think we would have heard if there was anything unusual.'

Mr Greaves looked at Hannah again, as if uncertain about something he wanted to say.

'How is your work going?' asked Eva, sensing that they needed more time to settle in.

'Quite well, actually. I had some ideas about gadgets which could be produced quite inexpensively that would help people with arthritic changes in their hands and fingers.'

'I'd be interested to hear how that goes; the application of such aids is so broad. I do hope your ideas can be taken forward.'

There was another pause.

Eva tried again, this time contributing something about herself to the discussion.

'You may remember that I'm on study leave this week.'

'Yes, of course,' said Mr Greaves. 'I hope it's going well.'

'Yes, it was a good decision to take a week off at this point.'

The next pause felt quite uncomfortable; but Eva sensed that the silence was important, and did not plan to break it. After a few minutes, she noticed that Hannah's head, which had been hanging forward slightly since she came, allowing her to gaze at her pitifully thin knees, swivelled round a little; and Eva imagined that her eyes were turned towards her father, who appeared increasingly uncomfortable.

At last he took a very deep breath and said, 'Last time we were here I told you about Dawn.'

At that point she heard his voice catch a little, and she gave him time to steady himself before replying.

'Yes, I'm glad that you were able to.' She wondered about saying more, but thought better of it.

He looked over to Hannah again, who still appeared to be resolutely studying her knees.

He took a larger breath than before. 'I don't have any photographs of her.'

There was a pause where the tension seemed unbearable, and then he went on. 'But I've brought with me the one thing I have that was hers.'

He seemed to slump in the chair, as if the effort of saying this had completely exhausted him.

Eva noticed that Hannah's bowed head had swivelled round towards her father, and her face was showing clear signs of astonishment. However, she wanted to concentrate her attention on Mr Greaves for now, so she said gently, 'Would you like to show it to me?'

He reached inside his jacket pocket, and brought out a purse made of velvet of a deep purple colour. Carefully he pulled open the stud on the front of the purse, lifted up the flap, and slowly pulled out a tiny white cotton vest. He unfolded it, and laid it on his knee, the knee that was nearest to Hannah. Eva could see a tear running down his right cheek, but felt it might be inappropriate to offer him a tissue at this stage. She did not want to risk doing anything that would get in the way of what he was trying to communicate. She turned her attention to Hannah who was staring and staring at the vest.

'My – wife – made – this – purse.' It was as if Mr Greaves were pulling the words out of his chest, and as if the pain of that were excruciating.

Eva felt in a quandary. She wanted to respond in a way which took into account the needs of both Hannah and her father. She knew how she would speak to Mr Greaves if Hannah were not there, and she knew how she would speak to Hannah if she were now alone with her. It was essential that she behaved in a way that addressed the needs of each, but enabled them to stay together.

'What a beautiful vest,' she said. 'Is it handmade?'

Mr Greaves' body shuddered, and the 'yes' that she heard sounded more like a sob than a word.

'Did Hannah's mother make that too?'

He nodded, unable to speak.

Eva was concerned. It seemed to her that this was the first time Hannah had known of the purse and the vest, and if that were so, then becoming aware of their existence at this moment and in this context, must surely be very shocking to her. She thought quickly.

'Did she make a vest like that for Hannah too?' she asked.

Mr Greaves nodded again. Hannah was looking even more pale than usual.

'We keep Hannah's vest in...'

'Noooooooo!' Hannah's voice was almost shrill.

She was by now alarmingly white, and there were bluish areas around her eyes.

'Noooooooo!'

Mr Greaves leapt out of his chair, and bent over Hannah with his back to Eva. In that moment Eva felt that she became invisible to them both. She could hear a sound as if Hannah's teeth were grinding together. Mr Greaves appeared suddenly quite calm and determined, as if this were a situation with which he was all too familiar. He had gathered Hannah up in his arms, and was rocking her from side to side, holding her head safely on his shoulder.

The grinding sound had stopped. Eva began to realise that she was hearing a low muttering sound from time to time. That sound increased a little. As it became more audible, Eva was sure that she could hear something that sounded like 'mu... mu... mu... m'.

Although she longed to do something practical to help, Eva knew she had to take a course that was more difficult for her, and that was to wait.

Eventually, Mr Greaves sat down on his chair with Hannah cradled in his arms. She was not so white now, the bluish colour around her eyes had faded, and she clung to his jacket with her thin hands.

Without looking at Eva, he looked straight into Hannah's eyes and said, 'I think we should try to talk here about Mummy. I know that I said we never would, but we have to now. We must,' he finished in decisive tones.

Hannah started to struggle in his arms, and Eva could see her start to throw her head from side to side.

Mr Greaves held her head firmly and gently against his chest, still looking into her eyes and repeated, 'We must.'

He picked up Dawn's tiny vest from the floor where it had fallen when he had leapt up to nurse Hannah, and he put it into her hand.

'Your mummy made a special vest for each of you. She loved you both very, very much. I'm sorry I've not shown you Dawn's vest before. You were right to tell me last time we were here that I had to talk about Dawn. We made a start on that. It was very, very hard for me, but you were right. And I had to be the one who spoke about her. Now it's time to start to talk about your mummy. When Dawn died we both lost your mummy, although she didn't go away until much later.'

An idea had been forming in Eva's mind, which she decided to voice.

'I'm wondering if you'd like to have a little time on your own at the moment? I think you might need a rest, and time to talk about Hannah's mummy and to decide what you might like to tell me about her. Because I'm studying this week, my time is quite flexible. I have to go on an errand some time today, and I was going to suggest that I could go now rather than this afternoon. You're welcome to stay here while I'm away. I'll be away about an hour.'

Mr Greaves looked at her gratefully. 'That would be really helpful. Would you like that, Hannah?'

Hannah nodded.

'I bought some apple juice in case you wanted a drink of anything. Do help yourself while I'm away. The bottle is on the worktop in the kitchen.'

Eva collected her coat and her bag, and was soon striding purposefully down the road. She certainly had some things to do, but she was beginning to think that she might postpone them and use this time to reflect on the morning's events. In the end, she decided to collect a book she had ordered from the library; and then return by a circuitous route to give herself the time she needed to think, and to ensure that Hannah and her father had ample time alone. All the signs suggested that something really important was about to be revealed; and that it concerned Hannah's mother, and the effect of her absence upon Hannah and her father. But what it was Eva could not begin to guess.

Much as she wanted to know, she was determined that she would do nothing to push either Mr Greaves or his daughter into revealing anything other than they decided. If they decided to reveal nothing further, she would respect that. She knew that to try

155

to hurry things might affect Hannah's condition adversely. It seemed clear there was something about the mother's absence that was crucial to Hannah's current illness and her almost total dependency upon her father; but Eva's intuition told her that their situation was far more complex than could be addressed by their simply telling her, a relative stranger, about the loss of Hannah's mother.

The hour had almost passed, and Eva made her way down the road to the front door of her house and let herself in. Hannah and her father were sitting in an attitude that indicated they had been waiting for her return. They greeted her, and she hung up her coat and sat down. She deliberately did not ask if they had taken any refreshment in her absence, as she felt that would be an inappropriate distraction from what they had to tell her.

'Hannah and I have been talking,' said Mr Greaves. 'I've apologised to her again for not having shown her Dawn's vest before, and I've talked to her about it. I've explained to her that I understand what a big thing it is for her to have to take in, especially as she'd had no warning about it at all. The problem was that with my own difficulties this was the only way I could take things forward. I lay awake many nights thinking about it. I knew that I shouldn't just produce it here when Hannah had previously known nothing of it, but it was the only way I could start to talk about the rest of the story. I went over and over it in my mind, but could think of no other way. Sometimes I resolved not to bring it; but then I realised that I was backing away from facing things that are very important to both of us, things that we need help with. It was the only way I had of helping me to the point where I could insist to myself and to Hannah that we must talk about her mother.

'We've agreed that the best thing now is to ask you if we can make another appointment to see you again quite soon. For now, what we need is to have some time together. There are some things we need to talk over, and decide what to do. Fortunately I can take some days off work straight away. Could we make a tentative arrangement to see you again in about two weeks' time? If we're not able to come then, I'll phone you several days in advance to let you know.'

'Let me see my diary,' answered Eva. 'From the mid-afternoon of February 3rd is free at the moment. Is that a suitable time for you?'

Mr Greaves made a note in his own diary.

'I'm very grateful for your help,' he said.

'Thank you.' Hannah's voice took Eva a little by surprise, but she concealed this and smiled warmly at her.

Not long afterwards, she stood at her front door, waving at the car as Mr Greaves drove away.

Chapter Twenty-one

Ellen sat in a corner at the left of the open fire in the Bull Inn. She had arrived in plenty of time, wanting to settle herself before Adam appeared. She had left the red book on its shelf in her library, as she knew it was safe there, and there was no chance of studying it this evening. Instead, she had brought a copy of the local weekly newspaper. Thinking that she had about fifteen minutes before Adam was due to arrive, she had just started reading an article about health problems relating to exercising dogs, and the plans of the Community Council to suggest a local system of voluntary dog licensing, along with a dog training scheme which offered an initial free session. The dog training business had been started by a young man who had been a pupil at the school where she taught until just after her father's death, and she was interested to read a little of what he was doing.

She was immersed in reading the article when a voice penetrated her consciousness. It was familiar. Looking up, she saw Adam. She jumped up and reached out her hand.

'I had not expected you so soon,' she apologised.

'I was lucky to have a clear run. The roads were very quiet. Can I get you a drink?'

'Thank you, I'd like some mineral water with lemon in it.'

Adam left his coat on the chair next to Ellen, and disappeared for a few minutes. He returned carrying two glasses, and handed one to Ellen.

'How was your lecture received?' asked Ellen politely.

'Very well, actually.'

'What was the subject?'

'It was a presentation of all the information I've been studying about the effects of soil compaction.'

'I'm afraid I'm completely ignorant of that,' Ellen confessed.

'Never mind. I'm sure that we can find some subjects of mutual interest. For example, what kind of music do you enjoy?'

Adam noticed that Ellen looked startled, but quickly composed herself. He wondered what had affected her. After all, he had made the question as general as possible. He thought it best not to ask anything more, and moved on to tell her about the experience he had had in the Traveller's Arms before he had decided to stay for dinner, and where she had subsequently joined him.

'A Blüthner piano,' Ellen mused, 'in an otherwise ordinary hotel. How strange.'

'Yes, and as I said, quite a selection of good classical music on the shelves in the same room.'

Encouraged by the fact that she did not appear to be in any way detached from what he was saying, Adam decided to tell her a little about Boris and their projects.

'Are you familiar with any of Bartok's music?' he asked.

'Yes, I know some of his string quartets.'

Here she stopped. She murmured, 'Please excuse me for a moment.'

She headed towards the Ladies' toilets, chose the end cubical, and locked herself in. She was shaking all over.

'*Stupid, stupid, stupid,*' she said to herself. 'Why did I say that? Oh no! What am I going to do now?'

As the shaking continued, she contemplated leaving the Bull through the rear exit, phoning them from her home, and collecting her things the next day.

'No, that wouldn't be right,' she muttered to herself through gritted teeth. She had clamped her jaw tightly to prevent her teeth from chattering.

Remember the conversation you had with Eva, she told herself. You mustn't run away. Just give yourself a few minutes to recover, and then go back and sit down again.

These thoughts calmed her a little; but then she found herself panicking about what she would say to him, something that would seem a valid explanation of her rather prolonged absence.

I know. I can say that I didn't have time for lunch, and that I'd forgotten, and wondered why I'd felt faint...

Having decided this, she was ready to return to her chair. She was grateful for the warmth of the fire. Being on the left-hand side of the fireplace was a comfort to her; it reminded her of her red book on its shelf on the left-hand side of the fireplace in the library at home. For a moment she even dared to remember the warmth of the room before her mother's death, when it was a music room, with the sound of Bartok string quartets filling the room as her parents played with their friends.

Ellen made herself look at Adam, and she said, 'I'm sorry, silly of me, I had no lunch. I wondered at first why I felt dizzy so suddenly. Could we get something to eat?'

'I was given something after the lecture, so I'm not particularly hungry; but I'd be happy to join you with something. What do they serve here?'

'There's usually a selection of cold salads. I find when I get like this, something based on rice is the best thing.'

'Let me go and get something for us,' said Adam helpfully. 'You sit here. I won't be long.'

He was soon back, carrying a tray bearing cutlery and two plates, one of which was piled with a rice mixture decorated with finely cut tomatoes.

'Here you are. Don't worry about how much you eat. I thought it was simpler to bring plenty rather than having to go back for more.'

Ellen was grateful, both for his sensitivity, and for the fact that her plan had helped her, thus sparing her any further embarrassment. She began to relax again.

Adam went on. 'I've brought myself a sandwich; that's all I need. Can I tell you a bit about my friend Boris, and what we're trying to do?'

'Yes, of course, I'd like that.'

'Last time I saw you, in the Traveller's Arms, I'd been just about to go out to stay with Boris again. He lives not far from St Petersburg. Actually, I'll be going out to see him again in a couple of months, at the end of March. When I go, I usually stay for about two months…'

Now it was Adam's turn to falter. Ellen noticed that he seemed to freeze. It was as if he had become a statue. Strangely, she was rather reassured by this. When he had mentioned his impending trip to Russia she had relaxed considerably, and now, seeing that he was struggling with something, she felt much more able to spend the evening with him.

'What is it that you are doing together?' she asked.

Adam found that he could move again.

'It's got a bit of a history to it,' he began.

He explained how they had been students together, and how, inspired by Bartok's work, they had collected Romanian songs, how they had come to light again, and how he was trying to find a publisher for them.

'How interesting,' said Ellen with some feeling.

Encouraged by her reaction, Adam went on to tell her a little about the far greater task he and Boris were attempting, working on the collection of Russian songs they had been amassing.

Ellen considered for a moment, and then decided to risk being a little more open.

'I'm impressed,' she said. 'I do hope that you have success in your ventures. Going back to the subject of Bartok, I believe that some of his travels led him to Biskra in Algeria, and while there he made some study of Arabian music. My father was a lecturer in Middle Eastern languages.'

Without giving Adam time to say anything, she rushed on.

'His father had lived in Arabia for about five years as a young man, and we – I – still have his collection of books from that time. It's rather fine.'

She stopped, exhausted. But she was proud of herself for managing to speak in a normal way about her father; and she had even referred to the library, although she had not named it as such.

Adam felt warmed by this unexpected, albeit tenuous, link. Having picked up that Ellen's father was dead, he decided not to ask anything in particular about him at this stage. His mind drifted back to the evening when Matthew had come round to see the plans for the conservatory, and how he had found he could speak to him about Maria. Sitting here now with Ellen, he was profoundly grateful for having had that evening with Matthew. It had certainly helped him to cope with the moment of panic he had had when he started to speak to Ellen about his trips to see Boris. He was happy to talk about what he and Boris were working on together; but he did not want to say anything about why he had been going to Russia every summer.

Adam chewed a piece of his sandwich reflectively.

'Actually, I went to see a publisher earlier this month, and there's a chance that they might be interested. The man I'd gone to see was ill, so I had to see someone else. He seemed interested; and he's going to speak to his partner when he's well again, and get back to me. Meantime I've sent him three of the manuscripts of Romanian songs that Boris and I have recently revised. The originals we wrote down as students were not as precise as they needed to be. Of course, at the time we wrote them, we had no idea that years later we'd be trying to get them published.'

'I wish you every success.' Again, Ellen encouraged Adam; and she knew she had a genuine interest in what he was saying.

With the subject of Bartok exhausted for now, Adam cast around in his mind for another topic of conversation, one which might also prove to be common ground. He noticed that Ellen was searching in her bag, and he wondered what she might be looking for. He said nothing. After all she may merely be looking for a handkerchief.

'I know it's in here somewhere.' She spoke in a quiet voice, half to herself. 'I put it in my bag just before I left the house.'

Now intrigued, Adam asked, 'What are you looking for?'

Ellen smiled at him; and Adam was struck by her warmth and genuineness. 'I'm looking for my pen. I put it in my bag before I set off.'

'I can lend you a pen,' said Adam as he felt inside his jacket. But before he encountered one of his three pens she shook her head.

'No, I don't need to borrow a pen,' she said. 'I've brought one to show you.'

It began to dawn on Adam what she might be talking about, and he waited patiently to see.

'Ah, here it is.' She triumphantly produced a small narrow box, and set it down on the table.

'I think I know what might be inside that box.' Adam was now more certain of the situation. 'Is it the pen you told me about on the train, like the one I dropped?'

'Yes, it is. Look.' Ellen opened the box for him to see.

Adam reached inside his jacket pocket once more, took out a pen, and laid it alongside Ellen's.

'The same indeed,' he said.

Adam was pleased that Ellen had brought her pen to show him. It was a pleasant surprise. And there was now no doubt in his mind that it had been a good thing to contact her to say he was going to be in the area.

As if reading his mind, Ellen said, 'Thank you for thinking of me when you knew you were going to be in the locality. I'm glad you wrote to let me know, and that it's been possible to meet.'

'And this is a very pleasant place you chose,' said Adam, nodding outwards into the room in which they were seated.

Feeling more confident, Adam decided to ask Ellen about the book she had been reading when he had seen her at the hotel in York. He was curious to find out more about it. Perhaps it would cast light on the dream he had had about her.

'Ellen,' he began, 'I'd like to ask you about that book you were studying when I saw you in the hotel in York.'

'What is it you'd like to know about it?' she asked.

'Anything you can tell me. You did seem to be completely engrossed in it.'

'I know,' she replied. 'I certainly was. I came across it when I'd completed most of the cataloguing of my grandfather's books from the Middle East. However, I don't think that it's part of that collection at all; I think it just happened to be among them. It's a very unusual book. At first I was very possessive of it. I didn't want to speak to anyone about it, and I preferred to carry it with me wherever I went. More recently, I talked about it to some of my closest friends.'

'Would you mind describing it to me?'

'No, not at all.'

Ellen told him of the embossed hard covers, deep red in colour, and of the blackened edges of the pages. She explained about the leaf-vein pictures, and about the pattern of the repeating numbers of blank pages; and how some of these pages, although blank, seemed to affect her. She went on to tell him about the day she had opened the book as if the back cover were the front cover, and how, for the first time, she 'saw' something on certain of the blank pages.

'I didn't actually see anything; but it was as if a design made up of pinpricks had been impressed upon my mind,' she finished.

Adam had been listening very intently to everything she had been telling him.

'Can you tell me any more about the pinprick designs?' he asked.

Ellen looked uncomfortable.

'It's all right,' Adam continued. 'I'm not trying to put you on the spot. It's just that I'm very interested; and I'll tell you why shortly.'

Ellen looked puzzled, but said, 'The nearest I can get to it is to say that the pinprick designs I "saw" in my mind reminded me a little of faint spore-prints. If you leave the opened cap of a mushroom or a similar fungus on a piece of paper overnight, you'll usually see a pattern on the paper the next morning. The colour of the pattern depends on the colour of the minute spores which have dropped from the cap on to the paper. The way the spores are laid out corresponds to the layout of the gills or the pores on the underside of the cap of the fungus. But the layout of the pinpricks was not like any spore print pattern I'd ever seen. In fact, if I were to name the form that was nearest to the ones I thought I was seeing, I'd use the word "spiral". But I can't be sure; the images were so faint, and seemed to be in my head rather than on the pages in front of me.' She paused. 'Now tell me why you're interested.'

Adam explained. 'It was shortly after I came back from seeing Boris in Russia. I returned at the end of September, so it must have been some time in October. I woke one morning having dreamed about you and about the book.'

Adam described the dream to Ellen. He told her how she had been sitting reading in a long room. He described how, when he tried to walk towards her, he did not seem to get any closer, and how she had seemed frightened when she became aware of him, and had disappeared through the wall behind her chair. He told her how, when he reached the chair, he picked up the book she had dropped, and could see only blank pages. He finished by saying, 'I'm sure it was the red book you've just been telling me about.'

He seemed at first to have said all he had to say; but then he continued: 'There's one more thing. More recently, when I felt restless and couldn't sleep, I thought there had been something on the pages after all, shapes of something, but of what I didn't know.

Also I had some association between the room in the dream and the room at the Traveller's Arms – the one where the piano was.'

Ellen was staggered. This person, whom she had met only three times before, had been dreaming about her, and about the red book. She could not think of anything to say. She needed time to get used to this information, and she felt an urgent need to talk to Eva and Jane about it. She was glad that it would not be many days before she saw them again.

She decided to be as honest as she could. 'Adam, I do feel quite shocked by what you've just told me.'

'I'm sorry if I've offended you in some way.'

'No, that's not what I mean. Remember that you've had months to get used to that dream, whereas I've only just heard it. I'm the central character; and although I may be symbolic of some other situation, it certainly sounds much like me.'

'I'm beginning to see what you mean; and I realise that when I described the dream to you, I didn't say that I woke up in quite a state afterwards. I hadn't intended to tell you about it when we met this evening, but I had begun to feel sufficiently relaxed that it seemed quite natural. Now I can see that telling you was quite out of step with the kind of contact we have. I also admit that it was wrong of me to tell you the dream without being prepared to tell you at the same time how it affected me. I should have waited to see if we had any further contact – contact in which the whole of it could be spoken about. I do apologise.'

Ellen was touched by his scrupulous honesty, but she knew that she could not talk to him any more now. Any further discussion would inevitably involve her having to put her reactions to all of this on one side. She needed to talk about it all to her friends, the people she knew well, and not try to discuss it with this person about whom she knew almost nothing. She looked at her watch. Ten o'clock. Adam noted her action, and could see the time on her watch. He did not have to look at his own.

'Ellen...' he struggled to find the words... He felt that it was now his responsibility to help her out of the position he had created for her by his ineptitude. 'I see that it's getting late. I want to thank you again for this evening, and to apologise once more for my error. Would you let me see you to your car fairly soon?'

Ellen found this approach to be something to which she could respond authentically. She had feared that she would have had to switch into rather formal, and almost ritualised, farewells.

'I'd appreciate that,' she replied. 'Before I go, can we talk a little about your further plans for your projects with your friend – I think you said his name is Boris?'

'There isn't much more to tell,' said Adam.

But as he said that, into his mind flashed the memory of the special tape which awaited his return to Boris' home, and the effect it had had upon him. He felt a longing to tell Ellen about it; but he said nothing, not wishing to make another mistake. He thought of something else he could say.

'The publisher said that they're investing a lot in the publication of ethnic music, so I think that increases our chances of their being interested.'

'I do hope they take up your manuscripts.'

'Thank you,' replied Adam. 'I plan to go back out to see Boris at the end of March, and we'll continue working on the Russian songs.' He added, 'That's earlier that I usually go.' Here he faltered, but made himself continue. 'I normally spend the summer there – part of July, the whole of August, and to the middle of September.'

'I think I'd like you to let me know how your negotiations with the publishers turn out,' said Ellen slowly. 'Would you write to me sometime when you have more news?'

'Yes, I'd be glad to. I appreciate your interest.'

Ellen reached for her coat, and stood up to put it on. Adam put out a hand to help her, but she turned slightly, in a way that made it more difficult. He let his hand fall by his side, and waited until she was ready. After that he walked with her to her car, said 'Goodbye,' and watched as she drove off into the darkness. He stood there remembering the sound of the train, and remembering the tape.

Ellen drove down the road for about a mile. Then she drew the car into a lay-by. She had realised that, although things had improved for her by the time she left, she certainly felt a bit shaky. And there was something at the back of her mind that she wanted to recall. She had been aware of it when Adam had told her about his dream, but she could not get hold of it. Ah, now she had it! When she and Eva and Jane were last at Jane's house, Eva had told her how she was fairly sure that she had mouthed the name 'Adam' during the state she entered as a result of looking at the spirals. She was beginning to think that this might be something to do with Adam Thomas after all.

If he could dream about her and her red book in such an intense way, then it was not beyond the bounds of possibility that *she* could have felt some similar connection with *him* when so deeply affected by the spirals. She had not forgotten that the name of the boy in Frances Ianson's book was Adam; and of course this could be the more significant of the two. At this stage, she had no way of knowing. Here her thoughts stopped; and she knew again that the next step was to talk everything over with her friends.

Adam had not booked a room anywhere. His intention had been to drive home through the night after seeing Ellen, and nothing had changed his mind. He drove at a moderate speed. He was in no rush to get back home; indeed, he valued the time spent that was neither in the pub with Ellen, nor being in his home. His mind was alert to the road, but more or less empty of other issues. The word he would use to most nearly describe his state was 'suspended', and he welcomed it. His journey was uneventful, and he eventually arrived home at 3 a.m.

He did not feel as if he wanted to be in bed yet. First he checked the phone to see if there were messages on the call-minder. Ah, there was one from Matthew. Again he sounded very crackly. He reran the message and was able to make out that Matthew was hoping to be back in the middle of next week, and was suggesting that perhaps they could meet the following weekend. '*Leave a message on my phone at home*' the message concluded.

Adam did not have to think about this. He phoned straight away, and left a message inviting Matthew round for the Saturday evening.

Next, e-mails. He made his way to his study. Minutes later, he felt a sense of eager anticipation as five new e-mails appeared. Disappointingly, three of these were 'junk' messages, an increasing problem of late. He must find out from Matthew how to deal with this. There must be a way of screening them out. Of the remaining two, one was from Boris, and the other was from Professor Barnes' e-mail address.

But he's abroad at the moment. He was to be away for months, said Adam to himself. And there's no reason for him to write to me anyway.

He clicked on the envelope, and immediately noticed the formal style of a letter-writer.

<Dear Mr Thomas,

I will be giving another series of talks after Easter. There is a place for you if you want to attend. Please reply to this address by the end of February.

Yours sincerely,

Edmund Barnes>

After an initial lurch of excitement, Adam was pitched into conflict. He was going away at the end of March, and had planned to be away for at least five weeks, preferably two months. That would mean he would not be back until the end of May. Professor Barnes' e-mail had not given any precise dates, but surely most of the talks would be over by the end of May. Realising that he had plenty of time to think about this, he turned his attention to Boris' e-mail.

<Hello old friend,

Have you any more news from Carillon Music? If they are indeed interested, perhaps I should meet them myself sometime?

No more tapes have arrived since I last wrote, but as you know we have plenty to get on with when you come.

Best wishes, Boris>

'No. No news from Carillon Music yet, but it's early days.' Adam said out loud.

Tomorrow he would work on some more of the Romanian songs. If the news from Gordon Quaver turned out to be good, then finished versions of all the songs would be needed. He had only completed three. There were at least another twenty. If he pushed ahead with these now, he could send them to Boris, who, as always, would suggest amendments. He had about ten days before he must start on the work that was lined up for him for the whole of February. He sent a reply to Boris.

<Boris,

No news yet, but scan the rest of the Romanian songs and send them to me. I will work on them over the next ten days and you can comment.

I am just back from meeting Ellen. We did not have very long together, and I know that I handled it really badly at one point, but overall I think it went well. You may be surprised to hear that she is interested in our projects, and has asked that I let her know how things go. I'll tell you more about the evening when I come to see you. I don't want to write about it in an e-mail.

Adam>

'Bed now,' he muttered. 'I've plenty to get on with tomorrow. I've two manuscripts here I can work on, and I hope to get more from Boris by the end of the day. I shall enjoy working in the conservatory again.'

Chapter Twenty-two

Ellen packed her small bag carefully, including the red book and her copy of the book by Frances Ianson. She was grateful to Eva for having obtained a copy for her, and she had gradually worked her way through it, making some notes as she went. She packed the notes along with the book. Jane's description of the content of the book had covered nearly all of the material that Ellen herself felt was significant as she read through it; but there were a few things that she wanted to discuss with Jane and Eva when they met. Tomorrow, after work, she would drive straight to Eva's house.

The next day passed pleasantly, and she felt contented as she drove out of the car park where she had met the man with the girl in the wheelchair. This time there was no delay. The car park was not busy so there were plenty of spare spaces.

She arrived at Eva's in the middle of the evening. Jane was already there. She had taken the afternoon off work, as this had greatly simplified her travel arrangements. Eva and Jane greeted her enthusiastically.

'We've been looking forward to your coming,' laughed Jane. 'We agreed we wouldn't exchange any of the important news until you arrived. It's been difficult to hold back, but we've managed! Just to reassure you straight away, I've brought the diary that contains the spirals, and I've got the envelope with all the photocopies in it.'

'And I've remembered to bring the red book,' Ellen added eagerly.

'Have you had anything to eat?' asked Eva.

'Well, no, actually.'

'I made enough for three just in case,' Eva went on. 'Jane and I have eaten ours, but you must have yours now. We can have a drink of something to keep you company. I've realised that we have quite a number of things on the agenda for this weekend, so I was going to suggest we make a list. We could do that while you eat, and then decide how to go about things.'

'That's a good idea,' Jane and Ellen agreed.

They settled themselves round the table.

'Jane, I'd like to hear any news you have about your stay with Clare and Emily. I'll put that as number one on the list. Is that okay?'

Ellen and Jane nodded in agreement. More ideas followed rapidly, and Eva continued to add to the list, which soon consisted of six items. It read:

1. Jane's news about Emily.

2. Ellen's news about her meeting with Adam.

3. Ellen's news about the red book.

4. Eva's news about Hannah, the girl in the wheelchair.

5. Discussion of the book by Frances Ianson.

6. Further study of the spirals.

'I think that must be everything now,' said Eva as she laid down her pen.

'I'm not sure.' Ellen's forehead was wrinkled with concentration. 'Let me see if I put a note in with the comments I made about the book. No, there's nothing else here. Ah, now I remember! The stick... your stick, Eva. We haven't spoken about it for a while; in fact I'd forgotten about it in the midst of everything else that's been happening. I think it's important that we spend some time talking about it.'

'I'm glad you said that,' replied Eva. 'I've nothing in particular to report, but I have noticed that recently I'm even more anxious than before about the possibility of losing it. I don't take it out of the house at all. I keep it upstairs, just beside my bed. Yes, I'll add it to the list.' And she wrote:

7. The stick.

She went on, 'The next thing to decide is the order in which to take these. Can I suggest that we ask Jane to tell us about Emily first? We have time to do that this evening.'

'Then can we hear from you about the girl in the wheelchair?' asked Ellen eagerly. 'I was thinking about her again when I set off from the car park earlier today. It happened to be the one where I saw her and her father.'

'That sounds okay,' said Jane, 'but I think that would be plenty for this evening. We may even need some time with that in the morning. I certainly have some interesting things to say about Emily. I wouldn't be surprised if you've a lot to tell us about the girl in the wheelchair, Eva.'

'Yes, I have; and I'm eager to do that before we move on to the spirals, because once we become immersed in them, there's no room for anything else.'

'I'm wondering if the best thing would be to leave the discussion of Frances Ianson's book until just before we concentrate on the spirals again,' suggested Jane.

Eva and Ellen agreed readily.

'And I think I should talk about my meeting with Adam and about my red book together,' added Ellen.

'Why's that?' asked Jane.

'If I start to explain now, it will take up time that we need for this evening's subjects. You'll understand why when I talk about it tomorrow,' replied Ellen.

Eva picked up her pen again.

'So I'll mark Emily and Hannah for this evening, and the red book and Adam for tomorrow morning. It won't matter if we take more time for this evening's subjects tomorrow morning. I suggest that we take a break tomorrow afternoon by going out for a walk. It gets dark early, and we can wind up any more discussion about those four items when we return. After we've eaten, we can devote the evening to the *Communications* book and the spirals. We'll have the freedom then to continue until as late as we want, or we can go to bed at a specific time and talk again on Sunday morning.'

'I think I'd prefer to stay up late on Saturday evening,' said Jane.

'I agree with that,' said Ellen emphatically.

'It's certainly good to be able to carry on as long as we want, without having to watch the clock,' said Eva. 'I think that where the spirals are concerned it's very important indeed to reduce any external pressures to a minimum.'

'We've a little more time this weekend,' Ellen reminded her friends. 'Because we're meeting here instead of at Jane's house, I don't have to leave until late afternoon.'

'That extra time may well prove to be invaluable,' said Eva.

'Why do you say that?' asked Jane.

'It just feels as if it's going to be, that's all I can say.'

The three friends moved into the sitting room, and Jane began to tell Ellen and Eva about the set of wooden shapes she had had specially made for Emily.

'What an excellent idea!' exclaimed Eva. 'You must keep me informed about this. There may be further shapes I could suggest you get made for her.'

'I'd be glad of your input.' Jane was relieved to have the support of her friend. 'Any ideas will be gratefully received.'

Jane continued with the story of her visit, and how much Emily had loved the shapes, insisting on taking them up to her cot with her; and how she had fallen asleep with a tetrahedron clutched in each of her hands.

'That's absolutely fascinating!' Eva was clearly involved in everything that Jane was saying.

'Have you spoken to Clare since you went home again?' asked Ellen.

'Yes, she phoned me last week. Emily is still using the shapes every day. She keeps them with her abacus, needing to know exactly where they are. George is due home again soon, and I'll be interested to hear what he has to say about it all. He may well have suggestions about which shapes to get made next. I don't mind getting more made soon if Eva or George come up with suggestions. The toy maker was certainly very involved in the whole idea. But I'd like to move on now to hearing what Eva has to tell us about Hannah and her father. There is nothing more I can think of about Emily, but we can go back to talking about her if you think of anything to ask.'

Eva began to tell her friends what had happened at the meetings she had had with Mr Greaves and Hannah. At times Jane and Ellen interrupted to ask a few questions, but in general they listened quietly.

When she had finished, it was Ellen who spoke first.

'I do think that you've made some progress there,' she said solemnly. 'It sounds as if the father and daughter have been struggling under an enormous weight of distress. They've had quite a bit of medical help, but they've been trying to cope with their distress alone. It's so obvious to me as an outside observer that they can't deal with all of that just between the two of them, and that Hannah's physical health has suffered greatly as a consequence.'

'I think there's a lot still to come when they return to talk to you about Hannah's mother,' Jane reflected. 'At this stage it's impossible to guess where she is, and under what circumstances she went away. We know that she had been traumatised by Dawn's death; and from the description we have she behaved only mechanically from then on.'

'I'm worried about how Hannah will cope with the need to start talking about her mother while her state of health is so precarious, but I respect Mr Greaves' decision to go ahead with this now,' said Eva. 'My hunch is that he's felt sufficiently supported in his meetings here to be able to start to face the need for him and Hannah to talk about her. And I think that having started to face it himself, he became resolute about helping Hannah with it, having some confidence that he could now support her through it. The difficulty for me is that I have to wait for each meeting, trusting that something positive is happening in between. It's really an act of faith on my part. But it is essential that I must enable them in their lives, and not intervene inappropriately.'

Eva sounded a little strained as she explained all this, but what she said was presented with confidence.

'You said they're coming to see you again quite soon,' said Jane. 'When will that be?'

'February 3rd.'

'What will you do if they decide not to talk to you about Hannah's mother?' asked Ellen.

'That will depend on a number of things,' replied Eva. 'The main thing I'll be looking out for is any small changes in their attitude towards me, and the way they relate to each other. Mr Greaves will have with him the results of the most recent hospital tests. I'll be taking these into account too, along with my own observations of any changes in Hannah's general state. I want to say how much I appreciate the interest you both have in this. I'm sure that kind and concerned involvement of informed people does have a beneficial effect in extreme cases like Hannah's.'

She paused for a while and then continued.

'I may already have mentioned this, but I want to go over it again. You'll remember that it was a colleague of mine who sent Hannah and her father to me. I may also have told you that one of the things I noticed in the notes she sent me was that she'd picked up very unusual configurations in energy fields around Hannah. She seemed pretty sure that this was, at least in part, something to do with Hannah's relationship with her father. I think that if Hannah and her father decide they don't want to talk to me about Hannah's mother, and if I can't detect any change for the better in Hannah's condition, I'll ask them if they'll see my colleague again, as I'd like information about what she can sense now. If she could sense some resolution in that area, then I'd be willing meantime not to press them about Hannah's mother, and merely ask them if they'd be willing to come to talk to me again from time to time.'

'I can see why you're thinking along those lines,' said Jane, 'although I couldn't have worked it out for myself.'

'Me too,' added Ellen. 'I'll look forward to hearing how things go at the meeting on the 3rd.' She yawned. 'Goodness! I'm beginning to feel quite sleepy. I'm worried that I won't be able to keep giving this my full attention.'

'I think we've covered everything now,' replied Eva. 'I'm tired too, and I think we should call it a day now. I'll make up the sofa bed down here. I've changed my bed upstairs. If there's anything else that either of you needs, don't hesitate to ask me.' She laughed, 'I'll let you take care of my stick for the night; and we mustn't forget to talk about it, although I don't know what any of us will be saying.'

They all slept well and were up early, ready to proceed with the next item on their list. Breakfast over, they were once more seated in Eva's living room.

'Over to you now, Ellen,' smiled Eva.

'Before I start I want to say that I'm likely to blurt this out,' Ellen warned them.

'Don't worry about that.' Jane was comforting. 'We've got plenty of time to sort it through afterwards.'

'Adam had dreamed about me and the red book,' Ellen said in a rush. She looked flushed. 'I got quite a shock, and I had to leave soon after he told me. He even seemed to know something about what's in the book.'

She struggled for a moment, and then sounding alarmed, burst out 'Actually, I feel really upset,' and she started to cry.

Eva passed her a box of tissues, and sat beside her with her arm round her. Jane went to the kitchen and brought a glass of water. When she returned, Ellen was sobbing uncontrollably, while Eva patiently handed her tissue after tissue out of the box.

It was some time before Ellen's sobs began to subside; and then Eva said authoritatively, 'I think that when you're ready, the best thing is to start at the beginning and go through it all slowly, bit by bit. We've got plenty of time.'

Jane nodded. 'We want to know what happened, and we want to help if we can.'

'Perhaps it would have been better if I'd phoned one of you straight afterwards,' said Ellen, her voice sounding wobbly. 'But because I was going to be seeing you both soon, I decided it wasn't necessary.'

'Another time, just lift up the phone to one of us straight away,' insisted Jane.

'I can certainly see the sense in that now,' said Ellen with a wan smile. 'Now, I'll start from when Adam arrived at the Bull.'

Having finished telling her friends exactly what had happened she said, 'I want to talk to you both about the pinprick designs that I see in my mind when I've been studying certain of the blank pages in the red book. At first I had some association between these and my memories of seeing spore-prints; and as you know, that's what I told Adam. I'm worried you might think I'm making something up now, but since that evening with Adam, I've been thinking that the pinprick patterns might be faint spiral patterns. Oh, I know it all sounds improbable, but I wanted to tell you. Actually I'd already said to Adam I thought they might be.'

'Why don't we all have another look at the book just now?' suggested Jane.

'It's in my bag upstairs,' said Ellen.

Jane went to get it for her and soon returned.

'Shall we start at the back like you did just before you first saw the pinprick patterns?' she asked. 'Just show us exactly what you remember doing.'

Ellen took the book and turned it over, so that the back cover was in the position that she would normally have the front cover. Then she began to turn over the pages. Here was one of those beautiful leaf-vein patterns. Seven pages – then another. Nine pages – then another. She went back to the first leaf-vein pattern and started counting the pages again. This time, when she reached the third page she stopped and gazed intently at the blank page for a while, then shut her eyes.

'Yes, I thought that was the first page to try,' she said. 'I can see a faint pinprick pattern now.'

'Can I have a look?' asked Eva.

Ellen handed the book across to her.

'I'll look at the page after the leaf-vein pattern first, and work my way to the page you've just been studying,' said Eva.

She stared at each page in turn for some time, and then either shut her eyes or looked away.

'No, I'm not aware of anything,' she said. 'Here Jane, you try.'

Jane took the book, and repeated the exercise.

While she was doing that Eva suddenly exclaimed, 'I think I *can* see something.'

'Don't tell us what it is yet,' said Jane urgently. 'Let me have some time to absorb this first.'

She had decided to work her way through the pages from the second leaf-vein pattern, but was so fascinated by it that she sat staring at it, wondering at its beauty.

'I'm so affected by this leaf-vein design, I think I'll leave the blank pages for now. Tell us what you saw, Eva.'

'I find it difficult to describe. I can see what Ellen means when she says that the pattern seems to be in her mind, not on the page. Looking at the page, I'm not aware of seeing anything at all; yet afterwards there's an impression in my mind of a very faint pinprick design. Yes, pinprick is a good word to use. I'm not sure that I'd associate the design with either a spore-print or a spiral.

The mass of pinpricks appear in a random design, and it's all too faint for me to be able to say anything else about it.'

'I know that we're planning to go out this afternoon,' Ellen reminded them. 'Do you think we could have an early lunch, so we can have a longer break? I hope you won't be offended, but I feel in need of being on my own. I'd like to take the bus to the shopping centre, and have a look round. I'm not thinking of buying anything, I just want to be in a crowd of people.'

'Do you still want to go for a walk, Eva?' Jane asked.

'Yes. Shall we go together? Let's get lunch then. Before we leave we should agree a time to be back here. Before I forget, here's one of my spare keys, Ellen. You'll find the bus stops just at the end of the road. The service is very good, about every ten minutes.'

It was not long before they were all ready to leave. Jane and Eva set off at a brisk pace in the direction of the river, and Ellen made her way to the bus stop. She was glad that her friends had been willing to walk without her. A bus came almost immediately, and before long she was walking slowly round the shopping centre, staring into the windows of the shops. There were a number of charity shops, and she searched these, looking through the bookshelves.

Jane and Eva soon reached the river bank and followed the path to the bridge, where they lingered, throwing sticks into the river and watching them caught in the twisting path of the eddies.

'Do you think Ellen will be all right?' asked Jane worriedly.

'Yes, she'll be fine. It was good that she could take the time for herself.'

As agreed, Jane and Eva arrived back at the house at dusk. They found Ellen there already, although she had arrived only minutes before them. She looked relaxed, and Jane forgot any anxieties she had had about her.

'Look what I picked up in a charity shop!' Ellen smiled as she handed a book entitled *Mathematical Models* to Jane. 'It looks a bit advanced; but you never know, you might see something useful in it. That reminds me, I bought a frame for that photograph you have of Emily. It's in my travel bag, I'll just go and get it.'

'Thank you *so* much,' said Jane gratefully, as Ellen handed first the book to her, and later the frame.

'The other thing I bought was this,' Ellen added with an air of amusement.

She produced a packet of crumpets out of a bag.

'I thought we could share them now, while we're talking about Frances Ianson's book. We can have our meal later, and then devote the rest of the evening to the spirals.'

Adam whistled happily as he tidied a few things away before his friend was due to arrive. He had been working on the manuscripts of the Romanian songs all week. Now it was Saturday and he had nearly finished the versions he was going to send to Boris. He was sure his friend would suggest a comprehensive list of amendments, but that did not worry him. He admired his precision, and was more than happy to accede to his views. Some of the minute changes amused and entertained him, and never caused him any feeling of impatience or irritation. He still had not heard anything more from Gordon Quaver. He had decided to wait until the middle of February, and if he had not heard anything by then he would either write or phone.

The doorbell rang, and he opened the door to Matthew, who was standing on the step, with a large grin on his face and a bag of nuts in his hand.

'Hello, Matthew, it's so good to see you again. I've been looking forward to this.'

'Me too.'

'Let me take your coat. I'd like to show you the finished conservatory before we sit down.'

Adam led the way through, and Matthew whistled admiringly. 'It's great,' he said simply. 'I see you're working in here. How do you find it?'

'It's just right – very quiet; and there's plenty of space to spread my things around. The insulation is very good, so it heats up quite easily. I'm working here at the moment on that music I'm hoping to get published.'

'Ah yes. How's that going?'

'The publisher I saw earlier this month hasn't got back to me yet, but he did seem quite encouraging. I thought I'd just go on with the preparation. It'll be disappointing if it doesn't work out with him, but it wouldn't be the end of the world. If they say "no", any delay caused by having to look for another publisher is really of no consequence. We aren't in any sort of rush. Anyway, come and sit down. I lit the fire in the sitting room about half an hour ago.'

The two men made their way into the sitting room, and sprawled in chairs in front of the fire.

'How have things been for you, Matthew, since we last met?' asked Adam.

'A bit mixed. I now know I won't be moved anywhere for at least another two years. It's a big relief to me, but I'll have to travel quite long distances, and will be away from home a lot. Staying away overnight has never appealed to me much. I put up with it, but I'm always glad to be home again. Sometimes work takes me near the home of a friend. That makes things a lot easier. I get in touch, and usually find there's a spare room I can borrow or rent.'

'I don't envy you,' said Adam sympathetically. 'I was away myself earlier this month, but opted to drive back home during the late evening, arriving here in the early hours of the morning. I had a lecture to give, and then I met up with an acquaintance. It turned out to be very interesting.'

'Tell me about it,' said Matthew, cracking a walnut with the nutcrackers he had thoughtfully brought with him.

He threw the pieces of shell into the fire, and handed Adam half of the contents he had extracted.

Remembering Matthew's sympathetic reception of his confidences about Maria, Adam found himself telling him all about his contact with Ellen since he had first encountered her on the train. During this he told him exactly what had taken place the evening he had spent with Ellen at the Bull. When he spoke about the dream and Ellen's reaction to hearing it, Matthew suddenly sat bolt upright.

'Ow!' he yelped. 'My back! Serves me right for slumping in the chair. Now, what's all this about how your dream was something that your friend almost recognised? That's spooky!'

'I'm not sure I'd use that word,' said Adam a little stiffly.

'Sorry. I'm not an academic myself, and I tend to use words loosely at times, especially when I'm suddenly affected by something. How about "synchronicity"?'

Adam blinked. Matthew had leapt from one extreme to the other. However, his reaction had not been surprising. Adam had had a long time to get used to his dream, and two weeks to think about his meeting with Ellen. Matthew was only now hearing all of this.

'She said to keep in touch about the music?' Matthew went on. 'At least that means there's a reason for contacting her, so you don't have to worry about whether to keep up the contact or not.'

'I must admit I'm grateful for that,' said Adam. 'I do very much want to keep in touch with her. As I said to you, I felt something unusual from that first meeting on the train, and, more recently, this business of the dream has affected me very deeply.

'I hope you'll forgive me for asking, but...' Matthew hesitated.

'Fire away.'

'Look, are you intending to try to get her to spend time with you. You know, go on holiday, that sort of thing...?'

Adam was taken aback, and his face showed it. Such thoughts had never occurred to him. Matthew sat cracking nuts and handing kernels across to him, which he ate mechanically. Of course, it was natural that Matthew might think along those lines. It would not have been surprising if he himself had been thinking that way. Perhaps what was surprising was that he had *not* been thinking that way. Not at all. There was certainly an attraction, a growing fascination, but it was complex and elusive.

'I expect this might sound a bit strange, but the nearest I can get to explaining how I feel about Ellen is that we have some kind of shared purpose.'

Matthew continued to crack nuts.

'I suppose such things do happen sometimes,' he said slowly; 'but what do you have to go on?'

'Nothing really,' replied Adam. 'Well, no solid evidence. All I have to go on is how I feel about it; and that dream.'

'That's good enough for me,' returned Matthew reassuringly. 'There's no harm in trusting your instincts, so long as you don't go at it like a bull in a china shop and do anything rash. Everything you've told me so far shows that you've put a lot of careful thought into it, so I think it's going to be okay, whatever it is.'

He stared into the fire for a few minutes.

Then he said, 'Hey, can we have a game of chess?'

'Yes, we can,' replied Adam. 'I'd like that; but remind me that I have one more thing to tell you.'

'What's that?'

'I've been to a talk by Professor Barnes.'

'Oh, excellent! He's a good guy, isn't he? Yes, I'll remind you when we've had a game.'

The time passed pleasantly. Adam thought how the sounds of the fire crackling, Matthew's cracking of the nuts, and the crunching of eating them, were very calming; but he realised that it was really the sense of trust and companionship that soothed him.

The game finished.

'Now tell me what you thought about Professor Barnes.' Matthew's voice broke into Adam's reverie.

How long had he been staring into the fire? Had he been dozing? His vision seemed disturbed. What was it? He felt a bit panicky.

'There's something odd happening,' he managed to say in slightly strangled tones.

'What is it, mate?' Matthew's voice helped to steady him a little.

'I think I'm seeing something that isn't there,' he said.

'Steady on! ' Again the sound of Matthew's voice was a comfort to him, but it seemed to fade out of reach, as he slipped into unconsciousness.

Ellen, Eva and Jane had cleared away the plates and dishes from their meal. They had enjoyed cooking together. Eva's kitchen was small, but they had managed to navigate around one another very successfully. For some time now, they had been discussing Frances Ianson's book. Jane had thoughtfully prepared a fairly lengthy synopsis of the text, and had begun by reading this out. Eva and Ellen had produced the notes they had made when they had each studied the book; and they had all discussed the points that they raised. There were many unanswered questions in their minds, and they found it stimulating to debate them.

'We could go on all evening like this,' Ellen said with enthusiasm. 'I find it extremely helpful to talk through my notes with you both. I can see other avenues of thought, and I want time

182

to pursue them. But I think we should perhaps be thinking of moving on to studying the spirals now.'

'I've certainly gone through the list of questions I'd made; and I've been making more notes as we've been talking. I feel I've got plenty to think about, and I'm happy to leave the book for now. I agree with Ellen; perhaps we should move on,' said Eva.

She laid her pencil on one side and looked across at Jane. 'What's your view?' she asked.

'That's fine by me. I have the diary and the photocopies here. I brought them downstairs while you were drying the dishes. Do you have a sheet handy, Eva?'

Eva produced a white sheet from a cupboard, and spread it out on the floor in front of them.

'By the way,' said Ellen playfully. 'I've brought your stick downstairs, Eva. I don't want it to be left out! We haven't yet decided when we're going to talk about it, and I don't want it to be forgotten because we're concentrating on all these other things.'

'It's good to see you so cheerful,' said Eva, smiling.

'Yes, I feel much better,' replied Ellen. 'I feel that something has lifted a bit after this morning. Thank you both for being so helpful.'

'Remember what I said, and phone one of us straight away if something else comes up,' Jane reminded her.

'And I know that you would do the same for one of us,' added Eva.

'Thanks a lot. Now, how are we going to go about looking at the spirals this time?' said Ellen, obviously keen to begin.

'I think we should have a bit of a review first,' Eva was cautious. 'The effect of the spirals on you was almost instant and was very pronounced when we last looked at them at Jane's. Added to that, a number of other things have been happening in each of our lives, some of which might have a bearing on how open we are to being affected by the spirals. In my recent studies I've not come across anything quite like our own situation; but I've read enough, and indeed had enough personal experience, to suggest that being involved in things that have intense emotional significance can lead to an increase in sensitivity to paranormal matters. I'm using the word "paranormal", not because I think it's exactly the right word, but because it's the only word I can think of at the moment for our reactions to the spirals.'

'It'll do for now,' Jane reassured her. 'And I agree with your proposal. I'd like to draw up another list – this time of the factors we can see that might be affecting us.'

Ellen felt in her bag and took out her pen.

'Okay,' she said. 'And just to show that I'm in total agreement with your approach, I'll write the list, using the pen that's like Adam's. Now, if we look first at my life, there's my recent contact with Adam, and yesterday morning's outpourings with you. The contact with Adam has revealed that there's some connection between him and me that I hadn't known about before. But getting used to the fact that he dreamed about me and the red book is taking me a long time.' She paused. 'And of course, he now knows about the pinprick patterns I see in my mind after looking at those particular blank pages.'

'There's something else,' added Eva. 'You've invited him to keep in touch with you. That's a big shift on your part.'

'Yes, that's true,' replied Ellen. 'I haven't forgotten how you made me aware of how I've been keeping myself politely detached from people who may want to develop a friendship with me. It gave me quite a shock when you told me, but I could see it was true. Yes, inviting him to keep in touch, albeit about the music, is a big shift on my part.'

'As for me, I think my situation is quite straightforward,' said Jane. 'The only thing we have to note is my growing involvement in Emily's development.'

'That may be true, but I think it may be affecting you in more ways than you think. I don't think that you're merely a potentiator in Emily's development. And I think that the eager collaboration of the toy maker has had quite an effect on you too,' Eva added wisely.

Jane coloured a little. 'I must think about that. And now you're helping me to talk a bit more about the whole situation, I think that the choice of shapes was significant. At first I'd thought of going to see a maths teacher to discuss the best shapes to try, but I abandoned that idea, deciding instead to follow my own instincts. That was a big step for me, because I remember very little of school maths, which I never understood anyway.'

'I'd guess that it's your own sense of connection with your niece that is guiding you,' Eva went on. 'You clearly love her, and want to see her for who she truly is. Anything you give her will be something that you've decided from that basis.'

Ellen nodded in agreement. 'It was obvious the first time you talked about Emily that you have a very important bond with her. That's why I offered to look for a frame for her photograph. I wanted to give you something that showed you that I respect and value your relationship with her. You'll always be very important in her life.'

Jane's eyes looked slightly red, and her voice sounded a little muffled, as she asked Ellen to make notes of all they had said, saying that she would find it helpful.

'And now to me,' said Eva. She turned to Ellen. 'Please will you keep making notes – it will help me too, I think.'

'Surely.'

'The most obvious place to start is my involvement with Mr Greaves and Hannah. There's so much in it that it would fill several pages. The important thing for me is that we spent time talking about it yesterday evening, so I know that both of you know everything that has happened there. I want to remind us that the two meetings took place here, in this room. Other things I want to take into account are my increased contact with the colleague who sent them to me – the long-lost childhood friend. The effect of the loss of her from my life was profound, and the gradual re-establishment of contact is affecting me a lot I know. That there is contact with her about Hannah's case makes the situation all the more intense… Ah, I'm glad I said that. I realise I must suggest to my friend that we spend an afternoon together sometime, perhaps visiting a museum or an art gallery. I can see now it's important that we have more time together that's not directly about Hannah. Hannah's illness has brought us closer together; but we must not rely on that as a means for continuing our relationship. That would not help us or Hannah.

'In addition to all of that there's my recent study of energy medicine. I read a lot during the week I devoted to the subject, and I know I've not absorbed it all yet by any means. Lastly, there's my stick, and my increased anxiety about the loss of it. I'm glad you asked me about it, Ellen. Alongside everything else, it didn't seem much, but now I can see it could be important.'

Ellen was scribbling quickly. 'I think I've got all of that down now,' she said. 'But I'm not taking the minutes of a meeting!' She laughed, still in a light-hearted mood.

Eva hesitated for a moment, and then decided to say something else.

'I want to mention one more thing. We're all more relaxed this weekend. We have a bit more time, and we're getting more of a grasp of everything. I just want to add that I know that at such times people are often more open and sensitive to other things.'

'You're right to raise that,' Jane replied. 'I could see you hesitating, not wanting to risk dampening Ellen's mood, but it would have been wrong not to mention it.'

'I agree. We must always say what we're thinking. That's the only responsible way of going about this; and we have to be able to trust each other,' said Ellen seriously.

Jane took her diary. She had an embroidered bookmark at the place where the first page of spirals was.

'Clare gave me this for Christmas,' she remarked. 'It's the letter "J", with flowers woven round it. It's really beautiful. I was very touched, and knew at once that I'd use it with my diary.'

She opened her diary, and passed the bookmark round for the others to admire.

'Eva,' she said, 'would you be the one to lay the enlarged spirals out on the sheet again? Ellen, perhaps it would be best if you looked away while she's doing it, since you were affected so quickly last time.'

'Good idea. I'll go and stand at the front door, and get a breath of air.'

Ellen stood up and went to the door. Opening it she stood outside, pulling it almost shut behind her.

Eva worked quietly on the floor, making careful measurements, and placing the spirals as indicated by the small diagram. Jane watched Eva at work, but did not look at the arrangement she was constructing. She felt a flicker of excitement and anticipation, but contained it, knowing that whatever happened must be controlled in a proper way.

'I think that's it now.' Eva got up from the floor. 'We can go and get Ellen. I know we should have spoken about this before; but since she's been so sensitive to the spirals, shall you and I agree not to study them yet, but to watch Ellen's reaction like we did before?'

'That's a very good plan,' agreed Jane. 'I'll go and get her now.'

She made her way to the front door and called to Ellen. There was no reply. She quickly opened the door and found Ellen standing there.

'Ellen,' she repeated; but there was no response. 'Eva!' she called anxiously. 'Will you come and help me?'

Eva moved quickly to the front door.

'Ellen,' she said softly, 'come inside now. I think there's something here you want to see.'

Ellen turned. Her eyes were open, but she seemed in some kind of trance. Eva felt her hand, and found her skin warm to the touch. She nodded to Jane. Jane noted that Ellen's face was a little pale, but not to a degree that caused her concern.

'Ellen,' repeated Eva, 'why not come and sit down?'

She took Ellen's hand and led her back to her chair; she helped her to sit down, and stood in front of her so that she could not see the spirals. She could hear the sound of Jane's pencil on paper. She knew that Jane would write as precise an account of what was happening as she could. It was a relief to her to remember that since it was Jane herself who had first seen the spirals, and indeed had probably drawn them, the effect of them upon her now was likely to be quite different from any effect on herself or Ellen. She thought how, when she had been laying out the spirals, she had been so engrossed in the measurements she had to make that she was less focussed upon the spirals themselves than upon the overall layout. Maybe the reason why she had not been affected by the spirals while laying them out was that her mind was concentrated in a purely practical channel.

This whole situation is absolutely fascinating, thought Eva, although I'm not sure what to do next. It's important that I don't do anything that risks causing harm.

At this point she noticed that the slightly pale colour of Ellen's face had been changing, and her skin was now a healthy pink.

This is a good sign, she thought. She motioned to draw Jane's attention to it, but found that Jane was already making a note.

'Are you ready to see the spirals now?' Eva asked Ellen.

To her surprise, Ellen answered in a low voice. 'Yes.'

Eva moved to one side so that her body no longer obscured the spirals from Ellen's view. She sat down, picked up her notebook and pen, and waited.

Ellen sat and looked at the spirals with what seemed to be almost a beatific glow on her face. Jane and Eva stared wonderingly at her. Her mouth started to move slightly, but no sounds came at first. Gradually, Eva was able to pick out some sounds. This, in addition to her lip-reading skills, allowed her to make out enough to start writing.

'Adam.' That was certainly one of the words. 'Sound.' 'Light.' Yes, she was more certain this time. She could be nearly completely sure that Ellen was saying, 'Sound of light.'

But there was more.

'Veil.' 'Behind.' No, she had got those the wrong way round. Ellen was saying 'Behind a veil', or was it 'Behind the veil'? She was not sure.

Eva thought how fortunate it was that Ellen was repeating the things she was saying, and repeating them a number of times, almost as if she were devising a mantra.

'Sound of light', or was it 'Song of light'? Eva recorded both versions. Was it 'behind' or 'beyond'? Eva could not be certain, and again she recorded both.

She glanced across to Jane, who was watching Ellen's hands intently. Eva returned to her own observations. It was good to see that there were no signs at all of the strain Ellen had manifested on previous occasions. Instead, it was as if her whole being was emitting a radiance which manifested visually as a soft, almost imperceptible glow, and it seemed to Eva as if Ellen were bathed in a gentle, warm light.

She realised that she had lost all track of time. She knew that time was not important, except in that there was no pressure at all. How sensible it had been for them to meet at her house, so freeing Ellen to be able to stay the whole weekend. Ellen seemed to be speaking other words, but she could not make them out. Eva kept trying her best, but the most she could do was to try to work out how many of them there were. She watched Ellen without looking at her notebook, and made marks at different places on a clean page to denote different words and the frequency in which they came.

At length, Ellen became completely still, with her hands together in her lap, and her head bowed.

'I think I'll get another sheet and put it over the spirals,' whispered Eva to Jane.

She moved carefully over to the cupboard, selected another white sheet, and with Jane's help, covered them in a way which least disturbed them.

Eva and Jane waited quietly until Ellen started to stir. She lifted up her hands and rubbed her eyes.

'But I thought I was standing outside the door,' she said. 'And where are the spirals? There's just a sheet on the floor.'

She looked from Eva to Jane and back again.

'Oh,' she said, 'have I...?'

'Yes,' replied Eva gently. 'Jane and I have been making notes again, and we can go through it all with you when you're ready.'

'There's no rush,' added Jane.

'I'd like to know now,' said Ellen. And then, with surprise, 'I don't feel cold this time; not at all. This is quite different. And I don't feel shocked like I did before. Yes, let's go through it all now. But first, tell me why the spirals aren't here on the floor. Have you put them away?'

'No,' replied Eva, 'we've just covered them over with another sheet.'

'What a good idea. It'll be easy to return to them if we want to.'

Eva and Jane explained to Ellen how, when they had gone to get her from outside the front door, she had been in a trance-like state. They explained how they had brought her in, and had been making notes as before. They went through Jane's notes first.

'I watched your hands very carefully all the time, because of what I had observed last time,' Jane told her. 'This time, you positioned your hands in the same way, but they were largely still. There was a short period at the beginning when they seemed to vibrate, but after that I saw nothing unusual. I just heard a very low humming sound.'

Eva looked surprised. 'I didn't hear anything.'

'No, I don't expect you did,' answered Jane. 'I have an unusual capacity to hear low sounds. About three years ago I had a serious ear infection, and I was worried in case it had damaged my hearing. In fact I became rather obsessed with the idea,' she admitted. 'It was then I decided the best thing was to get it tested. The audiologist was very reassuring, explaining that it was not uncommon for people to have such anxieties. He gave me a completely clean bill of health for my ears. In fact he said I was very lucky to be able to hear very low notes. I was surprised. I'd always been used to my own hearing, and didn't realise that others don't hear in quite the same way.'

'How long did that low hum last?' asked Ellen.

'I could hear it most of the time you were sitting looking at the spirals,' answered Jane. 'The only other thing I noted is how you looked so well this time, almost radiant in fact.'

'Yes, I noted that too,' added Eva. 'Apart from the beginning, when you looked a little pale, you looked very well. When I held your hand your skin was warm. I agree with Jane's observation of radiance. In fact I would say that I felt almost bathed in a kind of warmth that seemed to radiate from you as you watched the spirals.'

'Now Eva, tell me, did I say anything this time?' asked Ellen.

'Yes, and I'm a bit more confident about having picked up what you were saying. You were mouthing as before, and there was sound, but it was very quiet.'

Eva read out the words and phrases she had noted. She then went on to explain how she had observed other words, five in total, three of which predominated. 'I think that one of them was either "grief", "grieve" or "grieves",' she said.

'If it was "grieves",' said Jane suddenly, 'it might have been the name Greaves.'

'You're right,' agreed Eva. 'I hadn't thought of that.'

Ellen suddenly said, very determinedly, 'I feel sure that it was the name Greaves.'

'What makes you say that?' asked Eva, startled.

'It just came into my head,' answered Ellen. 'I seemed to see the name written in my mind.'

At first Adam could not understand why he seemed to be lying on his side, looking at a pair of feet.

'Any longer and I'd have had to phone a doctor.' He heard Matthew's voice, trying to sound cheerful, but failing. 'Good job I'm a trained first-aider. No, don't try to get up yet, just lie there for a minute; then I'll give you a hand to get up slowly. We don't want you keeling over again.'

Adam was thankful not to have to move yet.

When he was safely back in his chair, Matthew asked him if he could remember anything.

'We'd finished our game of chess.'

'Yes, that's right.'

'Then I was just sitting eating nuts you had handed over to me, thinking how nice it was in front of the fire. I suppose I must have dozed off. Then I woke up on the floor.'

'That's some of it,' said Matthew. 'I'd better fill you in. Earlier on you asked me to remind you to tell me about Professor Barnes once we'd finished our game of chess. I'd just said something to remind you, and you seemed a bit disturbed. You said that something odd was happening. The last thing you said before you passed out was that you thought you were seeing something that wasn't there!'

Adam stared at him, looking stunned. 'You certainly reminded me about Professor Barnes, but I don't remember anything after that. Are you sure you heard me speak?'

'Yes, and I'm quite sure of what you said.'

'My vision does seem a bit odd at the moment,' mused Adam.

'Is it blurry?' asked Matthew.

'No, it's as if there's a multitude of pinpricks just in front of everything.'

He stopped for a bit before going on. 'Remember what I was telling you about my meeting with Ellen at the Bull? She told me about how she was seeing pinprick designs after looking at some of the blank pages in her red book.'

'Yes, I remember you said that. If I'd read it in a book, I don't think I would've believed it; but because it's you, and someone who's important to you, I'll try.'

'It's beginning to fade now.'

'I'm glad about that,' muttered Matthew. 'Do you think we can have a chat about Professor Barnes now? I want to know what you thought of him.'

Adam told Matthew of his visit to Professor Barnes' house, and how disappointed he had been when the rest of the talks were cancelled because the professor had been called away abroad.

'But I've recently received an e-mail from his address to let me know that there are more talks after Easter. I won't be able to go to the first ones because I'll be away staying with Boris, but I think I'll be back in time for the last two or three at least. The e-mail didn't give precise dates. I've to let them know by the end of next month.'

'Let me know what you decide. As you know, I was impressed by the guy. I like his manner too; he never talks down to anyone, and always takes what anyone says seriously.'

'That's right. And his house is an amazing place to visit. The rest of the gathering were friendly people I thought; but I was surprised to see that all of them were men.'

'Funny that,' replied Matthew. 'It was like that the time I was there too. Probably just a coincidence.'

'Maybe so and maybe not,' was Adam's response.

'Look, mate,' said Matthew, 'I've got a suggestion.'

'What's that?' asked Adam.

'I'm worried about leaving you on your own after you passed out like that. Tomorrow's Sunday. I don't have to work until Monday, when I have to drive off early to another far-flung place.' He groaned at the thought. 'How about you coming over to my place to stay, or I could stay here if you prefer?'

'That's really good of you to offer. I think I feel okay now, but I'd like you to stay. The bed in the spare room is made up, although I have papers spread all over it. I can easily move them. I have spare pyjamas, and you are a similar size to me. I'll just go and get them.'

He got out of his chair, eager to get things arranged, but quickly sat down again. 'I feel a bit sick. Do you mind if we sit here a bit longer?'

'That's exactly why I was worried about leaving you on your own. We can sit as long as you like, and then take things slowly.'

When Adam woke the next morning, he knew he had slept well.

He looked at the clock and saw it was nearly midday. He could hear a cheerful whistling sound, and realised he could also smell burnt toast. He got up to the bathroom and heard Matthew call out.

'How're things this morning?'

'I feel fine, thanks. I slept very well.'

Later, eating some fresh toast, Adam asked Matthew about his plans for the rest of the day. This was a conversation which led to their deciding to enjoy a walk together before Matthew had to go home to get himself ready for the early start the following day. His last words before they parted had been to remind Adam to leave a message on his call-minder when any news came from the publisher.

The evening saw Adam, much refreshed, settling down once more in his conservatory to work on the few remaining manuscripts. He wanted to get these completed and sent across to Boris, as it was now nearly February, and the start of his next assignment from his former employers.

After discussing what had happened to Ellen as far as they could, her friends had decided to leave the spiral arrangement on the floor of Eva's living room, still covered by the extra sheet. They had agreed that they would decide in the morning if they were going to take the study of the spirals any further this time. It was fortunate that Eva had arranged them on an area of the floor that was not needed for the sofa bed.

The night had passed uneventfully, and the three were again gathered in Eva's living room, having enjoyed a light breakfast.

'I listened to some music on the radio this morning while I was waiting for you two to appear,' said Eva.

'What was it?' asked Ellen.

'I didn't catch what the announcer said, and it wasn't anything that I recognised. I can look it up in the *Radio Times* later.'

'I was thinking when I was lying awake,' Jane began, 'that one of the things I'd like to do now is to try to broaden the subject of the spirals a bit.'

'What have you got in mind?' asked Eva interestedly.

'I don't know why it hasn't occurred to me before, but there are a number of spiral forms which occur in nature. Up until now we've concentrated entirely on the spirals in my diary, which we've assumed I wrote while either asleep, or barely conscious. Since I did that after reading the beginning of Frances Ianson's book, we've only studied the spirals in relation to that book. Of course, the book reveals how when the son feels a sense of connection, he is freed to become very creative; and part of that is expressed in the spiral forms he uses when growing plants in the garden. However, we have no further detail about that. We may be right in assuming a connection between that and the spirals I drew; although by the time I drew them, I hadn't reached the part of the book where the son is growing vegetables and other plants; and there's nothing in the synopsis which refers to spiral forms, so I had no prior knowledge of it.'

'Good thinking,' said Eva encouragingly.

Jane continued. 'While I was lying awake, I mentally listed a number of spiral forms. Can I go through these with you both, and perhaps you can add to the list?'

'I'll be in charge of writing them down.' Ellen picked up her notebook and pencil.

Jane began. 'I remember going to an exhibition of Aboriginal art, and I'm sure there were some spiral forms there. I remember too that a friend of mine told me that from the air, Spinifex grass appears as spirals consisting of dots; and that Aborigines, who have never seen the grass from a plane, depict these forms quite clearly in their art.'

'That's fascinating,' breathed Eva. 'Can you tell us any more about it?'

'I'm afraid not; that's all I know about that subject. But there are obviously other groups who use spiral forms. I remember noticing a book in a second-hand bookshop once, which had a spiral form on the front cover. As far as I can remember, the book was the story of an African woman from a particular tribe. Part of it was a description of her relationship with her mother. I remember this spiral on the cover had words following the path of the spiral. They were inside it, going round and round.'

'Do you have the details of that book?' asked Ellen, as she wrote.

'Again, that's all I can say. I wish now that I'd made a note of it. Finally, there's something on my list that I read quite recently, some months after the spirals appeared in my diary. It was something I might not have taken particular interest in, had it not been for my own spirals.'

'What's that?' asked Eva, eagerly.

'I'd picked up a book in the library about the life of a transplant surgeon. There's a chapter where he refers to a number of developments in the understanding of anatomy. I learned that it was a Spanish GP, who was interested in the anatomy of the heart, who first discovered that the muscle fibres form a spiral; and that this explains why the heart, when it contracts, displays a twisting movement.'

'Amazing!' said Ellen and Eva together.

'All of these examples give considerable food for thought,' mused Ellen, as she finished writing down the final details. 'I haven't got anything of my own to contribute. How about you Eva?'

'I think I've one, but I'll check it. It's a seed pod.' She stood up and went over to a large set of shelves laden with books. She selected one, and searched its pages. 'Yes, here it is, "*Medicago lupulina* – black medick: seed pod coiled in almost one complete turn",' she read.

'I don't know where all this takes us,' Ellen commented, 'but it certainly opens things out. I wonder how many more examples we'll come across, now that we have a reason for noticing them?'

'I'm certainly going to keep a note of anything from now on,' said Jane. 'Are both of you willing to do the same?'

Ellen and Eva readily agreed.

'Because I've had an intense reaction to the spirals so far, we've concentrated almost exclusively on that,' Ellen went on. 'We've had no time yet to study the intricate strokes that make up each spiral, or indeed to study the direction in which each spiral is formed. And there's that amazing double spiral too.'

'I do look at the spirals sometimes at home,' said Jane quietly. 'I usually become quickly immersed in the strokes that make them up. I have a belief that there's a language embodied in them somehow; but I've no proof of that, nor indeed any way of understanding it if it is. I haven't laid out the enlargements. I look at them individually, or look at the pages in my diary.'

'I think it might be best if I don't look at the spirals again myself on this occasion,' Ellen decided. 'Shall I continue to take notes while you and Eva look at them together? I could turn my chair round, so that I don't catch sight of them.'

Having agreed on this as a sensible idea, Ellen moved her chair, Jane and Eva carefully removed the sheet that Eva had spread over the spirals the night before, and then laid it to one side.

Jane addressed Eva. 'I feel quite emotional about seeing them laid out as indicated by the diagram. I'm glad that you're able to do it with such precision. As I said earlier, when I'm at home, I sometimes look at them in my diary, and sometimes I look at the enlargements individually. Although the strokes that make up the spirals are less well defined in the enlargement, they're still clear enough.'

'Yes, I see,' answered Eva, who was looking at the layout and then glancing at some of the spirals in the diary. 'It's good to have access to both versions, though. Would you mind if I copy the pages of your diary? What I'd like to do is to keep a full copy of the enlarged spirals here, together with a copy of the spirals from your diary.'

'Is there somewhere locally with a photocopier?' asked Jane.

'Yes, the local supermarket has one. We could walk along to it before lunch, if you don't mind. I'd also like to take photographs of the pages in your diary.'

'I'll walk along to the shop with both of you, but I won't take any copies home with me,' said Ellen after some thought. ' I think it's best if my exposure to the spirals is only when both of you are present, for the time being at any rate. But we still haven't talked about your stick, Eva. Can we spend some time on that before we go?'

'The shop is open until five every Sunday, so we've plenty of time,' said Eva. 'We can certainly talk about my stick, but I don't know what else to say about it.'

Ellen picked it up from where she had placed it in the corner of the room when she brought it downstairs from Eva's bedroom.

'After you'd first looked at the spirals at Jane's house, you said you'd been affected by them in a way that was similar to the effect of the drink you'd had before you chose this stick.'

'That's a point. So the drink had helped me to choose this stick?' said Eva. 'I suppose it's possible, but there doesn't have to be that link. After all, it's a very nice stick. Both of you have admired it. Even if I had not had the drink, I might still have chosen this one. But I'll bear this in mind. I do remember I had no interest in any of the other sticks, and that's a bit unusual. I'm normally a person who looks carefully at each item before making a choice.'

'I suppose if we continue the line of thought which says that the drink helped you to choose the stick, then maybe the effect of the spirals is going to help you to make a right choice. You seemed pretty sure that the effect of the drink and the effect of the spirals was similar, if not the same.' Jane's contribution surprised Eva and Ellen into silence. 'And in Ellen's case,' Jane continued, 'it's possible that there's a link between the effect of her red book, and the effect of my spirals on her. There's so much we don't know or understand. Much of what we're saying is conjecture; but it could prove to be correct. And what about that carving on Eva's stick?'

She took it from Ellen and peered closely at the carving.

'It does seem to depict two people discussing something. What does that mean? Is it a generalised symbol? Or is it specific to something?'

'I wish now that I'd examined all the other sticks,' said Eva with a hint of frustration. 'I don't know if any of the others had carving. If they did, I don't know if they'd be similar or different.'

'Shall we take it for an outing to the supermarket?' asked Ellen, trying to lighten Eva's mood.

She was unsuccessful, as Eva suddenly appeared panic-stricken.

'*No*. No. Definitely not!' she gasped.

'I'm so sorry; I shouldn't have suggested it. It was insensitive of me after you'd told me how anxious you are about its safety.' Ellen hurriedly tried to calm her friend.

'I'll take it back up to your bedroom before we go out.'

'I'm sorry,' said Eva, miserably. 'That's the first time I've had a bout of panic about it. It took me completely by surprise. Yes, please take it upstairs, and let's go out.'

The outing to the supermarket was brief, but was a welcome

break. Lunch followed immediately. Ellen offered to drive Jane to catch the five o'clock bus, as she needed to leave about that time herself. This meant they had a little time left, and were able to use some of it to go over all they had covered since Friday evening.

'I don't know when we should fix to meet again,' said Eva. 'I'll be seeing Hannah and her father on February 3rd.'

'That's quite soon,' Ellen remarked. 'I don't know when I might hear from Adam again. It all depends on when he gets a publisher to take a serious interest in his projects.'

'I think the three of us should keep in contact by phone,' said Jane. 'I don't know when I'll have more news of Emily. Apart from that, this weekend has been packed with so much, that I for one need a lot of time to turn it over in my mind.'

'It's a good idea to have a definite arrangement to keep in touch by phone. I'll probably find it easier to contact you both if anything comes up, rather than feeling I should wait, and risk getting into a state again,' said Ellen, smiling ruefully.

'As far as I'm concerned, I think meeting at my house has worked well, and I'm happy for us to use it as a base next time. What do you both think?' asked Eva.

'It has worked well for me, because it has meant that I don't have so far to travel, and there's more time. I think that really helped this weekend,' replied Ellen. 'How has it been for you, Jane?'

'The journey here is fine for me, and I agree that it's been good to have the extra time; but do remember that my home is open to you both at any time. I'd better start getting my things together now, so that I'm ready for when you leave, Ellen. It's good of you to give me a lift to the bus station. It means I don't have to use the local bus to get to it. The Sunday service is rather sparse.'

Chapter Twenty-three

Monday morning dawned. Although the curtains were drawn, Ellen was surprised to see so much light creeping round them. When she pulled them back, she immediately saw why. It had snowed; and it was quite deep. Her journey back yesterday had been straightforward. Thank goodness it had come after her return. It had been forecast for later in the week, but had very obviously arrived early. She did not like to drive in snow. She did not like to drive even when there was only a little snow. Normally she would have braced herself, and forced herself out of the door to clear the car, in preparation for driving off to the first destination of the day.

Today was different. Almost without thinking, she picked up her diary and opened it at the front, where there was a long list of contact phone numbers. She lifted the phone and keyed in a number.

'Hello, Gladys. This is Ellen speaking. Sorry to phone you at home, but I wanted to catch you straight away. The snow is really bad here, and I don't want to risk it. I'm sorry about that. I'm at home, so if you want to phone to check on anything, please do.'

'Thanks for phoning, Ellen, I'll phone round the others. Maybe we can postpone this morning's meeting. Most of the items on the agenda are not urgent. I'll get back to you later, and let you know what has been decided. Can you give me a few times that might suit you in a couple of weeks?'

Ellen consulted her diary, and suggested alternative dates.

'Thanks, Gladys, I'll hear from you then,' she finished.

She lay down on her bed again. Although the room was cold, her thick winter-weight dressing gown kept her warm enough. She had surprised herself, and needed to think. How on earth she had managed to phone to say that she would not make it to the meeting she did not know. Gladys' response had been immediately supportive and helpful. Her sensible suggestion of postponing the meeting was one which would, until now, have been likely to result in Ellen's insisting on trying to make her way there this morning after all; but she had felt no urge to protest – none at all. Thinking about what had just happened, she felt staggered at the change in her behaviour.

Gradually, an idea formed in her mind. I'll get up and lay a fire in the library, she thought. Then I'll light it, take my breakfast in there, and just sit and think.

Breakfast was finished and the fire was burning brightly. Ellen knew that she had made exactly the right decision. This is where she needed to be. She sat and reflected on the relentless lifestyle she had pursued in recent years. The more she reflected, the more she knew that it would have to change. She was glad that she had been able to contribute to helping people less fortunate than herself, people who had no home and little food, people who were uncertain about a future outside prison or hospital; but now she needed some time to reassess her own position. She realised that she had been behaving in a driven way, moving from meeting to meeting, from project to project. She knew that the quality of what she had contributed was adequate, and could even admit to herself that it had been good. But now she realised that she had done this by denying that she needed something too. Her scrupulous honesty told her that she had clung to this driven pattern in order to numb the unbearable feelings of the loss she had suffered when her father died.

'But I can't go on like this.' She startled herself as she heard herself speak this out in clear, firm tones.

She thought about how distressed she had been on Saturday at Eva's house, when she was about to tell her friends about the evening she had spent with Adam. Again, her scrupulous honesty made her face that one of the things that had affected her so much about seeing him again was the fact that he had dreamed about her in the way that he had. However, there had not been the slightest suggestion of his making any inappropriate assumptions from that; and he had tried his best to make amends for telling her about the dream when they hardly knew each other. Overall, she was glad that he knew about her red book; but she felt anxious about the way she had told him, feeling that too much had been revealed too soon.

Then her honesty prevailed once more, and she knew that at root she felt comfortable with this man, and wanted to have the opportunity of developing a friendship with him. She also knew that she had a lot of very difficult feelings she would have to face along the way if she continued her contact with him. In truth, none of these feelings could be attributed to anything he had done or said.

However, such problems were not necessarily only hers, she reflected, as she remembered how he himself had hesitated in their conversation, and had appeared distinctly discomfited. She felt a little better about herself as she remembered this.

'But I must not dwell on that at the moment.' Again she spoke out loud and startled herself. 'I must look at my own situation. Something has to change. My contact with Eva and Jane was intended to be about the spirals, but now I can see many other things coming into the picture. Apart from the stick, there's Hannah and her father, Emily, Adam Thomas, and I suspect there are other things yet to come. I feel much closer to Eva and Jane because of all this.'

She sat and watched the fire. She felt soothed and helped by the random movement of the flames, and the spitting noises, as wood and coal cracked or splintered. This fireplace was something that had been a constant in her life, and although she had no power to bring back her father or her mother, she could bring the fireplace alive. Its appearance was now just the same as it had been when they had been there.

'Silly of me not to have realised that before,' she said, once more startling herself. 'I've been lighting it on the cold evenings whenever I've been at home after father died, and I've never consciously realised before what it has meant to me.'

She stood up out of her chair.

'And I've never shared this fire with anyone since father died!' she exclaimed.

She was astounded when she realised this. More than seven years had passed, and the library had been hers and hers alone. She had always shown any visitor to the front sitting room, and any tradesmen to the kitchen; and she had ensured that no one stayed more than a few hours. The weekends she had spent with Jane and

Eva had begun to make her realise how very lonely she was. She spent a lot of time with people in her work. She saw and spoke to many people each day; but she was lonely, terribly lonely. She sat down again, and felt tears run down her cheeks.

I must take some time now to think of something I can do to try to change this, she thought.

Ellen slowly picked up her diary and found the pages that were headed 'Notes'. Helpfully, they were blank. She wrote:

I know that I am getting closer to Eva and Jane. We have agreed to keep in touch by phone until we meet again. I must keep in touch with them both. I made a gesture of friendship towards Adam by asking him to let me know when he has news of publishers for his projects. When he contacts me I must be sure not to behave in a way that appears distant.

Encouraged by rereading what she had written, she picked up her writing pad and wrote a short letter to both Jane and Eva, thanking them for their help over the weekend. She moved on to say that she would look out for references to spiral forms, and that she looked forward to any news of spiral forms they found. To Jane's letter, she added a sentence asking her to tell her more about the interest in the needlework she shared with her sister, Clare. She put on her boots to take these letters to the postbox straight away. She put the guard round the fire, and was soon trudging awkwardly down the pavement.

Ellen lived at the end of a long terrace of Victorian houses. There were many rooms in her house, most of which were quite spacious, and the ceilings were high. The height of the ceiling meant the library had the capacity to hold a very large number of books. As she returned home, her errand accomplished, she suddenly became very sure that the next step she must take was to work out how to invite someone round to sit and enjoy the library with her. This was entirely logical and sensible, but the challenge immediately filled her with feelings of dread. How could she possibly do that? Steadying herself with a firm statement that these feelings were to do with her past and not her present situation, she sat down with the 'Notes' section of her diary open once more. She was relieved to find that she felt connected to a feeling of companionship with Eva and Jane as she strove to make a list. The lists made in Eva's house came back into her mind, and seemed somehow to spur her on to try to make this next list. She wrote a heading which was in the form of a question to herself.

Whom to invite to share the fire in my library? (And how to go about it.)

She was surprised and pleased to find that an idea came into her mind almost immediately. As she had written the heading, she had felt anxious that she would not be able to think of anything. But already she had an image of a group of people meeting in her library. Every week, perhaps? No, it would be best to start with a more modest plan. How about each month? Yes, that felt better. The next thing would be to decide what interests would bring such people and herself together. If Jane lived locally, perhaps she could have suggested that a needlework group might come. But Jane did not live locally, and needlework was not something that Ellen knew anything about so far. Music?

No! She flinched. Not yet… not music… no… I can't… I can't. She took some deep breaths and steadied herself.

Books. That sounded all right. Perhaps I can find an antiquarian book society. I don't suppose there'd be a local group, but there may be one not too far away. I'll make some enquiries… She brightened. Although most of the books here are probably not old enough to interest them, I do have a number which would. There are certainly some very old ones amongst my grandfather's collection, and some of these my father never got round to cataloguing.

She hesitated. Then she took another deep breath. If I find such a group, and if they are people I like and can trust, I'll show them my mother's collection of first editions, she decided.

Ellen's mother had made a small collection of nineteenth-century first editions, which Ellen kept in a glass-fronted cabinet that formed part of the library.

Ellen felt the better for having made these challenging decisions, and she promised herself she would spend time in the afternoon looking in the Yellow Pages for antiquarian bookshops, with a view to finding a group of antiquarian book-lovers.

When she returned to work the next day, she would put her

mind to the task of devising ways to reduce her commitments gradually, to a level where she had more time to herself while she continued to reassess her life.

Chapter Twenty-four

Adam had completed the revision of the manuscripts of the Romanian songs; and his mind was very much on his work assignment for February. He must complete this by the end of the month; not only because the project demanded it, but also because he wanted to have the first two weeks of March completely free to prepare for his return to Russia to be with Boris.

He went to pick up the pile of mail from behind the front door. The 'junk' mail was easy to deal with. He did not bother to open it, and put it straight in the bin. That left two bills and a letter. The postmark of the letter was blurred, giving no clue to its origin. He opened it with the paperknife, and immediately saw the heading 'Carillon Music'. He read on.

> *Dear Mr Thomas,*
>
> *Further to our meeting, I have consulted our co-director. We are both very interested in your work and would like to take this matter further. As you know, we are a relatively small firm. Our schedule is full for the next few months. We hope, however, that you would be willing to wait until we have time to attend to your project.*
>
> *We would like to offer you a provisional date of May 28th for a further meeting. Please will you let me know if you wish to take up this offer. If you are in agreement, it would be helpful if you would complete your revision of the manuscripts by that date, and bring them with you.*
>
> *Yours sincerely,*
>
> *Gordon Quaver*

Adam felt a lurch of excitement. There was no mention of the Russian songs; but if the Romanian project was successful, then Carillon Music might be willing to consider them. May 28th – that was ideal for him. He would not be long back from Russia, but would have had time to collect himself. He and Boris would have the opportunity to discuss the whole matter while he was out there. All he had to do at the moment was to e-mail Boris about the letter. He set about doing that straight away. When he heard back from him, he would reply to Gordon Quaver.

He rubbed his hands together. He realised what a good thing it had been that he had worked on the revision of the manuscripts straight away, and that that was completed. A thought struck him: I must let Matthew know; he'll be interested.

He went to the phone and was soon speaking to Matthew's call-minder.

And now, back to the papers for February's task, he told himself.

Many hours later, Adam decided to take a break.

There's a lot to go through in these files, I must keep at it, he said to himself determinedly. I think I should sketch out a timetable for the month. There are the visits I have to make which are already fixed, and I must organise myself around these. This week I have a lot of background reading to get through.

Eating his supper while reading the paper in the evening, Adam was satisfied with his progress through the day. He felt tired but content.

'If I keep to my schedule as I've managed to do today, I'll be fine,' he murmured.

It was not long after that he began to feel a little uneasy, and became convinced that he had forgotten to include something important. He checked his schedule. There was nothing that worried him there. What could it be? He turned the radio on and smiled as he heard the announcer introducing a Bartok quartet. It was then that it struck him.

'Adam Thomas, you fool!'

He banged his fist on his knee with a force which he instantly regretted.

'Ellen asked you to let her know when there was news from the publishers. I *must* write to her…' he said aloud.

Staggered that he could have temporarily forgotten something that was so important to him, he decided to write immediately. After a sentence to say how pleased he had been to see her again, he copied down the content of the letter from Gordon Quaver. Next, he decided to give her the date of his flight out to St Petersburg, and to say that he hoped to be back by May 21st at the latest. Then he thought for a while, sucking the end of his pen in an absent-minded way. He finished off by saying that he would be glad to hear from her, as he would like to know how she was, and he asked about any plans she had at the moment.

He reread the letter, and, satisfied with what he had written, put it in an envelope, and left it in a place where he could not avoid seeing it in the morning. Checking his e-mails, he found one from Boris. It was very short, and was written in a way totally uncharacteristic of his friend.

<HOORAY! YES. B>

Adam picked up his pen once more and wrote to Carillon Music, confirming that he would be attending the meeting, and would bring the completed manuscripts. After this, he returned to his computer. Now that he was more certain of his movements, he could respond to Professor Barnes' e-mail. He wrote thanking him for getting in touch, and saying that unfortunately he would be out of the country until May 21st, but would be keen to attend any talks that were still to take place after that date. He sincerely hoped that there would be at least two in the series that he could attend, but there was always the possibility that the talks would have finished, or that the place would be given to someone who could attend the whole series.

He sent the message off, and was curious to see the contents of another message from Boris which appeared in the in-box. Clicking on the envelope, he opened it to discover that his friend had had an idea that excited him.

<Dear Friend,

I have been thinking. I could arrange to travel to the UK with you on 20th May when you return, and stay for two weeks. We could go to the meeting at Carillon Music together. We could take with us some of the manuscripts of the Russian songs at the same time.

What do you think?

Boris>

Adam keyed in a quick reply.

<Excellent plan. You will stay here with me of course.>

He sent it off, but his mind rushed on. Perhaps they could go together to a talk by Professor Barnes? Unlikely, but it was a good thing to hope for.

Chapter Twenty-five

Eva had been looking forward to seeing Hannah and her father again. Not only was she interested to see how they were, but also she liked them, and respected their honesty and dignity in their difficult situation. She knew that the meeting might throw up unforeseen difficulties for her, but she was more than willing to face whatever emerged.

As before, they arrived a few minutes early, and she opened the door in welcome. Mr Greaves carried his daughter from the car, but when they came through the door, Hannah patted his arm and looked meaningfully into his face.

'Are you sure?' he asked.

Hannah nodded. Mr Greaves gently lowered Hannah, and Eva watched as she stretched out her feet towards the floor. Mr Greaves stood behind her with one arm under each of Hannah's to support and steady her. Hannah braced herself and took not only one but two steps, before falling on to the chair that Eva had put out for her. Throughout, Mr Greaves had helped her, so that her fall did not harm her in any way. Her pale face had flushed momentarily, before it returned to the colour which Eva had been used to.

'That was very good,' said Eva matter-of-factly, with a carefully placed tinge of warm encouragement. 'Thank you for wanting to show me.'

She turned to Mr Greaves.

'It's good to see you both again.' And then, quite directly, 'How are things now?'

Mr Greaves turned to Hannah, who nodded her head and smiled fleetingly. 'Hannah and I have talked a lot about her mummy since we last saw you. We've agreed that I'll tell you a bit about how she disappeared, and what happened after that.'

'Thank you,' Eva replied. 'I'd like to hear about that.'

'You'll remember how I told you that after Dawn died my wife was distraught, but after that she soon entered a detached – almost mechanical – state. She did everything that was required of her, and to those who didn't know her well, she appeared a normal, loving person. However, it was clear to me that she was just acting this "normal" behaviour. I lived alongside her as best I could.

'Soon after Hannah started school, my wife disappeared. She left a note on the kitchen table. It said: "I have to go. Don't try to follow or find me."'

'From that time on, Hannah found eating a trial. She had never found it very easy at the best of times, unless I fed her with a spoon. I was not always there, and I knew that her mother was uncomfortable about my feeding Hannah in this way. After she disappeared, everything got even more difficult. Hannah hadn't been at school long, and the staff had never seen her mother, as it was always I who took her and collected her. Hannah could not bear my telling the staff that her mummy had gone away. When asked about her, I'd have some story ready about how she was away helping a sick relative. For a long time, Hannah believed that she would be coming back soon.'

'I can understand that,' Eva said encouragingly.

Mr Greaves continued. 'She had always been a slender child, and no one commented on this. We managed somehow between ourselves to cope for about two years. After that, Hannah was terribly pale, and her growth in height made her look as if she'd been stretched. She slept more and more, and she started to miss a lot of schooling. After about six months, we had to see doctors because the education department required it, and, frankly, I was very worried myself. Hannah insisted that I should not talk to anyone about the note her mummy had left, and that I should always talk about her being away helping someone. I went along with this, because that's what I wanted to do as well. I couldn't face doing anything else.'

'I can perfectly see how that happened,' said Eva helpfully.

'Because I'm a nurse, I was able to convince the hospital and the education department that I was able to look after Hannah. Everyone could see what a close, trusting relationship we had. A formal diagnosis of myalgic encephalitis – or M. E. – was made at some stage. I felt relieved by this, knowing that I then had something to say to people, without having to talk about my wife, and without Hannah having to go through the trauma of talking about her mother. If Hannah had had to do that, she would have been facing the fact that she had not contacted us, and showed no signs of coming back. You already know how I eventually started my own business, so that I could work from home and be there to look after Hannah.'

Eva waited. She sensed that Mr Greaves had not finished. She saw him hesitating, apparently trying to formulate what he was going to say next. But it was Hannah who spoke.

'We've decided to find out where she is, haven't we Daddy?'

Mr Greaves faltered and swallowed.

'Yes, we have.' He turned to Eva and said, 'We both know how difficult it may prove to get information about where she is, and what has happened to her. She may have gone abroad, for example.'

He stopped, and added in a low voice, 'She may be ill, or even dead.'

There was a pause, after which his voice was stronger and more decisive. 'But we want to know, Hannah and I. We want to know.'

Here Hannah took over. 'If we find Mummy, she may not be able to recognise us.'

Eva knew then that Hannah and her father had not tried to deny any of the quite real possibilities.

'I wish you well in your search,' she said.

Mr Greaves and Hannah looked at each other again.

'We want to ask if we can come back and tell you how we're getting on with our search,' Mr Greaves said earnestly. 'Would that be possible?'

Eva felt tears spring into her eyes, and she replied, 'That's what I'd like, but I didn't feel in a position to ask.'

'Could we make a time to come in about two to three months?' Mr Greaves asked as he took out his diary.

'How about towards the end of April?' suggested Eva. 'Could you come on the 21st?'

Mr Greaves carefully wrote the date in his diary.

'Thank you for seeing us again today,' he said.

'I have something for Hannah in the kitchen. Can I just go and get it before you go?' Eva asked.

She had in the kitchen some very small bottles of apple juice that she had seen in a shop the previous week. She had bought them, not sure that the circumstances would be right for her to give them to Hannah. Now she felt quite certain that it was the right time. She put them in a small but strong carrier bag, and brought them into the living room.

'Here you are. When I saw these, I thought of you. Perhaps they might come in handy.' And she left it at that.

Hannah peeped inside the bag, shut her eyes tightly, and then looked again. 'Thank you,' she said.

'Shall I carry them out to the car for you?' asked Eva.

Hannah nodded. Mr Greaves helped her to the car rather than carrying her. She needed a lot of help, but it was obvious that she wanted to try.

This time Eva stood beside the car while Mr Greaves started the engine. 'Bye,' she said to Hannah, through the window.

She was sure that she could see the little white hand waving as the car disappeared out of view.

Chapter Twenty-six

Adam worked to his timetable throughout February, completed his report on time, and posted it off. Now he was able to concentrate entirely on preparing for his flight, which he had booked for March 15th. There were always a number of things to see to when he was going to be away for a relatively long period. At least there was no worry about frozen pipes at this time of year. He liked to clean the house before he went, and leave everything tidy. He paid outstanding bills, and left instructions at the bank about any that were to be presented while he was away. He cancelled the newspapers well in advance, picking up a paper each day until he left. Any mail delivered while he was away would be well out of sight. The outer front door had only a very small window in it. It was oval, made of stained glass, and was quite high up in the door. No one could see through it. However, as usual, he arranged with the neighbour, who kept a spare key, that he would check the house at least twice each week. He arranged for a taxi to collect him in plenty of time to take him to the train to the airport. He had a sense of eager anticipation as he looked forward to seeing Boris again.

Three days before he left, he received a letter from Ellen. Although absorbed in his preparations, he was delighted when he saw the now familiar handwriting on an envelope behind his door. She thanked him for his note, and wished him a safe journey. She said she hoped his meeting on May 21st would be fruitful. The next lines were about herself. She had been reorganising her life a little, and had decided to open her home to a meeting of an antiquarian book society. At first he was surprised; but then he remembered how she had referred to a collection of books that had been her grandfather's. There was the red book too, of course. Perhaps she had a number of other books that she had not mentioned when they met in the Bull, or perhaps she was interested in antiquarian books but did not have any. The meeting was to take place while he was away. She went on to say that if all went well, she hoped it would become a monthly event in her life.

On an impulse, he slipped the letter into a file of papers that he had in his travel bag. He wanted to be able to look at it again while he was away, and maybe he would show it to Boris. There was quite a lot to tell Boris about Ellen when they saw each other. He could talk to him about it one evening. He looked forward to their daily routine of working on the tapes together, walking in the afternoon, working again, and then cooking and eating later in the evening. Late in the evening would be an ideal time to talk about Ellen.

Adam realised he had mixed feelings about hearing the special tape again, the one Boris had carefully placed on the top shelf by the delicate glassware. It had now been nearly six months since he had heard it. It had affected him very profoundly at the time. Would it affect him in the same way when he heard it again? On one hand he was eager to hear it again, but on the other, he felt a sense of caution bordering on anxiety. And there had been Boris' dream too. Adam had almost forgotten about that. What exactly had Boris written in his e-mail about that dream? Adam was glad that he had saved the e-mails he had exchanged with Boris since his last visit. He decided to find his account of the dream and take a copy of it in his bag, in the file where he had put Ellen's letter.

As he searched for the e-mail, he began to remember that Boris had that dream on the same night as he himself had dreamed about Ellen, and that he had sent an account of it to Boris. Yes, now he remembered: Boris' e-mail about his dream had come down when he sent his own e-mail off to him of his dream about Ellen. He decided to make a copy of both e-mails, and put them in the file in his travel bag. It did not take him long to locate them. He ran off the copies, and read through them again prior to packing.

It all came back to him… Although the dreams had been noted several hours apart, they had certainly taken place on the same night. Both dreams had involved seeing intense white light that had no apparent source; and it was clear that both he and Boris had been deeply affected by their respective dream experiences. Having these copies in his file would prompt him to raise this for discussion with Boris. In any case it was likely to come up when he started to talk about Ellen.

March 15th soon came round. Adam's journey, although tedious at times, passed without any problems. Boris was waiting for him at the airport as arranged, and the two men hugged each other enthusiastically as they met.

'Nine weeks here and two more in the UK!' Adam did not attempt to conceal his obvious delight at the prospect.

Boris smiled broadly. 'I booked my flights as soon as we had agreed my plan.'

'We have got a lot of ground to cover on this visit, but I relish the thought of immersing ourselves in the Russian tapes once more,' said Adam enthusiastically.

'That is exactly how I feel. It has been a long wait, but at last we can continue,' replied his friend.

'Have any more tapes arrived recently?' asked Adam.

'Yes, but not many. A few weeks can go by without any new ones arriving, then there can be two or three. There is no way of predicting when they will come, of course. I have stored them all safely.'

'Have you listened to any of them?' Adam asked.

'Of course not. That was our agreement, and I would not break my word about that.'

Boris sounded a little offended, and Adam hurried to pacify him.

'I'm sorry. I only asked that because had I been the one who was collecting and storing the tapes, I think I'd have been tempted to listen to one or two. I wouldn't, of course, but I would have been tempted,' he said honestly. 'I wonder how many we'll manage to go through this time?'

'It is difficult to estimate,' Boris replied. 'As you know, some tapes have only one or two songs on them, whereas others have several.'

'One thing's certain,' said Adam. 'This is a job that can never be rushed. We have our nine weeks here, and we'll just work through as many as we can. We can maybe do a few more when you're in the UK with me, unless of course by some miracle we've done them all by then.'

Adam loved the peaceful surroundings of Boris' home. His own house was quiet, and the conservatory was a very pleasant place to work; but the surroundings could at times produce more noise than he would have wished. Too many people had dogs, people who did not really know how to care for them. The barking of an agitated dog could be extremely irritating. Youths driving too fast for the suburban streets could also cause unwanted noise. Apart from the large vegetable garden around Boris' house, there was a vista of fields and trees stretching away into the distance. And the house was at the end of a track, so there was no passing traffic.

'Shall we have a game of chess tonight?' asked Adam, as they arrived outside Boris' house.

Boris smiled, 'I hoped you were going to suggest that, my friend,' he said, 'but if you had not, I would have. Of course we shall, and then tomorrow we shall work.'

Adam took his bag to the room he always used when he stayed here. He took out the file, and laid it on the bedside table. He paused for a moment, but decided not to open it. He returned to the living room. Boris was laying out the exceptional pieces of the chess set his grandfather had carved.

'Look,' he said, 'I brought out the chess board which goes with these pieces, you have not seen it before.'

Adam studied it with admiration.

'The decoration round the edge of this board is amazing,' he said. 'Did your grandfather make this too?'

'No, and I think you will find it hard to guess who made it. I am sorry I did not get it out last time you were here; I do not know why it did not occur to me.'

Adam made a wild guess which he was sure was not the answer.

'Your grandmother made it.'

'How on earth did you know?' Boris was clearly astonished.

Adam looked embarrassed. 'I thought from what you'd said that there was no chance I'd guess correctly, so just for something to say I thought of the person who, in my mind, was the least likely to have made it.'

'My grandmother was very impressed with the pieces her husband was carving. Every day, she would ask him to show her what he had done. One day, she told him about a plan that had been forming in her mind. At first he had been dismissive of it, but he soon became enthusiastic and encouraged her. There were times when they would sit side by side, each working at their part of the whole project. If you look underneath the board when we have finished this game, you will see her initials carved in one corner. You have to look carefully, because she made them very small.'

Adam traced his finger admiringly round the interwoven design around the edges of the board. The board was substantial, about four centimetres thick. Boris watched Adam intently as he explored the design. Then, for no apparent reason, it occurred to Adam to examine the sides of the board. He was glad he had, as he discovered further carving, the quality of which was quite outstanding. In his discovery, he completely forgot about the game he was to play with Boris, and became totally absorbed. Boris, continuing to observe his friend, said nothing. Having examined the side that was close to him, Adam worked his way round the two sides. The pattern was different on each. The side nearest to him appeared to portray a large gathering of people. The side to the right of this was a series of low buildings of a simple style. The side to the left depicted tangled undergrowth. By now, Adam was curious to see the side that faced Boris. He reached out to turn the board round so that he could see, but was surprised to find that his friend took both of his hands and said simply, 'Wait…'

Adam sat back in his chair and waited.

Boris began to speak. 'It was not by accident that I did not bring out this board when you were here before,' he said. 'There are not many people who have seen this since my grandmother's death. I value it very highly, and the only people I wish to see it are people who I feel will truly understand its significance. My grandfather was more than eighty years old when he carved the chess pieces. My grandmother went to him with her proposal of the board on the eve of the 49th anniversary of their wedding day. The board took her a nearly a year to complete, and she put the finishing touches to it on the eve of their 50th wedding anniversary. The side nearest to you depicts their wedding day, the side to the right, their first home. The side to the left symbolises the undergrowth they had to clear in order to make a living. I wanted you to know all of this before you see the fourth side.'

At this, he slowly turned the board round, so the side that had been facing him was now facing Adam.

The first thing Adam noticed was that this side was plain by comparison to the other three sides, except for a small knob in the middle with a letter on either side of it. The single letters were beautifully decorated, but there was no further design on that side. On the left was a letter 'O' and on the right was an 'A'.

'My grandmother's name was Olga and my grandfather's name was Alexei,' explained Boris.

Adam turned his attention to the small knob. He took hold of it, and pulled very gently. A shallow drawer slid out, revealing a folded piece of paper.

He looked at his friend who nodded and said, 'Yes, you may read it.'

Very carefully, he unfolded the paper. The date on it showed that it was nearly a hundred years old. Adam guessed that it was a document that confirmed the date of the marriage of Boris' grandparents. Feeling that he was witnessing something that was not really his to see, Adam refolded the paper, gently rearranged it in the drawer, and slid the drawer shut, making sure that the paper did not catch in it.

'Thank you, my friend,' he said, 'for trusting me with this. I feel honoured.'

Boris inclined his head, but said nothing for a while.

Then he said, 'I am very glad that you are here again. We will play chess many times.' He added, apparently as an afterthought, 'The glassware on the top shelf in that cupboard was theirs too.'

Two weeks had passed. Adam and Boris had quickly resumed the routine they had devised on Adam's last visit. Their work was going well; it was satisfying, and they greatly enjoyed each other's company. They said very little as they worked; but their walks, together with their shared cooking ventures and late evening relaxation, were full of discussions, jokes, reminiscences and storytelling. There was seriousness, and there was laughter.

Late one evening, Adam addressed Boris in a serious tone. 'I've been thinking that there are a couple of other things to attend to, and we should try to decide a time for these before long.'

'Yes, indeed. I have not spoken myself, because both of the things I think you have in mind are ones that affect you greatly. I thought therefore it was for you to raise them when you were ready.'

'I appreciate that. I needed time to get back into our routine; but I feel ready to think about them now.'

'Which shall we start with?' asked Boris. 'The tape, or Ellen?'

Adam was grateful that Boris had named the two subjects. He knew his friend would not have forgotten; but it was a relief to know that he had been thinking about them, and had been sensitive in waiting for him to raise them himself.

'I don't know which to choose,' he said slowly, and then added, 'but if you don't mind, I'd like to talk a bit about both of them this evening. Perhaps tomorrow evening we can come to a decision about what to do.'

'Will you say something about Ellen first then?' asked Boris.

Adam straightened himself in his chair.

'You remember that I met up with her in January? I want to tell you about that meeting. I wanted to wait until we were together before I talked it over with you. Since then, she and I have exchanged a couple of letters, and I've brought her most recent one to show you. It arrived only a few days before I left to come here. The other things I've brought with me are a copy of the e-mail I sent to you about the dream I had about her, and a copy of the e-mail you sent to me about the dream you had on the same night – the dream about the intense light round the shelf where you keep the tape.'

'Ah yes,' said Boris. 'It would be good to look at those dreams together. One of them is related to one of the subjects we want to discuss, and the other is related to the other. And the two dreams happened on the same night.'

'Going on to the subject of the tape,' Adam continued, 'we should spend some time talking over exactly what happened on the day I was so affected by it, and how I was after that. I know that you were affected by it too, and I want you to describe that to me, now that I'm more able to concentrate on it.'

'Yes, we do need to take some time with that before we decide how and when to listen to it again,' Boris agreed.

'A thought has just occurred to me,' said Adam. 'We have the option of leaving it until we're both in the UK, or at least leaving it until nearly the end of my time here. I am worried that if I'm affected so intensely by it again, it might disrupt the flow of our work. Although we're not rushing to complete the tapes, we certainly want to get as much done as we can on this visit. That way, we'll know more clearly what we might say to Carillon Music about our Russian project when we see them at the end of May.'

'I have a suggestion to make,' said Boris. 'I think the best thing might be to take some time soon to talk over what happened when we last listened to the tape. Then we may realise how we want to proceed with it. However, it is equally important that we take time to talk about your friend Ellen, and about our dreams.'

Adam became decisive. 'I think we should make a start tomorrow evening after we've eaten.'

The following evening, after another fruitful day, the two men settled themselves down for a serious discussion.

'The first thing I want to ask you, Boris, is how you felt about the whole tape episode. I know that I was in some state for quite a time after I knew that something had happened. I was able to work a little the next day, but I didn't feel right, and I think it was very wise of us not to pursue it any further on that visit.'

'To tell you the truth, Adam, I was very alarmed. I tried to appear calm throughout, because I knew you needed something ordinary around you; but it was hard for me to see you like that, especially as the tape had affected me too.'

'Can you describe that to me?'

'It is very difficult to put into words. I felt that the music reached to the depths of my soul. I have been deeply affected by music before, many times, but never to that extent. For a fragment of time, it even felt as if I had some greater knowledge about the whole universe. I did not remember what that knowledge was, but I certainly remember the feeling associated with it.'

'Of course,' said Adam, 'all this was taking place in a context where we'd been working very closely together for many weeks. Not only were we in the same room, but also we were sharing the same life, and the same purpose. And now, we're doing the same once more.'

'I think that was part of the reason why we were both affected so deeply by hearing the tape. It is my guess that if I had heard it somewhere else, and in circumstances where I was less close to the people I was with, it would still have affected me, but not to the same degree,' Boris concluded.

'I'm inclined to agree,' said Adam. 'And something else has occurred to me. I'd spoken to you about Ellen earlier in that visit. You showed a genuine interest, and I remember you ended by saying you were sure I'd be seeing her again, and that that time was not very far away. A lot has happened since then. I know that it might be purely coincidental, but the dreams we had on the same night – mine about Ellen, and yours around the shelf where the tape is kept – could mean that there's some link between the significance of Ellen in my life and the effect of the tape on me.'

'That is certainly one explanation as to why you were more affected by it that I was,' said Boris. 'But an equally possible one is that you are the one who is in a foreign country when you are staying with me, and there are many things that are different, which in turn might have led to your being more open to the effect of that tape.'

'You're right,' agreed Adam, 'but I don't want to forget what I just said. When I tell you about my meeting with Ellen in the Bull, perhaps you will see why.'

Adam went on to tell Boris everything he could remember. Boris was certainly impressed when Adam told him about Ellen's description of her red book, and how that had fitted with his memory of the book she had been reading in the dream.

'I also want to tell you how I had quite a difficult moment when I was with Ellen. It was when I was talking to her about my trips out to see you. I was suddenly nearly completely overwhelmed with feelings about Maria's death. To be honest, the only thing that saved me was the fact that I have two good friends who know a lot about my loss – yourself and Matthew.'

'Matthew?' questioned Boris.

'He's a neighbour of mine. I hope you'll meet him when you come to stay. He's away from home a lot with his work, but he might be around. He came round one evening to see the plans for the conservatory I was having built. I felt relaxed in his company, and later that evening, I found I was able to talk about Maria.'

'I am very glad to hear that.' Boris' voice was genuine and warm. 'I have been glad to be someone in whom you could confide; but I have worried a little as the years have gone by that not only do you not speak to me about her any more, but also you do not appear to talk to anyone else about her.'

The two men were silent for a while.

Then Adam said, 'Actually, I realise there's something I should tell you about Matthew's most recent visit. He came round and spent another evening with me. I showed him the completed conservatory, and then we sat together for the rest of the evening. We played some chess.' He laughed. 'Matthew can't really play chess, but we just have a bit of fun with it.'

'Do you want to tell me now or later?' asked Boris.

'I want to leave it until later. First I want you to tell me again what I was like when I went into that state when we listened to the tape together.'

'You had been working on the tape and brought it to my attention. We listened to a little of it together, and I said something about it, agreeing that it was very moving. We listened to it again. We held hands as we listened, and I felt your hand growing cold.'

Boris went through the whole experience again, bit by bit. He described how Adam's eyelids had drooped, how his lips began to move slightly, and then more obviously. He told him again how his throat began to move, as if he were singing, but no sound came.

'And you told me later in an e-mail that you thought I had said the name "Ellen",' said Adam.

Adam thought for a while, then he went on. 'Remember how I told you that it was only some time after my dream about Ellen that I became sure that I had seen something faint on the blank pages of her book?'

'Yes.'

'Well, I wondered for a while if I was inventing some construction to put on the whole thing. It nearly blew me away when Ellen told me at the Bull that she had found some of the blank pages had left faint pinprick designs in her mind.'

'As you know, I had not been certain that you had said Ellen's name, and because of that, I did not let you know until later. It helps me to hear your account of your experience of those blank pages you saw in the dream, and of Ellen's experiences with blank pages of that book of hers.'

There was another silence as the two men reflected on all that had been said.

'Could you tell me the rest again now, please?' asked Adam.

Boris went on to say how the tape had finished, and how Adam's lips had stopped moving; but that he had stayed in that cold state with his eyelids drooped for more than half an hour.

'I kept hold of your hand,' he said. 'It meant that I could feel if you were still cold, but also I did not want to startle you. When you started to come round and warm up, I stayed beside you until I was sure you knew where you were. If you remember, you were not aware that anything had happened until I told you.'

'Yes, I remember; and that brings me to the point where I think I should tell you about what happened when I was last with Matthew.'

Adam described how he had felt very relaxed.

'I think I was possibly dozing a little,' he said. 'Matthew had just reminded me that I was going to talk about Professor Barnes, when apparently I passed out. I came to on the floor.'

Boris looked worried, but said nothing.

'After I'd come round enough to get back into my chair, Matthew and I talked about it all. Matthew said that just before I passed out, I'd said I was feeling strange, and I thought I was seeing something that wasn't there. I have to say I have no memory of having said that at all. However there's no reason why Matthew would invent such a thing, so I do believe him. One thing I can remember is that my vision seemed blurry once I was back in my chair. It was like having a whole lot of pinpricks in front of my eyes. Matthew was sufficiently concerned about me that he spent the night in my spare room, for which, I admit, I was grateful.'

'Pinpricks?' said Boris. 'Do you think that was anything like the kind of thing Ellen was talking about?'

'It could have been,' replied Adam. 'I'd like to have the chance of talking to her about it. I want to ask her more about what she sees after looking at those pages of her red book. Since she describes the effect as pinpricks, I could well have been seeing something similar.'

'Can you tell me about Professor Barnes?' asked Boris. 'Who is he?'

'I hope you'll meet him when you come to stay,' said Adam. 'Sorry, I'd better start from the beginning.'

He told Boris about the leaflet he had picked up in the library – the day after he had the dream about Ellen. He told him more about the visit from Matthew that evening, and how it had emerged that Matthew had met Professor Barnes; and how he had been very encouraging about Adam's plan to try to attend the talks. He told Boris about the talk he had gone to, and how disappointed he had been when the professor was later called away, so there had been no further talks that term.

'But now, I'm waiting to see if I can go to one after we get back. In fact, I'm hoping that we can both go to one, you and I.'

'Please explain. You are going a little too fast for me to follow.'

'Sorry, perhaps the best thing would be for me to check my e-mails from here, and see if I have an answer yet.'

Using the Internet on Boris' computer, Adam was pleased to see a message which had come from Professor Barnes' address.

<Dear Mr Thomas,

There is a talk on May 24th, and one on May 31st. Those are the last two of that term. I have put your name down for both of these. There are still a few places available.

Best wishes,

Edmund Barnes>

'What do you think, Boris?' asked Adam eagerly.

'I will willingly follow your advice,' Boris replied.

Adam quickly sent a reply to include Boris, explaining that he would be staying with him for two weeks while visiting the country.

'I wonder if Matthew will be around too?' he said. 'There's no way of telling. Hang on, I think I have his e-mail address in my diary. I'll forward Professor Barnes' message to him, and tell him what I've arranged so far; then it's up to him to decide what to do.'

'We have spoken about so many things this evening,' Boris

reflected. 'I think that we should leave the decision about when to listen to the tape for now.'

'You're absolutely right,' Adam replied. 'In fact, I think we should put it on one side until next week, and then think about it again. We still have plenty of time.'

Chapter Twenty-seven

Ellen was looking forward to the weekend with a mixture of trepidation and eager anticipation. Her idea about contacting a group of people whose interest was in antiquarian books had been successful so far. The second bookshop she had contacted through studying the Yellow Pages had provided an immediate link, since the proprietor was himself a member of a group that usually met only five miles from Ellen's home. He had been immediately enthusiastic about her offer, and said that he would contact the rest of the group to get their view. However, he had also said that was merely a formality, as the group always took up such offers. Indeed, they had seen many interesting collections of books over the years because of their eagerness and flexibility.

Ellen had reiterated that she was not sure that any of her books could be termed antiquarian, but that the library itself was a pleasant venue for a meeting. She had emphasised that she would be more than happy to host such a meeting. Daringly, she had even added that it might be possible to arrange a further meeting there, should the group find her home congenial.

The meeting had been arranged for a Saturday evening, and now it was only two days away. Ellen had planned to provide some light refreshments, and had made a list of things she would need. She could easily collect these on Saturday morning.

The punishing work schedule she had devised for herself, and had followed for a number of years, had been changing. Slowly but surely, she had decided what hours she truly could sustain, while still keeping a balance between work and possible recreation. This change was still in its early stages, but she was beginning to feel some benefit already. At first, it had been very difficult. She had delegated work to free some time for herself. Her colleagues had been very supportive of this; and she had learned from them how worried many of them had been about her, and how they themselves had tried to think of helpful ways to approach her about their concern.

Having made some time for herself, she had found that she was painfully aware of her father's absence once more, and was tempted to clutch on to activities which would push this out of her mind. She had had to be very firm with herself, learning how to cope with this, while trying to develop a balanced view of what she might enjoy doing for herself. She had been greatly encouraged that her plan about the antiquarian book society had led to something; and, with that to look forward to, she had looked at other things to try. She had been for a walk with the local ramblers' group, and had added her name to their contact list. She did not think she would go with them regularly, but she certainly wanted to keep in touch. Thinking about Jane's expertise in needlework, she had made some abortive attempts to do some cross-stitch. The next project after that had proved to be more successful. She had bought material and thread and a simple pattern for making a top for herself for the summer. She had found that struggling to understand and advance this was something she could do while being at home. An inconsequential conversation with a neighbour in the queue at the local supermarket had revealed that help was at hand regarding sewing at least, and she left that conversation feeling a sense of triumph that her efforts had borne fruit.

Ellen had been glad to hear from Adam about the date of his meeting and of his travel; but she had laid the note aside, and its importance had receded in her mind until it was almost too late to reply before he left the country. She had been pleased that she had something concrete to say about her own life, in addition to wishing him well in his.

The shopping completed in the morning, Ellen started laying out on the kitchen table all the things she needed for the evening gathering. She had been told that nine people would be arriving. She put the radio on and listened to a play as she worked. When that ended, she found some cheerful music to suit her mood.

Time passed quickly, and soon she heard her doorbell ring. All traces of the occasional anxiety she had felt earlier in the day disappeared as her guests arrived and introduced themselves. She was pleased to discover there was a wide range of age amongst them. She guessed that the youngest, a serious-looking man with owl-like spectacles, was in his early twenties; and that the person who appeared to be the oldest was a woman with two sticks, whom she guessed was in her eighties. She had considerable difficulty in walking, and Ellen was glad that the ground floor of her home was all on one level. Once inside the house, there were no steps at all, not even at the back of the house, where the kitchen and a small cloakroom were situated. She showed the woman to a comfortable upright chair in the library, which meant that she would have minimal difficulty in getting up and sitting down.

Ellen felt so comfortable with these people that she decided on the spur of the moment to tell them how this room had been a music room until after the death of her mother. She then explained how it had been gradually converted to a library; and gave them a description of how she and her father had struggled to get boxes of books down from the loft where they had been stored since the death of her grandfather years before she was born. The fire she had lit before the arrival of the group burned brightly in the grate. She felt confident that she had made the right decision.

She handed round some samples of her books, and found that the group was very appreciative, making observations which further stimulated her own interest in the collection. She had been right in her guess that much of the library consisted of books that had no antiquarian status, but there were later editions of some which kindled considerable discussion. Lastly, she came to her mother's collection of first editions, kept in the glass-fronted cabinet. She invited Mr Holden, the bookshop proprietor who had provided the link to these very pleasant people, to open the cabinet and examine the books.

Mr Holden stood up from his chair, and joined her at the cabinet. She watched him as he carefully picked up the books one by one. He examined each of them with gentle precision, and then addressed her, together with the assembled group, giving the title, author and origin of the book, along with his assessment of its condition. She stood spellbound as he worked through the books on the top shelf. As she watched, she realised that no one had even touched, let alone examined, these books since the death of her mother well over twenty-five years ago. The group was silent throughout this, as if they sensed the deep significance of the event.

Having carefully replaced the last book on the far right of the shelf, Mr Holden turned to Ellen and said:

'Miss Ridgeway, you have a very fine and valuable collection here. This evening we have time only to note the ones on this shelf, and give each a brief examination. I would advise you to catalogue them if you've not already done so, and have them valued for insurance purposes.'

'But...' Ellen stopped herself just in time. She had been about to say, 'But mummy's books are priceless,' and managed to convert it into, 'But I had no idea.'

The woman with the two sticks turned to her and said, 'He's absolutely right, my dear. I know that these things can come as a surprise if books have been in the family for a long time. One regards them as familiar furniture, rather than objects of monetary value. But you should take his advice. In fact,' here she smiled, 'you don't need to look any further to find someone whom I would firmly recommend for the job.'

Mr Holden looked embarrassed and rather uncomfortable.

'I must make it clear Miss Ridgeway,' he flustered, 'I did not come here to try to get work for myself.'

Ellen hurried to reassure him. Her dealings with Mr Holden had shown him to be scrupulously honest and trustworthy.

'Mr Holden, not only am I grateful for your brief assessment of these books, but also I know that I'd be very glad to engage your services to value them for me, if indeed you have time to do that.' She turned to the rest of the group and went on, 'I see that we must finish soon, as it's nearly ten o'clock. Before you go, I'd like to say how much I've enjoyed having you here this evening. Please do feel free to contact me if you'd like to come again sometime.'

She blushed as everyone clapped.

Mr Holden addressed her. 'On behalf of us all, I want to thank you for opening your home to us this evening; and I'm sure that we'll take you up on your offer of a further visit. Can you leave it with us, and we'll be in touch?'

Ellen smiled. 'Yes, of course,' she said.

'Returning to the matter of the valuation of the books in this cabinet, I can telephone you next week to discuss a mutually convenient time,' Mr Holden said.

'Fine. Now, can someone give me a hand to get all the coats, and we can warm them at the fire for a few minutes,' said Ellen brightly.

The serious young man with the owl spectacles jumped obediently to his feet, and followed her silently.

Her guests departed, and Ellen tidied away the crockery they had used. She felt almost euphoric. Not only had she had a group of total strangers in her library all evening, but also she had told them how the library had come to be, and had opened her mother's book cabinet for them.

'And,' she exclaimed out loud, 'they're really nice people! And they'll be coming back again!'

The phone rang: it was Jane. 'Hello Ellen, I remembered that this is the evening you were having the antiquarian book group round. How did it go?'

'Oh, thanks for phoning,' replied Ellen. 'It went very well indeed; so well that I'm feeling quite high. If you have time, I'd like to tell you all about it.'

'Surely,' answered Jane, and she listened with obvious interest as she heard Ellen's account of the evening, interjecting questions from time to time.

'Well, that's the story so far,' Ellen concluded. 'Thanks for phoning. I really needed to tell someone about it. I realise I've been talking for a long time.' She glanced at her watch, 'But if you've a bit more time, I'd like to hear if there's any more news about Emily and your project of the wooden blocks.'

Jane chuckled. 'Yes, there is. George, her father, came home soon after I left, and he's become so involved in it that I've rather taken a back seat. I've given him the details of the toy maker, and he contacted him direct. They have long and involved discussions about what to make next! By the way, I also handed on to him that book you picked up at the charity shop when we were last at Eva's, and he sends his thanks. Clare tells me she often finds him studying it late at night. To be honest, I think it's better that Emily and her dad are doing this together. He sees her much more often than I do, and after all he is her dad.'

'I think you're right,' Ellen agreed, 'but you must never forget how important you've been in starting this.'

'No, I can't forget,' laughed Jane. 'Every time I speak to Clare on the phone she tells me more about it, and thanks me again. I'm not sure when I'll next visit them, but I expect I'll get quite a surprise when I see all the new additions to the set, even though I've already had them described to me.'

'That all sounds like good news to me,' said Ellen. 'Can I phone you next week? I might not have anything particular to report, but I'd appreciate a chat.'

'Yes, of course. Bye for now.'

Chapter Twenty-eight

Another week had passed. Adam and Boris had continued to concentrate their energies almost exclusively on the tapes, and were more than satisfied with their progress. They still greatly valued their walks, and the time they had late in the evening to relax and turn things over together.

One evening, Boris raised once more the subject of his dream.

'I have been thinking,' he began, 'the intense white light in my dream was certainly emanating from where I keep the tape, but of course my special glassware is there too.'

'Could you get it out this evening and let me have a look at it?' Adam asked. 'I haven't studied it as closely as I'd like.'

Boris stood up from his chair and went out of the room. When he returned, he was carrying a wooden tray. He carefully took down the glassware, piece by piece, placing it on the tray. Adam noticed that the sides of the tray were a little higher than normal, and commented on this.

Boris nodded. 'I don't want to risk dropping any of these. This particular tray is the one I use for anything that is vulnerable.'

He carried the loaded tray across to where Adam was sitting.

Adam took the tray with great care, and examined the pieces one by one. He wished he knew something about glass engraving, but he did not. It was clearly a set of stemmed glasses. Each glass bore a slightly different design of a trailing vine bearing bunches of grapes.

'Do you know anything about them other than that they belonged to your grandparents?' he asked.

'I'm afraid not,' Boris replied. 'It is one of those things I wish I had asked my grandmother about before she died, and there is no one now that I can think of who might know.'

Adam handed the tray back to him, and Boris returned the glasses to their shelf.

'I'm still unsure about the best time to listen to that tape again,' mused Adam.

'There is also the question of how much of the tape to listen to,' added Boris.

'What do you mean?'

'The tape is unusual in that the recorded material continues through the whole of the first side,' replied Boris.

'Yes, of course, you're right,' said Adam, 'but where does that take us?'

'Have you had any other tapes that have so much on them?' asked Boris, 'because I certainly have not. All the tapes I have been working on carry five songs at most, but most of them have only one or two.'

'I think I've had one with seven on it; but, like you, I've found that most of them carry one or two. What are you getting at?'

'Nothing in particular. I'm just trying to think about that tape.'

There was a silence, and then he continued, 'I wonder if there is anything on the other side of the tape?'

'I hadn't thought of that,' said Adam. 'Are you thinking we might play it and see?'

'I suppose we could,' said Boris slowly, 'but I would like to think about it a bit more first. If I remember correctly, it was a sixty-minute tape, which means the full side would take thirty minutes to play.'

Adam became decisive. 'I think we should check side B of the tape.'

Boris did not try to deter him as he collected the tape, and ran it to the beginning of side B.

'Here goes then.'

Adam switched the tape on. There was no sound, and he reached over to switch it off, but Boris stopped him.

'No, let it run for a while, in case there is something farther on,' he said.

The gentle swishing noise of the tape continued until Boris himself switched it off. Then he ran it on to the end with the 'fast forward'.

'Perhaps we could listen to just the end of side A?' Adam spoke only half-heartedly.

Boris replied, 'I think we should put it away now and go to bed. Neither of us is sure enough about how to approach this. We have taken a step forward this evening. In a way nothing came of it, but in another way something did.'

'What do you mean? There was nothing on side B.'

'Precisely, we have established that. And before this evening we did not know, and we had not thought to check. In fact, before this evening, although we had known that we had listened to music filling the whole of side A, neither of us had commented on that fact before.'

'I see what you're getting at.' Adam was impressed by his friend's attention to detail. 'And I think you're absolutely right. We should put it away now, and sleep on it. I'm sure that as time goes on we'll feel clearer about what to do. At the moment, we aren't.'

That night, Adam woke bathed in sweat. His heart was racing uncomfortably. He tried to think if he had been dreaming, but could remember nothing. He sat up, and took a few sips from the glass of water on the table beside him, in the vague hope that it would help in some way. It had no effect. There was no bedside light; this was something that had never bothered him before when he was staying here. Now, suddenly, it did. He needed a light. Not the main light: that was no good. He got out of bed, put on the dressing gown from behind the door, and started to go through the living room towards the kitchen. Strange, there seemed to be a glow coming from a corner of the room. He glanced across, and realised that the glow was coming from the region of the shelf where the tape and the glassware were stored. He turned immediately, and went straight to Boris' room, knocking gently on the door. Boris, who was a light sleeper, woke straight away; and realising that he should follow Adam's directions, he put on his dressing gown, and followed him into the living room. They stood there in total darkness.

'What is it?' Boris whispered.

Adam was too confused to say anything except to ask for a candle. Boris quickly provided one from a cupboard in the kitchen.

'Thanks, Boris. Perhaps we can talk a bit in the morning before we work,' said Adam, and returned to his bedroom.

Adam woke very late the next morning. He was astonished when he saw it was nearly noon. He dressed quickly, and went to find Boris, whom he discovered wearing a coat, and sitting on the doorstep at the front of the house.

'Hello, Adam.' There was relief in his voice. 'I decided not to disturb you, but I did check on you from time to time.'

'Thanks; I think you were probably right to let me sleep, I had a rather odd experience in the night, or at least I think I did.'

'Do you want to tell me about it now, or leave it until later?' asked Boris wisely.

'I think I'll leave it until this evening,' answered Adam. 'I'd rather have something to eat, and go out for a bit. Perhaps we could have a shorter walk than usual, and then get on with some work.'

The day passed uneventfully, and Adam found it easy to immerse himself in their established routine. By the time they were cooking, he felt in good spirits, and was satisfied that he had done something useful with the day.

As always, they sat and relaxed in the late evening. Boris waited a while before prompting his friend.

'You were going to tell me about last night.'

Adam jumped in his chair. 'Yes,' he replied vaguely. 'Sorry, I was nearly dozing. What did you say?'

Boris gently repeated his question.

Adam looked perturbed. 'I remember that I slept until nearly noon today, but I'm not sure there's anything else to say.'

Boris hesitated, and then said, 'I think that something happened last night, because you came and woke me up. You were going to talk to me about it this evening.'

Adam looked blank.

'Wait here a minute,' said Boris.

He got up and left the room, but soon returned, carrying a candle in its holder.

'What have you brought that for?' asked Adam. 'We don't need a candle at the moment.'

'This is the candle I gave you last night,' said Boris.

'What do you mean?' asked Adam. 'What would I want with a candle?' Then, realising that Boris was looking worried and perplexed, he added, 'Look, tell me what's on your mind.'

Boris recounted the events of the night before, and added that when Adam had spoken to him in the morning, he had said he would like to talk about what had happened, but had opted to wait until evening.

'I have to believe you,' said Adam, as Boris finished what he was saying, 'but I can't remember any of it. This all reminds me a bit of what happened after I came to, that evening Matthew was round and I passed out.'

'Yes, I have been thinking of that,' replied Boris.

'I think I'd just like to have a game of chess, and then go to bed,' said Adam. 'I don't think that thinking about this any more tonight will help at all. Can we use that wonderful chess board again?'

Boris was happy to turn to a game of chess, and soon the two friends were immersed in the exciting possibilities of the game.

Later, tired and relaxed, they bade each other goodnight, and made their way to bed.

Adam woke in the night, bathed in sweat again. His heart was beating violently, and missing beats. He looked at the clock and discovered he had not been asleep for long. Had he been dreaming? He could not remember. He lay on his back feeling very agitated. Slowly, he remembered what Boris had told him of the night before, and how he had woken Boris up and asked for a candle. How could it be that he had erased this from his memory?

'I'm very glad that I trust Boris completely,' he muttered to himself.

He got out of bed and went to the bathroom to splash cold water on his face and neck. That felt a little better. He wished that he had a bedside light.

'Wait a minute!' he exclaimed. 'That is what I thought when I woke last night.'

He felt excited; now he was remembering having woken the night before. He went back into his room and sat on the edge of the bed.

'I wanted a light because I felt agitated. I thought a light would settle me. I went through the living room and…' he paused '…I saw a light emanating from the shelf where the tape and the glassware are kept.'

Now he was getting somewhere.

'I went to get Boris, but when he came into the living room with me, the glowing light had gone. Boris got me a candle and I went back to bed, thinking I'd talk to him in the morning.'

He got up from the bed, and started walking decisively towards Boris' room, but he stopped short of the door.

'No, I don't need to disturb him. No sense in us both losing sleep. I'll get something to write on, and I'll write it all down. That way, I don't need to wake Boris up; and if I've forgotten all this by the morning, I'll have the account here to remind me.'

Very pleased with his decision, Adam put on the main light in his room, and sat writing everything he remembered on to a piece of paper. He felt much calmer now, and his heart felt entirely normal. He finished his task, put out the light, and got back into bed.

The next morning, he was up early. Boris could hear him singing in the kitchen as he made his breakfast.

'You sound very cheerful this morning,' he said as he made his way through to join him.

'Yes,' replied Adam. 'I woke in the night, feeling terrible, but I remembered all that had happened the night before.'

'Why didn't you wake me?' asked Boris.

'I didn't want to disturb you, and it really wasn't necessary. I wrote it all down on a piece of paper. I'll just go and get it. You stay here, I won't be a minute.'

He soon returned and read everything out to Boris who was listening intently.

'A glow from that shelf…' Boris repeated. 'When I saw the light emanating from there in my dream, it had a quality that was different from the glow you describe, it was a very intense white light.'

'I know, I remember,' replied Adam. 'And the light I saw was definitely a glow, a yellow glow. I wish I knew what this means. I had that experience after we'd sat up trying out side B of the tape. As I told you, I felt really terrible when I woke. At first my heart was racing, and I was bathed in sweat. I wanted to calm myself, and I thought that getting some kind of small light by the bed would help. I was intent on finding one, when I saw the glow and came into your room. Now I'm trying to think how I felt about seeing the glow.'

He pondered, his face screwed up with concentration.

'It's odd,' he said at last. 'I can't remember feeling anything about the glow at all. Seeing it made me come to find you, but that's the only way I remember being affected by it.'

He thought some more, then said decisively, 'I know what I want to do. I want to get the tape out tonight, and I want to listen to side B again.'

'But there is nothing on it,' Boris reminded him.

'Nevertheless, I want to listen to it again.'

Adam seemed so confident and determined that Boris found himself willing to fall in with his idea, and they agreed that they would do it just before they went to bed. This decided, Adam found that he concentrated well on his work that day.

When night-time came, saying nothing, Boris collected the tape from the shelf, and ran it to the start of side B. He and Adam sat in silence as the tape played right through that side. Silently, he put the tape in its case and back on the shelf.

'I hope you sleep well,' he said, as he made his way to his room.

'Thanks,' Adam called after him.

When Adam woke next morning, the first thing he was aware of was a feeling of well-being. His pulse was steady, and his breathing was slow and deep. Boris put his head round the bedroom door.

'How did you sleep?' he asked.

'Fine,' replied Adam. 'I didn't wake up at all, and I'm not aware of having had any dreams.'

'That is good then.' There was relief in Boris' voice.

Over breakfast, Adam suddenly said, 'I think I'd like to listen to side A soon. What do you think?'

Boris, who was feeling grateful that things seemed to have returned to normal, started, and then resumed his usual posture of outward calm.

'I'm not ready,' he said firmly, looking across at Adam.

'Why not?'

'You have had a good night; but during the two nights before that, you woke in a bad state. I think we should leave it for at least another week before we try listening to side A.'

Adam was disappointed. He could see the sense of what his friend was saying, but he wanted to learn more about the tape, and its effects upon him. Then he realised that he was being selfish and almost petulant, and he felt ashamed.

'I'm sorry, Boris,' he said. 'I was getting a bit carried away. It must be hard for you. I go into strange states that you either witness or get an account of. Are you worried?'

'Some of the time, yes.'

'Then we must take this more slowly than I was suggesting. I certainly would like to listen to side A again before we leave for the UK, but I'll leave it up to you to say when you're ready. If you don't get to that point, I'll be very disappointed I know, but I'll have to deal with those feelings. I'll not blame you.'

Boris' expression lightened.

'I think I just need more time,' he said. 'I too would prefer to listen to it again while we are still here. We are due to leave on 20th May. Let us aim for the beginning of May. And of course I would like to keep talking about it before then from time to time.'

'I'm very happy to agree with that,' replied Adam. 'Let's get on with the other tapes now.'

Chapter Twenty-nine

Jane had found Ellen in good spirits when she phoned her the week after the visit from the antiquarian book society. Ellen had told her that another visit had now been arranged for the middle of June, and that Mr Holden had made an appointment to come and value the books in the cabinet next month. She had cleared a day in her diary so she could be there, and she showed obvious signs of looking forward to discussing the books with him. She had made a start on her sewing project, and had invited the neighbour who had previously promised her some help to come round for an evening. Jane was glad that Ellen was taking so many steps to broaden her life, and she had said so. Ellen had thanked her for her encouragement, but had surprised her by suddenly questioning her about her work. Ellen had been very blunt with her, saying that although she respected Jane's choice of occupation, she felt that Jane was more intelligent than the job required.

Jane had been mostly silent while she listened to what Ellen had had to say. She knew in her heart that Ellen was right, but it was hard for her to hear it.

Although Jane knew that her parents had loved and encouraged her, she had always felt that their real interest was in Clare. Clare had always been bright and popular at school. She was the one who had gone on school trips, while Jane had never been keen to go away from home. Clare had gone to university and had gained a good degree, while Jane had opted for secretarial college. Before she had Emily, Clare had had a number of exciting jobs, whereas Jane had stayed in one job – as a quiet mainstay to her boss. She did not dislike her work, but Ellen was right; it did not stretch her in any way. She had been able to buy the bungalow she lived in only because she and Clare had inherited money from a great-aunt who had never married. She had taken out a small mortgage that, together with the inheritance, had enabled her to buy it. She could not imagine ever moving from it.

There had been times when Jane regretted the fact that she had not gone to university; but she knew she had not had the confidence. Although she enjoyed the company of people, she was not gregarious like Clare. The social side of university life had not appealed to her, and in any case, she had worried about whether or not she would be able to keep up with the course-work.

Not long after her conversation with Ellen, Jane had received through the post a circular from the Open University. In the past, she had only given such items a cursory glance before dropping them into the bin. This time, she had hesitated. There was a tear-off reply slip for obtaining further details. On an impulse, she had completed it and sent it off. She had felt cautiously excited when a brochure arrived. In fact, she had felt quite encouraged, and had moved on to serious consideration of choosing a taster course.

She then phoned Ellen, and after the initial greetings, she went on to describe what Ellen's 'bullying' had led to.

'And now I've told you about all that,' she said, 'I wanted to start thinking of dates we could suggest to Eva for our next meeting.'

'How about some time towards the end of April, or the beginning of May?' asked Ellen. 'The first weekend in May would suit me very well. How about you?'

'I'll just get my diary. Hang on. Yes, that should be fine. Shall I phone Eva, or will you?'

'We both can,' laughed Ellen. 'But on the front of the arrangements, how about I phone her soon? I'll get back to you to confirm the date, or to find an alternative.'

'If I remember correctly, she's seeing Hannah and her father again towards the end of April,' said Jane.

'I think you're right. So the beginning of May might be a good time for her. She'll probably have more news for us. By the way, I have to admit that I'm afraid I haven't collected any references to spirals yet. My mind has been taken up with so many other things, I haven't really been looking. Perhaps I'll be able to once we have our meeting definitely fixed.'

Eager to advance the arrangements, Ellen phoned Eva later that day, and found that she was glad to have their next meeting the first weekend in May.

'Good. I'll phone Jane again and let her know,' said Ellen. 'She thought that you were seeing Hannah again sometime fairly soon.'

'Yes, that's right; Hannah and her father are planning to come on 21st April.'

'By the way, how are you feeling about your stick these days?' asked Ellen.

'Thanks for asking; I'm feeling far less anxious about losing it, and I've been taking it out with me recently, because I enjoy having it with me. Actually I've had one or two experiences where I've felt that it has helped me.'

'What do you mean?' asked Ellen.

'It's one of those things that one can't be sure about,' Eva began, 'but I'll explain what happened on one occasion. I was walking along the river bank one day, and I started to feel uneasy. The stick seemed to tremble in my hand, and I almost dropped it. Without knowing quite why, I took a few paces away from the bank, and walked close up to the fence of the field on the other side of the path. Just then, a section of the bank gave way and slid into the river.'

'That's amazing!' said Ellen. 'I can see how you ended up feeling that the stick had helped you. What was the other time?' she pressed.

'I was in the bathroom getting ready for bed. I had propped the stick up in the corner of my room – you remember, you saw where I kept it. I heard a clatter from the bathroom, and went into my room to see what it was. The stick was on the floor, but it was farther away from the corner of the room than if it had just fallen. The handle was pointing towards the door, and the end was pointing towards the window. I had a strong feeling that I should shut the window. I went over to it, and outside I could see the dark shape of a figure in the part of my garden that is to the side of the house. I sensed there was something wrong, and phoned the police immediately. My next-door neighbours had been away for several weeks, and I was concerned about their house. The police came very promptly, and caught someone at the back of the house; he had just prised a window open.'

'Goodness! It was certainly a good thing that you heard the stick land on the floor.'

'I can't work out how the stick fell where it did,' said Eva. 'I've tried pushing it over when it's propped up in that corner, but I can't get it to land where I found it.'

'This sounds like something we should talk about when we're all together again in May. I'll remind you,' Ellen volunteered. 'After all, I was the one who was keen to put it on the list of things to discuss when we met last time. I'll tell Jane when I speak to her – if you don't mind.'

'Please do,' Eva replied.

'You must remember to ask Jane about her news when you next speak to her,' Ellen continued.

'What news?'

Ellen chuckled. 'I think I'll wait and let her tell you. It's good news.'

'All right then. I can't think what it might be, so I'll just have to wait.'

Chapter Thirty

Eva had been back to the shop where she had bought the small bottles of apple juice, but she was disappointed to find there were none left. She had asked an assistant. No, they had just been a one-off line. She had scanned the shelves, and had eventually settled for a large bottle of juice made from crushed russet apples. The more she thought about it now, the more satisfied she was with her purchase. It felt right after all to have something different. Two weeks ago she had received a note from Mr Greaves confirming that he and Hannah would be coming on the 21st.

April is such a lovely month, she thought to herself as she admired the crocus flowers in the neighbouring gardens.

At the front of her house, her own garden was full of a mixture of daffodils and narcissi. She loved the bright yellows; she always felt these colours brought something alive in her. It had not been long after she moved into her house before she had started planting a selection of these bulbs. As a child she had always loved seeing them in her aunt's garden, and as she grew older, she had promised herself that when she had her own home, she would have some of these bulbs. She knew that even if she had no garden, she could plant some in window boxes.

Her thoughts ran on. My stick... The day I got my stick, I was on my way to stay with my aunt overnight on my journey home.

She liked the feeling that her stick was connected to thoughts of her aunt, even though the link was somewhat tenuous.

The next day was the 21st, and through her front window Eva saw Mr Greaves' car draw up, punctual as always. She could see Hannah in the back of the car, struggling to open the door by herself. She saw Mr Greaves turn round in his seat as if he were speaking to her in an encouraging way. Although it was clear that she was not yet strong enough to open the door unaided, Hannah was obviously determined to try. Eva opened the front door and stepped outside to wait. By this time, Mr Greaves was sensitively helping Hannah with the door of the car, giving her just enough help to enable her to continue to be instrumental in the task. Once the door was opened, Eva could see Hannah wriggling to the edge of the seat where Mr Greaves put his arm under one of hers, and helped her out.

'Hello, Hannah, Mr Greaves,' smiled Eva, and was about to step forward; but Hannah was by now showing signs of trying to walk towards her, so Eva stayed motionless and waited. Slowly, step by step, Hannah made her way forward with her father continuing to support her under one arm.

'Hey, that's really good!' said Eva encouragingly, stepping backwards through her front door as she watched Hannah's progress.

Hannah said nothing, as if she required all her concentration. She had by now reached the front door, and took hold of the door jamb to steady herself before stepping inside. She then made her way round the room to her chair by holding on to the furniture as she went, with Mr Greaves following close behind in case she needed further help.

When they were seated, Eva decided to introduce the apple juice straight away.

'Guess what I found when I was out shopping?' she asked.

Hannah and her father looked at each other.

'Apple juice?' guessed Hannah.

'Right first time,' laughed Eva. 'Do you want some now?'

'Yes please, and if there's any left over, can I take it away with me?'

'Of course you can. It's different this time; I'll just go and get some for you to try.'

Eva soon returned with the small glass. This time it was more than half full. Hannah took a sip and looked surprised.

'Daddy, you try it,' she said, handing her glass across to him.

'Mmm, I like this. Do you?' asked Mr Greaves.

'I like it a lot. Can you buy some for me, please?'

Mr Greaves smiled. 'Of course; I'll make a note of how to find the shop, and we can get some when we leave.'

'I have a large bottle of it here, and you're welcome to take it with you when you go; but I'll write down the address of the shop for you as well,' said Eva, glad that her purchase had turned out to be so successful.

Hannah looked across to her father, and said with touching dignity, 'Daddy, will you get the picture out now please?'

'Are you sure?'

'Yes.'

Mr Greaves opened the thin document case that he had carried in strapped across his shoulder, and pulled out something that looked a little like a greetings card. The front was blank, but Eva could see that the edges of it were slightly decorated. He handed it across to Eva who could then see that the front would open to reveal a mounted photograph.

'Is it all right for me to have a look?' Eva directed her question to Hannah.

Hannah nodded her head seriously.

'It's my mummy,' she said.

Eva looked inside, and saw a picture of a woman, probably in her mid-twenties. She looked relaxed and happy as she smiled towards the camera.

'I took this photograph of her when we'd known each other for only a few months,' said Mr Greaves. 'I do have a few more, but I like this one best.'

'So do I,' said Hannah emphatically.

'Hannah and I want to tell you how far we've got with our plans for looking for her mummy. When she left, she might well have gone abroad. She had many friends and contacts in different parts of the world. I have a number of addresses from years ago. Hannah and I have written a letter on my computer, and we have sent a copy to each of the addresses. I also have a couple of addresses of relatives of hers in the UK. We've written to them as well. Hannah and I thought very carefully about what to write. We did all of it together. We agreed that, at least to begin with, we want only to contact people who once knew her. If we get no news that way, then my next idea is to use the Internet, but that's very public, and we'll have to think again about what we'd write.'

Here, Hannah interrupted, 'Show her, Daddy.'

Eva assumed that Hannah was instructing her father to let her see a copy of the letter they had written together, but she soon saw that this was not the case. Mr Greaves had taken from his document case an unopened letter that Eva could see was addressed to him and Hannah. He handed it across to Eva.

'Hannah and I received this in the post only yesterday,' he said. 'We think it's a reply to one of our letters. We both had the same idea, and that was to bring it here today, and ask you to read it with us. Would you?'

'Please,' said Hannah.

'Of course,' replied Eva.

Mr Greaves continued, 'Thank you. It will help us.'

Eva looked at the envelope. It bore an Italian stamp, and was postmarked 'Milano'.

Mr Greaves explained. 'My wife had a cousin in Milan. I only met him once, but he did seem very pleasant. She usually wrote to him once a year, just to keep in touch.'

'Would you like to open the envelope?' Eva addressed Hannah. 'I have rather a nice letter knife. Wait a moment and I'll get it.'

She looked inside a small bureau that was standing about halfway along one wall of the living room, and produced a wooden paperknife with a carving of an owl on it.

'Thank you,' said Hannah, gravely, as she reached across for the letter and the knife.

Eva and Mr Greaves watched while Hannah very carefully slotted the knife into the corner of the envelope, and gradually opened it. Eva noticed that she took great care to check that the letter inside was not caught up in the knife. Once it was open, Hannah passed the letter across to her father, who began to read, silently. Eva could see that there were at least three sheets, possibly four. Hannah sat completely motionless, watching her father's face as he worked his way through them. Eva noticed that his face became grey and drawn as he read farther into the letter. Hannah must surely have noticed this too, but she remained motionless and completely silent, waiting for her father to finish.

After he had reached the end, Mr Greaves sat for some time with his head sunk down on to his chest. When at last he spoke, he was finding it difficult to control his voice.

'I didn't guess we would get so much news so quickly,' he said.

'I thought that the letter would be kind, but I really did not expect anything from it. I'd only written as an outside chance that he may have known something, or later heard something.'

Hannah appeared very composed. 'I want you to read it out now, Daddy,' she said.

Mr Greaves began to cry, silently. His body shook from time to time, but there was no sound. Hannah carefully stood up from her chair, and holding on to the arm of another chair, cautiously but determinedly worked her way across to her father. Eva was in a quandary; she was worried that Hannah might fall, but she sensed it was crucial that she did not intervene in any way. She knew that her place for now was as a caring witness, and not as a participant. Hannah, exhausted by her efforts, had reached her father's knees and flopped down on to the floor between them, clutching one of his legs on her way down. From her position on the floor, she stroked his feet.

It seemed a long time before Eva could be certain that Mr Greaves was no longer crying. Hannah was still stroking his feet. His head was still bowed on his chest, but he was not crying. More time passed; then Mr Greaves reached down and took Hannah's hands in his. His head was still bowed but Eva could see that he was gently squeezing Hannah's hands.

'Can you read it now, Daddy?' enquired Hannah.

At first Mr Greaves made no sign, but then he nodded, very slowly. He picked up the letter from where he had laid it on his lap, and began to read it out.

'Dear Colin, Dear Hannah,

'Thank you for your letter. There is no easy way to reply to it. I think it is best if I just give you an account of events.

'When Sarah left your home, she travelled from place to place. She worked in fairly menial jobs to pay her way. When she arrived at my door, she was very thin and looked quite unwell. I took her in straight away, of course. She would say very little at first, but I managed to glean that she had left you about six months prior to this. She was adamant that I must not contact you. She was convinced that her presence in your lives was harmful to you. I tried to persuade her that that could not be the case, but she would not be swayed from her belief.

'She would not see a doctor. I was sufficiently worried about her state of health that I used to keep my bedroom door and hers open at night, in case she called out. There were nights when I heard her calling for you both, and for Dawn. At first I thought that she was afraid of the dark, and was longing for dawn to come. I used to talk to her about this, and as the weeks went past she told me about Dawn. Then I understood.

'Each week I would ask her if I could contact you, but she always said no, and she made me sign an agreement, promising that I would never contact you. I still have it. I did not destroy it after her death. She never changed in her belief that it would harm you to be in touch with her.

'It was very difficult to get her to eat, and she was always very weak. One night, several months after I took her in, I heard her coughing. This was the beginning of serious bronchitis, and her continued refusal to see a doctor meant that by the time she was seen, she had pneumonia. She had no resistance, and, I believe, no real will to live. She died in the December. She is buried near my home. If you wish to come any time, you are welcome to stay with me for as long as you want.

'I expect there may be things that you want to ask me. Please feel free to write to me any time. I hope you will understand that by not contacting you, I was honouring her wishes. Now that you have contacted me, at last I am free to write to you.

'Giovanni, cousin of Sarah'

Mr Greaves laid the letter down on the floor, picked Hannah up, and sat her on his knee. Eva could hear them exchanging an occasional phrase or sentence as they sat with their arms round each other. She continued to sit as quietly as she could, not wishing to do anything that might risk disturbing something that she knew was of crucial importance to them both.

At length, Mr Greaves addressed her. 'Hannah and I are very grateful indeed for your kindness. We must go soon. There's a lot that we must see to, but it'll take time to decide, and to arrange things. Would it be possible for us to keep in touch with you by phone meantime?'

'Yes, of course,' Eva replied warmly. 'If you leave a message on my call-minder, together with suggestions of convenient times for me to return your call, I'll gladly keep in touch. There are times when I'm away from home, but generally I use a PIN number to access my messages.'

She wrestled inwardly with her feelings while Hannah and her father began to prepare to leave.

Then she said, 'I've something I'd like to suggest.'

They turned towards her.

'I...' she faltered momentarily, '...I've something you might like to have with you until your next visit here.'

Her resolve strengthened, and she picked up her stick from the corner of the room.

'Hannah, you're doing so well with your walking, but I see you still need a little help. Would you like to use my special stick until I see you again?'

Mr Greaves took the stick, and passed it to Hannah, who immediately noticed the small carving on it. She held on to it tightly.

'It feels so good,' she whispered.

'When you come again, I'll tell you the story of how I got that stick, and you'll be able to tell me where the stick has been while it has been with you.'

Eva was completely confident now of what she was doing.

Reaching out to furniture with one hand, and clutching the stick in the other, Hannah made her way to the door, with her father close behind in case she stumbled. Eva let them out, and stayed at the door while they opened the car and got in. As Mr Greaves drove away, Eva could see her stick waving at Hannah's window.

Chapter Thirty-one

'How many tapes are there still to do?' asked Adam as he began work on Saturday morning.

'I have been asking myself the same question.' Boris sounded amused. 'I'll go and get the box and count them. I have a feeling that there are not many left now.'

Boris brought the box from the cupboard in the hallway, and counted the remaining tapes. 'Ten.'

'We have about two weeks left,' mused Adam. 'If there's not much on these tapes, we should finish them all before we leave.'

'I know; but you can never predict how much there's going to be on them.' Boris sighed. 'To tell you the truth, I could do with a break. We have worked every day since you came.'

Adam, surprised, looked at his friend sharply.

'Is something the matter? It isn't like you to be like this,' he said. Adam knew his friend to be a creature of habit, and an indefatigable and methodical worker.

Boris took a deep breath, 'I just need a change.'

'It won't be long before you'll be in the UK with me.'

'I know, but I need a break now.'

Adam was astonished; his friend sounded almost petulant – something that was totally out of character for him.

He tried again, 'Are you sure that there's nothing the matter?' he asked.

'I don't want to have to listen to that tape tonight, that's all.'

Boris got up hurriedly out of his chair, snatched his coat from a peg in the hall, and went out of the front door.

Adam was stunned. Until Boris had said this, he had completely forgotten that it was to be this evening that they were going to listen to the special tape together. In addition, he had never seen his friend behave like this before. He ran after Boris and caught up with him as he turned the corner of the house, heading for the access road.

'Hey, Boris!' Adam took him by the arm. 'Look, we don't have to listen to that tape tonight. And we can have a day off today – that would be fine by me.'

Boris stopped. He seemed to sag a little.

Adam continued, 'Tell me exactly what you'd prefer to do today. I'll go along with anything you say.'

'I need your help,' Boris confessed. 'We will be travelling very soon, and it is a long time since I went anywhere for more than one night. I am embarrassed to say this to you, but I need your help in deciding what clothes to take, and what to pack them in.'

'You're just out of practice, that's all,' Adam reassured him. 'How about we look through what bags you have, and then draw up a list of things we think you'll need while you're away. Remember, it's because you let me use some of your clothes that I can travel here with very little luggage. When you stay with me, you're very welcome to use my things.'

Boris looked surprised. 'I had not thought of that,' he said, brightening.

'How about we spend the day talking about what we'll be doing when you're staying with me?' suggested Adam; and he saw Boris begin to relax.

The rest of the morning passed very pleasantly. Adam and Boris discussed the impending meeting with Carillon Music at some length. Their exchanges became light-hearted as they shared their hopes about the outcome. And of course there would be the two talks by Professor Barnes. Adam was looking forward to introducing Boris to Edmund Barnes. He very much hoped too that Matthew would be home some time during Boris' stay, as he wanted them to meet.

'Perhaps I can get Matthew round one evening,' he said. 'He's almost certain to arrive with a large bag of nuts!' He became serious. 'There's one other person that I'd really like you to meet.'

'Who is that?' asked Boris curiously.

'Ellen. Ellen Ridgeway. I don't for a moment think it's likely, but it doesn't stop me from hoping.'

By this time, Boris' spirits were much recovered. 'Why don't you write to her?' he asked.

'But she won't be anywhere near where I live when you're staying.'

'How do you know that?'

'She lives about five hours' drive away.'

'I see what you mean,' Boris acceded; 'but it doesn't mean you can't write to her.'

'That's true. I could write something rough just now, and read it to you. You can tell me what you think.'

He picked up a pencil and began to write.

Dear Ellen,

As you may remember, I am returning home later this month, in time for the meeting with Carillon Music. I will have my friend Boris with me. He will be staying with me for two weeks.

He sucked the end of his pen, noticed what he was doing, wiped it on his handkerchief and continued:

Please let me know if there is any possibility that you might be in the area during that time. Boris and I would be very pleased to see you.

Best wishes,

Adam

He read it out.

'That sounds fine to me.' Boris was encouraging. 'Would you like some of my notepaper? You could write it out, and this afternoon we can walk to the village and post it.'

Adam felt uncertain, but could see that there was no harm in writing it out on Boris' notepaper, and walking to the village with it. It was a pleasant walk. If on the way he felt he could not post it, then he did not have to.

In the event, by the time they reached the village, Adam had no problem at all about posting the letter.

Returning to Boris' house by a slightly different route brought more variety to their outing, and both were quite relaxed and jovial on their return.

'I think that we could listen to a little of that tape this evening after all,' Boris told his friend.

'I've been thinking about that,' replied Adam. 'Why don't we listen to some of it now, before we cook? We could listen to the first few minutes. After that we could cook and eat, and later in the evening we could listen to more if we wanted.'

'That is a very good idea,' Boris replied.

He hung his coat on a peg in the hall, and went to get the tape. Then he and Adam sat down to listen. Soon the sound of the rich tenor voice filled the room.

'Speak to me! Quickly – say something!' There was urgency in Adam's voice.

Boris looked at him, and saw immediately that his eyelids were beginning to droop.

'*Adam,*' he said firmly, 'we are going to cook some vegetables now. Adam Thomas, this is your friend Boris speaking to you. We are going to cook some vegetables now, and I am about to switch off this tape that is full of beautiful music.'

He reached across and switched it off.

'*Adam Thomas. Adam.* We can listen to some more later, but it is time to cook now.'

He took hold of Adam's hand, and shook it a little.

Adam appeared pale, but spoke. 'That was a close one! This time I felt myself going, and was able to ask you for help. It's amazing how quickly it happened. One minute I was sitting with you; then the music started, and the next minute something strange started to happen.'

'What exactly was it?' asked Boris.

'Do you remember that after this happened last time, the only thing I could say was that I'd had a feeling of wanting to talk to you about something?'

'Yes, I do.'

'Well, this time I had that feeling again, although I haven't a clue what it was that I wanted to say. No, hang on a minute, there's something else. I had a vague sense of being able to see something.'

'What did it look like?' Boris asked.

'I can't be sure, but I think it was some kind of faint pattern or design. Phew, I feel exhausted!' Adam finished.

Boris was intrigued. 'When you told me about the time you passed out when Matthew was there, you said that when you came round, Matthew told you that you had said something just before you lost consciousness. What was it?'

'Thanks for reminding me… He told me I'd said I could see something that wasn't there.'

Boris went on. 'The other thing I remember your saying about that whole event was that after you were sitting back in your chair your vision was disturbed.'

'How could I forget? You're absolutely right. When I told Matthew, he asked me if it was blurry. I said not, because the nearest I could get to describing it was as a multitude of pinpricks in front of my eyes. It was then I remembered what Ellen had described to me in the Bull about the effect that some of the blank pages of her red book were having on her. And of course there is my own feeling about that book I saw in my dream – that there had after all been something on the blank pages. I didn't get round to talking to Matthew about that.'

'Was what you could see after hearing the tape this time the same as when you came round after passing out with Matthew?' Boris said, keen to grasp exactly what had happened.

'No, but the whole thing was somewhat similar in that I could see something that was between me and everything I knew was there. I can only repeat that it appeared to be a faint pattern or design. The pinprick effect I was aware of when I was with Matthew was not organised in any way.'

'This is fascinating,' said Boris eagerly. 'Perhaps next time you are affected, you might see some patterns.'

'I suppose that's possible.' On this occasion, Adam was more cautious than his friend. 'Look, if you don't mind, I'd like to do something practical, rather than talking about this any more at the moment. Can we get on with the cooking, and we can decide what to do about this once we've eaten? I hope we can listen to a bit of that tape again later, but I'm not sure yet.'

Chapter Thirty-two

Ellen arrived at Eva's looking relaxed, and better than Eva had seen her for a very long time.

'It's good to see you looking so well!' Eva exclaimed, as she let her friend in.

Ellen replied confidently, 'Yes, I am well, and I'm sure it's because I've done so much recently to improve my life. I've reduced my working commitments to four days a week, and I don't do any work in the evenings. In my free time I'm seeing more of the local people, and joining in with the various activities. That is, of course, in addition to particular things I arrange, like coming here, seeing the antiquarian book people, and so on. I'm quite clear in my mind that this way I'll be able to give my time more effectively to projects for the homeless and the people in halfway houses. I notice too that I have some more creative ideas these days to introduce into the schemes, one or two of which have been a great success, and have been adopted long-term.'

'I'm very interested to hear that,' Eva replied. 'Perhaps you'll tell Jane and me something about it over the weekend.' She glanced at the clock. 'Her bus arrives at the shopping centre in about an hour.'

'If I bring in my bag, I could drive there now, and meet her,' said Ellen enthusiastically. 'Would you like to come? There'd be time to look round one or two of the shops together before the bus arrives.'

Twenty minutes later, Ellen and Eva were browsing round a charity bookshop that was on the side of the shopping centre that was next to the bus station.

'I notice these shops are becoming much more common,' Eva said as she skimmed a section on gardening.

'Yes, this is the one where I bought the book on mathematical models that I gave to Jane.'

'We must keep an eye on the time,' said Eva. 'It's easy to get lost in one of these shops, and I don't want to miss Jane.'

In the event, Jane's bus arrived rather late, and Jane disembarked looking stressed.

'It's good to see you,' Ellen welcomed her.

Eva's concern spilled over, 'What happened?'

'There was a bit of a delay. There was a problem with the bus as we set off. We had to stop and wait for a relief bus to come. I'm sorry I couldn't let you know; I haven't got my mobile with me. I don't always carry it, and I didn't think to bring it.'

'Well, it's good you're here now,' said Eva, smiling. 'We can go back to the house, cook our meal, and then decide how we're going to spend our weekend.'

The evening was cool. The three friends elected to walk along the river bank, to be out long enough to watch the sunset. Ellen had brought a camera.

'I'm practising,' she said awkwardly, 'but if any of these come out okay, I might get enlargements and frame them to hang in my house, to remind me of the times we've been together.' She turned to Eva, 'I was hoping that you'd let me take a photograph of your stick while I'm here.'

'I haven't got it at the moment.'

Ellen was astonished. 'What's happened to it?'

'You'll find out when we talk about my recent meeting with Hannah and her father,' said Eva, mysteriously.

'We'll have to contain our impatience,' Jane joined in, 'but I don't think we'll have to wait long before we hear. As soon as we get back to the house, I want to know the full story. Ellen, would you take a photograph of this bridge for me? Can we get Eva standing on it first?'

Back at her house, Eva told her friends about the improvement in Hannah's health, about the letter, and how, on a sudden impulse, she had offered her the use of her stick.

'I have to say it was a bit of a struggle to get myself to do it, but it was almost as if there was a voice inside my head saying "lend your stick to Hannah", over and over again. And by the time she was going away with it, I felt perfectly at ease, knowing that it was exactly the right thing to do.'

'That's amazing,' said Ellen; 'given how anxious you've been about losing the stick.'

'Not only do I know that it's in very safe hands, but also I know it's in the right place,' said Eva confidently. 'By the way Ellen, I spoke to Jane on the phone soon after I spoke to you, and I told her about the way the stick had seemed to help me with the river path, and also the incident about the burglar. Silly of me, I should have shown you both where the path had fallen into the river. It was farther along than where we were this evening, though.'

'I've thought a lot about all of that since I heard,' said Jane. 'It made a big impact on me. I certainly would like to see the section of the bank that collapsed.'

'Shall we get on with the list for this weekend now?' said Ellen as she produced a notebook out of her bag, together with a pen. 'My special pen, of course,' she commented. 'At the top of the list I'm going to write "Ask Jane about her studies".' She looked across at Jane meaningfully.

'Thanks.' Jane sounded pleased. 'I'd love to tell you both how I'm getting on with that, and what I'm planning. I'm grateful to you, Ellen, for pushing me in the right direction.'

'Good,' said Eva. 'And if the weather forecast is correct, it's going to be a beautiful day tomorrow. Can I suggest that we make a picnic, and spend the day walking by the river and exploring some of the woodland nearby. There are still some paths I haven't investigated.'

Ellen and Jane agreed with alacrity.

'We could concentrate on the spirals in the evening,' Eva concluded.

'I think the evening is a good time for that,' Ellen agreed. 'I'm so glad that we eventually fixed to meet this weekend – the first weekend in May... and everything outside is bursting into life.'

The weather forecast proved to be correct. The day was glorious, and was filled with the pleasure of the countryside. Ellen took innumerable photographs, making no excuses for doing so. Flowers, butterflies, fishermen, Eva and Jane, views of fields and trees; and, of course, the collapsed river bank. They returned to the house tired and somewhat dishevelled, but profoundly glad that they had chosen to spend the day as they had.

Checking her call-minder, Eva found there were two new

messages. One was from the roofer to say that he would come on Monday morning to do the annual check of the roof. Eva made a note of this while she started to listen to the second message. She listened intently, and then saved the message. She turned eagerly to her friends.

'There's a message here from Hannah and her father.'

'What does it say?' asked Jane and Ellen together.

'Mr Greaves said there was no need to return the call; and that they were just phoning to let me have a piece of news, and would be in touch again. Then Hannah's voice said they would soon be going to Milan to stay with her mother's cousin, Giovanni, for at least a week. She ended by saying she would tell me all about it later.'

There were tears in Eva's eyes as she related this message, and she could see that both Ellen and Jane were deeply affected.

It was Jane who spoke first. 'Although I've never met them, I do feel very involved, and I'm so glad that things are going better for them.'

'That's exactly how I feel too,' added Ellen. 'You must phone us both when you next hear from them.'

Jane nodded, and said emphatically, 'Yes, you must.'

'I will,' Eva promised.

That evening Eva took out the photocopies of the spirals in preparation for laying them out once more as planned.

'I haven't looked at them since we were last together,' she said. 'Have you been studying them, Jane?'

'Yes, I do get out this diary from time to time, and study the strokes and patterns that make up the spirals. I don't reach any conclusions; but I'm still fascinated by them, and I've never lost the belief that there's a language embodied in them. I haven't ever made a layout on the floor from the photocopies. That only happens when you do it, Eva.'

'I'm aware that something is likely to happen to me again,' Ellen said, in matter-of-fact tones. 'After what's happened before, it would be strange if it didn't. Last time my body didn't go into shock, so perhaps things are changing. I can't feel anything at the moment, but I won't go out of the door this time. I'll just sit here while you lay it out, Eva. One more thought,' she added. 'I'll hold my pen between my fingers. If I start to change, and my hands move into the position you described to me before, then my pen will drop to the floor.'

'I'll start watching you now, while Eva is putting the spirals out on the floor,' Jane reassured her.

Eva began to concentrate all her attention on her task, while Jane watched Ellen intently. Ellen sat with her pen between her fingers, watching Eva's concentration, rather than looking at the spirals themselves. She had a vague sense of being able to hear something faintly, and realised that the best thing was to mention this to Jane.

'Can you tell me more about it?' asked Jane, as she jotted something in her notebook.

'No, I wish I could; it's just a sense of being able to hear something, but having no concrete knowledge of what it is.'

'Is it a particular kind of sound?' asked Jane.

She noticed that Eva had almost completed the layout of spirals, and that they were in Ellen's line of view, although Ellen was still looking at Eva.

Ellen's pen fell to the floor.

'Song of light,' she said in clear, precise tones. 'The sound of light.'

Eva indicated to Jane that she would do any writing, and Jane continued with her questions.

'Do you want to tell me any more about it?' she asked gently.

Ellen's face had the same glow that it had manifested the last time she had been affected by the spirals.

'Beyond a veil,' she whispered; and then more faintly, but still audibly, 'Adam'.

'Thank you for telling me,' said Jane, uncertain as to what to say next. 'I am always interested in what you have to say. If there's anything else you want to add, I'm here listening to you. I won't move from this place.'

She could see a slight vibration in Ellen's fingers as she sat with them in exactly the same position as when she was previously affected.

'Adam,' Ellen whispered again. 'Greaves, Mr Greaves.'

'Thank you for telling me,' Jane repeated. 'I'm glad that we are all here together talking about these important things.' Here Jane could not think of anything further to say, and opted to repeat her last sentence slowly and gently, several times.

Ellen made no further indication of trying to speak. Jane noticed that her fingers had stopped vibrating; and soon after this, her hands fell into her lap, and she sighed.

'Something happened again, didn't it?' said Ellen, as she looked from Jane to Eva and back again. 'And actually, something is still happening, because… I was going to say I can't see properly… but there's something I can tell you about it – it's the same sort of effect that I get after looking at the special blank pages in my red book. Let me just stay with this until it fades; and then you can tell me what happened to me this time.'

Eva and Jane sat quietly, while Ellen appeared to be staring at a point not far in front of her face.

'I can't tell you anything more about it,' she said at length, 'but it's faded now. Will you tell me what you saw happening to me?'

Eva and Jane went through their account of what they had seen and heard.

'Mm,' said Ellen, 'it seems that I was able to speak more clearly this time.'

'Yes, that's right; there was no doubt about it this time,' Jane confirmed.

Chapter Thirty-three

Their meal over, Boris and Adam were settled back in their comfortable chairs. 'Are you sure that you want to listen to it again now?' asked Boris.

'Yes, I'm sure.' Adam was clearly determined. 'But I think it's wise to stick to the first few minutes again.'

'Shall I switch it on?'

Adam nodded, and Boris leaned out of his chair to run the tape back to the beginning. Then he switched it on. Once more, the sound of the glorious tenor voice filled the room.

'Will you take hold of my hand again, quickly?' asked Adam, urgently.

Boris immediately reached across and took his friend's hand gently but firmly in his.

'The music is so beautiful, the feelings I have are almost too intense to bear,' murmured Adam. 'But there's something else... I can hear something behind the music.'

'Can you tell me what it is?' asked Boris slowly.

Adam did not reply, but was saying something else: 'I can see something too.'

'Just tell me anything you want,' said Boris, encouragingly.

He maintained his gentle hold on Adam's hand and squeezed it from time to time, hoping to reassure him of his continued presence.

'I don't know... I don't know.' Adam's voice carried a sadness which Boris found almost unbearable.

Boris was now in a quandary. He and Adam had agreed to run the tape for only a few minutes. Those few minutes had passed. What should he do? To reach the switch for the tape, he would have to let go of Adam's hand. Mentally, he kicked himself. Why had he not thought of this before? He could easily have positioned the tape player closer to his chair. He made a decision. Maintaining his grasp of Adam's hand, he stood up from his chair, and moved in front of Adam, taking hold of his other hand.

'Stand up for a moment, my friend,' he said firmly. 'We have something to do.'

Adam stood up obediently, and Boris backed round to the tape player, taking Adam with him. He freed his left hand, and switched it off.

'Now, we can sit down again, and I will wait with you until you can see me again,' said Boris.

He manoeuvred Adam back into his chair, and sat on the arm of the chair, now holding Adam's left hand in both of his. He waited. Adam's hand did not feel cold, in fact it felt quite warm, but his face looked very sad. It was a long time before he spoke. Boris had not counted the minutes; but he noticed that he was reaching the point where his leg was likely to cramp because of the odd angle at which he was sitting.

'I feel terribly sad. Terribly, terribly sad,' said Adam. Before Boris had time to think of anything to say he went on. 'I feel terribly sad that I don't know – I don't know what to say to you. I never remember feeling as sad as this. Not even after Maria died. I didn't think I could be any sadder than I was then, but I am. It's even beyond tears.'

Boris waited.

Adam went on. 'I want to know what I heard, and I want to tell you. I want to know what I can see, and I want to tell you. But I can't. I don't know, and I can't tell you.'

He slumped in his chair.

Boris waited again. He knew that there was nothing he could do or say that would change how his friend felt, and he sensed that even if there were, he should do nothing to disturb what Adam was going through.

At length, he felt he could make a contribution.

'The way I see it, Adam,' he began, 'is that something is emerging in your life. We do not know what it is yet, but when signs of it come, each time they are a little stronger. Although I cannot be sure, I do believe that this will all become clearer, given time. And I think we both agree that whatever is happening cannot be hurried.'

'I'm eternally grateful for your support and your wisdom in this.' Adam's thanks could not have been more genuine.

'For my part, I am glad to be with you,' Boris replied.

'I feel so very tired now.' Adam's voice was weary. 'I think I must go to bed.'

Tired as he was, Adam spent a restless night. Whenever he woke, he thought he had been hearing the sound of a train. He woke the next morning with his night clothes damp, feeling totally exhausted.

'I'm not up to doing any of the tapes today,' he confided at breakfast.

'I guessed that you would not be,' said Boris sympathetically. 'I sometimes heard you shouting in the night.'

'What was I shouting?' Adam was immediately interested.

'I could not make it out. I was half asleep myself.'

Disappointed, Adam went on to tell Boris about the sound of the train. Boris listened with obvious interest.

'Do you think that this is to do with the time you first met Ellen?' he asked.

'I do. Something similar to this happened to me before at my house, a night or two after I'd had that dream about Ellen, and you had your dream about the intense light around the shelf where you keep the tape and that glassware. That time, I couldn't fall asleep. My mind kept filling with memories of Ellen, of the dream, and questions about the whole puzzle. I seemed to spend the whole night hearing sounds as if I were in the railway carriage. That sound has come into my mind on a number of other occasions too.'

'I think you need to rest today,' advised Boris. 'I have a plan. I have logs to cut. I think I will spend the day doing that, and you can join me whenever you want to. I would appreciate any help you can give me, but you can feel free to go and rest whenever you like, or just to sit and talk from time to time. What do you think?'

'That's really helpful,' answered Adam gratefully. 'Let's get started. I'll join you to begin with, and then I'll go and lie down for a while.'

Boris' plan worked very well, and by evening Adam was feeling a great deal more able to contemplate the rest of his stay, and the work they still hoped to advance. Boris was glad to see the improvement in Adam; and the mounting heap of logs in his shed was a welcome outcome of their efforts of the day.

After some discussion, they decided to spend the next ten days alternating between the cutting of logs, and processing more of the few remaining tapes. They agreed that the intense physical activity was what they needed more of now; and this had the advantage of helping Boris to be well advanced in his preparations for the following winter.

The last two days before travelling to the UK were left free for final arrangements, such as preparing to close down Boris' house, and packing their things.

Chapter Thirty-four

Ellen had dropped Jane off at the bus station late on Sunday afternoon. As she drove the long journey back to her home, she reflected on the events of the weekend. Certainly her reaction to the spirals seemed to have progressed a little, but there were so many unanswered questions about the whole subject that she did not even try to begin to list them. She was glad to have had plenty of time earlier in the day for discussion with Jane and Eva. These were times she valued very highly, and she was always left with much food for further thought. She realised how much she was looking forward to hearing more news of Hannah and her father. Jane had promised to phone her sister to ask about Emily; but, more importantly, she had confided that she had definitely decided to apply for an O.U. degree course that would start in February of the following year. Ellen had been delighted to hear this news. She had felt a little guilty for putting pressure on Jane to think about her career prospects, but now she could say goodbye to that.

She was not long home before one of her neighbours knocked on the door, carrying some warm scones in a dish. She was surprised and delighted at this gesture. The neighbour could not stay to talk, but thrust the dish into Ellen's hands, saying how glad she was to see her back safely. Ellen was very touched by this, and made a mental note to think of something she could do in exchange, some time in the future.

She phoned both Jane and Eva to say that she was back, and then set her mind to preparing for the week's events. There was much to occupy her, but there was also time for plenty of thought and reflection. This was the week when Mr Holden was due to come to value her mother's books. She checked her diary. Yes, he was due to come on Thursday.

It was May 16th. Ellen got out of bed, and stretched her arms high above her head. The month was already halfway through. Mr

Holden's visit had been very satisfactory. Ellen had greatly enjoyed watching him valuing the books that had been her mother's. It was so obvious to her that the monetary value he attributed to each book was only part of the total value he placed on them. He had handled them in a way that she could only describe as loving care. Before he had left, he had promised her written confirmation of his opinion, and said how much he looked forward to the next meeting at her house, which was to be on the 16th June. He had asked her permission to talk to the group at that meeting about some of these books. She had been more than pleased to agree to this, and added that she too was looking forward to that meeting.

She went downstairs, and picked up the post from the floor behind the door. Here was a letter that looked as if it must be the written valuation from Mr Holden. But what was this? There was a letter with a strange stamp and postmark. She examined it more closely. The postmark was smudged, and could not be deciphered, but the stamp was clearly Russian.

'But I don't know anyone in Russia,' she said out loud.

Then she stopped, instantly realising that this must surely be from Adam. She took a knife out of the kitchen, opened the envelope, and read the note she found inside. Her first reaction was one of panic, but she noted that this was small, compared with any panic she had felt about him earlier. It soon passed, and she involved herself in checking a number of things. He was hoping that he might see her – and Boris would be with him. The first thing she checked was her road atlas. A journey to Adam's locality would take about five hours, but at this time of year there was much daylight, which made the prospect of such a journey more agreeable. Then she checked her diary. She had four days completely free right at the end of May.

'So it would be possible,' she said slowly; 'but this is something that I don't want to decide on my own. I'll think about it today, and then phone both Eva and Jane this evening to talk about it.'

She was surprised to find that by evening she had almost made up her mind to write to Adam's home address to let him know about these dates, and to say that she would like to meet his friend, and that although she had not planned to be in the area, she was willing to drive down. She was glad to discover that both Jane and

Eva encouraged her; so later that evening, she sat down and wrote to Adam:

> Dear Adam,
>
> Thank you for your note. Although I had not planned to travel south in the next few weeks, I find I do have some free days at the end of the month. I would be glad to travel down to see you, and to meet your friend. Please let me know if these days are convenient for you. I could travel down on the 28th, the day of your meeting at Carillon Music. I am sure that I can find accommodation locally, and perhaps we can meet up the following day.
>
> Let me know what you think.
>
> I look forward to hearing from you,
>
> Ellen

Decisively, she put the note into an envelope, and having addressed it to his home, she attached a first class stamp.

Chapter Thirty-five

The taxi drew up in front of Adam's house. Adam paid the driver, while Boris took their luggage out, and put it on the pavement. The friends were travel-worn, and had not bothered to shave.

'That's the worst journey I've ever had travelling to and from your home,' said Adam through gritted teeth. 'I've heard people talking about having to sleep on the floor in an airport, but I've never had to do it before! Let's get inside, and then we can start to unwind.'

Boris was silent. His face looked grey. Adam unlocked the front door, and added the small pile of mail from the floor to the larger heap on the small table in the hallway.

'Come on through. Here's your bedroom. Dump your things, and come to the kitchen.'

Adam pointed to the kitchen door.

'I'll put the kettle on, and switch the heating on for an hour,' he said.

He looked at his watch, and found it was just after midnight. Many hours ago he had adjusted it to take account of the change in longitude. It was useful to be able to see the time, but it helped very little with his confusion. The change in time, the delays of the journey, and lack of sleep had left him feeling muddled. But there was one thing he was sure about. He wanted to make his friend comfortable.

He put a hot drink on the table in front of Boris. He wondered whether to offer him something to eat, but thought better of it. He watched his friend sipping the hot liquid. Exhausted though he was, he felt anxious. Boris had said nothing during the last hours, and he looked ill.

Best to get him into bed as soon as possible, he thought. Then we'll see what the morning brings.

He waited until Boris had finished his drink, showed him the bathroom, and laid out some pyjamas. Returning to the kitchen, he made himself sit down and have something to drink, before checking to see if Boris was safely in bed. He was reassured to find him lying on his side under the duvet. His eyes were shut, and he was breathing evenly.

Adam undressed slowly. 'Won't be needing you!' he said to his alarm clock as he collapsed into bed.

Adam opened his eyes. Daylight showed round the sides of the curtains of his room. His copy of the Sisley hanging in its usual place told him immediately where he was, and he sighed with relief.

Home, he thought; and his mind flooded with images of the ghastly journey he and Boris had suffered.

He thought he could hear sounds coming from somewhere in the house, but he was not sure. He did not want to move, and realised with relief that there was nothing he had to do. Perhaps he could go back to sleep... He felt relaxed. But what about Boris? Adam suddenly remembered the grey pallor of his friend's face when he last saw him. If he had heard sounds in the house, that meant that Boris was up and moving about.

I'd better check, he said to himself.

He found Boris sitting in the conservatory with the portable radio beside him. Although it was switched on, the sound was so low that Adam only heard it as he entered the conservatory.

Boris smiled. 'Good morning, my friend,' he said.

His face looked quite normal, Adam noted.

He sat down beside Boris, who continued: 'This is a very pleasant place to sit.'

He had opened two of the windows. The air was warm and filled with birdsong. The remains of a packet of plain biscuits sat on the desk.

'I see you found something to tide you over until we go shopping,' Adam said.

'Yes,' replied Boris. 'I was very hungry. If you remember, I could not eat much on the journey. I did not want to wake you, and I did not want to go out to look for a shop as that would have meant leaving you.' He smiled. 'You have been asleep a long time.'

Adam realised that until now, he had assumed that it was

270

morning. Suddenly, he was not so sure. 'What time is it?' he asked.

'According to the radio, it is just after 3.30 p.m.' Boris watched Adam with amusement, as an incredulous look spread across his face.

'Half past three?' he echoed.

'Yes, half past three.'

Adam spluttered. 'I feel such a fool!'

Boris smiled indulgently. 'I am glad you slept, you needed it.'

'You're right. And there's nothing we have to do today except buy some food. There's a supermarket about a mile away that's open until late, so there's no rush.'

There was a pause.

'By the way,' Adam continued. 'I did the work on the Romanian songs in here at this desk.'

'I gathered that,' replied Boris. 'And although I am still recovering from our journey, I am looking forward now to our meeting with Carillon Music.'

'Less than a week to go now,' said Adam. 'And we'll be taking with us not only the completed Romanian songs, but also the ten Russian songs we brought back with us.'

'Yes, I think we chose them well.' Boris sounded confident. 'We have music from a number of different communities amongst those ten songs. I am satisfied that the selection gives some indication of the considerable variation that we have found.'

'I'd like to get washed and dressed now,' Adam said as he stood up. 'After that we can walk up to the shop, and get something for our evening meal.'

Boris could hear Adam whistling as he moved between his bedroom and the bathroom. It was not long before he returned, clean-shaven.

'I'll just have a couple of these biscuits with a drink of mineral water, and then we can set off. Is that okay?' asked Adam, as he disappeared briefly into the kitchen for a glass and a small plate.

'Just take your time, there is no rush,' Boris reminded him. 'I could make a list while you are eating.'

The shopping trip went well, and the friends returned laden with all the things they needed.

'Put the bags on the kitchen table. I'll put the perishable things in the fridge, and we can leave the rest,' said Adam. 'Let's take the snacks we bought into the conservatory and put our feet up. I'd prefer to cook later on as we did in your house, if that's okay with you.'

'Yes, that is fine for me,' answered Boris.

'If you don't mind, I'll bring the post through, and see what I must deal with.'

They sat in the conservatory. Boris read a book, while Adam looked at his mail. As always, there was a heap of junk mail that he did not bother to open. He started to sift this out first. He was not far through the heap, when he stopped.

'Boris, there's a letter here from Ellen!' he exclaimed.

Adam slit open the envelope, and Boris could detect a slight tremble in his hand as he unfolded the sheet. His eyes scanned the writing, and he relaxed and began to read out loud.

'That *is* good news,' said Boris when Adam had finished.

'Yes, it looks as if she's willing to come down, and that means you'll meet her. I'll write back straight away. I wonder if she has anywhere to stay. I'll give her my phone number, and she can get in touch if there's a problem. There are a couple of nice places not far from here. You'll remember that when we met at the Bull she seemed interested in our project, and I'm glad that we'll be seeing her soon after our meeting at Carillon Music.'

He took a pad out of his desk, and wrote his phone number at the top of the sheet.

Dear Ellen,

It is good to hear that you can come. Boris and I have just arrived back. Here is my phone number. Perhaps you would like to give me a ring, and we can make the final arrangements.

If you are unsure about accommodation, I can suggest a couple of places you might find suitable.

Yours sincerely,

Adam

'Unfortunately, the last collection has gone for today. We can walk along to the box later this evening. I'll have a look through these other letters now.'

Adam continued with his task, and Boris returned to his book. Only a few minutes later, Adam came upon a handwritten note that someone had pushed through his letter box in his absence. He opened the sheet of paper, and discovered that it was from Matthew. He read it, and found that Matthew had been sent to a job in North Wales for a month.

'Sorry to miss the chance of the meetings at Prof. Barnes',' he had written.

Adam turned to Boris, 'I'm afraid there's no chance of meeting Matthew while you're here,' he said. 'I have a note from him.'

Adam read the note out for Boris.

'That is a pity,' said Boris.

His reaction was one of genuine disappointment.

'When I see him again, I'll let him know that you were sad to have missed him,' said Adam. 'It's only a couple of days now before we'll be at Professor Barnes' for the evening,' he continued. 'As you know, I haven't been given the title of his talk, but it's bound to be fascinating.'

The two spent the evening in the kitchen, glad to reconnect with the pleasure of their shared cooking activities.

On May 24th Adam had woken early to the sound of the birds. He was content to lie there. It felt good that Boris was here. They were both looking forward to their meeting with Carillon Music – only four more days to go. Today they would work on some of the remaining tapes they had brought over with them. He waited until he could hear Boris moving about, and then he got up to join him.

They were enjoying a leisurely breakfast together when the phone rang.

Adam lifted the receiver. 'Hello,' he said.

He heard the voice at the other end say, 'Hello, is that Adam Thomas? This is Ellen Ridgeway speaking.'

'Hello, Ellen, it's good to hear you. So you got my note?'

'Yes, it's just arrived. I thought I'd phone right away. You say you have some suggestions about accommodation. Could you give me the details please?'

'I'll just go and get them.'

Adam laid down the receiver, and went to get a small heap of leaflets that were in a drawer of his desk.

'Here we are,' he said when he returned to the phone. 'There's a quiet guest house about half a mile from here, and a small hotel about the same distance away but in the opposite direction.' Adam read out the details slowly over the phone, giving Ellen a chance to write them down.

'Thanks,' said Ellen. 'I'll get on with that straight away. The only other thing is to arrange a time to meet.'

'What time do you think you'll arrive?' asked Adam.

'It'll be some time in the late evening,' Ellen replied.

'Perhaps we could meet up the following afternoon?' Adam suggested. 'If you phone and let us know where you're staying, Boris and I could walk round and meet you. How about around three o'clock?'

'That suits me,' answered Ellen. 'If you're out when I phone back, I'll leave a message telling you which place I've booked.'

'Boris and I will look forward to seeing you then,' said Adam, and he replaced the receiver. He turned to Boris. 'I expect that you can see that I have a very large smile on my face!'

'I gather that was Ellen, and that we are going to meet her the day after we go to Carillon Music?'

'Yes, that's right. It couldn't be better,' added Adam.

The two finished their breakfast, and planned their day's work, taking into account that they would have to eat early that evening, so that they could get to the talk in time.

'I'm sure it starts at half past seven. If we leave at seven, that'll leave plenty of time,' Adam calculated.

Reassured that everything was going according to plan, Adam found he could concentrate well on his work with the tapes, and Boris worked quietly in his usual way beside him. This was the first time they had worked together here. Adam realised how important this was to him. Here they were, sitting together in his conservatory; the windows were open, allowing the soft spring air to circulate freely around them. The phone rang in the house, but he was so engrossed in his work he was barely aware of it. It was only later that he realised that it might have been Ellen, phoning to let him know where she would be staying. He checked his call-minder. Yes, it was a message from her, letting him know that she would be staying at the Rookery, the small hotel he had suggested. He did not disturb Boris, but waited until lunchtime to let him know.

At seven o'clock, the two men set off down the road to walk to Professor Barnes' house. As they walked, Adam reminded Boris of his last visit there, so that he had some idea of what to expect. However, as they came in sight of the house, Adam was surprised to see a group of about eight men and women filing in through the gate. They were talking animatedly, and did not notice Adam and Boris until they joined them at the door. One of the women rang the bell, and the door was soon answered by Professor Barnes himself, who looked exactly the same as he had the last time Adam saw him.

'Good evening, friends,' he greeted them. 'Do come in.'

He beckoned them through the door, and into the hall. Adam and Boris followed the others in, shaking hands with him on their way.

'Take the first door on the right,' he said.

The group made their way into the room. It was a large room with a bay window; well lit and comfortably furnished. The seating was predominantly arranged round the walls. It was a mixture of straight chairs with upholstered seats, low armchairs, and settees. Adam noticed that about half the chairs were already taken, but he found two straight chairs, side by side, for himself and Boris.

Professor Barnes followed them into the room, and closed the door behind him.

'I think that's everyone now,' he said, as he took up his position beside a table in the centre of the room.

There were a number of boxes on the table, some made of cardboard and some of wood, together with a small pile of books.

'As some of you will know,' began Professor Barnes, 'I have a collection of fossils. I thought that this evening could be an introduction to some of these. I've brought specimens through for you to see. You can hand them round, and I'll give you an idea of what they are, their age, and how I came by them. Most of those I have here tonight I found myself; so if you're interested, I can tell you the story that lies behind each of them.'

A hum of interest went round the group. 'Yes, please do,' said a number of voices.

275

The professor began. 'The first box contains specimens of fossil plant material from the Triassic era, which was approximately two hundred million years ago. I collected these about forty years ago from a part of the Rhaetic, Coombe Hill in Gloucestershire. You will see that there are fragments of horsetails and ferns; but there is also an aberrant lycopod of which I am immensely proud.'

He passed a box to the woman sitting nearest to him, indicating that she should pass it round.

Then he continued. 'The second box contains brachiopods and crinoids from marine facies of the Carboniferous era. I collected these from a number of sites in Britain. Most of you probably know that that era lasted about sixty-five million years, and it began about three hundred and forty-five million years ago.'

Again, he passed the box to the woman nearest to him.

By the time the first box had reached Adam and Boris, Professor Barnes was recounting a story of sitting in a waterlogged tent overnight, waiting for a storm to pass; and describing the kind of camping equipment that was available in his youth. This evoked much laughter from the company. Not only was the professor very knowledgeable, but also he was a highly accomplished and amusing speaker. He was the kind of person who could bring a subject alive to almost any audience. Boris and Adam were sad when the evening began to draw to a close with the offer of the usual cup of tea and a biscuit.

'I am so glad you arranged that I could come here,' said Boris. 'This man is so inspiring. It is good that we can come to one more talk next week.'

'Yes,' answered Adam. 'I'd like to know what he's going to talk about. I think I'll ask.'

He walked across to the professor, who was standing talking to a man of about his own age.

'Excuse me, sir,' he interrupted, 'I want to thank you for this evening, and to ask you what the title of next week's talk is.'

Professor Barnes turned to Adam and said, 'I enjoyed sharing some of my fossil collection; but I'm afraid I don't yet know the title of the next talk.'

The other man took over. 'Perhaps I can explain,' he said. 'When Edmund retired, he promised himself that he would only give talks that he hadn't had to prepare. After a lifetime of careful preparation for lectures, he wanted to be different. People who know him already know this.'

Professor Barnes smiled. 'That's correct. You'll always be welcome, whenever I have a place available, but I'll never be able to tell you in advance what I'm going to talk about.'

Adam thanked him again, and returned to Boris to explain, while they prepared to leave.

'I'm puzzled as to why we were shown to a different room,' said Adam to Boris on the way home.

'And more than half the guests were women,' added Boris. 'You had told me that it was only men when you went before, and I am sure you told me that Matthew had said the same.'

'The décor of that room tonight was so different; it was as if we were in another house,' Adam continued.

'The house is very large,' said Boris. 'There is another room at the front on the left-hand side of the entrance. It also has a bay window. And when we were in the hall, I saw that there were several doors leading off. I could see as we approached the house that the first storey must be the same size as the ground floor.'

Chapter Thirty-six

Ellen had reserved a room at the Rookery for two nights. She had been pleased she had remembered to check if there would be a room available after that. She wanted to be able to continue her stay after meeting Boris and Adam, but did not want to be committed at this stage. The receptionist had reassured her that there would be no problem. After that she had left a message on Adam's call-minder. Now, on the eve of her departure, she felt the need to phone Eva or Jane, as there were things she wanted to talk over. She tried Eva's number first, and was pleased to hear her familiar voice.

'Hello… Oh, it's Ellen. I'm glad to hear you; I was thinking of phoning you. I have some news of Hannah and her father. But tell me why you phoned.'

'I'm setting off tomorrow to meet Adam and his friend Boris, and I wanted to tell you about it,' explained Ellen.

'Thanks for letting me know,' said Eva. 'How are you feeling?'

'Actually, I'm looking forward to it very much,' replied Ellen. 'I've booked a room in a local hotel for a couple of nights, but I might stay a bit longer. I'll see how it goes.'

'How long is the drive?' asked Eva.

'It's about five hours. I intend to set off first thing in the morning, and make my way there by the middle of the evening.'

'I have an idea. I have the day off tomorrow,' said Eva. 'Shall I meet up with you somewhere on your way? Or if you want, you could detour by my house. It would add more than an hour on to your journey, but it sounds as if you've plenty of time.'

'What a good idea!' exclaimed Ellen. 'I'd love to do that. I could set off earlier than I had planned. That way I could spend several hours with you. I'll come to your house.'

'Shall we leave the rest of the talking until then?' asked Eva.

'Yes. I'll get my things together, and have an early night. Expect me to arrive some time around eleven.'

The following day Ellen arrived at Eva's well before eleven. She had set off very early, eager to spend time with her friend.

'Can we walk down by the river again?' she asked. 'I need to stretch my legs.'

Eva put on her strong shoes, and they set off.

'Now tell me what your plan is,' she said.

'Today is the day that Adam and his friend Boris are seeing someone about the songs they're hoping to get published. It's a big day for them. I'll spend the night at the hotel, and we've arranged that they'll walk along to meet me in the afternoon. After that, there's no definite plan. I know I'll enjoy discussing their music projects with them. I'm looking forward to that.' She added, a little guardedly, 'I've got my red book with me. I thought I'd show it to Adam.'

'A good idea,' replied Eva, encouragingly. 'After all, he's seen you with it, and he's dreamed about it. I'm sure he'll appreciate the chance of having a look at it.'

'That's what I thought; but I also know it's important to me that he looks at it.'

Eva looked at her keenly. 'You're probably right.' She thought for a minute, and then added, 'Do you think you'll tell him about Jane's spirals?'

Ellen started, and then coloured. 'Why did you ask that?'

'It occurred to me that if things go well between you, you might want to tell him. After all, sharing your red book is a big thing for you. Depending on how that goes, you may well start thinking about the spirals. They're a big thing in the lives of all three of us. We don't yet know what they mean, or indeed what the full effect of them is on each of us; but it's you who's the most obviously affected. And it's without doubt that you say the name Adam during the time you are in the trance-like state.'

Ellen became defensive. 'But Adam is the name of the boy in Frances Ianson's book.'

'I know it is,' replied Eva, 'but Adam Thomas is of direct importance to you, and it may well be him,' she persisted.

'I know, I know,' said Ellen irritably. 'I know you're right, and I know that I should think about all of this in advance. Have you any advice?'

Eva thought for a moment. Then she said, 'I think Jane should be back from work before you leave here. How about phoning her to tell her what's happening, and to ask her if she feels comfortable about the idea of your talking to Adam about her spirals?'

'I hadn't thought about that.' Ellen sounded a little alarmed. 'You're right, of course. I should have her permission; and then, if I do feel I want to tell Adam the story, I won't suddenly feel in a quandary about it. Have you anything else you want to say?'

Eva continued, 'All I can say is that I'm sure you'll know at the time if it feels right to tell him about the spirals or not. I do think that a lot of it will depend on how he relates to you about your book. Your account of the evening you spent with him at the Bull suggests to me that he'll be very pleased to have the opportunity to see it. You'll just have to take things from there.'

'Thanks very much. This conversation has been very helpful,' said Ellen. 'Perhaps we can come back to it all later. Can we talk about Hannah now? You said you had news of her.'

'Yes, I do. Mr Greaves phoned me the other day. He and Hannah had come back from their stay in Milan. I spoke to both of them. Hannah told me about how they had all gone to her mother's grave. She had chosen some special flowers to take there. When they arrived at the cemetery, she got her father and Giovanni to help her walk to where the grave was. She sounded so proud of herself. "Mummy didn't realise how much we loved her," she told me. "That's why she went away. I think she thought it was her fault that Dawn died, but it wasn't. Dawn just didn't have to be here very long, that's all." She told me all about where Giovanni lives, and the room where her mother had stayed. Then she told me about some of the things she had seen in the locality, and other things they had done together. She said, "Giovanni said we can go back to see him again, and Daddy says we can go quite soon."

'Mr Greaves told me how he was feeling more settled now. He said that he and Hannah would make regular trips to Milan, and that he hoped Giovanni would come and stay with them soon. He said how well Hannah was looking now. "Her cheeks are nearly always pink, she keeps taking me for walks round the garden, and there's a lot of apple juice and soup being consumed in this house." His voice sounded light, as if an enormous load had been lifted away. Before they rang off, they asked if they could phone again some time soon to make a time to come and see me. Hannah still goes for hospital checks, and I'll encourage them to continue with that, but it does look as if things are on the mend now.'

She turned to Ellen, and saw that there were tears in her eyes.

'Yes, I cry too,' she said. 'I've been affected very deeply by them.'

'Is there any news of your stick?' asked Ellen.

'Silly of me to leave that out! Hannah told me that she took it to Milan, and had it with her when she went to the cemetery to see where her mother was.'

Ellen's voice was solemn. 'The stick was in the right place,' she said. 'Have you had a chance to tell Jane the news about Hannah and her father yet?'

'Yes, I phoned her last night to let her know you were coming here today. I told her then. Shall we go back to the house now? We could have something to eat, and then it won't be long before you can phone her about the spirals.'

They returned to the house, where they baked some scones, which they enjoyed with Eva's home-made fruit spread. As Eva had predicted, it was not long before it was time that Ellen could phone Jane. Jane was happy to hear of her trip to see Adam, and had no reservations about her talking to him about the spirals if she found she wanted to.

'Good luck with it all!' Eva called as she waved goodbye to Ellen. 'Phone me when you want; I'll be looking forward to hearing your news.'

Ellen arrived at the Rookery at eight o'clock, a little earlier than she had predicted. It had been easy to find from Adam's directions. She booked in, and settled herself in her room. This evening she would relax with her red book, and tomorrow morning she would go out and get some idea of the area. Before long she was settled on her bed, engrossed in her book.

Chapter Thirty-seven

The last three days had passed uneventfully. Adam and Boris had continued to work on the tapes that they had with them, but not the same long hours as before. Adam had been keen to show Boris some of the surrounding countryside; and one evening they had gone to a concert in the local Town Hall that had been given by an amateur ensemble from a neighbouring town.

It was now the morning of their meeting with Carillon Music. They had arrived at the car park in plenty of time, and sat talking for a while before going across to the office block. Having spoken to the receptionist, they did not wait long before Gordon Quaver came down a corridor to meet them, accompanied by an older man, whom he introduced as Peter Brown.

'Come this way,' he said warmly.

He led them to a door at the end of the corridor from which he had emerged, opened it, and ushered them inside.

'Please do take a seat. Would you like a glass of water?' he asked as he filled four of the glasses from a bottle of mineral water.

Peter Brown spoke as he opened a file of papers that lay ready on the desk.

'I'm sorry to bring you all this way,' he began, 'but I did want to meet you both.'

Adam's heart lurched. Did this mean that Carillon Music were not interested in them after all? he wondered.

'Yes,' he went on, 'when I saw the samples of your work, I was immediately interested. I could have had all the necessary contact with you by letter and phone, but I didn't want to give up the opportunity of meeting you. Have you brought the rest of the songs with you?'

'Yes,' replied Adam. 'I have them here.'

He opened the thin case he had used before, took out two folders, and handed one to Mr Brown, who opened it eagerly, and studied its contents.

'Yes, yes,' Mr Brown repeated, nodding his head as he did so. 'Is this a copy you can leave with me?' he asked.

'Of course,' replied Adam.

'And you have another folder there, I see.'

It was Boris who answered. 'These are some songs from our Russian project,' he said hesitantly.

He turned to Adam, 'Do you want to talk about these now?' he asked.

Adam nodded and began: 'We brought these in case you made a firm decision about the Romanian songs. Gordon may already have told you, we've been working for several months now on tapes of songs that have been collected from all over Russia. It's a much larger project. We wondered if you might be interested.'

'Mr Thomas, Mr Ivanov,' Mr Brown said sincerely. 'It's beginning to look as if we are embarking on a long and fruitful association. I'm delighted that you have brought us some of your other work. Can you leave it with me to study, and I'll phone you in a couple of days?' Adam and Boris readily agreed, and Mr Brown continued. 'Would you be willing to go over the background to the Russian project?' he asked. 'Gordon certainly mentioned it to me, but we didn't discuss it.'

Gordon nodded.

Over the next half-hour, Adam and Boris described their project from its inception, while Mr Brown and Gordon Quaver listened, interrupting with an occasional question.

The meeting was concluded as Adam passed the second file to Mr Brown, who reiterated that he would phone in a couple of days.

Back in the car, Adam and Boris were jubilant.

'We must celebrate!' said Adam. 'I know of a restaurant where we can get a good lunch. I'll take you.'

It was later that evening, over a game of chess, that Adam began to feel unwell.

'I'm sorry, Boris,' he said. 'I think I'll have to go to bed. I feel exhausted, and I can't see properly.'

He looked at the clock, and noticed that it was only nine o'clock.

'If I go to bed now, perhaps I'll be okay in the morning. Just help yourself to anything you need.'

He stood up, swayed about, and sat down again.

'Would you mind giving me a hand?' he asked.

Boris came across, took his arm, and helped him to his room.

'I will come back and see you in a little while,' he promised.

When he returned, Adam was already asleep. Boris switched off the lights, and pulled the door to. He felt concerned. Adam had seemed fine all day. Whatever was affecting him had come on very suddenly. He made a mental note to check his friend again later, before he went to bed.

When Boris woke the next morning, he could hear Adam moving briskly around the house. He got out of bed, and found his friend cleaning the kitchen floor.

'I will do that with you if you will wait,' he told Adam.

'No, don't bother,' said Adam cheerfully. 'I feel full of energy this morning. Our meeting yesterday went so well, and this afternoon you'll meet Ellen.'

Boris stared at him. 'I was worried about you last night,' he said.

'Worried about me?' questioned Adam. 'What for?'

'You weren't well.'

It was Adam's turn to stare at Boris. 'Will you tell me what you mean? I'm fine,' he said.

Boris explained. When he had finished, Adam sat down heavily on one of the kitchen chairs.

'I don't remember any of that at all,' he said, and then paused. 'I'm beginning to think it sounds a bit like what happened when Matthew was last here, only I didn't pass out on the floor this time. Perhaps I should get a check-up with the doctor just in case there's something wrong with me.'

'I think that is a good idea,' replied Boris. 'I would feel easier if you did. I cannot see any reason why this happened.' He stopped, and then went on, 'Unless it has something to do with Ellen's visit. But I think you should get checked anyway.'

Adam was silent. He was thinking about what his friend had said... Ellen... But he would phone the doctor's surgery, and make an appointment.

Chapter Thirty-eight

Adam and Boris arrived at the Rookery at exactly three o'clock. The building was supposed to be about a hundred and fifty years old; and judging by the style, Adam had no doubt that that was correct. They found Ellen sitting in the foyer. She smiled, stood up, and started walking towards them. She took Adam's hand. This time her touch was open, and she was in no hurry to let go of his hand.

'You must be Boris,' she said, turning to him. 'I'm so glad to meet you.' She took his hand, and shook it warmly. 'There's a pleasant sitting room at the back of this hotel; perhaps you know it?' she asked Adam.

'No, I don't, but let's give it a try,' replied Adam.

Ellen led the way. The room was indeed pleasant. It looked straight out to a large walled garden. There was an extensive lawn surrounded by a wide herbaceous border, and there were many fruit trees trained against the wall. Although the room was not a conservatory, most of the wall that looked out to the garden was glass. The room extended along the whole of the back of the hotel, and must have been at least forty feet long. It looked as if it was an extension to the original building, and that it must have been built quite a long time ago. They had entered through a door at the far right of the room, and walked down most of its length to a quiet area next to the inner wall.

'How was your journey back from Russia?' Ellen asked when they were seated.

The two men laughed ruefully. 'We have agreed that it was the worst journey we've ever suffered.' They went on to entertain her with the story of their struggles.

'I'm sorry to hear all that.' She turned to Boris. 'I do hope that your return journey will be more comfortable. How long are you able to stay?'

'My return flight leaves early on June 4th,' he said. 'I wish I could stay longer, but I have to get back.'

Adam looked at his friend appreciatively, 'Boris, I'm so glad you were able to come, and I'll miss you when you go.'

Ellen noted the strong link between the two men, and was impressed by it.

She continued, 'My drive down yesterday was very pleasant. The way it worked out, I had time to call in on a close friend on the way, and we spent several hours together. It broke the journey for me.'

'That was good,' said Adam. 'How did you find your room last night?'

'It was very comfortable,' Ellen replied. 'I had all that I needed. I arrived at around eight. I didn't bother with a meal – I didn't feel hungry. I expect it was because my friend and I had been baking in the afternoon! Because I'd had an early start, I was quite tired, and lay down on my bed.' She paused. 'I lay and studied the book I told you about when we met at the Bull.'

Ellen was glad to note that telling Adam this had not been difficult, or caused her any agitation. Adam saw that she appeared to be comfortable as she referred to her book, and he guessed that it would be all right to include Boris.

'Because Boris is a trusted friend,' he said, 'I did tell him what you told me about your book. And I've also told him about that dream I had about you.'

Ellen leaned back in her seat, and digested this information. Her overall reaction was one of feeling reassured.

Adam was looking at her a little anxiously, so she smiled at him and said, 'I'm so pleased that you can confide in Boris. I have friends I trust in that way too. In fact, Eva, whom I visited on my way here, is one of two such friends. Although neither of them lives close to me, I sometimes meet up with them for a weekend; and of course we phone each other. I'm lucky to meet you, Boris, because you live so far away.'

Boris had been sitting quietly throughout this exchange. Although he had not been worried by anything Adam had already told him about Ellen, he had concerns and questions in his mind about what exactly was happening in their lives. He had seen Adam having some very intense experiences, and it seemed that these had some link to her; although by ordinary standards, they were hardly more than acquaintances. He felt a little reassured by his impression of Ellen as someone of integrity. This quality in her might prove to be essential, if they were ever to discuss something of what had been happening to Adam. Already she had mentioned her book – the one Adam had already described to him, first in the dream, and later after his meeting with Ellen at the Bull.

Boris spoke to Ellen. 'Yes,' he said to her. 'We work so well together, and enjoy each other's company so much, that it's hard that we live so far apart. We do keep in touch by e-mail, but it's no substitute for real contact. It's lucky indeed for me that you were able to come when I was over here. This is the first time I have been in Britain since I was a student here.'

'But your English is excellent!' Ellen exclaimed.

'I was brought up to be more or less bilingual,' explained Boris, ' and I have made sure that I have not lost my English.'

'I'm impressed. I'm afraid that my Russian is non-existent.'

'Do not worry about that,' Boris reassured her. 'Adam took a very long time before he was sufficiently fluent. It was a good thing that he persevered, otherwise we could never have worked on the Russian songs together.'

'The songs...' said Ellen. 'Now, tell me how your meeting went yesterday.'

Boris and Adam took it in turns to describe to Ellen the meeting with Gordon Quaver and Peter Brown. Confident about the outcome, they took obvious pleasure in telling the story in the most amusing way they could, allowing Ellen plenty of opportunity for laughter. When they had finished, she asked them many questions about the songs themselves, finishing with a challenge.

'Well,' she said, 'when you have finished the Russian songs and had them published, what will you be doing next?'

Boris and Adam stared at each other. So engrossed had they been in their two projects for nearly two years, they had not considered what would happen afterwards. It was Adam who spoke first.

'You'll have to give us time to recover from discovering that Carillon Music are interested in our projects,' he said. 'I think both of us are in a state of shock and exhilaration!'

'I was teasing you,' Ellen replied. 'But seriously, now you have the link with that publisher, you might want to think of another project after the Russian one is complete.'

Boris looked at Ellen appreciatively. 'Thank you for your thoughts,' he said, 'we will remember to think about that when we can, won't we, Adam?'

'Yes, indeed. This conversation will certainly start me thinking.'

'Shall we order some tea?' Ellen suggested.

Adam looked at his watch. It was five already.

'How about you, Boris?'

Boris nodded. 'Yes, good idea.'

Adam stood up and said, 'I'll go and find someone.'

He went off, leaving Boris and Ellen, who sat and exchanged comments about particular valued recordings of music they discovered they had in common. Adam returned, and was soon followed by a young woman carrying a tray with their tea.

'We've made no plan yet for the rest of your visit,' Adam commented, as he poured Ellen a cup. 'How long are you able to stay?'

'My room is booked for tonight,' Ellen replied. 'After that, I could stay another night, and travel back on the 31st if I wanted. The hotel isn't busy.'

Since meeting Ellen today, Adam had noticed that she was not edgy at all. And now she was offering the possibility of staying on a day longer than he had hoped. He remembered that she had certainly indicated in her letter that she had a few days free, but had not suggested that she stayed here for all of them. He decided to be direct.

'I'd really like it if you'd stay on,' he said.

It was obvious to Ellen that his statement was completely genuine, and she looked across to Boris.

'I too,' he said simply.

'Will you allow me to reserve your room for the additional night?' asked Adam.

Ellen allowed herself to agree. She had quickly reminded herself that if she felt anxious at all, she could phone Eva or Jane; but at the moment she felt totally at ease with the situation.

Adam disappeared for a few minutes once more, and when he

returned he said, 'That's fixed then.' He went on, 'Ellen, I've something to ask you.'

'What is it Adam?'

'You've brought your book with you. Would you be willing to let us see it some time before you leave?'

'I'd be happy to show it to you both. I'm glad you asked. I'd like to see what you think of it. I have it here in my bag. I can show it to you now, but we should put some time aside if you want to study it properly.'

She unzipped a section at the back of her bag, produced her book, and put it on her lap. She took out a tissue, and wiped the table before carefully placing the book where Adam and Boris could reach it. Then she returned to her bag, and took out a pen and a notebook.

'You'll see that I've brought my pen as well.'

She smiled across to Adam, who immediately reached for the inside pocket of the light jacket he was wearing, and produced his own pen.

'Look, Boris,' he said, reaching across to hold his pen next to Ellen's. 'They're identical, just as I told you.'

Boris examined them carefully, and nodded. 'You are right of course; and as you said, the design is unusual.'

'What's the notebook for?' Adam asked Ellen.

'I think that it's sensible to have something on hand when anyone new is studying this book. There may well be things that we want to make a note of. To be more specific,' she continued, 'it was not long after I saw you at the Bull, Adam, that I decided to take the book with me to show my friends, Eva and Jane. We'd arranged a weekend at the end of January together at Eva's house. I'd already told them about my chance meetings with you, and I found myself telling them about our conversation at the Bull, and what you told me about your dream. They were very interested of course. I confided that since seeing you at the Bull, it seemed to me that the pinprick patterns I saw after that seemed even more like faint spirals. After that we looked at the book together, starting from the back. I looked for the first blank page that had affected me on earlier occasions. Again I saw a pinprick pattern. It was Eva who looked at the book next. She worked her way through the blank pages to that same page, but saw nothing until a little later, when

Jane was examining the book. Her reaction to that page had been delayed. She seemed to see a slightly different pattern from the one I saw, but she saw it in the same way as I had: as if it was in her mind, not on the page.'

'What pattern did she see then?' asked Adam.

'She said that the pinpricks appeared quite random.'

'And what did Jane find?' asked Adam, eagerly.

'She was completely transfixed by the second leaf-vein pattern, and she did not want to study the blank pages.'

'*Ellen*,' said Adam, urgently.

Ellen and Boris looked at Adam, who was sitting rigidly in his seat.

'I've just realised something. I've told each of you that when I looked back on my dream, I not only thought I'd seen something on the blank pages, but also that I had some kind of association between the room in the dream and the room at the Traveller's Arms where the piano was.'

Ellen and Boris nodded.

'I'm amazed that I haven't realised it before, but the room we're in now is very like the room in the dream. In fact, we're sitting in almost the exact position where Ellen was sitting reading in the dream.'

Boris looked stunned. Ellen appeared composed; but inside her thoughts were in turmoil.

What *is* all this? she thought.

Remembering the experience she had gained through study of the spirals with Eva and Jane, she felt she should take charge of the situation.

'We need to think through all of this very carefully,' she said, authoritatively. 'I still want to show you my book, but I think we should plan in advance how to go about it.'

Confident about having gained the prior approval of her friends, she decided to tell Boris and Adam something of the puzzle of the spirals, and how profoundly she had been affected by them. Briefly she told them how she had heard from Jane about the spirals in her diary, how she and Eva had visited Jane to see them, and how since then they had met from time to time to study them again. She described the kind of state Eva and Jane had observed her in.

'So you see,' she went on, 'after the first time I was affected by the spirals, we were very careful how we went about looking at them again. It's because of this, and what I know Adam has already experienced because of his dream that included my book, that I insist we approach looking at my book together only after careful planning.'

'You are wise,' Boris said. But then he went on, 'There is something else we should bring into the picture here. Adam,' he addressed his friend, 'it is clear to me that the next thing is to talk to Ellen about what happened when you were with Matthew, and indeed what happened to you last night.'

Ellen looked anxious. 'Have you been unwell, Adam?' she asked.

'Last night I did begin to wonder if there was something wrong with my health, and I've planned to go to the doctor for a check. I'll still go; but after hearing what you've said about your experiences with the spirals, I don't think that I've anything physically wrong with me. Boris,' he turned to look at his friend, 'can we also tell Ellen about the tape?'

'We *must* tell her,' Boris replied. 'And we must tell her before any further consideration of looking at her book. We *must* talk about all these things before attempting to study the book together. If I am to be honest, I have heard so much today I need to think about, and I will have to turn to something less intense for a while.'

Adam nodded. 'How do you feel, Ellen?' he asked.

'It's a little different for me,' she replied. 'I'm already familiar with my book, and I've been part of the story about the spirals right from when Jane first told me. But it has been emotionally draining even putting it all into words for you. And now I have learned that you have something to tell me that sounds similarly profound. It's clear that I have much to learn... Yes, I too need time to think about all of this before we continue.'

'Perhaps Boris and I should leave you now?' suggested Adam. 'It's after eight, and we should all eat. I'd like to suggest that we eat dinner together here, but as we all need time to think, I doubt if that would really be appropriate. How would you feel about Boris and me collecting you at about ten thirty in the morning? You could come to my house, so that we can talk about everything.'

'I'd like that,' Ellen replied.

291

She put her book and her pen back into her bag, and stood up.

'I'd like to walk with you both down to the end of the road, and we can say goodbye there.'

The three slowly made their way out of the hotel. The late sun warmed them as they strolled along together in silence.

Back in the hotel dining room Ellen ate sparingly. She did not feel hungry at all, but realised that she should eat something. Her mind was whirling. What was it that Adam and Boris had been experiencing that could be in any way similar to the story of the spirals? Later, in her room, Ellen realised that she should speak to Eva or Jane, and she reached for the phone. It was important to talk to one of them before she saw Adam and Boris again, and heard their story.

'Hello Eva. I'm glad you're in.' Ellen was relieved to hear her friend answer the phone.

'What is it, Ellen? Is something wrong?' Eva had noted the urgency in Ellen's voice.

'Nothing is wrong,' Ellen reassured her. 'It's just that there's so much happening I can hardly keep track of it all. I wanted to tell you about it before I see Adam and Boris again tomorrow.'

'Will you give me some idea of what you're talking about please? Then we can decide what to do.'

'Well, Adam and Boris came up to the hotel here yesterday afternoon as planned. I was very glad to meet Boris, he seems a really nice person, and he and Adam are obviously close friends. It was good to see them together. It emerged that Adam had told Boris everything he knew about me, and that made the conversation easier, of course. I told them about how you and Jane are close friends of mine, so they know I confide in you. We got round to talking about my book, and I took it out. I explained how it had affected us all. I also said something about how the spirals had affected me. It was in this way that I convinced them we should make notes while we studied the book, and also discuss how to go about it.'

'That sounds right to me,' said Eva.

'But there's more,' Ellen continued. 'Adam and Boris told me things have been happening to Adam too. I was astonished. Fortunately, I had the presence of mind to suggest that we parted until tomorrow morning, so that we all have time to think.'

'What kind of things?' asked Eva.

'I didn't ask. All I know is that something happened to Adam when he was with a friend called Matthew, and also things have happened when he was with Boris. In fact, one incident happened last night. I realise, now I'm telling you, that it must have been when I was lying on my bed, studying my book!'

'This is intriguing,' said Eva. 'I think you were absolutely right to suggest a break. Of course, I'm eager to know more straight away; but like you, I'll have to wait. By the way, you haven't told me yet how they got on at the publisher's.'

'That went very well. It seems they've established a good link.'

'What's happening in the morning?'

'They're coming up to collect me mid-morning, and we'll go to Adam's house to pick up where we left off.'

'I'll be thinking about you all then,' said Eva. 'I think it's good that you're taking it all slowly. I can't add anything, except that I'll let Jane know what's happening.'

'Thanks, I'd like that. Give me a ring in the evening if you want. I'll be here.'

'I will. I'll make sure I do. Thanks.' Ellen rang off.

Having spoken to her friend, she felt easier, and was able to get ready for bed, looking forward to the following day.

Chapter Thirty-nine

'Breakfast!' Adam called to Boris, who was still shaving.

'All right. I'll be there in a minute.'

They sat at the kitchen table, keen to have a few more words about the events of the day before, and about their impending meeting with Ellen. They had resisted the temptation to sit up turning it all over late in the evening, and had limited themselves to running through what Ellen had told them so far.

'I have to admit that I'm impatient to get a chance to study Ellen's book,' said Adam. 'I can see the sense in waiting, but it doesn't mean that I'm not impatient.'

'I can see why you are,' replied Boris. 'But promise me that you won't do anything to rush this,' he added earnestly.

'I'm not planning to,' Adam reassured him. 'But if you think I'm getting carried away at any time, I give you full permission to say so straight away.'

'Thank you,' said Boris. 'That helps me. As you know, I have been anxious about you at times, and I have to admit that I feel anxious about today. There is no way of telling what might happen.'

'Point taken,' said Adam, now studying his friend with a serious expression on his face.

'Let's tidy up a bit. It'll soon be time to go and collect Ellen.'

It did not take them long to clear away the breakfast things. The day was clear and bright. The sky was the intense blue that was so characteristic of this time of year, and the birdsong was varied. Soon they were strolling along the road towards the hotel.

'We are early,' said Boris.

'I know, but I prefer that.'

As they turned up the drive of the hotel, they could see Ellen standing at the front, waiting for them to arrive. When she caught sight of them, she immediately started walking down to meet them.

'Hello,' she greeted them. 'What a beautiful day!'

Adam noticed that she was carrying the same bag as the day before, the one with the zip compartment from which she had produced the red book.

Noticing his obvious interest in her bag, Ellen smiled and said, 'Don't worry, I have it with me.'

Adam felt a little embarrassed, but went on to ask her how she had been since they parted.

'I decided to phone Eva for a chat,' she said. 'I thought it best.'

Boris nodded.

'After that I slept very well,' she continued. 'How about yourselves?'

'We talked through what you told us, and we've been looking forward to seeing you again, hoping to learn more from each other,' said Adam. 'I slept very well myself. How about you, Boris?'

'I was a little restless. I realise that I was anxious until after we spoke this morning.'

'Why was that?' asked Ellen.

'I know that Adam is keen to see your book. I do not know what the effect will be. When we talk to you about the things that have happened to him that we cannot explain, I think you will understand. But I felt better this morning once he and I had spoken about that.'

Ellen nodded. 'This is a very pleasant area where you live,' she commented. 'Of course I haven't had time to look at any of the surrounding countryside, but the immediate area looks almost ideal. I spent some time yesterday morning walking round it.'

'There are very few drawbacks to living here,' Adam replied, 'I'm very lucky to have found this place. The surroundings are very good – there's easy access to open fields and woodlands. A little farther afield, there are places of interest to visit such as a small church dating from Norman times.

Reaching his house, Adam unlocked the door.

'Just go on right through to the back,' he said to Ellen. 'We can sit in the conservatory. It might get too hot in the afternoon, but we can start off in there. Would you like a drink of something?'

'Water is fine for me.'

Adam brought glasses and a jug of water for them to share, and sat down in one of the easy chairs he had moved through for the purpose.

'I have a suggestion,' he said. 'Yesterday you told us a little about the spirals. I've a lot I'd like to ask about that whole subject. But I know that Boris and I agreed to tell you about the tape.'

Boris interrupted. 'What I said was that we should tell Ellen about it before we decided about studying her book. Ellen, perhaps we should ask you to choose whether we tell you about that now, or you tell us some more about the spirals.'

'Mm. It's difficult to decide. There's certainly a lot more I can tell you about the whole subject of the spirals. However, I do think it best if I learn something about your side of things before we continue with that, so please will you make a start.'

'It's helpful that you already know of our two projects,' Adam began, 'and how we've worked closely together on them for months. The story of the tape began one day when, having picked out a new tape from the Russian collection, I began to listen to it, and immediately realised that it was very different from the others I'd been working on. I was so struck by it that I interrupted Boris.'

Here Boris spoke. 'That had never happened before. We never interrupt one another when we are working together. We work in the same room, but do not speak. Of course, we would discuss the project as we walked or cooked together, but never while we were actually working on the tapes. Because of this, I knew straight away that it was something very important.'

Adam continued. 'We listened to it together, and were both deeply affected. Boris,' he looked across at his friend, 'you'd better take over here.'

Boris described exactly what had happened, with precise details of everything he could remember of the state Adam had been in.

'When Boris first told me about it, I wasn't able to take it in,' said Adam. 'You see, I had no memory of it at all. All I knew was that I felt rather cold.'

'There is one more thing,' said Boris. 'It is something I did not feel I could tell Adam at the time.'

'Yes, that's right,' said Adam. 'I could not be sure at the time,' Boris continued. 'That is why I said nothing about it. In fact, I only told him after he had e-mailed me his account of the dream he had

had about you and your book. The same night that he had that dream, I too had an intense dream. After thinking about the two dreams, I decided to let him know. When he had been in that strange state, I had tried to make a note of the few words I thought I recognised of what he had mouthed. And your name had been one of them.'

Ellen had been sitting very still, listening intently. Now she said, 'I can see why you wouldn't have said anything to him until later, Boris – when he'd had that dream about me. I'd like to know what *you* dreamed on that same night. I'd also like to go through what you've told me so far about Adam's reaction to the tape. I want to make sure I've taken everything in.' She turned to Adam. 'You were going to tell me about something that happened when Matthew was visiting you here. But first, I think I must tell you precisely how the spirals affected me the first time I saw them. Of course, what I'm going to tell you is mostly Jane and Eva's account, because like you, Adam, I have no conscious memory of it myself. Like you, all I remembered was feeling cold when I came round.'

She began: 'I told you before that Jane had explained to me how the spirals appeared in her diary. Perhaps I should explain that she was reading a particular book at the time. I'll tell you more of that later. Months later, she had hurt her ankle, and couldn't come to a meeting where Eva and I had hoped to see her. We went to visit her afterwards, and it was then I first saw them. When I saw them, the last thing I remembered was looking at the double spiral, which, according to the insert we think is a layout diagram, is central.'

'When you talked about them yesterday, you told us that there were nine, which appeared over five pages of her diary, and that each was made up of tiny pen strokes. Can you say more about the pen strokes?' asked Boris.

'You really need to see them,' replied Ellen. 'They're extremely complex.'

'Leave that for now, then,' he said, 'and tell us exactly what you were told about what happened to you.'

Ellen told them what Eva and Jane had described to her after she was first affected by the spirals.

'It wasn't until the second time I was affected that Eva was able to work out some of what I was mouthing,' she said. 'You'll be interested to learn that one of the words was "Adam".'

Adam and Boris stared at her.

'Adam?' said Adam. 'You mean me?'

'I can't be sure,' Ellen replied. 'There's another Adam involved in this.'

'Who is that?' asked Boris.

'He's a central character in the book Jane was reading just before the spirals appeared in her diary.'

'Why do you think there's a connection there?' asked Adam.

Ellen laughed.

'Why are you laughing?' Adam sounded hurt.

'I'm sorry, I shouldn't be laughing. You'll see what affected me when I explain. The book Jane was reading is called *Communications*, and the central issue in the book is about the connection between a mother and her son, Adam. I felt odd when you started asking about a "connection", almost as if you knew it had a double significance, and I laughed to try to conceal how I felt.'

'Who wrote the book?' Boris asked.

'Frances Ianson,' Ellen replied. 'I should tell you that it's an account of how the mother struggled to understand her son, who was only able to make sounds that no one could understand. She knew he was trying to communicate something. His behaviour sometimes appeared aggressive, but she realised he was frustrated and distressed. When she eventually established a connection with him, he became calm, and subsequently transformed their neglected garden. He arranged plants in spiral layouts.'

'Spiral layouts!' Adam could not contain his astonishment. 'Were they like the ones in Jane's diary?'

'Unfortunately, we don't know. The book didn't describe them in detail.'

'Do you have a copy of this book?' asked Boris.

'Yes, but I haven't got it with me,' replied Ellen. 'Would you like me to send my copy to you once I get home?'

'Do you happen to know if it's still in print? I'd prefer to buy a copy,' said Adam.

'It was Eva who got mine for me,' answered Ellen. 'Jane offered to lend hers; but Eva and I both wanted our own copy. As far as I remember, Eva ordered them on the Net.'

'I have a list of websites that are very good at getting books new or second-hand,' said Adam as he jumped up. 'If you don't mind, I'd like to see to it straight away.'

He scribbled on a piece of paper.

'I'll leave you two for a minute, and see what I can find.'

It was not long before he returned.

'I've got it on the screen now. Boris, would you like me to order a copy for you as well?'

'That would be a great help. But can you get a copy sent to my home?' asked Boris. 'Remember that I will be leaving here soon.'

Adam looked sad. 'Of course I will; but I'd forgotten that you were going away so soon.'

He disappeared again, and came back later, looking pleased.

'That's it fixed,' he said. 'Can you tell us more about the book, Ellen?'

'I think I'd rather leave it, and let you read it for yourself,' she said.

'Okay. Well, at least tell me which Adam you think was the one you were talking about when you were affected by the spirals.'

'I'm not sure,' said Ellen slowly, 'but it could be both. At first I thought I had to work out which one it was; but the more I think about what's been happening, and about Jane's book, the more I've been wondering if I meant both you and the Adam in the book. I didn't know the son in the book was called Adam until after I'd been mouthing the name...'

Adam broke in, 'Yes, and with all that's been happening, I'm not surprised that you don't see that as a reason for discounting the possibility that you were referring to him.'

'You're right,' said Ellen. 'That's exactly what I think.' She turned to Boris. 'Would you mind telling me about your dream now – the one you had the same night as Adam dreamed about me and my book?'

Boris told her all he remembered of his dream, and then added, 'As you will have gathered, both my own dream and Adam's included intense white light.'

'Yes,' replied Ellen. 'Adam saw the light around me, and you saw the light around the tape – or at least the shelf where you'd put the tape.'

'So it's not unlikely that the intense white light in the dreams could indicate a connection between the tape and your red book,' said Adam. 'And we've been discovering that there's a link between my experience with the tape, and yours with the spirals.'

'The red book, me, spirals, the tape, and you,' mused Ellen, looking at Adam.

'There's that pinprick pattern as well,' added Adam. 'And I haven't told you yet what happened when Matthew was round here.'

'Yes. I think it is time we told Ellen about that,' agreed Boris. 'It could be very significant.'

'We've already talked about my experience of the pinprick patterns and Adam's feeling of something being on the blank pages when he looked back at his dream,' said Ellen.

'That's right,' Adam continued, 'but when I passed out when Matthew was here, I had quite an intense experience of pinprick patterns like you'd described.'

'You passed out!' Ellen was alarmed.

Here Boris interrupted. 'I did wonder if you were going to pass out again the other night, Adam.'

'You mean after you'd been to Carillon Music?' asked Ellen. 'That was the evening I was lying on my bed in my room at the Rookery looking at my red book. Oh!'

'You might be thinking exactly what I'm thinking,' said Adam. 'Perhaps whatever link there is between us meant that on that evening, your study of the special blank pages in your red book was affecting me here in my house.'

'When I was speaking to Eva last night, I realised I must have been looking at my book around the time you felt strange,' Ellen mused. 'Can you tell me when Matthew was round and you passed out?'

'Mmm. Let me think. I've been at Boris' for a couple of months, and before that I was tidying things up here, and getting ready to leave... Hang on. I know; it was not long after *our* meeting at the Bull.'

Ellen took a small pocket diary out of her bag, and searched through the pages. 'Was it a weekend?' she asked.

'As a matter of fact it was,' Adam replied. 'It was a Saturday evening. What made you ask that?'

Ellen looked at him meaningfully. 'I spent the last weekend in

January at Eva's with Jane,' she said simply. 'In the daytime, I told them about our meeting at the Bull. I remember being upset. I hadn't realised that I had needed to talk about it.'

'I'm not surprised you were upset,' said Adam. 'When I look back on that meeting, there was a lot going on for both of us. But go on.'

'We talked quite a lot about my red book that day. That's what I was telling you at the hotel yesterday. Do you think it could have been the last weekend in January that you were with Matthew?'

'It could well be… Let me think… Yes, it must be… Just afterwards I started on an assignment I'd agreed to do for work. And that's another thing: I must make a note to phone them. I'd said I'd be away for three months. They'll be expecting me to be available again next month.'

He hurriedly scribbled a reminder to himself, and laid it on his desk in a prominent place.

'The way I'm feeling now, I hope they haven't got anything lined up for me for a few weeks. I'm sorry Ellen, I got distracted. Will you continue please?'

'That same evening was when Eva arranged photocopies of the spirals on the floor. She copied the layout that was indicated on the same page of the diary as the double spiral. It was the first time she'd done that. I was standing outside the door, and apparently I was affected by them even there. Eva and Jane had to lead me back inside. Apparently I said a number of things as well as "Adam".'

'What were these?' Boris asked.

'I can't make sense of them yet, but Eva said it was something like "sound of light", or "song of light", and "behind the veil", or "beyond the veil". I said the name "Greaves" as well. During a subsequent meeting one weekend, apparently I said all these things quite clearly when again affected by the spirals.'

'I am normally a cautious person,' said Boris, 'and at this point I think I should suggest that we take a break. But I don't want to. All I want to do is to get to the bottom of what is going on.'

'That might not be possible,' said Adam.

'I know,' replied Boris, 'but at least let us keep talking about it all, and see where it goes.'

'I agree,' said Ellen. 'I'm perfectly willing to continue.'

'Well,' said Adam, 'before I ask you more about the things you were saying, tell me more about the time you and your friends met again to study the spirals.'

'Of course,' replied Ellen.

'Can you first tell me exactly when that was, Ellen?' Adam asked.

'Well – yes.'

She turned the pages of her diary. 'Here it is, the first weekend of this month. So it was four weeks ago.'

'Tell me what happened,' instructed Adam.

'Apparently I spoke the words Eva had noted before. As I said, I spoke them very clearly.' Ellen described exactly what had happened, and finished by saying, 'and after I had come round, I could see the pinprick patterns in my mind.'

'Was this in the evening?' asked Adam sharply.

Ellen jumped slightly. 'Yes, it was.'

Adam turned to Boris. 'Boris,' he said, 'that was the evening when we listened to side A of the tape again, and I was sure I saw pinpricks.'

Ellen was silent for a moment while she took this in.

Then she said, 'I'd very much like to listen to that tape.'

'I'd like to let you hear it,' replied Adam, 'but it's in Boris' house, on the shelf where we keep it.'

'It's probably just as well,' sighed Ellen. 'Although I feel exhausted, I can't give up on this. Maybe it's a good thing you can't let me hear it.'

'As far as we've got, it looks as if there is definitely a connection between the spirals and the pinprick patterns,' said Adam.

'There is something else,' added Boris.

'What's that?' asked Adam.

'Ellen has told us how her friends said she seemed to *glow* when affected by the spiral layout…'

'I see what you're getting at,' replied Adam. 'The night after we ran side B of the tape through the player was the night I woke in a strange state and went off to look for a candle.'

'What happened?' asked Ellen.

'I saw a glow coming from the shelf where we keep the tape. Then I went to find Boris, and he got me a candle. By that time, the glow had gone, and I forgot about it until I woke again the next night. The way you describe what your friends said about the glow that seemed to come from you certainly reminds me of the glow I saw from the shelf.'

'Tell me what you mean about side B of the tape,' said Ellen.

'Side A is full of music – the amazing music,' said Adam. 'Because it had affected me so strongly, Boris and I were wary of running it again on my recent visit. Eventually we decided to make a start by running side B. It was blank, but nevertheless I think it affected me. I woke up that night in an agitated state, and found that glow coming from around the shelf.'

'Do you keep anything else on that shelf?' asked Ellen, suddenly.

It was Boris who replied: 'There is some fragile glassware there which belonged to my father's parents. I have only a few things that were theirs. The other things are a set of chess pieces that my grandfather carved, and a chess board that my grandmother made to go with it.'

'That's most unusual,' Ellen reflected.

'Yes, it is,' added Adam. 'If you could see the board you would be amazed.'

He went on to describe it to her.

Then he said, 'I'm sorry Boris, I got carried away. I should have let *you* tell Ellen about it.'

'It is all right. You described it very well.' Boris looked thoughtful. 'Adam,' he said, 'we have not told Ellen yet about that terrible sadness you felt after hearing side A of the tape again.' He turned to Ellen. 'Adam said over and over again that he was feeling a terrible sadness that he could not really describe. And he said that he wanted to tell me what he had heard and seen, but that he could not. I tried to reassure him. I have seen that something is trying to come out of him, and I feel that given time it will emerge. Such things cannot be forced.'

'It was far, far worse that the feelings I had after my wife died,' Adam reflected.

'How long ago was that?' Ellen asked.

'Nearly eight years,' replied Adam almost mechanically. He looked detached as he remembered. 'Not long now before the next anniversary of her death,' he added.

'Then this is another thing that we share,' said Ellen softly. 'I've not been married, but I lost my mother when I was very young. As a result of this, my father and I became much closer. He died very suddenly as a result of a road accident about eight years ago. It has taken me a very long time to develop a life without him.'

'I've spent my summers with Boris since Maria's death,' Adam told her. 'I couldn't bear to be here in Britain at these times.'

Ellen nodded with understanding.

The three sat and stared at each other.

It was Boris who spoke first. 'We should think about eating something,' he said. 'I have just looked at my watch, and it is already the middle of the afternoon.'

'I want to see your red book, Ellen,' said Adam, 'but I know now that I must wait. I have to absorb everything you've told me today, and how it connects with my own experiences. I agree with Boris. We should have something to eat. After that, with your permission, I want to know if you have any inkling as to the meaning of what you said when affected by the spirals. At the moment I feel I should read Frances Ianson's book before I study your red book. I don't know why, but I want to follow my instinct about this.'

Ellen expressed surprise. 'I can't see any reason why you should read *Communications* before you study my red book. There's no connection between the two that I'm aware of. As you know I've been studying my red book for a long time. I found it in my library long before I knew of Jane's spirals, and I didn't tell Eva and Jane about my book, or show it to them, until quite a while after I'd first been affected by the spirals.'

'I agree that there was no apparent connection at first,' Adam assented. 'But we've just been talking over the whole picture of how you and I have been affected by things over the last year or so. And it's been clear to us both that there are links between us – through my study of the tape, and your study of both the spirals and your red book. I still think that I should read *Communications* before I study your red book.'

'I think I can follow that,' Ellen said. 'I admit that I was thinking only of how I first discovered my book, and my earlier studies of it. It just shows how important it is to talk things over; there are so many angles, and I can't hold them all in my mind at once!'

Boris began to look concerned. 'I certainly see why you want to wait, Adam,' he said, 'but if you do, then I will not be here when you study Ellen's book. Ellen is leaving tomorrow, and I leave in a few days' time. I would prefer to be here when you see it,' he concluded decisively.

Adam looked upset. 'I keep forgetting that you're going away so soon, Boris. We've spent longer together than before, because you were able to come back with me. I seem to be assuming that you're a part of my life here now.' He turned to Ellen. 'Ellen, how much longer can you stay here?'

'As things stand,' she replied, 'I've one more night at the Rookery, which you kindly booked for me. I'd planned to make my way home in the morning.'

'Is there any possibility of your staying longer?' asked Adam.

Ellen thought for a moment. 'I think that would be difficult; but let me check my diary.' She turned the pages quickly. 'I've something I can't miss on the evening of June 1st,' she said, 'but it would be possible to rearrange the other things for that day. What are you thinking?'

'I just wanted to check. Would you be willing to go ahead and make those changes?'

'Yes... I could.'

'If the three of us have even one more day together, maybe something might shift so that I feel I can look at your book... It's just a hunch,' he added.

'If my experiences are anything to go by, I'd say that change can happen quite quickly, and when least expected,' said Ellen wryly.

'Can we move to the kitchen, and continue this conversation there?' asked Boris. 'I'm hungry!'

The others followed him, still talking.

'Boris,' said Adam, taking things out of the fridge, 'it has just struck me that tomorrow is the day we go back to see Professor Barnes.'

'You are right.'

'Who's he?' asked Ellen.

'He's a very interesting man... very interesting indeed,' replied Adam. 'We'll tell you about him.'

'I had heard Adam speak about him,' added Boris, 'and I went to one of his talks last week. I was most impressed. He is a very knowledgeable and accomplished speaker.'

'And he lives in a most amazing house,' Adam added. 'I'll tell you all I know about him while we eat.'

He told Ellen how he had picked up the leaflet in the library, and described his impression of the first meeting he went to. Then he and Boris went on to tell her about the recent meeting.

'I've just thought of something!' Adam exclaimed.

'What's that?' asked Ellen eagerly.

'You won't believe this, but I picked up that leaflet the day after I'd had that dream about you with your book!'

'That's probably just a coincidence; but it's certainly interesting,' replied Ellen.

Adam looked at her, half smiling. 'Did you hear what you just said?' he asked. 'Is everything else "just a coincidence" too?'

Ellen groaned. 'You're right to pull me up. None of us know what's really going on. We've noticed some amazing connections between things we've been experiencing. Who knows what a coincidence is anyway? What help is it to anyone to say "just a coincidence"? The important thing is to notice possible connections, and talk about them. We don't have to come to any conclusions. But none of us should try to discount any of them. Especially me!' she added emphatically.

'I have an idea,' Boris began. 'How about e-mailing Professor Barnes to see if he has any spare places for tomorrow?'

'It's unlikely, but I can certainly do that,' replied Adam. He turned to Ellen. 'Would you like to come with us tomorrow evening if I can arrange it?' he asked.

'I'd love to. I've been thinking about your suggestion of my staying on another day. Can I use your phone to sort out June 1st? If I do that, I can stay on until the middle of that day.'

Adam looked pleased. 'Surely,' he said. 'I'll send off the e-mail first, and then you can use the phone.'

'If I can't go with you to the talk I'll be disappointed; but it won't change my mind about staying on another night,' said Ellen, as she looked for the phone number that she needed.

The e-mail sent, Adam sat with Boris, while Ellen did her phoning. She returned looking pleased.

'That was very straightforward,' she said. 'Now where were we?'

'There's one more thing,' said Adam. 'I'd like to invite you to stay here tomorrow night, but you won't find it as comfortable as the hotel. I have a sofa bed in the sitting room…'

'I could use that,' Boris added. 'You could use the spare room, Ellen.'

'Thanks a lot,' smiled Ellen. 'You're both very kind. It would mean that we'd have a bit more flexibility, but I think I should stay at the hotel. I need plenty of time to think, and I must phone Eva or Jane for a very long talk!' She looked at her watch. 'It's nearly five,' she said. 'I think I should go soon. Will you come up for me in the morning again? I'll be ready at the same time.'

Adam felt disappointed, but he knew she was right. She could talk things over with her friends, and he and Boris could spend the evening discussing what they had learned today.

The two men walked Ellen back to the hotel, and returned to Adam's house, where they spent a quiet evening, reading, talking, and listening to music.

Chapter Forty

Adam woke to the sound of the phone ringing. He grabbed the extension beside his bed, thinking that it must be Ellen.

'Hello,' said a voice, a man's voice. 'Is that Mr Thomas? Peter Brown here.'

Adam sat bolt upright. Peter Brown! Of course! He had said he would phone soon.

'Er... hello. Yes, Adam here. Good to hear you,' he replied.

'I'm phoning to confirm our definite interest in your Russian project,' said the voice. 'I'm sending you a letter of confirmation. Meanwhile, can you let us know what your timescales are for completing this work, and maybe we can get together again in a couple of months to thrash out the finer details?'

'I can certainly do that for you,' Adam's voice sounded strong and confident. 'I still have Boris here with me. We'll write to you over the next few days.'

'I'll look forward to that. It's good to do business together,' the voice concluded.

'Thanks for phoning,' said Adam, and replaced the receiver.

He jumped out of bed, and rushed into the spare room where Boris was lying looking very sleepy.

'Was that Ellen?' he asked.

'No, it was Peter.'

Boris looked puzzled.

'Peter Brown. Of Carillon Music.'

Boris sat up. 'What did he say?'

Adam told Boris what had been agreed. 'We can work on it after Ellen goes back,' he added. 'I can't think about anything at the moment, except the things we're discussing with her. After she's gone, we can concentrate on what we're going to say to Carillon.'

'That is good. Very good.' Boris was now fully awake. 'And now we must get ready to go and collect Ellen. Have you checked your e-mails?'

'No, not yet. The phone woke me. I'll do it now.'

Still in his pyjamas, Adam went to the computer. He did not think there would be a reply from Professor Barnes yet, and was surprised to see that one had been sent late the previous evening. It was only one line, and said:

<On this occasion, I am willing to squeeze in an extra chair. Edmund Barnes>

'Hey, Boris,' he called out, 'Ellen *will* be pleased.'

'What is the news?'

'They're fitting her in. Remember I told you that numbers are always limited? Well, he says he's going to add an extra chair. I feel quite honoured!'

Walking up to the Rookery, Adam was thoughtful. I must remember to ask Ellen again about those things she said when affected by the spirals, he told himself. It could give me some clues to that intensely sad feeling I had the last time I listened to the music on our tape.

They met Ellen coming down the drive from the hotel. She looked bright and fresh.

'I've booked the extra night here,' she said, 'and I had a long talk with both Eva and Jane last night. It was well worth it. I feel it's cleared my mind, so that I'm ready for today. By the way, they both want to have the chance to meet you some time. Boris, will you be coming over again soon?'

'Er … I had not thought about it,' Boris replied.

'Well, I think we should all think about it right now,' Ellen said firmly. 'Or if not, then you and Adam must sort it out after I've gone, and then let me know. We need to keep in close contact; and you'll probably want to see the publisher again.' She winked at Adam. 'Make sure you get Boris organised,' she said playfully.

'Actually, we have some news for you about the publisher,' said Adam. 'He phoned this morning.' And he went on to tell her about it.

'That means you'll *have* to come back soon Boris,' she said.

'I have not thought about it…' Boris blundered. 'I…'

'Ellen's right,' said Adam decisively, 'and if the air fare is a bit pricey for you, I'll pay half. It would be great to have you back again later this year, Boris. I was going to phone to delay any work assignments that might be waiting for me, but I'll take something on straight away, and will gladly send you the proceeds.'

Boris looked tearful, and Ellen patted his shoulder as they walked along.

'I'd like to contribute too,' she said. 'I know you haven't known me for long, but I hope you'll let me. I want to see you again soon, and I want you to meet my friends. We all have a lot to share.' She stopped for a moment, and then continued. 'Then you could both see Jane's spirals. I know she'd be willing to let you see them. She said so last night; but I thought you wouldn't be here, Boris.'

'That's great that we can meet your friends,' said Adam. 'And I think I'm going to wait until we meet them before I study your book.'

Boris put his handkerchief back into his pocket.

'Thank you for your generous offers, my friends. It is hard for me to accept; but I do so much want to see you again. Perhaps today we can work out when I might be able to come back. Once that is fixed you can tell your friends, Ellen, and arrangements can be made for us all to meet. There is another thing too.'

'What's that?' asked Adam.

'When I come back, I can bring the tape with me – the special tape. And we can share it with our new friends.'

'That's settled then,' said Ellen happily.

She was glad to know that not only would she be seeing Adam and Boris again, but also they would be meeting Eva and Jane, with whom she had shared so much. This was ideal: the spirals, the tape, and her red book. They could study them together, and see what happened. There was much to learn.

'Ellen?' asked Adam. 'Could you talk to us again about the words you said when you were affected by the spirals?'

By this time, they had reached Adam's house.

'Could we walk on for a while?' Ellen asked.

'Of course. There's a nice river walk near here. There's a good path which is wide enough for the three of us.'

'I'd like that. Eva has a river walk near her house too. And at Jane's we walked round the local reservoir.'

The sun warmed them as they strolled along, while Ellen told them again what she had said. 'I'm sorry I can't explain any of it any more. I've told you about the Adam in the book. You'll be able to read about him soon when your copy arrives. The "song" or "sound of light" I can't explain, and neither can I explain "behind" or "beyond the veil".'

'I wonder if the veil has anything to do with the pinprick patterns?' mused Adam.

'It's possible,' Ellen replied. 'Certainly they seem to be something that you and I see that aren't visible to others; although Eva did get some slight sense of something of the same, after she had studied the blank pages of my book. Incidentally, I've been thinking about what you said yesterday about the blank side of your tape. It seems that you were very affected by that in the night. From what I know now, I would say that our sensitivity to these things that have been affecting us has gradually increased.'

'The "sound" or "song of light" seems to resonate with me when I think about the music on side A of our tape,' said Adam. 'I'm sorry, I should have replied to what you said,' he added. 'Yes, I agree.'

'I've just thought of something else,' Ellen continued. 'When you read Frances Ianson's book, you'll come across an account of how the mother started to hear beautiful music in her head, after she began to make the connection with her son.'

'That's fascinating,' said Adam. 'I can't wait for my copy to arrive.'

'I am looking forward to reading that book too,' Boris joined in, after a period of silence. He sounded more in control of himself again. 'Ellen,' he said, 'there was one more thing you told us you had said.'

'Yes, it was another name. "Greaves".'

'How do you know it was a name?' asked Boris with obvious interest.

'That's a good question,' Ellen answered. 'When Eva first told me, I had no idea. But soon afterwards I felt absolutely sure.'

'Do you know anyone of that name?' asked Adam.

'Not personally, but there is someone – well, actually, two people.'

'Can you tell us about them?' asked Adam.

Ellen told them about her brief meeting in the car park with the man and his daughter who was in a wheelchair, and how it later transpired that they were subsequently sent to see her friend Eva to see if she could help with the daughter's condition.

'Their name is Greaves,' she explained. 'Eva has kept us up to date with her connection with them.'

Adam looked uncomfortable. 'If your friend Eva is a practitioner, then surely she should not be discussing them with you.'

'I should have said at the beginning,' Ellen replied quickly. 'From the outset, she had Mr Greaves' permission to discuss his situation with anyone she thought might be able to help. He was glad to agree, because he was at his wits' end. His daughter had had endless tests, was attending the hospital regularly, and getting nowhere.'

Adam relaxed. 'Thanks for explaining that,' he said. 'So it's okay for you to talk to us about them, so long as our primary concern is their well-being.'

'That's right. I feel confident that talking to you both about them is a good thing, and I'd like to tell you all I know.'

'It would be good to hear what you have to say,' said Boris. 'And I hope that we may be able to offer some help, however small.'

Ellen gradually told them everything she knew.

When she had finished she said, 'I'd welcome any questions or comments.'

It was Adam who spoke first. 'It's clear from what you say that there's some connection between these people and your contact with your friends. And it all started with the chance meeting in the car park.'

'I should really tell you more about the stick that Eva lent to Hannah to take with her to Milan. I think I should tell you the story of how she came by it,' said Ellen.

They made their way slowly along the river bank, while Ellen recounted the story of the old couple, the special drink, and the collection of sticks; finishing with how Eva had been certain of which one to choose. 'There's a small carving on it about halfway up,' she said. 'We don't know what it means, but it's two figures sitting opposite each other, as if deep in conversation.'

'Let me get this right,' said Adam. 'Tell me again about how Eva felt she was affected by the drink.'

Ellen explained again, and added, 'When Eva was affected by the spirals the first time she and I saw them, she later said they affected her in a similar way.'

'That is very interesting indeed,' said Boris. 'And I have been wondering if the effect of the drink helped her to know which stick to choose.'

'It's funny you should say that,' Ellen replied. 'That's exactly what we all wondered too. And that stick seems to have helped her. She told me a couple of stories about that. Although she didn't say so, I think that's why she lent the stick to Hannah. I was surprised when she told me she had, because she had been very possessive of it, and was fearful about losing it.'

'Hearing about the story of that old couple reminds me of your grandparents, Boris,' said Adam. 'They came across as having that same kind of wisdom and connection.'

'You are right,' replied Boris. 'Once my grandfather allowed my grandmother to work on the chess board, they became very close indeed. That closeness was a validation of all they had shared in their life together. That is why I treasure the chess set and the board. It is not just because of the skill that has gone into making them, it is because of what they represent. I wish I knew more about the glassware I have on that shelf, because I have the same feeling about that.'

'I know I'm changing the subject a bit, but my mind is hopping about a little,' Ellen apologised. 'I'll be very interested to see how Jane reacts to listening to side B of your tape when we all get together.'

'Why is that?' asked Boris.

'Jane has unusual hearing,' replied Ellen. 'She's able to hear very low sounds. She could hear some low sounds when my hands were vibrating, while the spirals were affecting me.'

Adam and Boris looked at one another. 'We'll remember that,' they said.

'And on the subject of sounds,' Ellen continued, 'the Adam in the book made some strange instruments to hang in the trees in the garden. That's another thing you can both look forward to reading about, when you get your copies of the book.'

By this time they had reached a sharp bend in the river.

'We can keep following the river here,' said Adam, 'or we can follow the field path and circle right round, returning finally along the road that runs past the Rookery. What do you two think?'

'I quite like the idea of a circular route,' smiled Ellen. 'How about you, Boris?'

'I am happy to go along with that.'

Adam guided them to the field path, where they had to walk in single file, and further conversation was not possible until eventually they reached the road.

It was mid-afternoon by the time they finally arrived back at Adam's house.

'Can I lie down for a bit?' asked Ellen. 'I feel very tired, and I want to be fresh for the talk this evening.'

'You can lie on the bed I'm using,' said Boris.

He took Ellen to his room, and left her there. She lay down, and was soon asleep.

Ellen felt refreshed by her sleep. Adam and Boris had left her for as long as they could, before waking her in time to eat the meal they had prepared; and now the three were walking down the road towards Professor Barnes' house in plenty of time for the start of the talk. Although Ellen had been impressed by the description of the house given to her by Adam and Boris, she was even more impressed when she actually saw it. It certainly was imposing. The fact that it was largely screened from the road meant that the full impact of the building was not apparent until a visitor was inside the gate, walking along the path. They arrived at the front door just as a young man was ringing the bell. He turned and smiled when he heard them behind him.

'Hello,' he said to Adam, 'I recognise you from last week.'

Adam smiled and nodded in reply. The door was opened by Professor Barnes in his now familiar jacket complete with elbow-patches. He welcomed them, and let them into the hall.

'Take the first door on the right,' he said as he returned to the front door to let more people in.

'This is the room we were in last week,' Adam said to Ellen.

The layout of the room appeared much the same as the week

before. Adam, Boris, and Ellen found three seats next to each other along the wall to the right of the bay window, and sat down. Ellen looked around the room, and noticed the variety of chairs. She thought about the beautiful upholstery of the chairs in Jane's sitting room, and she looked to see if there was anything here that specially caught her eye. About half the seats had been taken. She looked intently at each of the empty ones. There were a couple in the far corner at the opposite end of the room that she would have liked to have examined, but felt it was not appropriate to go and look at them now. She made a mental note to do so after the talk was finished.

Adam looked at his watch. 'It's nearly time to start,' he said. 'There aren't so many people here tonight.'

'I wonder if there is any particular reason for that,' replied Boris. 'From what we know, these talks are very popular, and I would have expected the room to be full.'

Just then, they heard a babble of voices, and a large group of people hurried past the window. They were soon filing into the room, apologising for their lateness. Apparently they had come in a minibus, and had taken a wrong turning on a new section of the bypass about half an hour ago.

Professor Barnes came into the room and shut the door.

'Welcome, everyone,' he said. 'I'm glad to see all of you here. As most of you will know, this talk is the last in this series. I'd like to talk about ancient signs and writing. This subject is uppermost in my mind at the moment. Some friends in Israel have invited me out stay with them this summer. When rebuilding part of their house, they had to dig deeply below the existing foundations, and they found a relatively large fragment of sandstone bearing an inscription. From the photographs they have sent me, I would say that most of the letter shapes are of ninth-century Hebrew, but I can't be sure until I see it. There are some that appear to be more typical of seventh-century Aramaic and possibly Phoenician.' He paused, and then went on, 'But enough of that for now. It's no good my guessing. Let's get on to things I have seen and studied already.'

The time rushed past, while Edmund Barnes held his audience spellbound with stories of his study of Viking runes, Egyptian hieroglyphs, and much more. It seemed all too soon that he drew his talk to a close, and offered the usual tea and biscuits to everyone.

Ellen spoke to Adam and Boris. 'I'm going to ask him about spiral writing,' she whispered. 'His talk was fascinating. He knows so much. He hasn't said anything about spiral writing, but it doesn't mean he hasn't seen any...'

She stood up and walked across to Edmund Barnes where he stood talking to a man of about his own age. Adam could see it was the person he had met briefly last week, Professor Barnes' old friend.

'Excuse me.' Ellen addressed both the men. 'I apologise for interrupting, but there's a particular question I'd like to ask the professor.'

They smiled at her; and the professor said, 'Don't worry about interrupting. What is it, my dear?'

'Do you know anything about spiral forms of writing?' she asked.

'Yes, I do, as a matter of fact.' The professor looked a little surprised. 'It's one of the less usual forms. I didn't touch on any this evening, but I have seen some. However, I can't say that I know as much about it as I'd like.'

Ellen felt encouraged, and went on: 'I want to ask if you'd be willing to look at some spiral forms I've seen.'

The professor looked interested. 'Can you tell me a little more?' he asked. 'Then I can give you an answer.'

'A close friend of mine fell asleep one night last year while writing her diary of the day's events. When she woke, she found a number of spiral forms had appeared on the pages. I have seen them myself, and I can tell you that they are of a very intricate design.'

Professor Barnes was clearly interested – very interested. 'I'd most certainly like to see these,' he said.

He turned to his friend. 'Joseph, would you mind if I see if this young lady can stay on for a little while this evening?'

'Of course not,' his friend replied. 'I'd like to learn more about this too.'

'You haven't introduced yourself yet, my dear. What's your name?'

'Ellen Ridgeway.' Ellen held out her hand.

Edmund Barnes shook it, and introduced her to his friend. 'This is an old friend of mine, Joseph Harper.'

'Hello,' said Ellen, as she took his hand, 'It is good to meet you.'

'Ridgeway,' said the professor, as if to himself. 'Ridgeway,' he repeated, more audibly. 'I knew someone of that name; but I didn't have a lot of contact with him. He was an expert in Middle Eastern languages. He died a number of years ago. Are you related?'

Ellen felt a rush of emotion, and struggled to conceal it. 'It's likely that you are talking about my father.' She paused, and then went on, 'He died as a result of a road accident about eight years ago.'

'Sorry to hear about your father's death, but I'm very glad to meet his daughter. He was very well respected in academic circles.'

'I'm pleased you knew of him,' replied Ellen. 'It may interest you to know that we have a room in the house that became his library, and that I have kept it intact. There are many books there that his own father collected on his travels.'

'That's good to know,' replied the professor.

Adam and Boris were watching the conversation with interest from the other side of the room. 'Ellen seems to have made a good connection with the professor,' Adam commented.

'Yes,' Boris nodded.

'Do you think we should go and join her?'

'I am not sure,' Boris replied. 'I would rather wait.'

He continued to observe Ellen and the two older men.

At length, they saw Ellen turn and make a gesture towards them. Then she, and the professor and his friend came over, and Ellen introduced them.

'Please do call me "Edmund",' the professor encouraged them, '"Professor Barnes" is rather cumbersome.'

'Edmund has asked if we can stay on after the others have left. He'd like me to tell him more about the spirals,' Ellen said.

Adam and Boris looked at each other, and nodded assent. 'Fine by us,' they said.

'If you wait here, I'll show the others out,' said the professor. 'Then I'll join you. Joseph,' he addressed his friend, 'will you keep them company meantime?'

He began his round of bidding his guests goodbye, and showing them out of the front door. When he returned, he drew up a chair for himself and his friend so they could sit with Ellen, Adam and Boris.

'Now tell me more about this,' he said to Ellen. To Adam and Boris he said, 'Ellen has told me how some spiral writing appeared in her friend's diary. I'm interested to learn more of how this writing is made up.'

Ellen went on to describe what she remembered of the tiny dots, dashes, curved strokes, and delicate side-branches that made up each spiral; but she emphasised that she was not able to provide as detailed a description as she would have liked. She also explained that each spiral differed from all others.

'And you said that it seemed that some spirals were worked from the inside to the outside, and some were worked from the outside to the inside. How did you come to that conclusion?' asked the professor.

'Of course we couldn't be sure,' replied Ellen, 'but I'd say that it was to do with the particular style of the pen strokes.'

'Boris and I haven't seen them yet,' Adam added, 'but we hope to arrange it later this year.'

'I've already said to Ellen that I'd certainly like to see them myself,' Edmund said eagerly. 'Ellen, would you be willing to approach your friend on my behalf?'

'Of course I am,' Ellen replied.

'As you know,' Edmund continued, 'I'm going to Israel soon, and I expect to be there until mid-July, and possibly into August. If she's willing to let me see them, could you suggest a date at the beginning of September?'

He turned to Adam and Boris, 'When are you hoping to see them?'

'We haven't arranged a time yet,' answered Adam.

'I have to return to Russia in a few days,' said Boris.

Edmund looked across to Boris. 'Whereabouts?' he asked.

'The nearest city is St Petersburg,' he replied.

'I've been trying to place your accent, but you've kept me guessing. Your English is very good indeed.'

Boris looked at Adam and Ellen. 'My friends and I are already making plans for my return,' he said confidently. 'We have not settled dates yet, but I will try to aim for the end of August. Adam and I have a business meeting to set up first, and of course we too are waiting for Ellen to contact Jane about when she can let us see the spirals. Ellen, do you think that Jane would be willing to have all of us there at once?'

Ellen laughed. 'I don't know,' she said, 'but I'll ask her. I have a hunch that she would welcome the idea.'

Joseph, who until now had been sitting quietly throughout this exchange, said, 'I'd like to be included too.'

'It's too late to phone her now,' observed Ellen, looking across the room at the ornate clock on the mantelshelf. 'I can phone when I get home tomorrow evening. I'll contact you all after that. From what has been said so far this evening, if she's willing to have everyone at once, a date in early September might suit.'

'I'm here for another week,' said Edmund. 'Here are my contact details.' He produced a card from his pocket and handed it to her. 'I check e-mails regularly whenever I'm away.'

Ellen took the card, put it in her bag, and stood up.

'It's very late, and we should go,' she said.

'There's one more thing, my dear,' said Edmund.

'What's that?'

'I'd very much like to see your father's books some time, if you'd be willing to arrange that.'

'Of course. I host occasional meetings of an antiquarian book society there. I'll let you have dates of any future meetings. The next one is on June 16th, so you'll be away. But I'll keep you informed.'

Edmund and Joseph said a warm goodbye to Ellen, Adam and Boris at the front door.

As they walked out of the gate, Ellen said, 'Would you two mind walking me straight up to the hotel? I have to set out in good time tomorrow.'

'I only wish we had more time,' said Boris. 'Ellen is leaving tomorrow, and I leave three days later.'

'I think we should firm up our plans as soon as we can,' said Adam decisively. 'Ellen, will you phone us tomorrow evening after you've spoken to Jane? Once we know if she can give us a date at the beginning of September, Boris and I can plan his next trip here. Once that's decided, I'll write to Peter Brown of Carillon to suggest a date for our next meeting with him. I promised to let him know fairly soon.'

'Adam,' said Boris, 'if I can arrange to come for a couple of months, would that be okay with you?'

'Okay? It wouldn't just be okay, it would be brilliant!' Adam slapped his friend on the back affectionately. 'We've nearly finished the Russian tapes now. I don't think I told you, but I've had an e-mail from work, and they have an assignment for me that should keep me busy this summer. All the while, I'll be looking forward to seeing you again!'

He turned to Ellen. 'Can I invite myself to that meeting of the antiquarian book society in your library on the 16th? I don't know anything about antiquarian books, but I'd like to see your library and where you live. And I could stay at the Bull!'

Ellen laughed light-heartedly. 'I'm glad you've invited yourself. I had been wondering whether to invite you or not. What do you think, Boris? Shall I let him come, or should he wait until you come back again?'

'If I am to be honest, I will probably be envious if he sees your library first,' replied Boris, 'but I won't stop him.'

'That's settled then; I'll phone the Bull tomorrow, and book a night,' said Adam.

By this time, the three friends had reached the drive up to the Rookery, and they slowed their pace, reluctant to part.

'Now remember, Boris,' said Ellen, 'you're going to come back soon, and you're going to bring that tape with you. We're going to see Jane and Eva, and perhaps Edmund and Joseph will be there too.' She paused. 'If they are, they'll get a surprise, won't they? There's a lot more to the spirals than we've had time to tell them!'

'Yes, there is plenty to look forward to,' Boris said happily.

Ellen continued: 'Quite apart from wanting to hear the tape myself, I'm very keen that Jane has a chance of hearing side B. I want to know if she can hear anything. It was a low hum she heard when I was affected by the spirals.'

'Was that when your hands appeared to be vibrating?' asked Adam.

'No, it was the time after that. Jane told me that she heard a low hum, but that my hands weren't vibrating.'

They had now reached the door of the hotel.

'Remember to phone us tomorrow evening, when you've spoken to Jane,' Adam insisted.

'How could I forget?' Her words reassured him, as she went inside.

Chapter Forty-one

The next day Ellen drove home slowly, deep in thought. It was only fifteen months ago that she had first encountered Adam on that train to York. A chance encounter, yet so much had followed from it. She felt grateful for the support of Eva and Jane. Without this she was sure that she would have turned away from any prospect of friendship with Adam. Had she not allowed herself to stay in touch with him, she would never have met Boris, Edmund and Joseph. What she had learned from Adam and Boris during this visit was amazing. Through it she now had evidence of a greater link between herself and Adam. It was all quite extraordinary. After meeting Adam at the Bull in January, she had accepted, reluctantly at first, that Adam had indeed experienced some strange kind of connection with her through her red book. Now she knew that this was only a part of something much bigger. Hearing about how Adam and Boris had come upon that particular tape, and how it had affected Adam, had staggered her. The effect of the spirals on her, and the effect of the tape on Adam, seemed to be all part of the same thing. And during these experiences they had seemed to know that the existence of each other was important. What exactly was going on? She had no doubt that there was more to discover about all of this. Much more.

Ellen felt excited about the possibility of everyone meeting up at Jane's house in September. If it came off as planned, there would be seven people there, together with Jane's spirals and Adam and Boris' tape. There was no way of predicting where any discussions might lead, and indeed what might happen when both the spirals and the tape were available.

She arrived home just after 4 p.m. She unloaded the car and put her things away before trying to phone Jane. There was no answer, so she left a message. She was disappointed that Jane had not answered, but realised it was still a bit early for her to be in from work. Feeling in need of contact she phoned Eva, and was relieved to hear her friend pick up the phone.

'Hello, Eva,' she said. 'I'm so glad you're in.'

'It's good to hear you, Ellen. I've been wondering when you'd be in touch again. I've been thinking about you a lot,' replied Eva. 'Two days is a long time to wait for news when there's so much going on.' She laughed, and then continued. 'How did you get on at that meeting last night?'

'The talk was excellent,' Ellen told her. 'Professor Barnes is a very inspiring speaker. I can't wait to tell you what the subject of the talk was.'

'Go on, surprise me.'

'Ancient signs and writing.'

'Tell me more!' said Eva eagerly.

'I think I'll just tell you what happened after the talk. I had a very strong impulse to talk to the professor about Jane's spiral writing, so I did. He was very interested in what I said, and wanted to know more. By the way, he recognised my surname, and it turned out he'd met my father. He didn't know him well, but it meant a lot to me that they'd met. He asked if I'd stay for a while after the rest of the group had left, so Adam and Boris and I stayed on. The upshot was that he'd like to see the spirals, and I'm trying to get hold of Jane to see if we can fix a meeting at her house at the beginning of September. I'm sure she'll agree. There's a good chance that Boris will be back staying with Adam by then, so with luck we'll find a date that suits us all.'

'In my conversations with Jane, she's very obviously looking forward to meeting Adam and Boris,' said Eva. 'I've no doubt she'll want to include the professor when she knows he wants to come.'

'There's one more person,' Ellen added.

'Who's that?' asked Eva, sounding puzzled.

'He's a good friend of Edmund's,' replied Ellen.

'Edmund?'

'Professor Edmund Barnes. He asked us to call him by his Christian name,' explained Ellen.

'Right. Now tell me who his friend is.'

'He's called Joseph Harper. They've been friends for a long time I understand, and so they know each other very well. I phoned Jane before I phoned you, but she wasn't in. Can you look at your diary and suggest some dates at the beginning of September that suit you? I'll try her again when I ring off, and I'll get back to you as soon as we fix something.'

'I've got my diary here just by the phone. I'll have a look. The first weekend in September is clear. It looks as if I'm tied up on the Saturday of the next one, so that weekend wouldn't suit.'

'I'm free that first weekend too,' replied Ellen, 'Let's hope that's okay for everyone else.'

'Why not try phoning Jane again now?' Eva suggested.

'I'd like to do that. Once I've spoken to her, I'll phone the others and then get back to you.'

Ellen tried Jane's number again, and was pleased to hear her friend's voice.

'I'm just in, Ellen,' said Jane. 'It's good to hear you. What's your news? As you know, Eva's been updating me.'

'The main thing is that I'm hoping you'll agree to host a gathering some time over the first weekend in September.' Ellen was a bit uncomfortable about the way she had blurted this out, but she went on. 'Sorry, I should explain.'

She told Eva about the professor and his friend.

'So you see,' she continued, 'not only have we got Adam and Boris who'd like to see your spirals, but also we have Edmund and Joseph. What's your reaction?'

'It sounds as if there will be seven of us at our next meeting instead of three,' said Jane. 'I'm sure we can all fit in my sitting room. Let me check my diary for that weekend. Yes, it's clear. Shall I pencil it in? We could all meet for the Saturday afternoon and evening, and you and Eva could stay the night.'

'That's great,' replied Ellen 'I'll get back to you when I've managed to contact the others.'

She rang off, and phoned Adam's number. She noted his pleasure as he recognised her voice.

'Ellen… How was your journey? …You've spoken to Eva and Jane already? …The first Saturday in September? …I'll tell Boris right away… Yes, he's just here… We can start looking at a flight for his return now… You'll phone Edmund? Good. I'll assume it's on then. Oh, by the way, this work assignment I'm about to start – I'm afraid I'm not going to be able to come to you on the 16th after all. I'm disappointed, but it can't be helped. At least Boris will get his wish that I won't see your library before he does!'

Adam chuckled, and then went on.

'I'm looking forward to my copy of Frances Ianson's book arriving. I can't wait to read it. I can assure you it'll be well studied before September. Look, I know you're busy fixing things up at the moment so I won't keep you, but I hope we can speak again quite soon.'

'I'll write to you to give you some idea of my movements,' said Ellen. 'I think I need a week or so to get used to everything I've learned over the last few days, but after that I'd appreciate a chat. Give my love to Boris, and wish him a safe journey from me. He has just another couple of days left with you, hasn't he?'

'Yes. I'll do all of that. And I'll look forward to your letter. Bye for now.'

Adam rang off. Then he turned to Boris and gave him Ellen's message.

Ellen rang Edmund's number, and getting no reply wrote a note about the proposed date of the first Saturday in September. When she put her pen down she realised how disappointed she was that Adam would not after all be able to come to the meeting of the antiquarian book society on the 16th. The thought of seeing him again in just over two weeks' time had been very important to her. She got up and wandered around the room. How empty the library seemed this evening! She thought how this room had for so long represented a haven of seclusion for her. But it did not feel like that any more. An occasional meeting of the book society was a start, but there needed to be more life in this room than that. Her mind went back to those early musical gatherings that had been her life until her mother died. Perhaps she was ready to arrange something musical now? Cautiously, she pondered this thought. The more she thought, the more she realised she wanted it now. And she wanted it very much.

Another idea struck her. Instead of going to Jane's in September, perhaps everyone could come here? After all, her library would provide plenty of room. Jane and Eva could stay here, and the four men could lodge at the Bull. The only drawback she could see was that it would mean a lot of travelling for everyone. But Adam and Boris, and indeed Edmund, had already said they wanted to see her library. Perhaps Eva would be willing to drive across to pick Jane up, and then they could travel up together. Ellen picked up the phone decisively.

'Hello, Eva. Everything's falling into place quite well. I'm just writing a note to Edmund to confirm the date, but I've an idea that I want to run past you.'

Ellen went on to explain her proposal to Eva, who was immediately enthusiastic.

'I'd love to come up,' she said. 'Shall I phone Jane about it, while you check with Adam and Boris?'

Ten minutes later they were comparing notes.

'So it's on then,' said Ellen delightedly. 'You and Jane can stay Friday, Saturday and Sunday nights if you want. I'll leave it up to you both to decide. I'll finish my note to Edmund now and get it in the post, together with a leaflet about the Bull.'

'There's one more thing before you ring off,' said Eva.

'What's that?' asked Ellen.

'I just wanted you to know that Hannah and her father have been in touch again. They're calling in next week. They phoned to say they'd be in the area – a business trip, I think. They asked if they could call in to say hello and return my stick. I'm looking forward to seeing them again.'

'I'll be thinking about you all,' replied Ellen. 'Bye now.'

Ellen took the leaflet about the Bull out of her desk drawer and put it in an envelope together with the letter she had now finished writing. She included the details of Frances Ianson's book, suggesting that Edmund and Joseph read it before September. She gave no information about it other than that it was part of the story that had led up to the appearance of Jane's spirals. It was not long before she was walking briskly down to the postbox.

On her way back to the house she began to think again about music in her library. It was quite clear to her that she wanted to arrange something, but whom should she approach? The silhouette of the local secondary school on higher ground about two miles away gave her an answer. She resolved to phone the head of the school the next day. Perhaps there would be some small instrumental groups of pupils who would like the experience of playing in her library? Having decided this, she suddenly realised that she had been too busy to think of food, and her stomach began to protest. She would eat something light and go to bed. Tomorrow she would phone the school.

Chapter Forty-two

Eva had a surprise when Hannah and her father arrived. When the car pulled up, Eva saw that Hannah's face was a healthy pink colour. The visit went well. Hannah could walk unaided now, and seemed to have energy to spare. She even announced that she was hungry, and ate most of a bunch of grapes that Eva had bought. She returned Eva's stick, thanking her for letting her borrow it, and insisting that Eva told her how she had come by it. She told Eva how she was going to start school after the summer holidays. A tutor was coming to the house to help her to catch up on the work she had missed, and she was making good progress. She was clearly excited about the prospect of going to school. She told Eva about a friend who had recently moved into the area who would be starting school at the same time. When Eva asked them about hospital appointments, they had smiled at each other and said that the next one was in six months' time – a much longer gap.

On the way back to the car, Mr Greaves thanked Eva again for her help. She was genuine in her request that they keep in touch. As she waved goodbye, Hannah called out that she would phone and tell her about the school uniform they were going to buy soon.

Eva phoned Jane and Ellen that evening to tell them about Hannah and her father. Both had been delighted. Ellen had told her of her preparations for the meeting of the antiquarian book society. Eva had sensed an air of eager anticipation in Ellen's voice, and Ellen had gone on to confide about her plans for musical events in her library.

By the end of June, Ellen felt ready to arrange a time to speak to Adam. She felt a little guilty that she had not been in touch earlier, but the time had not been right. As promised, she had written to him soon after her return – a letter that listed some of her work commitments. She finished by saying that she would write again soon. She later decided to phone him and leave a message suggesting times they might speak. She was pleased when he phoned back the following evening.

'Hello, Ellen,' he said. 'It's good to speak again.'

'Oh Adam! I'm glad you could phone. I wasn't sure if you'd be away. I knew from what you'd said before that your work was taking you away from time to time.'

'Yes, that's right. I'll be away again for a few days next week. Tell me how the meeting went on the 16th.'

'It went very well. There were a few more people. Mr Holden had asked me if I'd be willing to let some old friends and colleagues of his join us. Of course I agreed, and we had a very pleasant evening. It was so good to see everyone enjoying my mother's collection of first editions. There won't be another meeting until the autumn – some time in October I think. Have you got Boris' return flight booked? And have you any news about Carillon Music?'

'The answer is "yes" to both questions. Boris is coming back on 23rd August, and he and I are going to a meeting at Carillon on the 30th. This will be the time when we start to make decisions about the presentation of the volume of Russian songs. Actually, I think there'll be two volumes.'

'I'm so looking forward to having everyone here in September; but it seems such a long way off.'

'It's surprising how quickly time passes though,' replied Adam.

'Yes, I know. By the way, I want to tell you about another project I've started,' said Ellen.

'What's that?' Adam sounded immediately interested.

'I approached the local secondary school to see if there were any groups of pupils who wanted to play chamber music in my library. I can't remember if I told you before, but when I was small, before my mother died, what is now the library used to be a music room. My parents used to invite friends round to play, and I was encouraged to join in. The tentative plan I presented to the head teacher has been taken up immediately.'

'Tell me about it,' Adam encouraged.

'A small recital will take place in my library about every three weeks. Sometimes it'll be in the afternoon, and sometimes in the evening. I'll invite a few local people in as an audience, and any donations will go towards the school instrument fund. We had the first recital last week. It lasted about an hour, and it was very good.'

'What did they play?' asked Adam.

'Some trio sonatas by Telemann and Loeillet.'

'I'm very impressed,' said Adam with obvious feeling.

'Thanks,' Ellen replied. 'And what news of Boris?' she asked.

'I e-mail him quite a lot. He sounds in good spirits. He's very excited about coming over for the two months. I must say that having him to stay here all that time will be wonderful. We get on so well together.'

'I know,' replied Ellen. 'I could see that when I was with you both. Can you tell me how much money to send for my share of the cost of his air tickets? I'm sorry I forgot to ask earlier. You must tell me. It means a lot to me to be involved.'

'I'll write to you about it soon,' Adam promised.

'I had a very nice letter from Edmund confirming that he and Joseph would definitely be joining us in September. He says they've booked three nights at the Bull.'

'That's good. I must phone and make a booking for Boris and myself soon. I'll e-mail Boris and see if he'd like to stay for the three nights.'

'Let me know what you both decide. I've offered Eva and Jane the use of my bedrooms for those nights, but I haven't heard yet if they can stay as long as that. I'll let you know once I hear.'

'Look, why don't I phone you again when I get back from my days away,' said Adam. 'It would be good to speak again.'

'Yes, of course,' replied Ellen. 'I'll look forward to it.'

'Perhaps then we could spend some time speaking about the spirals and the tape, and all the other things we discussed when you were here,' suggested Adam.

'I'd like that,' Ellen replied. 'I've been thinking about it all a lot.'

'So have I,' said Adam. 'I haven't tried to come to any conclusions, I just let it all float around in my mind – usually in the late evening, or when I go to bed. Are you still spending time looking at your red book?' he asked.

'I don't look at it quite as often these days. However, like you, I usually spend time in the late evening thinking about all the things that have brought us together.'

'Perhaps that's why I feel you to be quite close by at such times,' said Adam lightly.

Ellen sensed that his light tones belied a deeper feeling, and she was undecided about how to respond.

After hesitating, she said, 'Adam, the link between us through my reaction to the spirals, your reaction to the tape, and our link through my red book, is something that's beyond what we can understand at the moment.'

'You're right. I look forward to talking about this when we speak again,' replied Adam. 'I hope that all goes well for you until then.'

'You too,' replied Ellen as they finished the call.

Chapter Forty-three

A week later, Ellen received a letter from Adam. She opened it and, as she expected, he had sent details of the cost of Boris' air tickets. There was also a short letter:

Dear Ellen,

Here are the details I promised.

I know that we were to be speaking quite soon, but I'm afraid I have to be away a lot longer than I first anticipated. Can we postpone our call until my return? I am taking my copy of Frances Ianson's book with me. I should be able to phone you by the end of the month.

I hope you are well. Boris is fine, and I bumped into Matthew yesterday. He is still away a lot, so we haven't been able to spend an evening together for a long time. I told him a little of what we discussed when you were down here. He said 'Blimey'!

Best wishes,

Adam

Ellen felt a stab of disappointment at the thought of having to wait until the end of July before she spoke to Adam again. Mechanically she wrote out a cheque for her share of Boris' fares. After this she felt better. The delay was really of no consequence. There was no rush to discuss things. In fact, a longer delay could be beneficial. Meanwhile, she had many interesting things to attend to. Her work projects were going well, and her reduced working hours meant that more and more she was including other things in her life. Instinctively she knew that this could cast more light on the meaning of what had been happening to her and Adam than would their next phone call.

In the evening she phoned Jane.

'Hi!' she said. 'I thought I'd give you a ring. I haven't asked you about your course recently; and I wondered of you had any more news of Emily?'

'Hello, Ellen,' Jane replied. 'You'll be glad to hear that I'm still very grateful that you pushed me about doing some more studying. I love the work, and I'm meeting some interesting people at tutorials. I can fit the course work around my job – just. There's little time to spare, but I don't mind. After all, I'm doing what I want. I mustn't talk for too long because I have a long essay to finish by the weekend.'

'Let's just have ten minutes then,' said Ellen. 'It's good to hear you sounding so enthusiastic about what you're doing. Now, tell me about Emily.'

'She's coming along fine. Whenever I phone Clare, Emily always wants to say "hello" too. Her dad has added a number of blocks to her collection – much to her delight. Have you heard anything more from Adam?'

'I did have one conversation on the phone; but he's away a lot just now, so we won't be speaking again until the end of the month. He's got his copy of Frances Ianson's book now, and he's taking it away with him.'

'That's good. You'll be able to go over some of it with him when you speak again.'

'We hope to. And I hope he'll have read the whole book before then.'

Ellen suddenly felt very glad that she would not be speaking to Adam again before he had read the book. For a further discussion about the spirals to be effective, he really needed to have done that. Not only will he have read the book, but also he would have had a chance to mull it over. Excellent.

'I won't keep you now, Jane. You must get back to your essay,' she finished.

'Thanks for phoning. Bye for now,' replied Jane.

Ellen put the phone down.

I think I'll reread my own copy, she said to herself.

She took it from a shelf near the fireplace. In fact, it was next to the place she kept for her red book when she was not carrying it with her. It really was inspiring. It was good to read it, even if it might have no bearing on Jane's spirals. But there was no doubt in her mind that it *did* have a bearing on them. She wished there had been more detail about the spiral forms the son had used when laying out the plants in the garden once he felt connected to his mother. The book was predominantly about the commitment of the mother to her son in his distress and how she had connected with him, rather than about the spiral forms.

A thought came into her mind. I've been so overwhelmed by the effect of the spirals on me that I've tended to concentrate on that, rather than how they are constructed. When I tried to describe their appearance to Edmund, I could remember very little of the finer detail. I wonder if any of the side branches of the spirals resemble leaves?

At that point her mind filled with the leaf-vein patterns in her red book, and she realised it would be a good idea to talk this over with someone.

Phone Eva, she told herself, and lifted the phone once more.

'Hello Eva,' she said. 'I've been sitting here thinking about the spirals. Can you talk just now, or are you busy with something?'

'Hello, Ellen. I was thinking of phoning you this evening myself, but you've beaten me to it. What exactly is on your mind?'

'I had a note from Adam to say that he's to be away longer than he thought, so I won't be speaking to him again before the end of the month. At first I was disappointed, but then I realised that it was probably a good thing. He's got his copy of Frances Ianson's book, and he's going to be reading it. I'd rather speak to him once he's read it and had time to digest it. I phoned Jane for a chat earlier this evening, and after I'd spoken to her about it, I felt quite certain. Since then, I've decided to reread my own copy. I was just sitting here wishing that the book had a detailed description of the spiral forms the son used in the garden, when a number of thoughts started coming into my mind, and I wanted to speak to you about them.'

'Oh good,' replied Eva. 'Tell me about them.'

'I've very little memory of the intricacies of the spirals. I assume it's because I get so affected by them. I was just wondering if some of the side branches resemble leaves, when I started to get very strong images of leaf-vein patterns from my red book. This isn't like ordinary memory; it's very intense experience. I thought I'd better try to phone you for a chat.'

'You were right to do that,' replied Eva. 'I haven't had that association myself, but that doesn't mean that there isn't one.'

'Have you got the photocopies of the spirals handy?' asked Ellen.

'Yes, of course. Shall I get them out?'

'Yes please.'

'Hang on a minute then.'

Eva picked up the large brown envelope and took the nine sheets out.

'Got them,' she said.

'Now, can you describe some of the side branches to me?' asked Ellen.

'Okay. I'll talk first about the spiral that goes to the top of the layout... Oh, no I won't.'

'What do you mean?'

'Ellen, I'm not sure this is a good idea. Remember how easily you become affected by the spirals – you were standing *outside* my front door one time when I was arranging them and you were affected then. I know things have moved on quite a bit since then, but I don't want to take any risks. You're in that house alone, and I'm about four hours' drive away!'

'You're right!' exclaimed Ellen. 'How silly of me... and of course that's why I never brought a set of copies home with me.'

'I think we should save this until we're all together in September. By the way, Jane and I want to take you up on your offer of staying for three nights.'

'That's excellent! I hoped you'd be able to, but I didn't know how you'd be fixed. Edmund and Joseph have booked in at the Bull for the three nights, and Adam is checking with Boris whether to do the same.'

'There's a good chance that we'll all be up for the whole weekend then,' said Eva. 'I'm sure that's the best thing.'

'I'll just read through the book again, and I'll have a chat with Adam about it when he phones,' said Ellen. 'That's enough for now.'

Chapter Forty-four

Over the following weeks, Adam often thought of his friend Matthew, and how his work took him all over the country. These weeks had convinced Adam that he had no taste for that way of living. When he had taken on this particular project, he had no idea how much travelling it would involve. He had thought that much of his contact would have been done by phone or e-mail; but it became very clear that he would need to have more face-to-face meetings than he had imagined. It was a challenging time for him. He sustained himself by the thought that some of the money he was earning from this was financing something very important to him – Boris' return. And every evening before he went to bed, he read a chapter of Frances Ianson's book. He found it fascinating; and he looked forward to the end of each day, when he could study it again. After the first few chapters he had bought a small notebook, and had gone back to the beginning of the book, noting the points he wanted to raise with Ellen when he spoke to her again.

In the event, his return home was even later than he had predicted, and it was the beginning of August before he was able to sit down in his conservatory to phone Ellen to make a time to talk. First he phoned Matthew, and left a message on his call-minder.

'*Hi Matthew,*' he said. '*This is Adam. I'm here for the next three weeks. Hope you'll be around sometime soon. I can fit in with you – I'm writing things up and can fix my own timetable. Get back to me when you can, and let me know if you can come.*'

Then he phoned Ellen. There was no reply, so he left her a message too.

'*Hello Ellen. This is Adam speaking. I'm back home now, and working from here. I'm phoning to arrange a time to talk. I've finished reading Frances Ianson's book, and I've made notes of things I'd particularly like to go through with you. I'll be able to give you some of Boris' comments too.*'

Ellen phoned back the following evening.

'Hello, Adam,' she said. 'I got your message, but I was in too late to phone you back. How are you?'

'I'm *so* glad to be home again,' he replied. 'I'm well, and I've got a lot to write up. I don't mind that now I'm back. I know now that I don't like working from no fixed abode. How are you?'

'I'm fine. I've been busy with a number of things, and I've been rereading that book. I'm glad I did because there are a few points that have impacted on me this time that hadn't affected me the first time I read it. You say you've made some notes?'

'Yes, when I'd read a few chapters, I realised I wanted to, so I went back to the beginning again.'

'Let's make a time to discuss the book soon,' Ellen suggested.

'How about tomorrow evening around eight?'

'Yes, that would suit me fine,' replied Ellen. 'By the way, have you booked the Bull yet?'

'Yes – three nights for Boris and myself.'

'You'll be pleased to hear that Eva and Jane are staying the three nights too. They'll be here with me.'

'Great!'

'Before you go, I just want to run an idea past you. Have you got a minute?' asked Ellen.

'Go on.'

'I've been thinking about the meeting. You and Boris are bringing the tape, Jane will bring the diary with the spirals, and Eva will bring her stick. I'll get her to make spare copies of the photocopies and photographs of the spirals, so everyone can have some. I have my red book here. Everyone will have read Frances Ianson's book. All of that's fairly straightforward, but I've been wondering what to do about the fact that Edmund and Joseph know very little about the whole situation. I began to feel it might be a good thing to fill them in with some of the background before they come. What do you think?'

'Good idea,' replied Adam. 'But it's a very big project. What have you got in mind?'

'Last week I started work on writing something that might be helpful. It's as accurate an account of my conversations with you and Boris as I can produce. My idea was that if we sent a copy to Edmund, then he and Joseph would know much more of the whole story.'

'That's a big job,' mused Adam. 'How far have you got?'

'I think I'm about half way or more,' replied Ellen. 'Do you think I should keep going?'

'Yes, I do. And I'd find it helpful if you'd let me have a copy to look through. With your permission I could scan it into my computer and e-mail it to Boris. We should really get permission from your friends before sending it to Edmund and Joseph though.'

'You're right. I'll phone them to check. If they agree, I should let them have copies to see if there's anything they want to say about what I've written. Meantime, I'll keep writing. Thanks. I'll look forward to speaking to you tomorrow then.'

Ellen put the phone down. It was good to be in touch with Adam again. It was not long now before the meeting, and there was quite a lot to do. She spent the rest of the evening writing up more of her discussions with Adam and Boris. Although it was two months now since they had been together, she felt she remembered everything very clearly. She sat up quite late, oblivious of the time, and completely absorbed in her task. She was determined to finish it before she went to bed.

When she had eventually finished her writing, she leaned back in her chair to stretch herself before reading through everything she had written.

I'll just read it through before I go to bed, she said to herself. Tomorrow I can photocopy it and send a copy to Eva and to Jane. I'll phone them both tomorrow evening before I speak to Adam, to let them know it's on its way. I can explain why I wrote it, and ask if they feel okay about my sending a copy on to Edmund and Joseph.

Having reread it, Ellen was satisfied with what she had done. She glanced at the clock, and was astonished to find that it was 1.30. At first she thought there must be something wrong with the clock, but having checked her watch and the clock in the kitchen, she knew it was right. She noticed that she did not feel tired, in fact she felt wide awake. It was fortunate that tomorrow was a day with no particular commitments, so her wakefulness and the lateness of the hour were of no immediate concern to her.

She went upstairs and got ready for bed. Her room was still warm with the effect of the daytime sun, and the moon was clearly visible through her window.

It must be nearly full now, she thought as she stared at it.

She was about to get into bed when, on impulse, she decided to go back downstairs to collect the writing she had done. Once back in the library, not only did she collect her writing but also she picked up her copy of Frances Ianson's book; and, as an afterthought, took her red book from its shelf, and made her way back upstairs.

Still wakeful, she propped herself up on several pillows, and considered whether to look at any of the things she had brought.

'I won't read my account of my visit to see Adam and Boris again,' she murmured to herself. 'I think I'm satisfied with it. There's no reason to look at it again now.'

She picked up her book and studied the first leaf-vein pattern. She marvelled again at how beautiful it was. She never tired of it, and indeed of any of the other leaf-vein patterns. She gazed at a few of the special blank pages. Again the suggestion of faint spiral forms appeared in the pinpricks in her mind.

She got out of bed and wandered along the corridor, past the empty bedrooms, and back to her own room. She liked to have her bedroom curtains open, with the moonlight streaming in through the window.

This is very strange, she said to herself. I'm sure I can hear a kind of humming sound. I wonder where it's coming from?

She stood motionless for several minutes, and then walked down the corridor once more.

'There's a definite hum, but also there's some faint music mixed in with it. It isn't anything I recognise at all. I can't think what might be making these sounds,' she murmured to herself.

She paced slowly along the corridor, turned, and retraced her steps; then she turned again, and repeated this exercise. The hum with the music intertwined seemed to become a little clearer. Was it becoming clearer, or was it that she was becoming more used to hearing it? She looked out of the upstairs windows in turn in an attempt to identify the source of the sound, although she knew that she was unlikely to find the answer there. She resumed her slow pacing and gradually accepted that the sound was from no ordinary source.

'Jane heard a hum on one of the occasions when I was affected by the spirals,' Ellen reminded herself. '*Adam... Adam,*' she repeated his name.

She could feel something on her cheek and she reached up and touched it. It was a tear.

She found herself speaking again: 'The veil... the song... the light...'

Her chest felt tight, and tears were now pouring down her face. She wiped them on the sleeve of her nightdress as she walked towards her bedroom.

Then another thought struck her. 'The mother in the book!' she burst out.

She went straight to her bed and picked up *Communications*. Feverishly she searched through the pages to find the section where the mother was gliding along the landing each night before listening to the tape of sounds her son had made, and how this discipline had led to her son eventually feeling connected to her and finding peace at last. Sitting on the side of her bed, she read through the section again, and felt calmed by it. Adam ... the son's name.

'I don't know what's happening or why. I don't understand it. But I'm certain that it's very important,' she told herself, surprised at how confident she felt about this.

She found she could now get into bed and lie down; but she did not want to sleep. She knew she wanted to reread more of *Communications*. She reached for the pad of paper and a pencil that lay on a chair near her bed, thinking that she might want to jot a few notes to discuss with Adam when she spoke to him the next evening.

When Ellen woke, she could hear the clatter of daytime sounds outside her house. For a moment she felt disorientated. Had she overslept? Having reassured herself that this was a day without commitments, she relaxed and closed her eyes again.

'It's okay,' she told herself. 'Remember you were up very late last night, and you had quite an intense experience. Just give yourself time. You can doze here for as long as you want.'

She lay there about another hour before deciding that she would try to get up and get washed. She sat up and rubbed her eyes.

Communications slid off the side of her bed and thudded on the floor. Her pad was still there, face down. As she moved it to one side, she could see that there were some marks on it. She turned it over, and stared in amazement.

'A spiral!' she gasped. 'I don't remember writing anything before I went to sleep.'

Unlike her memory of Jane's spirals, this one was regular in design, and relatively simple. It was made up of a long series of strokes, each about a centimetre in length. The first stroke curved to the right of the direction of the spiral, the second to the left, the third to the right, and so on to the centre of the spiral, which was in the shape of a small five-pointed star. She desperately wanted to speak to Eva and Jane; but she knew they would both be at work, certainly until the late afternoon. Adam would be at home though. What about phoning him now? But they had agreed to speak this evening: perhaps it would not be right to change that arrangement.

'Get washed and dressed,' she told herself firmly.

She put the pad down and followed her own directions. Standing in the shower, she felt the need for immediate contact become less urgent, and she was gradually able to think about planning the day up until the time she could speak to her friends.

Adam had woken early. He remembered that in the evening he would be talking to Ellen about Frances Ianson's book, and he was looking forward to that. He got out of bed briskly, ready to continue writing his reports. He was just beginning to shave his left cheek with a careful sweeping movement when he stopped, his hand and his razor suspended.

'Wait a minute!' he exclaimed. 'I was dreaming last night, and it was important. It was more of that light – the intense white light I saw round Ellen in that dream.'

He let his hand down, and rested it and the razor on the side of the washbasin.

'This time all I saw was the light, nothing else.'

The phone began to ring. He rushed to the extension in the hall and grabbed it.

'Hello?' he said. 'Oh, it's you Matthew. You're back ... for a week? Excellent. You can come over? How about tomorrow evening? Great! See you then. There's plenty to talk about I can tell you!'

Wiping drips of shaving soap from his pyjamas, he returned to the bathroom and finished shaving.

'I'll e-mail Boris about my dream. I'm glad it's only another three weeks before I'll be collecting him at the airport. I can't wait! Ah, here comes the post.'

Adam dried his hands, and took the post through to the conservatory. He saw an envelope that looked as if it might be from Carillon Music, and quickly opened it. Inside was a handwritten note from Gordon Quaver.

Dear Adam,

Just an informal note to tell you that everything is going well, and that I'm looking forward to seeing you and Boris again at the end of the month. The time you suggested is fine.

Gordon

Ah, something else to tell Boris in my e-mail, he thought. Adam smiled. Ellen is phoning this evening, her writing should arrive tomorrow, I see Matthew that evening, and then not long before I see Boris. After that he and I go to Carillon, and then off to stay at the Bull; and we'll see Ellen again. Life feels good!

He sat down at the computer, and was soon sending an e-mail off to Boris about his dream, and about the confirmation of the meeting at Carillon.

'Breakfast next, and then to work,' he said cheerfully.

Apart from photocopying her account of her time with Adam and Boris to send to Jane, Eva and Adam and posting these off, Ellen had spent much of the rest of the day in her garden tidying up a few weeds, and hanging out some washing. It was a good drying day, and she took full advantage of this by emptying the contents of the washing basket and changing the sheets from her bed. She felt content to wait until she thought Eva would be home before she tried to talk about what had happened to her. At about 5 p.m., she heard the phone, and ran into the house to pick it up.

'Hello, Ellen, it's Eva here.'

'You must have known I wanted to speak to you,' said Ellen happily.

'As a matter of fact, I think I must have sensed it. You've been on my mind all day,' said Eva. 'Tell me everything.'

Ellen told her of her efforts to produce an accurate account of her meeting with Boris and Adam, and the reason for it.

'I posted a copy to you today first class. It should arrive tomorrow. Read it through, and make a note of anything you want to comment on. After that you can tell me if you agree to my sending a copy to Edmund and his friend Joseph.'

'That's a very good idea. I'll do what you say, and I'll let you know what I think as soon as I can. But what else is on your mind?'

'Quite a lot happened last night,' replied Ellen; and she went on to tell her friend everything she could remember.

'No wonder you wanted to talk to me,' said Eva when Ellen had finished. 'I hardly know what to say. I wish you hadn't been on your own.'

'Maybe it wouldn't have happened if I hadn't been alone,' replied Ellen; 'and I'm certainly glad it did happen.'

'In any case, I'm glad you're okay,' said Eva. 'Would you like me to tell Jane, or will you phone her yourself?'

'I'd certainly like to speak to her, but perhaps not this evening, because I'll be speaking to Adam. Yes, please do phone her to fill her in; and tell her I hope to phone her tomorrow evening if she's going to be there.'

'Of course I will. By the way, don't hesitate to phone me if something else starts happening, and you want to talk. I don't mind if you phone me in the night. I have the phone beside my bed you'll remember.'

'Thanks. I'll speak to you again soon. I think I'll go now. I'll get my washing in and tidy up, ready for my call with Adam.

Ellen spent the next hour or so dealing with her washing and making her bed. Then she sat in her library, thinking through some of the things she wanted to discuss with Adam. When the phone rang it startled her. She looked at the clock, and saw it was exactly 8 p.m.

'Hello, Adam,' she said, as she put the receiver to her ear.

'Hello, Ellen. I've been looking forward all day to speaking to you,' said Adam warmly.

'Adam, I've something I need to tell you before we start to discuss the book,' Ellen began.

Then she stopped. 'No, perhaps we should discuss the book first,' she corrected herself.

'Ellen, I think that something's bothering you,' Adam said kindly. 'Tell me what it is.'

'I had quite an experience last night,' replied Ellen.

'Why don't you just tell me about that now,' Adam said encouragingly.

'Well, it's connected with the material in the book, I'm sure,' Ellen replied.

'Although we haven't discussed the book between ourselves, I can assure you that I've studied it thoroughly,' Adam reassured her. 'I've also been thinking about possible links between the content of the book and the things that have been happening to us and our friends.'

'In that case I feel easier about talking about last night,' said Ellen; and she went on to describe everything she remembered.

Adam let out a low whistle. 'That's amazing!' he exclaimed. 'And you may not be surprised to hear that I've something of my own to add.'

'You have?' said Ellen. 'Tell me straight away!'

'I had a dream; and I saw the same kind of light in it that I'd seen around you in the dream I told you about before. I wish now that I'd got some idea of what time I dreamed it. All I know is that I woke early – about 5.30 a.m. At first I didn't remember that I had dreamed: I only started to remember when I was shaving.

'As I told you, I finished my writing at about 1.30 a.m.,' replied Ellen. 'I think I must have eventually gone to bed and fallen asleep at about three.'

'Have you been in touch with Jane and Eva today?' asked Adam.

'I spoke to Eva, and she's going to tell Jane. I'll phone Jane myself tomorrow.'

'Well, do be careful. I'm not sure it would be a good idea to discuss your spiral and Jane's ones on the phone, when you're in the house alone.'

'You may be right. I'll bear that in mind. In any case, Eva has said I can phone her anytime – day or night.'

'I'm very glad about that. I'd offer the same, but I'm not sure it would be the right thing, in case I'm being affected around the same time as you. It's better to speak to someone who knows about the situation, but isn't actually in it. Matthew is coming round to see me tomorrow evening, and I'm going to update him about everything. Is that okay with you?'

'Yes, indeed. Will you e-mail Boris and let him know what I've told you? The other thing is that I posted my account of our meeting off to you today, so I hope it will arrive tomorrow morning. I'm sure Eva and Jane will be happy for you to let Boris see it.'

'Thanks. I'll scan it, and e-mail it to him.'

'I should hear back soon from Eva and Jane to see if they agree to my sending copies to Edmund and Joseph. I don't think that Edmund will be back in the country until towards the end of the month, but it can be waiting for him when he returns.'

'I could send the scanned version to him by e-mail,' Adam offered.

'I'd rather you didn't, thanks,' replied Ellen.

'Maybe you're right,' said Adam.

'Adam,' said Ellen, 'I think I'd rather not discuss Frances Ianson's book in detail just now, after what happened last night; but I'd like to hear your thoughts and reactions to it.'

'Okay,' said Adam. 'I'll tell you a few things; and maybe we can leave it at that until we speak again. The book made an enormous impression on me. The intelligence and commitment of the mother brought tears to my eyes; the condition of her son fascinated me; and the resolution of the situation was breathtaking. I was left with what seemed like a thousand questions in my mind. When I go off the phone, I shall be thinking about what happened to you last night, and holding it in my mind alongside some of the mother's experience as detailed in the book.'

'Thank you,' said Ellen. 'Look, I hope it's okay with you if I ring off now.'

'I think we should,' replied Adam. 'I hope you have a good night.'

When he put the phone down he went immediately to the computer and wrote a detailed account of Ellen's experiences of the night before. Then he e-mailed it to Boris. He added that he hoped to be able to send Ellen's account of their time together in May across to him the following day.

Chapter Forty-five

Ellen slept well that night. She woke in the morning feeling refreshed; and she had a productive day dealing with a pile of mail that had gathered at the office of one of the charities to which she gave her support.

She drove home in the evening looking forward to a leisurely meal, followed by a chat with Jane. Checking for messages on her call-minder, she found there was one from Jane to ask her to phone after 9 p.m., as she had to complete an assignment for her course. Ellen smiled. She was pleased that her friend was so engrossed in her studies, and she hoped it would lead to a more stimulating job for her.

She phoned just after nine, and Jane answered almost immediately.

'Hi Ellen, I know it's you. I've got a "caller display" phone now,' she said cheerfully. She went on: 'Eva told me what happened to you. So, now you've got a spiral of your own!'

'Yes, I have,' replied Ellen. 'It gave me some surprise as you can guess. I'm wondering what will happen at our September meeting. I hope that having everyone together will shed more light on everything. *Light*... oh, you know what I mean!'

'Yes, of course I do,' laughed Jane. 'Before I forget, the thing you sent me arrived this morning, just before I left for work. I took it with me and read it at lunchtime. It looks fine to me. I think you should certainly send a copy to Edmund and his friend. Eva thinks the same. She left a message on my phone about that because she knew I'd be speaking to you tonight.'

'I'll see to it tomorrow,' replied Ellen. 'How's your course going?'

'I'm delighted with it. It doesn't seem like work to me. I can't wait for the next assignment now I've finished this one. And I've got some news of Emily for you. You'll be interested to hear that when she's out playing, she collects bundles of small sticks and lays them out in groups, as if she's trying to work something out.'

'That doesn't surprise me,' replied Ellen. 'I think we're going to be learning a lot from her.'

Matthew and Adam were sitting in the conservatory, deep in conversation. Matthew had arrived in the early evening, eager to make contact with his friend and catch up on events. His own life seemed mundane by contrast with the things that Adam was telling him, but he was not sure that he could entirely believe everything he was hearing. He was in a quandary. He trusted Adam completely, but how could he believe the accounts of these strange things? Adam had let him read what Ellen had written, but this confused Matthew even more. The account was written in a very sensible and objective way, but the subject matter was another thing. And then there was what Adam had told him about Ellen's recent experience. He shook his head as if to clear it, but it made no impression on his inner conflict.

'Look, mate,' he said to Adam. 'I think you're a totally honest man, but what on earth *is* all this? I have to admit I can't take it all in. If anyone else told me this, I'd run a mile. I know some of it's right, because I was here that night you passed out; and I saw what sort of state you were in and what you were saying.'

'I think I can understand how hard it must be for you,' replied Adam. 'My position is very different from yours. I've been involved in it for quite a while now, either directly or through my association with Ellen. I've had more of a chance of getting used to it; but I can feel very strange and uncertain at times. There's one thing for sure, though.'

'What's that?' asked Matthew.

'I value the contact I have with you about this enormously.'

'Do you?' Matthew was obviously surprised.

'Yes I do. It means a lot to me to be able to tell you about it all. You're somebody I can trust; and although you struggle to believe some of it, you don't rubbish me in any way. It helps me to sort out my own thoughts.'

'Well, if you can take me as I am, I'm happy for you to keep telling me things. I can't hide how I feel, but if that doesn't make it difficult for you, let's just agree you're free to keep me up to date as things emerge. From what you're saying, something pretty big is brewing with this meeting you're all having at Ellen's at the beginning of next month. Phew, if this was a film of a psychological thriller, I'd be expecting to see the ceiling of Ellen's library caving in while the seven of you are sitting muttering incantations about spirals!'

Adam burst out laughing. His whole body shook.

'That's what I like about you Matthew, your down-to-earth, upfront attitude,' he said. 'Seriously though, it does feel as if the whole thing is coming to some sort of climax; although what that will be is something I can't even begin to guess.'

'Rather than playing at guessing games, can we have another game of chess?' asked Matthew. 'I've become quite interested under your gentle tuition.'

'Suits me,' replied Adam.

He disappeared into the house, and returned soon afterwards, carrying the box of chess pieces along with the board. The two men were soon concentrating on their game. For the first time Matthew felt involved in it, and was pleased to be adding this to his repertoire. His lonely evenings working away from home might be relieved a little if he could feel a bit more confident with this game. Surely some of the people he met in small hotels or bed and breakfast places would be able to play?

'Hey, you're getting much more clued into this!' exclaimed Adam after the first few moves.

'Thanks. I haven't played it with anyone else yet, but I do think about it quite a bit when I'm driving along on a boring journey,' said Matthew.

'Well, at this rate, with a few more weeks of thought sessions, you'll have me beaten.' Adam smiled. He was glad to have brought something into Matthew's life that he now appeared to be enjoying. 'Hey, I don't see any nuts this time,' he said.

Matthew looked a little evasive. 'Um,' he said.

'You don't need to apologise,' said Adam hurriedly. 'I don't expect you to bring anything but yourself when you come.'

'Actually I would have brought some, but at the last minute I wondered if your collapse had been an odd reaction to eating nuts,' he muttered. For once, Matthew could not meet Adam's gaze.

Adam put his hand across and touched Matthew's arm. 'That

was very thoughtful of you,' he said. 'I appreciate your concern. You must have got a real shock when I passed out.'

'Yes, I did.'

'This helps me to grasp more of what Boris has had to cope with when I've gone into a peculiar state listening to that tape of ours,' said Adam. He looked straight at Matthew and said, 'I want to thank you again for your help the evening I keeled over, and for staying the night. I'm quite sure that my collapse was to do with the thing that's happening between Ellen and myself. I'm grateful you were with me when it happened. Thank you.'

'Okay mate,' said Matthew gruffly. 'But you don't need to lay it on with a trowel. Let's get on with the game now.'

'Of course,' Adam replied. 'How about I get some grapes from the kitchen? Do you like them?'

'Yes, I do. Especially the red ones.'

'Red they are,' replied Adam.

He produced from the kitchen a large plate of red grapes, and the two munched together as their game continued.

It was after midnight by the time they parted.

'Remember and let me know how the meeting with the music publisher goes,' said Matthew.

'Are you around at the end of the month?' asked Adam.

'I might be here for a couple of days. Why?'

'I'd like you to meet Boris. You didn't see him when he was over last time. Let's try and fix it this time.'

Matthew looked pleased. 'Okay. Shall we make a date then? I can phone nearer the time if I can't make it.'

'Yes. If you have to do that remember that Boris will be here for a couple of months, so we can arrange something for later on in his stay.' Adam grinned wickedly. 'If we didn't meet until after we go to Ellen's, we could both tell you all about it!'

Matthew pulled a face. 'Maybe you'd need to digest it a bit first,' he advised. 'But of course you might have changed into a werewolf by then! But I'll stick to what I said before. You can tell me any of it. Okay?'

'I know. And thanks again. Goodnight,' said Adam as he saw Matthew out of the front door.

Adam got ready for bed slowly. It would not be long now

before he would be at the airport collecting Boris. He was determined to put in the hours to ensure that his work reports were completed and finalised a few days in advance of that. Then he would have time to get the house tidied up and buy some food.

Chapter Forty-six

Adam made sure he was at the airport in good time for the arrival of Boris' flight. He could not stop smiling when he saw his friend. In fact he noticed that his cheeks hurt with the size of his smile. The two men embraced each other, and then walked side by side to find Boris' luggage.

'Ah, you remembered,' said Adam, as he noted the modest size of Boris' bag.

'Yes, I know I can borrow things from you, or if I am really stuck we can go shopping,' replied Boris.

'How was the journey?' asked Adam.

'It was absolutely fine,' replied Boris. 'I slept much of the way. The food was not too bad, and I was sitting next to a pleasant young man. We had some interesting conversations that passed the time quite well.'

'Anything of note?' asked Adam.

'We spoke mainly about his career plans. I said a little about my friendship with you, and he was genuinely interested.'

The drive back to Adam's house was largely taken up with catching up on more of what had emerged since Boris had left.

'Keeping in touch by e-mail is good,' said Adam, 'but it's never as good as having you here in the flesh, and having a real conversation.'

'I have felt rather isolated since I left,' said Boris. 'I feel such a part of what is happening here, and it was hard to be back at home at first.'

'I've spent most of my time making sure my work was out of the way before you arrived,' said Adam. 'I didn't want to have any of it in my mind once you were here. I wanted to be free to concentrate on our meeting at Carillon, and then our meeting at Ellen's. And there's a good chance you'll get to meet Matthew soon. I've fixed a date with him. I hope he can make it.'

'When is that?'

'It's the evening after our meeting at Carillon,' replied Adam, as he turned the car into his drive.

'Let's go in and put the kettle on,' he said. 'You're bound to be thirsty.'

'I am certainly looking forward to being in a place where nothing is moving underneath me,' Boris said with a note of relief in his voice. 'I would like a drink, and then perhaps we could walk for a while. I need to get my legs moving.'

The following two days passed pleasantly. The next day saw Adam and Boris preparing for the drive across to Carillon Music to see Gordon Quaver.

'It's just an informal meeting,' said Adam, 'but I think it's good to keep in touch this way.'

'I agree,' replied Boris. 'Personal contact is nearly always the best way. I have recovered from my journey now, and I shall enjoy the drive.'

Adam used the same car park as before; and not long after arriving there, they were seated with Gordon Quaver.

'Thanks for coming across,' said Gordon. 'As I said, this is a completely informal meeting. We don't usually ask to see people at this stage, but I wanted the opportunity of talking over with you again the background to your projects, both of which are quite unusual. I know some of the story, but just tell me again, right from the beginning, and don't leave anything out.'

Adam and Boris relaxed. They told Gordon of their early association as music students, and they regaled him with stories of their less worthy exploits as well as the story of how they had come to make their collection of Romanian songs. There was much laughter mingled with the more serious discussion.

Adam noticed that Gordon had been making notes as they spoke.

'I have been wondering about writing an introduction to your collection,' he said. 'There's certainly plenty of interesting material that could be included out of what we've been discussing. What do you think?'

'I would not be averse to that,' said Boris, 'but I don't want anything that will detract from the meaning of the songs themselves. What do you think, Adam?'

'I agree,' replied Adam. 'I think that an introduction could be an interesting addition for anyone who bought a copy of the collection, but it must be entirely in keeping with the songs, and not include anything that would really be a distraction.'

'Do you think you could draft something suitable?' asked Gordon.

Adam looked at Boris. 'I think we could do that together while you're over here, couldn't we?' he asked.

'Yes. I would like to do that,' Boris replied.

'And what about the Russian collection?' Gordon went on. 'Your ideas there are much more recent, aren't they? Shall we talk through some of that, and then perhaps I could leave you to draft an introduction to those volumes as well? By the way, after much consideration, we've decided to advise you to agree to dividing these songs into three separate volumes.'

Adam felt very comfortable sitting here with Gordon and Boris. He was glad that he and Boris had agreed to come. He was aware that his attention was slipping a little, and that Gordon and Boris appeared to be deep in discussion. He was vaguely aware that he could not hear what they were saying any more; but it did not seem to matter. He leaned back in his chair a little.

'Why am I feeling so cold?' he heard someone say from a distance.

'*Adam!*' said Boris urgently. '*Not now!*'

He quickly took a glass of water from the table and put it to his friend's lips.

'Here Adam,' he said. 'Sip this.'

Adam was aware of the glass of water, and of his friend bending over him, but could hear nothing. He obediently took a sip, and swallowed uncomfortably. This action seemed to reconnect him.

'Sorry,' he said. 'I think I was dozing off… It must be this August heat.'

'I'll open a window,' said Gordon, concern showing in his voice, 'but actually you said something about feeling cold.'

Adam looked startled. 'Oh… that's strange. I'm sorry, I haven't a clue what I was going on about…'

Boris was staring at him meaningfully.

'Perhaps we should be going soon,' he said. 'Remember we

have to be back because the plumber is coming to check that drain of yours later today.'

Adam stared at Boris stupidly. Then he said, 'Yes... oh yes.'

He turned to Gordon and said, 'Gordon, thanks for having us across today. We're a bit tied up over the next few weeks, but after that we'll be able to work on those introductions. Won't we, Boris?'

'That is correct,' agreed Boris.

'I must let you get on then,' said Gordon. 'Thank you for coming.'

He stood up and shook hands with Adam, then Boris, and showed them to the exit.

Back in the car, Adam and Boris sat to take stock of the situation.

'I think that you were starting to go into that state again – the state you go into with the tape,' said Boris.

'You may be right,' said Adam, worriedly. 'But it's never happened in front of someone I hardly know! Thanks for bringing in the plumber. At first I thought you were going off your head, but then I realised what you were doing.'

'Gordon was talking about the Russian songs,' Boris reflected.

Adam groaned. 'That might be it,' he said. 'Look, I think I'm still sufficiently affected that I shouldn't drive yet. Do you mind if we find a place to have a sandwich and some soup? We could sit and eat and talk things over until I've recovered a bit more.'

'I think that is sensible,' replied Boris.

'And on the way back I think we should stop a few times and just walk about a bit,' Adam added.

In the event, their meal and the journey back were unremarkable. By the time they reached Adam's house, he was chatting animatedly about some shoes he was thinking of buying before the winter. Boris was glad of this conversation, and took care to keep it in the same vein. Later, over the evening meal, he suggested that they go over the events of the day with Matthew the following evening when he came round.

'From what you say,' he reasoned, 'you have told him everything already. He may not have remembered it all, but at least he has some idea of what has been going on.'

'He would certainly be open to that,' replied Adam. 'Why don't we just relax with a game of chess this evening; then tomorrow I'll show you some more of the local places of interest?'

The following evening the doorbell rang at eight o'clock precisely. Adam went to the door and let Matthew in. He was carrying a large bag of nuts.

'I can see you've relented!' said Adam. 'And I've got a very large bunch of red grapes for you here. Come on through and meet Boris.'

Adam led the way to the conservatory where Boris was standing with his hand held out to greet Matthew.

'I am very glad to meet you Matthew,' he said. 'I am sorry we did not see each other when I was last here.'

'Same here, mate,' replied Matthew. 'And we've got quite a bit to talk about. I hear that you've had some trouble with my pal here.' He jabbed Adam in the ribs affectionately. 'I think we've got some stories to swap about this one!'

'Hmm,' said Adam dryly. 'Yes. And you won't be surprised to hear that something else has happened.'

'Oh no! Already?' exclaimed Matthew incredulously. 'Can't leave you alone for a minute! You'd better tell me about it.'

'Sit down then,' said Adam, pointing to a chair.

He and Boris told Matthew of their meeting with Gordon at Carillon Music. Matthew listened intently while they went through it, and then waited for a moment before saying, 'So? And…?'

'We have not finished yet,' explained Boris. 'You tell him what you remember, Adam, and then I will add to it.'

When they had finished, Matthew stared at Adam.

'You'd better be careful, mate. That was a close one. You wouldn't have expected anything like that to happen there. If it can start that easily, I think you should have Boris with you all the time when you're out. At least until after you've had your meeting at Ellen's.'

'I have already made up my mind about that,' said Boris. 'I was waiting until you came before I said it, just in case Adam tried to object.'

'I'm not objecting,' said Adam. 'I think you're both absolutely right. Not only do I want to be with Boris until after that meeting, but also I'd like to ask him to stick close to me for a while after that. Are you willing, tovarish?'

'Yes, I am!' replied Boris emphatically.

'Well that's that fixed, then,' said Matthew. 'It's a load off my mind. Even without that funny turn you had at the meeting with Gordon, I was worrying about what might happen to you before and after the meeting at Ellen's.'

Adam looked at his friends gratefully. He felt very lucky to have people who were so concerned about him.

'The next thing to talk about,' said Matthew, 'is how you're getting up to Ellen's.'

'What do you mean?' asked Adam. 'I'm driving up, of course.'

Matthew looked at him and raised an eyebrow. 'Driving up?' he repeated.

'What are you trying to say?' asked Adam. 'Come on. Spit it out!'

'I'm trying to get you to think about whether or not it would be sensible for you to drive,' replied Matthew. 'That's all.'

Boris nodded. 'That is wise,' he said.

For a little while Matthew appeared lost in thought. Then he continued speaking.

'I've just been thinking – I might be able to help out a bit here. When exactly do you leave?'

'We're due to be at the Bull by early evening on Friday. I had planned to leave fairly early on the Friday morning, but I'm wondering now whether to take a couple of days over the journey, so we can take plenty of breaks,' said Adam.

'It's Tuesday now…' said Matthew slowly. 'Yes, I think I could fix it.'

'Fix what exactly?' asked Adam.

'It's a bit of a detour for me,' Matthew reflected.

'What is?' asked Adam.

'What I could do is to come up with you nearly all the way on Friday,' Matthew offered. 'I have to use a hire car, but I could fix to pick one up in Alnwick instead of setting off in one from home. The first one of my assignments is in Newcastle on Monday.'

'But that would mean you'd be away for a whole weekend when you could have your feet up.' Adam was clearly puzzled.

'Yes, but I'd know that you were both safe, wouldn't I?' said Matthew. 'I can't come back down with you because I'm based in Newcastle for the week, but you could make your way back down quite slowly, I should think.'

'That's a really kind offer,' said Adam. 'Can I have time to think it over?'

'No, you can't,' replied Matthew decisively. 'I'm telling you that's what's happening.'

'Thank you very much indeed,' said Boris. 'Your help and companionship are most welcome.'

'Okay,' said Adam. 'And since that's settled, I have an idea. Why don't you join us all for the evening meal at the Bull that evening? You can meet everyone then, and you could stay there overnight. Shall I phone Ellen and see if you might spend the rest of the weekend with us as well?'

'Steady on, mate!' said Matthew hurriedly. 'I don't think I'm up for all that stuff. I could stay at there that night if they have a room. I'll find out where the nearest car hire firm is, and work it out from there.'

'Yes, we can sort that out,' said Adam. 'I'll phone the Bull tomorrow, and you can fix the car hire. It's great that you're going to meet the others.'

'Let's have a game of something now,' said Matthew. 'Pity we can't have chess for three!'

'How about playing cards then?' Adam suggested.

The three spent the rest of the evening working their way through all the card games they could remember.

The following morning Adam phoned the Bull, and booked a room for Matthew. He then phoned Ellen's number. To his surprise, she answered.

'Hello, Adam. Good to hear you. All's well here. I'm expecting Eva and Jane to arrive some time on Friday afternoon. When do you think you'll get to the Bull?'

'I'm not sure,' said Adam. 'I'd guess late afternoon. There's something I want to ask you about it.'

'What's that?'

'You remember I spoke to you about my friend Matthew? I'm in the middle of fixing for him to travel up with us and spend the night at the Bull. Would you mind if he joined in with the meal we'd planned that evening?'

'Of course not. I'd be very pleased to meet him.'

'Do you think the others would agree?'

'I'm quite certain of that. I'll phone them to let them know, but just assume it's okay.'

'Have you heard anything from Edmund and Joseph?'

'Yes, I have. I had a letter from Edmund last week thanking me for the writing I sent. He was just back home. He said he'd be speaking at a conference in Birmingham this week, and would travel straight up from there with Joseph after it finishes on Friday.'

'Good,' said Adam. 'I'm glad you've heard something from him; so now we know he got back safely.'

'Not long to wait now,' said Ellen.

'Thank goodness! In some ways the time has passed quite quickly, but in others it has seemed a long wait. Apart from the meeting itself, I'm very much looking forward to seeing you again. Incidentally, Matthew offered to combine some of his travelling for work with offering himself as a co-driver, after he heard of my most recent experience.'

'What was that?' asked Ellen anxiously.

'Boris and I were at our meeting with Carillon Music. Gordon Quaver had got on to talking about the Russian songs, and I found myself feeling very cold. I slipped almost completely into another state. Fortunately Boris spotted what was happening and brought me out of it in the nick of time, without having to explain anything to Gordon. When we told Matthew about it, he was very worried about my driving the whole journey up to you, and he offered to co-drive, so long as he can get a hire car for Saturday to drive back to Newcastle by Monday at the latest. I'll phone him now to tell him he definitely has a bed at the Bull.' He hesitated for a moment before adding, 'I'll see you very soon.'

Adam felt warmed by his conversation with Ellen. It was a while since they had last spoken. He felt some anticipation of the elucidation of the unusual and as yet undefined connection they shared. He picked up the phone again to try to get Matthew.

'Hi! Is that you Adam? I was just dashing out... You booked the room? Great! What time shall I be ready on Friday morning? Ten? ...Yes, I'll be at the door. See you.'

Adam put down the phone and turned to Boris.

'That's all fixed, then,' he said.

It was Friday at last. At 10 a.m. precisely, Adam drew up outside Matthew's house. Matthew was standing on his front drive with a bag at his feet.

'Shall I put it in the boot?' he called out.

'Yes, there's plenty of room,' replied Adam.

Matthew loaded his bag in, and got in next to Adam.

'I'm pretty sure of the route,' said Adam. 'Shall I take the first hour and see how we go?'

'Fine by me,' replied Matthew. 'But be sure to pull in if you feel odd at any time, and I'll take over.' He turned round to speak to Boris. 'You're taking that tape up with you, aren't you?' he asked.

'Yes, I have got it safely wrapped in several layers of clothing in my bag,' replied Boris.

'And I'm not going to ask to listen to it,' said Matthew determinedly. 'For one thing I don't want Adam driving off the road, and for another I'm not sure I want to hear it anyway!'

'You might change your mind sometime,' said Adam. 'But for now, I think you're right not to hear it.'

The roads were relatively quiet, and they made good time. At eleven, Adam drew in at a lay-by. He was surprised to find that he was glad to hand over to Matthew, as he already felt weary. They changed seats, and Matthew set off. After only a short time Boris noticed Adam's head start to nod forwards. Soon he could hear deep regular breathing.

'Adam's asleep now,' he said quietly to Matthew. 'Can you keep your speed down a bit, just in case we need to stop?'

Matthew understood exactly what Boris meant, and slowed the car. Boris continued to keep a watchful eye on Adam.

Adam slept for most of three hours. When he woke he asked cheerfully, 'Is it my turn yet?'

'You can take over if you want,' replied Matthew, 'but I'm fine, thanks.'

Adam looked at his watch. 'Hey!' he exclaimed. 'Why didn't you wake me up? I thought I'd just dozed off for a few minutes.'

'We knew it was best not to risk startling you,' said Boris quietly.

'You don't need to treat me like a glass doll,' said Adam, sounding irritated.

'I think it is perfectly reasonable to be cautious under the circumstances,' Boris said evenly.

'I'm sorry,' Adam said apologetically. 'I shouldn't have said that. You're behaving in a responsible way, and I'm behaving like a thoughtless adolescent. You have my safety and the safety of us all at heart, and I thank you for that.'

'That will always be a part of my friendship with you,' replied Boris, seriously.

'You could take over for half an hour now if you want,' said Matthew.

'I'd like to,' replied Adam. 'I feel fine. Looking at the map, I think we'll be there within the next couple of hours.'

'I drove quite slowly while you were asleep,' said Matthew.

'Thanks,' replied Adam.

'Hey, guess what?' said Matthew. 'I think I'm looking forward to meeting your friends. I think we're going to have a good evening together. What sort of food does that place dish up?'

'There's a good range as far as I can remember,' replied Adam as he took the wheel.

A traffic hold-up delayed their progress, and it was already 6 p.m. by the time they arrived at the Bull. They unloaded their bags and booked in.

'Let's go up to our rooms, and then I'll phone Ellen to say we've arrived,' said Adam.

'I think I'd like to walk around outside a bit,' said Matthew. 'I need to stretch my legs.'

'Can I join you?' asked Boris.

'Of course, mate,' Matthew replied, looking pleased. He turned to Adam. 'Come and find us when you've finished phoning.'

Boris and Matthew were soon strolling along the quiet road.

Having found a phone, Adam rang Ellen's number. An unfamiliar voice answered, and he felt confused until he realised that this must be one of her friends.

'This is Adam,' he said. 'Am I speaking to Jane or Eva?'

'Hello, Adam. This is Eva. I'll get Ellen for you.'

'There's no need. I'm phoning to say we've just arrived, and we're looking forward to seeing you all soon.'

'Okay. I'll pass the message on. Bye for now.'

Adam put the phone down, and went to find Matthew and Boris. As he went out of the front door, he noticed a car draw up with two older men in it.

'Ah, I wonder if that's Edmund and Joseph,' he said to himself. 'I hope so.'

He walked across to the car, and as he got nearer, the driver got out.

'Hello, Adam. Good to see you. Have you been here long?'

It was Edmund. He held out his hand to Adam, who shook it warmly.

'No, as a matter of fact we've only just arrived ourselves. Matthew and Boris have gone for a walk.'

'Ah, you've brought your other friend with you. I remember reading his name in the notes that Ellen sent to me,' said Edmund. 'He'll be joining us for the weekend?'

'He's only here until tomorrow morning,' Adam replied. 'Then he's going on to Newcastle. He has work there.'

'At least we'll see him this evening, then,' said Edmund.

'That's good,' Joseph added. He had got out of the far side of the car, and had come round to join them.

'I'll go and catch up with Matthew and Boris now,' said Adam. 'We'll see you later. Ellen and her friends should be along in about an hour I should think.'

'Edmund and I will book in and have a rest,' said Joseph. 'We've got quite a number of questions to ask now that we've both read Ellen's notes, but I think we should leave them until tomorrow.'

Edmund nodded. 'There's so much more in the notes than I had learned when I met Ellen in May. I'm so glad you all felt you could trust us and include us like this.'

'I had a sense I could trust your integrity from the first time I met you at that talk I came to last autumn,' said Adam. 'Matthew had already spoken very highly of you; and when Ellen spoke to you we learned that you'd met her father. I know she's very glad to have the opportunity of having you here – not only to see her father's books, but also for your wisdom and experience. We're glad that you'll be a part of our deliberations about the meaning of the spirals, the tape, the stick, and the events that surround them which have drawn us all together this weekend.'

'I am honoured,' replied Edmund.

'I must go now,' said Adam. 'I'll see you both in about an hour.'

Ellen, Eva and Jane got into Ellen's car to drive down to the Bull.

'I feel excited and calm, both at the same time,' said Ellen.

'That sounds about right,' said Eva. 'You put it very well. I'm about the same.'

'I feel quite nervous,' said Jane. 'I'm not used to this kind of setting. I'm not used to eating in large groups; and I'm going to be meeting some people who know a lot about me and my spiral writing.'

'I think it's best to use this evening as a social gathering – getting to know one another in as ordinary a way as possible,' said Eva.

'I agree,' Ellen said.

'I think that would help me a lot,' said Jane. 'I wonder how the others are feeling?'

'We'll soon find out,' replied Ellen. 'We'll be there soon.'

When she drew up at the car park she was glad to see Adam and Boris sitting outside on chairs near the front of the Bull, with what looked like Edmund and Joseph sitting beside them. As she pointed them out to Eva and Jane, Adam stood up and walked across to where she was parking the car. He was smiling broadly. He waited while all three got out of the car.

'Hello, Ellen. It's good to see you and to meet your friends at last. I've been looking forward to this for a long time.'

Ellen first introduced him to Jane.

'Jane,' he said. 'I'm so pleased to meet you. And I'm indebted to you as the author of the spirals which have been such an important part of Ellen's awareness of her connection between my life and hers.'

'It's good to meet you too, Adam,' Jane replied, her feelings of nervousness dispersing rapidly. 'But remember, I may not be the author of the spirals. They certainly appeared in *my* diary, but that's all we can be sure about.'

'You're right to correct me,' said Adam. 'We must be as accurate as we can about everything.' He turned to Eva. 'You must be Eva,' he said.

'Good to meet you, Adam,' she replied, holding out her hand.

'There's a lot to talk over,' said Adam. 'But the four of us here were going to suggest that we keep this evening as a social gathering, and save serious discussion for tomorrow.'

'That's exactly what we were saying on the way,' said Ellen.

Adam continued. 'We do all need time to get to know one another; but there are other things to take into account. The dining area here is not entirely private, and I for one would prefer to keep our discussions to our immediate group. Added to that, although Matthew is more than happy to be meeting everyone, and to know about the whole picture, he's clear that he doesn't want to be involved in the deeper discussions.'

'That's absolutely fine by us,' said Ellen. 'Let's go across and join the others now.'

They made their way across the car park to where the four men were seated, and then spent some time with introductions before going inside for something to drink before their meal.

The Bull had provided a large oval table, which gave the greatest possibility of conversation between all of them. Matthew suggested that they change places at least once throughout the meal, thus producing an even greater opportunity of getting to know one another. By the end of the meal, they were all quite relaxed with each other.

Secretly, Matthew began to regret the firm stance he had taken about his need to leave in the morning. He felt so comfortable and at ease, that he thought how he would have liked to spend the whole weekend with these people. But when he thought about what they would be discussing tomorrow, he knew he had made the right decision. It was all very well having a social evening with a group of interesting people, but tomorrow would be a very different matter, and he knew he was not up to it.

Ellen turned to him and said, 'It's so nice having you here Matthew; it's a pity you aren't free to stay on.'

'Yes,' he replied, gruffly. 'Maybe another time then. Excuse me a minute, I think I need some air.'

He stood up and wandered off outside for a while to wrestle with a number of conflicting feelings.

At the end of the evening, Ellen stood up and addressed the group.

'We'll have to go soon,' she said. 'I'd like to suggest that you all come up to my house for lunch tomorrow; then we'll have the whole of the afternoon and evening together. Eva, Jane and I have organised all the food we'll need. Matthew, I don't know what time you have to leave, but if you can come up for lunch and see where I live, you're very welcome.'

'Thanks,' replied Matthew gratefully. 'My hire car will be delivered in the morning, but I don't need to leave for Newcastle until the afternoon. I'd certainly like to take up your invitation.' It felt good to him to be included like this.

'Good night then, everyone,' said Ellen.

'We'll see you tomorrow,' added Jane and Eva.

Chapter Forty-seven

Adam woke early, with a sense of eager anticipation. He looked across at Boris, who was still fast asleep in the other bed. Carefully he slipped quietly out of bed and along the corridor to the bathroom, where he washed and shaved and put on his clothes. He wanted to get out for a walk before breakfast.

As he left through the front door he encountered Edmund striding purposefully down the steps to the car park.

'Good morning, Edmund,' he said.

'Ah, good morning Adam,' replied Edmund. 'I'm just going for a walk. Would you care to join me?'

The two men walked briskly along the quiet road. It was some minutes before Edmund broke the silence.

'I'm glad to have this time with you,' he said.

'Maybe we're having similar thoughts,' said Adam. 'Let's talk and see where we're at.'

Edmund began. 'My main concern is that we all spend some time straight after lunch discussing some general points about how we're going to approach these very complex matters.'

'I'm thinking along exactly the same lines,' replied Adam. 'It may reassure you to know that Boris and I, in our dealings with the tape, soon began to realise that it's crucial to have that kind of discussion. We can check with Ellen, Eva, and Jane, but I have the impression they have been doing something similar when they have met to look at the spirals and Ellen's red book. What we need to do is to be sure to allocate some time preparing for the detailed discussions.'

'I don't say this to alarm,' said Edmund, 'but it does seem to me that there are dangers inherent in what we're hoping to approach.'

'I agree,' said Adam immediately. 'Ellen and I have had very intense reactions at times, and sometimes these reactions have been simultaneous, even from a distance. Boris, Eva and Jane have had lesser reactions. Ellen and I have definitely needed help with ours.'

'At the meeting this afternoon and evening, we'll have seven people. Matthew will have left by then. Joseph and I are involved, but less so than any of the rest of you,' said Edmund. 'It's my suggestion that Joseph and I take some overall responsibility, and that if either of us feel that events are intensifying in a way that worries us, we should be free to take steps to remedy that.'

'That's a generous offer,' said Adam. 'Each of us must take our responsibilities very seriously. That's paramount. But if you and Joseph were both willing to take the role you're suggesting, that would make the situation even safer. Can we agree then that we'll discuss this with the others after lunch?'

They turned to each other and shook hands. Then they retraced their steps to join Matthew, Boris and Joseph for breakfast. Boris had managed to acquire a number of newspapers, and he shared them out. The rest of the morning was taken up with reading and puzzling over crossword clues.

Ellen had a feeling of fulfilment as she welcomed everyone into her house for lunch. She showed them into the library straight away.

'Here are all my father's books,' she said. 'Do have a look at anything that interests you. If you want to search the catalogue, it's over here.' She motioned towards a large file. 'I'll just finish laying out our lunch in the kitchen. Come through in about fifteen minutes.'

Matthew sat down heavily in a chair. 'I've never seen anything like this in someone's house,' he said.

'It's certainly impressive,' replied Adam. 'It's difficult to know where to start.'

'I don't think I will,' replied Matthew. 'It's lunch for me, and then I'm off. I hope you lot will be okay without me.'

'I've already had a chat with Edmund about that,' replied Adam. 'We have some ideas about how to make sure things don't get out of hand.'

'Phew. What a relief! It's been worrying me. Now I can enjoy my lunch, and leave with an easier mind,' said Matthew.

He and Adam made their way to the kitchen. The others followed them, although Edmund was clearly reluctant to replace the book that was absorbing his attention.

After lunch, Ellen stood up. 'I don't want to embarrass you Matthew, but I want to thank you for coming up with Adam, and I want to say how nice it's been to meet you and have you here.'

The others smiled and clapped, and Matthew looked uncomfortable.

'Thanks. Well, I'll be off now. Look after yourselves,' he said.

'You too,' replied Ellen. 'I hope you'll come again when you're in this part of the country. In fact, you might want to use one of my spare rooms. I don't usually have people staying. Here's a note of my address and phone number.'

She scribbled on a piece of paper and handed it to him.

After this, they all went out to wave Matthew off in his hired car. He realised that this felt okay. In fact it felt really nice. Maybe he *would* contact Ellen when he was up here again. She had seemed genuine in her offer, and he much preferred not to stay in anonymous bed and breakfast places.

Ellen watched Matthew's car disappear, and then turned to the others and said, 'I think it's time we got to work. Let's all go back to the library.'

The others followed her back through the house. She had arranged a number of comfortable chairs in a loose circle, and she waited until everyone was seated before addressing them in quite a formal way.

'Welcome to my library, everyone,' she said. 'I've been looking forward to this day for weeks. It's so good to have my special friends here together. There'll be plenty of time for those who wish to look at the books to do so tomorrow. As you know we're here today to discuss a number of important subjects, which are linked by a common thread. I do hope that further understanding will come through the examination of all we know so far.'

She indicated a table that stood beside her chair.

'I have here Jane's diary containing the spirals, my copy of Frances Ianson's book *Communications*, Eva's stick, a photograph of Emily and her mother, and a photograph of Hannah and her father. Boris, do you have that tape with you?'

'Yes, I have.'

Boris felt inside his jacket pocket and produced an audiotape. He stood up and put it on the table with the other things.

'Do you think I should add the spiral that appeared on my pad recently?' Ellen asked the others.

'I think that for completeness that would be important,' said Edmund.

'I'll just go up and get it then,' replied Ellen.

She returned quite quickly with her pad and put it on the table.

'I have other items with me,' said Boris.

Adam looked at him, surprised. 'You didn't tell me,' he said.

'I was not sure what to do,' said Boris. 'I decided in the end to wait until we were here. I am sorry I did not let you know.'

'What have you brought?' asked Ellen.

Boris reached inside his jacket pocket again, and produced a small packet of photographs. He passed them round, one by one.

'This is a photograph of the shelf where we kept the tape after the first time it affected Adam so deeply. You can see the delicate glassware on the shelf. The other photographs are of the chess set my grandfather carved, and the chess board which my grandmother made to go with it.'

Everyone studied the photographs carefully, and agreed that they should be on the table with the other items.

'I see that you've all brought your copy of *Communications*, and my detailed account of those long conversations I had with Adam and Boris in May,' said Ellen. 'I think that's everything I wanted to say to begin with. Would someone else like to take over now?'

Adam and Edmund looked across at each other.

'Yesterday, Edmund and I had a bit of a chat,' said Adam. 'It led to Edmund making an offer on behalf of himself and Joseph.'

Joseph nodded. 'Edmund, do you want to explain?' he said.

'Of course,' replied Edmund. 'Joseph and I are relatively new to what has been happening in your lives. The first we knew of all of this was in May, when Ellen told me of the existence of the spirals. I was immediately interested, and you have all kindly agreed that Joseph and I could join your meeting today. I have been abroad until very recently, and on my return I found waiting for me Ellen's very clear and detailed account of her conversations with Boris and Adam. Joseph and I have studied this carefully several times. I will say straightaway that it is all outside my own experience. However, I do believe everything that you have documented, my dear,' he said, smiling at Ellen. 'And the presence of all of you here further confirms it. There are a number of things I have read about, or indeed heard of, that have given me a basis through which to consider all of this, and I may contribute some of it to your discussions. But I think that the most important thing Joseph and I have to offer is something outside the discussions. It's clear to us both that Ellen and Adam in particular have entered some deep states of altered consciousness. It is paramount that such a process should be supervised as much as possible. Fortunately, through your mature approach to this so far, and apart from the recent occasion when Ellen's spiral appeared, you have each had appropriate companionship when in an altered state. Exposure to the likely stimuli, such as Jane's spirals for Ellen, has been clearly defined and limited.

'Joseph and I wish to offer to be supervisors for today's meeting. We offer this on as informal a basis as possible. We would like to contribute to the discussions; but more importantly, we would want to be the people who help you to devise the framework for the discussions, and have the power to limit them, if we feel it to be necessary for the overall safety of the situation. Could I ask if you are all in agreement with this?'

All five agreed immediately, and Ellen thanked Edmund and Joseph on behalf of them all.

'I should say one more thing before we proceed to the next stage,' said Edmund.

'Joseph and I do want to have the opportunity to study the spirals and Ellen's red book, but we believe it would not be wise for us to do this until tomorrow. If we are to be affected by them, it would be best that it is *after* this meeting and not during it.

'Of course, you will no doubt be viewing them. I expect that we will also run the tape some time today, and we must agree careful guidelines for that before doing so. The other items I believe are easier to mediate, as the effects of them upon those who are sensitive are likely to be much less profound.'

Boris indicated that he wanted to say something.

'Yes?' asked Edmund.

'Professor, I am most grateful to have you and Joseph involved in this way. I feel no longer alone in my responsibility for the potential effects of the tape.'

'I feel the same about the spirals,' said Eva.

She turned to Jane, and noticed that she looked as if she might cry.

'Do you want to say something too, Jane?' she asked.

'Yes, I do,' Jane replied. 'It's an enormous relief to be here with everyone. I know that the story of what has been happening to us since I shared my spirals is fascinating; but at times I've felt frightened with the weight of responsibility. I know I spoke about it once, and it seemed to shift a little then, but it all came back. I've felt very alone in it.'

'You should have said.' Ellen touched Jane's arm. 'You shouldn't have kept it to yourself.'

'I couldn't see any way of changing the way I felt,' said Jane miserably. 'The facts remain. I read Frances Ianson's book, the spirals appeared in my diary, I shared all that with you, and look what happened to Ellen.'

Ellen stared at her aghast.

'But you're seeing it only from one narrow perspective,' she said. 'What you say is true, but it's only one small part of the whole picture. Maybe if I hadn't met Adam on the train, I wouldn't have been affected by your spirals, or only a little bit. If I hadn't had this red book and been studying it, maybe I wouldn't have been affected by your spirals. Maybe Eva's stick potentiated it all too. Maybe there are things that we don't yet know about that have been affecting me in a way that made my reaction to the spirals very intense.'

Here Adam broke in. 'Personally, I'm absolutely certain that the events that have happened to Ellen and myself are not only connected, but have been interdependent. And none of *my* process could be attributed to you, Jane.'

Jane was sobbing now. Ellen held her arm while she cried.

When she could speak again, she said, 'Thanks all of you for talking about this. I can see now how in-turned I had become about it. I do understand and accept what you're all saying.'

'Can I make a general point here?' asked Joseph.

The others all turned to him.

'To me, this demonstrates a clear need to spend more time in preparatory discussions. Here is one misconception being aired.

369

No doubt there are others, some of which you may not yet be aware. Perhaps Edmund and I could spend the next hour or so leading the kind of conversation which might bring more of them to light.'

There was immediate agreement amongst the others.

'Jane, would you like to continue?' asked Joseph.

'Not at the moment, thank you,' she replied. 'I feel there's a big shift in the way I'm thinking.'

'Don't hesitate to come back to it if you need to later,' Joseph encouraged.

'Can I raise something?' asked Eva.

'What is it?' Joseph asked.

'I'd like to talk a bit about Hannah and her father. The way they came into our lives is remarkable. Ellen has encountered them in a car park – Mr Greaves' car was blocking her in temporarily. Ellen was just setting off to spend a weekend with Jane and myself. It was not long after that I first saw Hannah and her father. They had been sent to me by someone who was a long-lost childhood friend.'

'It's difficult to see that situation as only a string of coincidences,' said Edmund.

'Yes,' said Eva. 'And the unravelling of the problems in the underlying connection between Hannah and her father was a complex story. I'm still not sure if their appearance in our lives was just something in its own right, or a part of the whole puzzle we're trying to understand. My contact with Hannah certainly brought a lot into my awareness that I hadn't concentrated on adequately before.'

'Although I didn't meet Hannah and her father, I did feel very involved with them,' said Ellen.

'That's true of me as well,' added Jane. 'And perhaps it would be a good thing for me to say a little about Emily now.'

'Go ahead,' said Edmund.

'My contact with Emily opened my mind in ways I couldn't have predicted,' said Jane. 'It's difficult to put words round this. All I can say is that we shared a particular wavelength. I know that sounds silly, but that's as near as I can get to what I want to say.'

'Not silly at all, my dear,' said Edmund. 'We know about this kind of link between people. It often involves small children. I think your link with her could have been one of the factors that led to your openness to the rest of the events that have been coming into your life since the appearance of the spirals in your diary. It's my view that there have been a number of factors in the lives of each of you that have potentiated your sensitivity to each other and to the items on the table. It's unlikely that we would ever be able to identify many of these. But for you, Jane, I think your link with your sister's daughter has been one of these factors. Boris, I think that the link to your grandparents through the glassware, and particularly through the chess set, has been something that has affected you in this way. I can see from the photographs that the set has been carved with great dedication. It is my belief that the resonance of such dedication lives on around objects such as these. The objects are carriers of it, and those who are open to deeper sensitivities are affected by it.'

'You have just put into words something I've been trying to articulate,' said Boris, gratefully.

'Yes, that's very helpful,' said Eva. 'I'm sure my stick falls into that category too.'

'There are two things we haven't got on the table,' said Adam suddenly.

He reached inside his jacket and produced a pen. It was the pen Maria had given to him. He addressed the others.

'This is a pen my wife gave to me some years before she died. When I met Ellen I discovered she had a pen exactly the same that an old friend from college had given to her. I'd like to put my pen on the table, as a reminder of what Maria brought into my life that opened me to so much. I must confess that I was very blind to some things she tried to show me, and it's only since her death that I've become more aware. I'm sad she's not here to see the difference she made.'

'I won't bring my pen down,' said Ellen. 'I think the pen Maria gave you is the one that's directly relevant to today.'

Adam went over to the table, and put his pen next to the tape.

'I wonder if we should all take a break now?' said Joseph. 'We've covered quite a lot, and we should perhaps take time to think through what has been said. Personally, I'd like a glass of water and a stroll outside.'

371

'Let's all go to the kitchen and have something to drink,' Ellen offered. 'After that, do feel free to wander around inside or outside the house. Shall we agree to be back here in about three quarters of an hour?'

Having served out iced fruit juices to her friends, Ellen went to the bottom of her garden and sat down on the grass. The sun was very hot. She noticed a butterfly fluttering around the few flowers she had in a border. She thought how lucky they were to have Edmund and Joseph here. They clearly wanted to be involved; and their presence was certainly an asset. She wondered how things would develop after the break.

By the time she returned to the cool of her library, she felt refreshed and keen to continue. She looked around the others and sensed an atmosphere of eager anticipation.

'I wonder what would be the best order to take things in now?' she asked Adam.

'The most obvious things are the spirals, the tape, and your red book,' he replied.

'Although I'm keen to listen to it, I think we should leave the tape until last,' said Ellen. 'When we play that, Edmund and Joseph will be exposed to it too, so I do think we should leave it for now.'

Edmund joined them. 'I agree entirely,' he said. 'My suggestion would be to let Adam and Boris see the red book next.'

'I'd like to do that,' replied Adam. 'But let's just check with the others first.'

'That's fine,' said Jane and Eva who had overheard the conversation. 'But remember that we haven't had much time with that book ourselves, so I think the four of us should take it in turns.'

Ellen passed the book across to Adam, who was now sitting next to Boris; and they all sat in silence while they slowly worked their way through the pages. After a while, they reversed the book and turned the pages from the back as if it were the front. Then they handed it across to Eva and Jane, who looked at it in the same way.

'How are you feeling now, Adam?' Joseph asked, as he noticed the colour change in Adam's face.

'Just a little cold,' Adam replied.

Boris looked at him sharply, and took hold of his hand.

'You *are* a bit cold. I think you should come out into the sun for a few minutes,' he said firmly.

He stood up, pulled Adam to his feet, and taking his arm, took him outside. Ellen followed them out into the sun, with the others not far behind.

'What can you see Adam?' she asked.

'Pinpricks,' he answered in a monotone. He started to cry. 'I feel so sad,' he said. 'So very, very sad.'

'What is it Adam?' asked Edmund kindly.

'I don't know… I don't know… I can't see it… I can't hear it… I feel so sad. I want to tell you, but I don't know.'

Ellen touched Adam's face. It looked quite grey.

'He's terribly cold,' she said. 'I'll go and get a blanket. Keep him in the bright sun and stay with him. Eva, will you come with me?'

'Yes, of course. What is it you want me to do?'

'I have a hunch that we need to get the spirals out,' said Ellen quickly. 'Can you bring them outside and start arranging them? I'll get the blanket and speak to Edmund and Joseph about what we're intending to do.'

She ran upstairs, collected a blanket and returned to Adam, wrapping it round him.

'Edmund,' she said, 'I've got a very strong feeling that Eva should arrange the spirals, and that I should sit looking at them. Would you agree with that?'

'Let's try it. It sounds as if you're being directed to do that. Boris and I can keep a close watch on Adam if the others will stay close to you.' He looked at Adam. 'No, wait a minute. It looks as if he's coming out of it.'

Adam was sitting on a garden seat. Boris was holding his hand. His face no longer looked grey, and Boris confirmed that his hand was beginning to warm up. Everyone stood quietly waiting while Adam began to return to his normal appearance.

When he eventually spoke, his voice was full of relief. 'Oh, that's better! Thanks, everyone, for sticking with me.'

'Tell us what you remember, Adam; but just take your time,' said Edmund.

'It was such an intense experience,' replied Adam. 'I felt I wasn't going to survive it. What was happening was difficult, but the intensity was beyond anything I've ever known.'

'Can you tell us any more about it?' asked Edmund in calm tones.

'I remember looking at the leaf-vein patterns with Boris, and the supposedly blank pages. I felt calm, relaxed and interested. We handed the book across to Jane and Eva, and I was sitting there thinking about everything Ellen had told us about the book and its effect on her, along with that dream I had about it. Then everything started to change. Boris, do you remember that time with the tape when I said I felt terrible sadness?'

'Yes. Go on.'

'Well, that sadness was relatively insignificant when compared with the sadness I experienced this time. It became more and more intense. Each level of intensity was more unbearable than the last. Then something seemed to break, and I was at the same time here with all of you, and also somewhere else. The only words that come into my mind are that I was behind a veil. This lasted only for a fragment of time before I found myself able to hear ordinary sounds again.'

'What do you mean? What sounds had you been hearing?' asked Ellen.

Adam looked at her blankly. 'I don't know,' he said.

'I was worried about you,' said Ellen.

'We all were,' the others added.

'I was going to get Eva to arrange the spirals. I didn't know why, but I think now that it was in an attempt to join you – wherever you were,' said Ellen.

'It may have been that your intention to join him was sufficient to help him to return to us,' said Joseph softly.

'Shall we go back to the library and sit down?' Boris suggested.

When they were all seated, Adam said, 'Something has just come into my mind, and I want to talk it over with you all. I don't know what it means, but it's as if I've been given a sequence of events to suggest that you follow. First we should allow more time to get used to the idea of what has just been happening. Then we should spend some time studying the sounds of the tape together. We should work through any effects that become apparent, and then take a break. My final image was of me with the red book, Eva arranging the spiral layout, and Ellen studying it, while the tape is being played.'

'That's a lot of ground to cover,' said Joseph. 'I notice that it doesn't include any time for Boris or yourself to study the spiral layout.'

'I know that,' replied Adam. 'It may be that we can't see the layout until later.'

'What does everyone think?' asked Edmund. 'I have to say that I feel concerned.'

'I'm willing to study some of the tape,' said Eva. 'How about listening to some of it, and then reassessing things?'

After some discussion, everyone was able to agree to this, and they decided to start with side B. They were keen to discover whether anyone could hear anything on it. When the tape was started, there was almost complete silence, apart from the slight sound of the tape spooling round. However, it was not long before Edmund noticed that Jane was leaning farther and farther back in her chair. Her face looked deeply relaxed, and her skin seemed to glow with vitality.

'Jane?' he called softly to her. 'Jane?'

'Yes. What… is… it?' she answered in low tones.

'Can you tell us what's happening?' he asked.

He looked across at Adam and saw that he was sitting bolt upright, staring at Jane.

'It's so beautiful. So, so beautiful,' Jane murmured.

'What is?' asked Edmund quietly.

'This sound, of course,' she replied.

Adam relaxed back in his chair. He felt such a sense of relief. Jane had become a part of the resonance of a sound that had been inaudible to him, but which had affected him. How he knew this, he did not know. He just did.

'Can you see anything?' Edmund asked Jane.

'The light,' she replied simply.

Joseph turned to Edmund. 'How long do you think we should leave the tape running?' he asked softly.

'I think we should just let it run on until the end,' replied Edmund. 'I think it may be too disruptive to stop it.'

When it came to the end, they all sat and waited to see what would happen to Jane. When it came, the change in her was very gradual and very gentle.

'How are you feeling now, Jane?' Joseph asked after a while.

'I feel completely restored,' said Jane. 'I know that might sound a strange thing to say, but those are the words that come into my mind.'

'Do you remember what you told us?'

'Yes, I do. I told you of the beautiful sound … and the light. Why are you asking? Didn't you all hear it too?' She looked around. 'Oh! You mean that I was the only one who was hearing it? And didn't anyone else see the light?'

Jane stared at the circle of her friends, and could see straight away that she had been the only one to have this experience.

'Jane?' said Ellen. 'Remember how you're a person who can hear exceptionally low frequencies?'

'Yes. I remember the audiologist telling me. I was very surprised.'

Ellen continued. 'I wonder if that extra capacity of yours means that you're more open than the rest of us to other qualities of sound?'

'I suppose that could be the case,' mused Jane. 'If so, it's truly amazing.'

She thought for a minute, and then went on.

'Look, I'm fine now. Why don't we just go ahead with the spirals?'

'How's everyone else feeling?' asked Joseph, as he looked round the circle.

There was some deliberation, and in the end it was decided that they would wait until after they had had their evening meal. The food was easily produced, as Ellen and Eva had prepared salads earlier in the day. They ate in the kitchen as before. Then Eva returned to the library to arrange the spiral layout.

'I'll come with you and run the tape back to the beginning,' said Adam.

After a while, the others joined them and sat down.

'Everyone ready then?' asked Adam. 'Here goes.'

He started the tape running again, and went back to his seat with Ellen's red book. Eva had arranged the spirals so that all Ellen would need to do was to turn her chair round to see them.

The library was completely quiet. Edmund and Joseph watched each of the others carefully. Ellen felt quite relaxed as she stared at the spirals. In a strange kind of way, it felt as if at last she was looking at them in the right place, in the right way, and at the right time. Everything felt right. If anyone had asked her months ago what would be her chosen way of viewing them, she would not have known what to say. She had been happy to see them at Jane's bungalow, and at Eva's house, but she had no idea then that she needed to see them here, in her own home, in her library.

This room embodied so much for her. It was the room that had meant family life when her mother was alive. It was the room that had later meant the growth of a deeper bond between her and her father. And it was the room where she had isolated herself in her grief after her father's death. Now it was the room where the people to whom she felt closest were gathered together. They had come together because of something that was very important, something that none of them could properly understand. And now they were intent on entering a state that might bring them nearer to the meaning of it all.

Adam felt a little anxious at first when he resumed his study of Ellen's red book. He did not want to have to face the same intensity of feeling again. He knew Boris was watching him carefully, and he valued that. But this time it did feel different. He felt closely connected to both Jane and Ellen, whereas earlier today he had been fully absorbed in his study of the red book. He had been aware of Boris, but not of the others. This time, he felt connected to Ellen and Jane, and in a way that was equal to his feeling of concentration on the red book. He was very aware of the difference. And it all felt right.

Jane had half expected to re-enter the same awareness of the beauty of her last experience; but this time was different. She heard beautiful sound, but at the same time she felt an equal beauty within the sense of her connection to Ellen and to Adam. This time, instead of the beauty filling her from inside, she perceived the whole room, and herself, to be full of the beauty of the sound and the light. Surely the others must be as aware of it now as she?

'Perhaps my mind is wandering?' thought Edmund to himself. 'It is as if I can see amazing colours, but none that I can describe; and my eyes see only this library and its occupants.'

He felt mildly uncomfortable. Here he was, supposed to be an objective observer, but he seemed to be greatly affected by something. As he looked from person to person, he noticed that his sense of colours was most pronounced when he looked towards Ellen, Adam or Jane. As he pondered on this, he became aware of sound – a kind of music. But where was it coming from? And what kind of instruments could make such sound? It was as if the sound originated only from inside his head. He wondered if this was akin to what Jane had described earlier, and if anyone else was experiencing the same kind of thing. He did not feel he could ask anyone. It did not feel right to say anything. Words were not right. He felt strangely affected, and realised he was on the verge of tears. Tears of great sadness, but of intense relief too. He could see out of the corner of his eye that Joseph's hands were trembling slightly; and he wondered if he too was experiencing something similar. The intensity of the sound increased. He found it almost impossible to concentrate on his task of observing the others. He hoped that they were all right, as he felt unable to offer help or direction.

Joseph noticed how his hands were trembling, but he could see the same was true of Eva and Boris. The sensation was not unpleasant or alarming in any way, but it felt very strange. He had never experienced anything like this before. It seemed as if there were sound in his arms and hands. It was as if they were 'singing'. But how could that be? Hands and arms do not sing. Yet that was the only way he could describe it. It was a most beautiful experience, once he had accepted that this was what was actually happening. It was as if the senses in his hands and arms were heightened to the point of ecstasy. Yes, ecstasy, that was the word. He wondered if the same was happening to Boris and Eva, but he could not ask. The use of words felt all wrong; and in any case, he felt he had none.

Ellen felt tears running down her cheeks. She felt so sad, so terribly sad, but it was an oddly beautiful sadness, full of light and beautiful sound. Her whole body felt as if it were bursting with the most beautiful light and sound imaginable. Was this similar to what Jane had been experiencing? Was Jane experiencing this right now?

Where is that sound coming from? Adam had become aware of sound beyond anything he had ever dreamed or known. Was it coming from the book? No. Was it coming from Boris? Unlikely. Where was it coming from? It filled his head, it filled his body, it filled the room, and it was light. The sound of light? He did not understand, but neither did he feel he had to. He knew that the only thing that mattered was to dwell in this experience. He felt tears pouring down his cheeks, and he moved his head so his tears would not fall on the red book.

Ellen, aware that it was as if her body had been transformed into an emitter of light and sound of unimaginable quality, and her face awash with tears, managed to turn her head sufficiently to see each of the others. She saw that each of them seemed to be cloaked in a radiance that she could only compare with memories of some ancient religious paintings she had seen. But no painting could really capture this radiance that she was seeing now. And she seemed to be hearing it too. But how could she be *hearing* radiance? That could not be true; yet it was the only way she could describe it. She could see that the others, like her, had tears pouring down their cheeks, and that these tears seemed to be of a purity that she could not describe. She was *so* sad, but it was a beautiful sadness, and a cleansing sadness.

Boris was thinking back to the effects of the tape upon Adam when they had listened to it together at his home in Russia. He remembered the agony in Adam's sadness then, and the desperation in his need to tell something that he could not grasp. He saw Adam's face, now awash with tears, and tasted the saltiness of his own as they reached his mouth. He felt an immensely beautiful sadness, full of sound, exquisite sound, and light of a quality that was far beyond that which he knew from the shelf at home where they had kept the tape. He was sure now of the reason why they had all been brought together. It was only through being together like this, after their experiences thus far, that they could together reach this deep level of awareness that had formerly been completely inaccessible, but which had gradually become available to them. The explanation did not matter any more. The important thing was that they were within this state together. He felt something happen inside his head, and suddenly he knew that the others too knew what he had come to know, and that they were all thinking the same thoughts, and had all reached the same level of knowledge.

Ellen thought about the music that had come to the mother in *Communications*, the music that had led to the fundamental change in her situation with her son. She was sure that what she was experiencing now was something similar, perhaps even the same.

As Ellen thought this, she knew instantly that the others were sharing the same thought. She had no anxiety about tomorrow, the day when they would be parting. She had no fear of the future. She knew that something profound had changed in each of them, emerging from their buried selves, now opened to a shared state of enlightenment that meant their experience of life from now on would be different. There was an unbreakable link between them, forged in a reality of beauty so pure that the pain it carried felt unbearable, but which could be borne because of its truth.